WHAT IF HOLDEN CAULFIELD WENT TO LAW SCHOOL?

Selected Legal Fiction and Nonfiction

by

Stephen M. Murphy

Foreword by Sheldon Siegel

Also by Stephen M. Murphy

FICTION

ALIBI

NONFICTION

THEIR WORD IS LAW: BESTSELLING LAWYER-NOVELISTS TALK ABOUT THEIR CRAFT

WHAT IF HOLDEN CAULFIELD WENT TO LAW SCHOOL?

Selected Legal Fiction and Nonfiction

PRINTING HISTORY
LawyersWriting trade paperback edition/June 2007

Visit our website at www.LawyersWriting.com

Library of Congress Cataloguing-in-Publication Data

Murphy, Stephen M.
What If Holden Caulfield Went to Law School? / Stephen M. Murphy with a foreword
by Sheldon Siegel
p. cm.
ISBN 978-0-6151-4096-4
1.   Legal stories-History and Criticism. 2. Legal stories-Authorship. 3. Law in
literature. 4. Novelists, American-20th and 21st centuries-Interviews. I. Title.

PRINTED IN THE UNITED STATES OF AMERICA
10 9 8 7 6 5 4 3 2 1

To my fellow lawyer authors, who skillfully arrange words to inspire, entertain, teach, and ultimately achieve justice through truth.

"Lawyers are all right, I guess – but it doesn't appeal to me," I said. *"I mean they're all right if they go around saving innocent guys' lives all the time, and like that, but you don't do that kind of stuff if you're a lawyer. All you do is make a lot of dough and play golf and play bridge and buy cars and drink Martinis and look like a hot-shot... How would you know you weren't being a phony? The trouble is, you wouldn't."*

-The Catcher in the Rye by J.D. Salinger

TABLE OF CONTENTS

FOREWORD

There is a common misconception that the lawyer-novel was invented by mega-selling contemporary attorney/authors such as Scott Turow and John Grisham in the late eighties and the early nineties. In reality, the legal fiction genre was popular long before the "legal thriller" became a staple of mass market fiction. Erle Stanley Gardner was writing Perry Mason books sixty years ago. *Anatomy of a Murder* was written in 1958 (which was, coincidentally, the year that I was born).

San Francisco lawyer/author Stephen Murphy is a gifted novelist who is also the preeminent chronicler and historian of the modern lawyer novel. In addition to some of Steve's own compelling fiction, this volume includes many of his thoughtful reviews of the works of many of the lawyer/authors whose books are available at your local bookstore. It also contains Steve's insightful interviews with many of the same attorney/writers. In a sense, this book helps to answer two questions. First, why are so many lawyers writing fiction? Second, why do people have such a fascination with fictionalized accounts of the legal system?

Like most lawyers, I have my own opinions on both issues. With respect to the first, I would hypothesize that most of us write stories because there is something in our genetic make-up that causes us to do so. We write because we must (or we think we must). We also have healthy egos (it comes with the territory when you're a lawyer) that allow us to believe that we actually have something interesting or entertaining to say. We are also used to writing lengthy (and often deathly-dull) legal tomes, so we have some capacity for parking ourselves in front of our computers for extended periods of time. Some of the more ambitious attorney/authors use their books to provide commentary on the legal system and contemporary society. All of us fancy ourselves as story tellers.

With respect to the second question, I believe that people continue to read lawyer novels because the genre is an ideal vehicle for the key elements of drama. It is difficult to imagine more compelling setting than a courtroom during a murder trial. The heroes are heroic and frequently flawed. The villains are evil. The players must operate within a profoundly imperfect system. The stakes and the tension are high. The prosecutors have a lot at stake in trying to prove a defendant's guilt. The defense attorneys have perhaps even more at stake in trying to preserve the client's freedom. Moreover, for better or worse, in the post-O.J. world, courtroom drama has become a form of reality-based entertainment where entire TV networks (often using prosecutors, defense lawyers and (gasp) novelists as commentators) devote substantial chunks of their programming hours to courtroom maneuvering and legal issues with decidedly mixed results. The good news is that the public is more educated about the criminal justice system. The bad news is that people are perhaps hastier to jump to conclusions and expect instantaneous DNA analyses to solve every murder.

In the pages that follow, Steve Murphy provides answers to these questions. If my guess is correct, a hundred years from now, lawyers will be writing fiction and readers will be buying their books.

-Sheldon Siegel
San Francisco, California

INTRODUCTION

Since my graduation from law school in 1981, legal fiction has exploded in popularity as a writing genre. Bestseller lists commonly boast more than one book by or about lawyers. America's fascination with our courts of law and those who practice in them continues unabated, even while public perception of lawyers often is less than positive.

It was soon after passing the bar that I first became interested in legal fiction, but my initial interest was piqued by a movie, not a book. I saw *The Verdict*, a film about a down-and-out lawyer who, out of a blend of desperation and conscientiousness, accepts a medical malpractice case against a Catholic hospital. In particular, the scene in which a roomful of defense attorneys sits around a huge conference room plotting to vanquish poor, outmatched plaintiff lawyer Frank Galvin stayed with me. When Galvin managed, despite mistakes along the way, to bring in a large plaintiff's verdict, I was hooked. The David-versus-Goliath theme stuck with me, not only in my later creative writing efforts, but also in my own legal practice.

The true turning point came when I learned the film was based on a book written by Boston lawyer Barry Reed, who happened to be an alumnus of my college, Holy Cross. I was fascinated by the simple revelation that a successful trial attorney could also write such a compelling novel. This was something to aspire to, I decided. But then the reality of my task set in: I had to learn first how to be a lawyer. It would require more than getting good grades in law school classes. I had to actually practice law. Learning to practice law took time, and learning to practice law well and effectively took even longer. I was determined to be a good lawyer and worked diligently toward that goal. In 1988, my hard work paid off when I was made a partner in my firm, Bianco Brandi & Jones. It was at that point that I encountered another trial novel written by a lawyer. The novel was *Presumed Innocent,* and the author was Scott Turow.

As with *The Verdict*, *Presumed Innocent* immediately grabbed my attention. I found the writing to be thoughtful, nuanced, and intelligent. This story of a prosecutor caught in the tangled web of the same criminal justice system he once represented was literature, plain and simple. And then I learned that Scott Turow continued to practice law. If he could do both, then why couldn't I? I'd had a brush with fiction writing while looking for a job after law school. On a week-long trip to San Francisco, after going on a dozen interviews, I was feeling cynical about the whole process of job hunting. I sat on a beach in Alameda, across the bay from San Francisco, and sketched out a story. The result was the title story in this collection, written from the perspective of a wholly alienated character, which is how I felt going through the interview process. *The Catcher in the Rye* was one of my favorite books in high school, and the character of Holden Caulfield has stayed with me ever since.

There was a big gap - as far as my writing was concerned - between 1982 and 1988. In 1988, I embarked on what would become a second and subsequently a third career. My first career, of course, was practicing law. I loved representing plaintiffs - the injured parties - in personal injury and employment cases. The conflicts were not much different from that seen in *The Verdict* (though I never had the defense hire a beautiful female attorney to seduce me, as happened to Frank Galvin).

My second career was writing my own novel, a legal mystery based on a murder trial I observed in New Hampshire soon after graduating from law school. The novel's original title was *Dutch Treat,* after the protagonist Dutch Francis. When attracting an agent became problematic, I changed it to *Friendly Deception*, which, to my ear, sounded more appealing. It worked, at least as far as getting the attention of Susan Kelly of the William Pell Agency. But when she managed to sell the book to Jove, a PenguinPutnam imprint, the title changed again, this time to *Alibi.*

My third career involved interviewing lawyer authors. I embarked on this career as a direct result of Scott Turow. While he was in San Francisco in 1988, I managed to obtain an interview with him. The piece was published in *San Francisco Attorney Magazine* and was the first of about forty interviews of lawyer authors I would undertake. These interviews formed my first book, *Their Word Is Law*. But the real advantage of this exercise went beyond publishing the interviews themselves. It was an opportunity to talk to successful writers about writing. I quizzed them on plot, character development, all the crossroads decisions a writer faces in the course of creating a fictional world. It was a wonderful tutorial, and it lasted nearly twenty years.

INTRODUCTION

Even after the book was published, I continued interviewing lawyer-authors. Many were writers I hadn't been able to interview before, thanks in large part to my work schedule. So I'm pleased to bring you in this volume interviews with prominent lawyer-authors such as Brad Meltzer, Philip Margolin, John Osborn, and of course, Sheldon Siegel, who has been both an inspiration and a supporter. Also included are three interviews with non-lawyers. Clifford Irving and John Lescroart are established writers who have published successful novels without a legal theme. But they've gone on to carve a niche for themselves in the legal thriller market. Lescroart in particular has been enormously successful with his Dismas Hardy series set in San Francisco. The book's concluding interview is with the late Hal Lipset, a legendary San Francisco private eye.

An essential aspect of conducting the interviews was reading the author's latest book. I read nearly a hundred legal novels in that time. As many writers teach, reading thoroughly and prolifically breeds good writing. I found in my case that I could not read fiction without writing about it so I wrote reviews of many of the books. On occasion it was a bit unnerving criticizing authors I had interviewed. After sending Barry Reed my review of *The Deception*, for which I gave a mixed review, he wrote back with a list of the reviewers who loved the book. But that's what makes the world of legal fiction--of literature of any ilk--so interesting. There's room for an array of styles, approaches, subjects--and, of course, reviewers.

It was with some hesitation that I decided to include those reviews in this book. Reviews usually have a short shelf-life; they serve a time-sensitive purpose at the time the book under review is in circulation following its initial publication. These reviews were previously published in different forms in the *San Francisco Chronicle*, *Legal Times*, *Mystery Review*, *San Francisco Attorney*, and *Barrister Magazine*. After re-reading my reviews, however, I decided they had some lasting value. I put a lot of effort into writing the reviews and tried to impart some background on the author, a sense of the plot and the characters, and analysis on how the themes related to current events. In short, I tried to go beyond merely critiquing the books. I hope you think I have succeeded in this.

Armed with tips garnered from my many unwitting tutors as well as from my reading of their work, I made steady headway on my own novels, first *Alibi* and eventually its sequel. I tried to incorporate the lessons learned from these interviews into both books, but I must admit it was not easy. Writing fiction is a difficult business. The amount of thought and planning that goes into writing a novel can be overwhelming. I grew to envy writers who could focus on their work. You know the ones: they churn out a new novel every year. It took me ten years to write my first novel. On average I wrote one or two nights a week. Often I'd go weeks or months without writing a page of fiction. This made it difficult to generate any momentum. It sometimes would take me a few hours just catching up on where I'd left off.

In the decade it took to write *Alibi*, the world changed. When I began in 1988, cell phones and personal computers were the exception, rather than the rule. By the time I finished, they were everywhere. This development, in turn, required that I go back and revise my plot. I also changed in that time, both as a person and as a writer. I like to think the responsibility of raising four children helped me to grow and mature, but my kids may dispute that. I also like to think I improved as a writer. After all, I was learning on the job, both by writing and by interviewing.

To be sure, I wrote other things during this time, some examples of which are included in this book. The story, *Honky*, is based on a real event. An African-American girl refused to give up her seat to an Asian woman on the streetcar. What is the proper reaction to such rude behavior? And what should a civil rights lawyer, on the verge of receiving an award for his representation of minorities, do? As might be expected, the story explores racism in thought and action.

The short story *No Room Available* arose out of frustration with being called to trial only to be told there was no courtroom available. In my first decade of practice, before California went to a fast-track system, I would prepare a case for trial four or five times before actually seeing a jury. It could suck the life right out of you, not to mention the psychological toll it took on clients. The story looks at what might happen if the scenario were applied to a medical setting. What if you were scheduled for surgery, but it had to be postponed because there was no operating room available?

Have Gavel, Will Travel also arose out of frustration, this time with a new trend in civil litigation: private mediation before retired judges. The story is cynical by design and in no way represents my actual experience with mediators. But I had noticed a built-in conflict with mediations in which a mediator gets repeat business from a corporation or law firm. Wouldn't such a mediator be tempted to tilt the negotiations slightly so he could keep getting cases? (The same is true for arbitrators who actually make decisions on cases.) Most mediators insist they'd never do such a thing. But the conflict is there, and it's not a conflict that exists in the public justice system. In fact, if a sitting judge has a financial interest in the outcome of a case or any business relationship with the parties, that judge usually is disqualified. In many respects, private justice has turned the basic notion of justice on its head.

In the end, this book is a tribute to legal fiction of all kinds, the thriller, the mystery, as well as the literary novel. I have had the opportunity to meet with many fascinating people and experience the camaraderie that comes with sharing not one, but two professions: lawyer and author. I am proud to be a member of both. Both writers and lawyers operate with the understanding that words have the power to touch a person's heart and move them into action. When the writer *is* a lawyer—and his aim is to shed light on injustice in one of its many forms—his words have the power to change the world.

-Stephen M. Murphy

STORIES

Honky

Jack Sloane stood before the full-length armoire mirror, carefully adjusting his red silk tie. He pinched the knot so the fold was just so and, with a satisfied grin, slipped on his gray pinstripe suit jacket. He wanted to look his best at the Bar Association luncheon. Today he would walk to the podium to receive the Litigator of the Year Award, in honor of his vigorous representation of employees who had suffered the sting of discrimination and harassment.

To many women and minorities, Jack Sloane was a godsend, an avenging angel willing to stand with them in their David-versus-Goliath battles against corporate greed and bigotry. Although a prominent white male, Jack empathized with the plight of minorities who were denied access to jobs, education, and other benefits solely because of their gender or race.

Brian, his best friend and football teammate in high school, had been black. He had received fair grades, slightly lower than Jack's. But while five private colleges sought after Jack, Brian was forced to attend state college. After comparing Brian's grades and SAT scores with his own and those of his other classmates, Jack could find only one reason for his friend's lack of success: racism.

As an eighteen-year-old Jack was powerless to help Brian, but he decided to find a way to gain that power. He settled on becoming a lawyer and devoting his career to helping minorities avoid the injustice that had befallen his friend. Now, after Jack had pursued his dream for a quarter of a century, his fellow lawyers were recognizing his devotion.

Swelling with pride, Jack tucked his briefcase under his arm and began the three-block walk to the streetcar. He strolled at a leisurely pace, shouting good morning to his neighbors, again feeling glad he'd ignored his real estate agent's advice. She'd told him that the Ingleside District was full of unemployed blacks dealing crack outside iron-gated houses, the facades pocked with bullet holes from drive-by shootings. What she'd neglected to say was that the northwest triangle of the district, where Jack now lived, was populated by hard-working, middle-class blacks and Asians.

Jack and Liz loved the neighborhood. On cool, foggy evenings they walked hand in hand with their twelve-year-old daughter, Allison, stopping in front of neighbors' houses to ask how everyone was. Allison chatted about school. She was in sixth grade at St. Kevin's, earning top grades and starring on the class CYO basketball team. Jack recognized his own fighting spirit in his only child.

At the streetcar stop Jack, thinking of his cute girl, joined the crowd. When Allison kissed him goodbye that morning, showing off her new polka-dot dress, she had smiled sweetly and said, "I'm so proud of you, Daddy. I just can't wait to see you get your award." Jack had reserved a seat for Liz at the luncheon but had never thought to invite Allison. Liz had astounded Jack when she said she would pull Allison from school early for the event. "Your daughter should see what a great man her father is."

Jack climbed the steps into the K-Ingleside car and showed his FastPass to the driver, a stern, serious Chinese man he recognized from other commutes. The car was crowded. Riders stood jammed together, clutching the overhead rails. In the rear Jack noticed a group of black kids, maybe thirteen or fourteen years old, sitting amidst a few empty seats. He took an aisle seat three rows from the back and pulled a hardback novel from his briefcase.

One of the black girls, sitting in a double seat by herself, adjusted her blue and black bandanna, twirled a patch of straight black hair around her fingers, and yelled to her friend (even though she was only a few feet across the aisle), "Yo, bitch! Where my mothafuckin' pick?"

Her friend scowled at her, then reached behind her head and yelled back, raising her arm, "You want this shit, bitch? Catch yo' ass." She threw the black plastic pick into her friend's lap.

The girls continued shouting back and forth, oblivious to the other commuters. Then one of the boys yelled to the girl with the pick, "You gonna need more than a pick for that ugly-ass do." The boys laughed.

"Up yours, mothafucka!"

Jack frowned at the language, an obvious sign of inadequate parental guidance, and opened his book. Hoping the girls would quiet down, he removed his bookmark and settled in to relax.

Out of the corner of his eye he noticed an Asian woman walk past in a navy blue suit, carrying a soft leather briefcase. She stopped near the girl with the pick, who leaned against the wall and rested her foot on the empty seat beside her. "May I have this seat?"

The black girl's reply was hostile and Jack looked up, not sure he'd heard correctly. The girl stroked her hair with the pick, staring at the Asian woman with narrowed, defiant eyes.

The Asian woman said nothing. She hovered over the seat, not sure what to do.

"I said," the black girl spat, "you gonna hold onto my leg?"

Jack straightened and stared at the black girl, stunned. His biceps tightened as he watched the Asian woman slink away.

The girl leaned back, smirked, and stretched both legs over the double seat. "Mothafuckin' gooks think they can push niggas round. We don't have ta take that kinda shit."

No one moved. The only sound was the scratching of the wheels, the slow shifting of the streetcar along the rail. Fury rose in Jack. Above all else he was a fighter, especially for people unable to fight for themselves. The Asian woman backed up and now stood next to him, staring out the window. She clutched her briefcase to her chest, hands trembling.

Closing his eyes, his body tense, Jack considered the possibilities: sit quietly and let the teenager get away with her rude behavior, or do something about it. He gritted his teeth and squeezed his eyes tightly shut. He knew he had to do something.

His eyes still shut, Jack played out a scenario in his mind: what would happen if he tried to play the hero?

He'd slam his book shut, stand, and tap the Asian woman on the shoulder. "Please," he would say, "take my seat." The woman would nod, grateful, and sit down. He would then walk toward the black girl and stand over the empty seat.

"Excuse me," he would say politely, "please move your leg so I can sit down." Although he would try to sound polite, the rage, he knew, would boil inside him.

The black girl would glare. "Oh, so you wanna hold my leg, huh?"

And Jack would smile. He would have to think about where this would go. But after taking the first step, how could he turn back? He would have no choice. Otherwise the girl would make not only the Asian woman look foolish, but Jack as well.

"Either move your leg or I'll move it for you," Jack would say. What else could he say? Could he still pretend to be polite after the girl challenged him so directly? Could he try to reason with a girl who obviously knew nothing of reason? Plainly, all she knew was brute force, success through intimidation. It was sad, Jack thought, that the girl was raised in such an environment. It was not her fault that she had been poorly educated and inadequately socialized, leaving her unable to deal with another human being on the most basic level. But it also wasn't Jack's fault that the girl was this way. He had to take her as he found her. He would fight force with force, intimidation with intimidation. So he would clench his fists and the muscles in his arms and shoulders would become taut, ready to strike.

He would hover over the black girl, striking his tough-guy pose— the same one he regularly gave a witness during deposition when the witness tried to avoid answering his question. "I didn't ask you that," Jack would tell the witness, staring into his eyes. "Don't evade my question. Answer the question I asked you." Most witnesses, usually a client's supervisor whom Jack claimed was guilty of discrimination, would back down, not used to being addressed in such a hostile tone.

But this girl was not like those supervisors. She would not be intimidated. What she *would* say, flat and even, with no intonation, was, "Honky mothafucka." Just like that. "Honky mothafucka."

The words would send Jack's rage bubbling over. He would be unable to control himself. How dare this uncouth girl disrespect him? Who the hell did she think she was? Jack was used to people obeying him. When he told a company to pay his client money, they paid. Big, powerful corporations feared Jack Sloane, but not this ... girl.

With a sweep of his arm Jack would knock the girl's leg off the seat. What other choice would he have? He would sit down, his knees brushing against her thigh. The girl's eyes would widen and she would scowl, a menacing, mean, ugly scowl. Then she would turn toward the crowd standing in the aisle.

"He hit me," she would scream. "Y'all see that? This honky mothafucka hit me." When no one moved, not one passenger coming to her defense, she would turn her anger on Jack. "You think 'cause I'm a nigga you can touch my ass? You wouldn't do that to no white girl, honky mothafucka."

Still seething, Jack would stare at her, embarrassed as the whole streetcar listened. The car would squeak to a stop in West Portal station.

Jack would turn away, ignoring her. Why should he dignify her vulgarities with a response?

Before he could see it coming, the girl would get him. She would swing her arm at his face, claw-like, digging her nails in his neck and cheek.

"Ouch, sonuvabitch!" Jack would scream, putting his hand to his neck and looking at the blood on his fingers. Again the rage would roil— at the black girl's rude behavior, the racial epithets, the embarrassment. He couldn't ignore her now. She asked for it. Instinctively, he would raise his right hand and slap her on the side of the head.

The girl would wail. "Help, the honky's beatin' on me. Help me, you mothafuckas."

Instinct would take over. Jack would no longer be a thinking, calculating attorney. He would be a man who had been embarrassed and humiliated by a stupid, ignorant ... black girl. He would strike back. He would show her who's boss. He would teach her a lesson. Without hesitating, overcome with anger, Jack would follow the first blow with a left hand to the other side of her head. He would put a little more force into it, smack this ... bitch good, get her attention. She wouldn't mess with Jack Sloane again.

By now the driver would stop the car and walk to the back. Jack tried to put himself in the driver's position. The man wouldn't like disruptions in his car, especially this early in the morning. As he made his way through the standing passengers, all he would see was some white guy in a suit slapping a little black girl. The driver would grab the white guy around the neck, get him in a headlock, and hold him down. All the passengers would yell . . . so many frantic voices he wouldn't be able to make out what they were saying. With the white guy struggling to get out of his grasp, the driver would pull his radio from his pocket and call the police.

This was the last memory Jack would have. Before, his reverie had looked like a movie. Now the scene froze on an image of the driver shouting into his radio. Then the screen went blank, like a slide projector shifting from one slide to another.

The next image was also frozen. It was afternoon and Jack had missed the Bar Association luncheon, missed his award. He stood outside the Taraval police station, staring at the sidewalk newspaper rack. The headline of the San Francisco Examiner read: "Prominent Lawyer Arrested for Racist Assault on Muni." The front page color photo sent a wave of nausea over him. He could barely recognize the man being held by the Muni driver, his arms pinned behind his back. The man with the sad eyes and pale skin, and the crooked red tie.

The streetcar stopped abruptly, knocking Jack's book off his lap onto the floor. His eyes popped open. He reached down to pick up the book and realized his palms were sweaty. His hands shook as he slid the book into his briefcase.

"We are now approaching Montgomery Station," the driver announced over the loudspeaker.

The car was nearly empty. The black girl and her friends and the Asian woman were nowhere in sight. Sweating, Jack picked up his briefcase. He made his way out of the streetcar and up the escalator, drained, empty, almost as if he were floating to the surface. At the top, beside the window of a bank, he glanced at his reflection. The nausea he had felt so strongly in the streetcar returned. He barely recognized the frightened man looking back at him.

In his office that morning Jack had difficulty concentrating. His thoughts kept returning to the black girl who had gotten away with her rude behavior, and the Asian woman who had suffered the girl's abuse silently. Worst of all, he had done nothing.

He closed his eyes. What a hero he was! Some champion of the oppressed he had turned out to be! He had thought the situation out fully, deliberated on the consequences, and in the end had done nothing. By deliberating so long, he had managed to avoid making any decision. The situation had called for action and he had wimped out.

Jack was twenty minutes late to the luncheon. He had debated whether to go at all, but in the end decided he couldn't leave his wife and daughter there alone.

The luncheon was being held in one of San Francisco's oldest and most glamorous hotels. The walls glistened with Italian marble, the ceiling shone with gold trim. When Jack opened the door to the grand ballroom, he was momentarily stunned. The room was packed with at least fifty tables, each holding a dozen diners. Over five hundred people were there.

They were halfway through the first course of Polynesian chicken. Servers scurried from table to table. The room buzzed with conversation. As Jack tried to see over the diners' heads to locate his family near the podium, he watched in horror as all faces suddenly turned toward him.

The Bar Association president, Marshall Preston, a tall, handsome black man, who had always reminded Jack of his old high school friend, was at the podium talking into the microphone. "And here's our guest of honor now, fashionably late." He waved. "Jack! Come up here, Jack. Your family would like you to join them for this happy occasion."

Awkwardly Jack made his way to the front. He stopped to shake hands with lawyers he knew, many of whom he had litigated against. They all wished him well, shouting their congratulations. When he got to the front, Liz and Allison were on their feet. They hugged him, saying how worried they were when he hadn't shown up on time. Jack mumbled an excuse about a conference call going overtime. Then he circled the table, shaking the hands of half the Bar's board of directors—and the presiding judge of San Francisco Superior Court.

Sitting between Liz and Allison, Jack picked at his food and engaged in small talk. Every few minutes a judge or lawyer walked over from another table to shake his hand. Even though he was the center of attention, his mind was elsewhere. He couldn't stop thinking about the incident in the streetcar, turning it over and over in his mind. He was not proud of himself, not only for his inaction but also for his thoughts. He could barely swallow and had a hard time keeping his food down when he managed it.

Finally, after what seemed to Jack an eternity, Preston took the podium to present the award. Liz grabbed Jack's hand. "I'm so excited, I can't stand it!"

Allison had his other hand. "Me too! I'm, like, totally psyched."

Preston spent a few minutes summarizing Jack's achievements: how he had forced a major insurance company to promote female adjustors to supervisor positions, how he had humiliated a wealthy fast food franchise for refusing to serve blacks. At the mention of each case, applause broke out in the audience. Jack thought about each one and of his own dedicated efforts, fighting the big firms with superior skills and hard work. He was proud of his results, but he wondered about his motives. Why had he fought so diligently?

"And now I take great pleasure in presenting our Litigator of the Year Award to Jack Sloane."

The room erupted in applause. Allison and Liz hugged Jack together. Everyone at his table smiled and clapped. When the noise died down, Jack remained seated. His body suddenly felt heavy, as if he were carrying a great weight. Liz grabbed his elbow and whispered to him to get up.

Slowly Jack rose to his feet and made his way to the podium. The room was still. Preston made another show of handing the award plaque to Jack and there was more applause. Jack held the plaque against his chest and stood behind the podium. He adjusted the microphone, looked out at the crowd, and waited a full five seconds before he spoke.

"I am deeply honored to be given this award. I have been anticipating this day ever since the award was announced weeks ago. When I kissed my wife and daughter goodbye this morning, I believed this would be one of the happiest days of my life. The pride and love in their eyes told me my life had been a success. Then something happened this morning that convinced me I cannot accept it."

A cloud descended over the room. No one moved. People asked their neighbors whether they had heard correctly.

Feeling the emotion well up inside of him, Jack took a long sip of water and cleared his throat. "Today I had the chance to prove that I deserve this award, that I really am a fighter for the underdog. Here's what happened." Haltingly, stuttering as he'd never done before, he told the story.

"I finally grasped my own thoughts. I started out thinking of this girl just as a young girl . . . then as a young black girl. But by the end, after my mind became enraged—and I dared not admit this even to myself—I thought of this girl, maybe not deliberately, not even as a girl, but as a—a nigger."

Almost in unison the crowd looked down at their laps, stunned. Jack looked at his wife and daughter, tears running down their cheeks. He whispered, "I'm sorry."

Placing the plaque on the podium with a thud, Jack walked to the table. He tapped Liz and Allison on their shoulders and directed them to the exit. Allison choked back tears and Liz dabbed at her eyes with a handkerchief. Head down, Jack walked ahead of his family, who were barely breathing, past the tables of silent lawyers and judges. They almost reached the exit.

"Wait, Jack Sloane!" Preston shouted into the microphone. "I have one thing to say to you."

Jack's throat tightened. He turned to face Preston. The eyes of the crowd moved from one man to the other.

"You, Jack ..." Preston's voice was full of emotion. "You are the most honest man I have ever met. We both know that racism permeates this country but few ever admit it. We will never defeat racism until all of us do what you have just done: confess it openly and honestly." Preston stared at Jack as if they were the only two people in the room. As if he could see through everyone else. As if he could see, really see, only Jack.

Jack was unnerved, and more so when Preston started clapping. First slowly, then forcefully and more rapidly. He moved his hands closer to the microphone. Others joined in. Not many at first. Then more people, until the sound was deafening.

Jack looked at Liz, who had stopped crying and seemed totally bewildered. He wondered if he were imagining this scene, as he had imagined the confrontation with the black girl in the streetcar. Allison buried her face in Jack's chest. Holding his daughter close to him, he reached out for his wife and put an arm around her. They remained that way while some of the crowd got to its feet and gave Jack a standing ovation. But Jack most noticed the seated ones who were slowly clapping or quietly staring into space. If he had been in the audience, Jack knew without a doubt, he would've been sitting with them.

No Room Available

The ticking was driving Danny crazy. For twenty minutes he had been riveted to the clock, waiting for the doctor. He rubbed his lower back, numbly impressed by the persistency of the pain that shot down his leg. He stared at the clock. It hung on the wall above a gold-colored crucifix, the arcing pendulum threatening to scalp Christ with every pass.

Danny surveyed the waiting room – a man with a walker talking loudly to a woman wearing a cervical collar, two men sitting togther on the edge of their seats, one leaning on a cane. An older woman across the room flipped through a *Cosmopolitan*. A man with a cast on his arm peered over her shoulder at the magazine. He put every one of them at close to retirement age.

The nurse slid open the plastic window. "Mr. Mathews, the doctor will see you now." He strode a little unevenly into the examination room, slipped into the gown the nurse had given him, and sat on the exam table. The magazines piled on the window sill far outdated the ones in the waiting room.

Danny liked Dr. Gregory. He was energetic and open-minded, never afraid to try new approaches to ease Danny's back pain. But several weeks of physical therapy had achieved nothing. Danny would feel fine during the therapy, but the next day his pain would return. And although the drugs helped with the pain, they fogged Danny's mind. He could think clearly enough, but everything was a movie playing in slow motion. It felt so good to be pain-free that Danny convinced himself he was fine—people just moved more slowly than they used to.

Yesterday he had decided to return to work at Century Plastering. His boss, Mr. Dixon, was reluctant to let Danny mount a scaffold, but Danny assured him his back was fine. "I can do it good as ever," Danny maintained. "You'll see."

Mr. Dixon had insisted a co-worker carry Danny's bucket up to the platform. Meticulously, Danny applied mud to the wall and smoothed it with his trowel, like an artist applying the finishing touches to his masterpiece. An hour later, Mr. Dixon came by to see how Danny was doing. His work on the wall was beautiful, not one flaw--except he'd completed only four square feet. Mr. Dixon told Danny to go home, see his doctor.

As he sat on the edge of the examining table, swinging his legs slowly back and forth, Danny opened one magazine after another, rifling through the pages. His mind replayed the disappointment of his failed effort to work; on the other hand, he thought, he was lucky to be alive at all.

Two months ago Danny didn't think he'd ever get back on a scaffold again. It was a short fall, only six feet, but it had scared him silly. Someone had stupidly removed a cross-brace. Danny took one step onto the platform, and the next thing he knew he was laying flat on his back, looking up at planks and beams hanging askance from above. His bucket barely missed his head. It could have been a lot worse, everyone said. If that sixty pound bucket had fallen on him. "Just my back," Danny would assure himself. "Nothing serious, just my back."

His wife, Susan, wanted him to sue the scaffolding company. "You could've been killed," she told him time and again. But Danny remained optimistic. "I'll be alright, soon as the doctor fixes me up." Susan scoffed at what she considered Danny's foolishly misplaced faith in the medical profession.

But Danny's belief in Dr. Gregory was unflagging, which helped account for why Danny didn't mind waiting, as usual. He tossed aside the last magazine, suddenly aware of the goose pimples on his arms. The flimsy gown was no match for the chilly room, especially the cold metal frame around the table. Dr. Gregory walked in, his head down, thumbing through a pile of records attached to a clipboard. Danny didn't know how much longer he could stand the cold, the pain in his back, the pins and needles running down his legs all the way to his knees.

Laying flat on his back, Danny lifted one leg, keeping it as straight as possible, then the other. He stood up and bent over at the waist as Dr. Gregory commanded - left, right, forward, backward. When Danny bent too far, the pain pierced his back. "Ooooh," Danny groaned.

"We'll take care of it," Dr. Gregory said. "Don't worry." He picked up the clipboard and jotted down a note.

"We'd better schedule you for surgery," he said. "You see this vertebra?" Dr. Gregory pointed to an X-ray positioned on a light box. Danny could make out nothing.

"We call this the L-2. It's the second lumbar vertebra. If you compare your L-2 with the other lumbar vertebra, you can see that it has slipped over L-3. See here. You can barely make out where the disc is. That's what's causing your pain."

Danny nodded.

"The surgery will involve moving that vertebra away from the nerve roots. Then I'll use a piece of bone-- probably from your hip--to give it more support."

"That sounds risky, doc. Moving bones around." Sweat beaded on Danny's forehead. He wiped it away with his sleeve. "There a chance this won't work?"

"There's a slight risk the bone won't hold, and in that case we'd have to operate again. But it's a minor risk, really."

"Isn't there somethin' else we can do?"

"You want to be free of the pain?"

"'Course."

"Then this is your only option."

The surgery was scheduled for Memorial Hospital in two weeks. Susan made arrangements for her mother to take care of two-year-old Laura so she could go to the hospital with Danny. Mr. Dixon was happy. "Just in time for the summer rush," he said when Danny told him the date.

On the morning of the surgery, Danny received a call from Jack. "Hey, big brother, good luck today. We need you back in the lineup for the playoffs. All the guys send their best." Softball was a big part of Jack's life.

Susan insisted on driving to the hospital. "You just take it easy," she said. "I'll be driving you around the next few weeks anyway." She pulled into a parking space at the garage, shut off the car, leaned over, and gave Danny a long kiss on the lips. "I can't wait to get my man back," she said, lifting an eyebrow.

They arrived at the waiting room at seven thirty, two hours before the surgery was scheduled to start. "Better early than late," Susan said.

Danny waited in line at the window for the pre-surgery papers, then sat down with Susan on the hard plastic seats. When he handed the forms to the receptionist, she said, "The anesthesiologist, Dr. White, will be here in a few minutes. He'll want to ask you some questions."

Danny could feel his heart pounding. Finally, he was going to get his life back in order. He looked over at Susan, who had her head buried in a magazine, and smiled, the pain in his back ebbing momentarily.

Half an hour passed and still there was no sign of Dr. Gregory or Dr. White. Susan stood up to stretch her legs and walk the halls. She had barely left when she hurried back into the waiting room. "I just saw Dr. White," she said. "He was at the receptionist's window and I noticed his name tag. I couldn't tell what he was saying, but he sounded upset. He told the receptionist, 'That's Gregory's problem' and then he went into the surgery suite. What do you suppose that means?"

Danny shrugged. "We just have to be patient."

An hour later, at nine o'clock sharp, Doctor Gregory walked in. "I'm terribly embarrassed. This has never happened before."

"What's wrong?" Danny asked.

Dr. Gregory looked at the ceiling, avoiding eye contact with Danny. From his back pocket he pulled out a handkerchief, removed his glasses, and wiped the lenses.

"I have no idea how this happened. Our operating rooms are completely booked. There's no place to perform your surgery."

"What!" yelled Susan. "How can that happen?"

"I should have suspected something was wrong. Usually you have to book non-emergency surgeries three weeks in advance. But they told us they had an opening today."

"But my back," Danny protested, the pain evident in his expression. "I can't bear it much longer. And I've got to get back to work. My boss won't--"

"This is ridiculous!" Susan snapped. "He must have this surgery."

"I'm sorry, Mrs. Mathews. It's out of my hands. Unless his life is in danger there's no way Danny can have the surgery today."

Susan threw the magazine to the floor, folded her arms across her chest, and glared at Dr. Gregory.

Danny hung his head, distraught. "Can we reschedule it right away? I suppose I can last another three weeks."

Dr. Gregory shook his head. "I'll be on vacation. My wife and I bought nonrefundable cruise tickets. But maybe my partner could step in for me?"

"No, no," Danny muttered. "You know my case better than anyone."

"I'll be back in a month. Let's schedule it for the day after I return."

"And what are we supposed to do while you're out playing shuffleboard on a yacht?" Susan demanded.

Dr. Gregory shrugged his shoulders and said nothing. After phoning the administrator's office to schedule the surgery, he bid the Mathews goodbye.

At home, Jack's voice came from the answering machine. "Hello, Susan, I hope everything went okay with Danny's surgery. I'll stop by tomorrow first thing after work. Wish him my best, okay, hon?"

Danny and Susan were startled by a loud "ugh" that came from the top of the stairs. "My God, what are you doing here?" asked Pauline Tardy, Susan's mother. "You should be in the hospital."

"Not today," Susan snapped. "No operating room available, they say. I've never seen such incompetence."

"That's crazy. Danny, what're you going to do?"

"Right now I'm going to bed," Danny said softly as he slowly mounted the stairs.

"Wait. You got some phone calls. Your mother wanted to bring you some magazines at the hospital tonight. And your boss said they just got a huge contract, so there'll be plenty of work for you."

"That's great, just great." He could barely get the words out. "Susan, could you..."

On the day of the surgery, Danny took a cab to the hospital. Mrs. Tardy had to return home (her garden needed tending), and the teenage babysitter Susan had hired called to say she had the flu. Danny marched numbly through the corridors to the surgery suite. He knew the route by heart and didn't even glance at the directional signs.

Arriving at the entrance to the waiting room, he gasped. The place was packed. Not an empty seat in sight. "This looks like an airport terminal," Danny said. Nobody paid him any mind. A small boy in the corner groaned pitifully, a low guttural sound. Were all these people here for the same reason he was? Danny looked around and shook his head. They wouldn't be here unless they--or someone they knew--were having surgery.

The receptionist recognized him. "Mr. Mathews, hi," she said haltingly. She offered him a brown clipboard, but quickly pulled it back. "Maybe I should wait until Dr. Gregory gets here. Why don't you go into the waiting room."

Danny felt a lump in his throat. He braced his back against the wall and sank slowly to the floor. The room was eerily quiet. Danny stretched out on the floor and fell asleep. He dreamed of his church and the Stations of the Cross. Danny marveled at the strain apparent on Christ's face as he labored along the dirt road under the weight of the cross, heard him groan and gasp with the effort. Christ ascended the hill in agony, stopping to catch his breath every few yards. Then He stumbled and fell, the cross landing on his back, barely missing his head. Danny stretched out his arms, wanting to help Christ with his burden, to relieve the painful weight of the cross on his back. Just as his hands were about to grasp the splintered wood, Dr. Gregory grabbed his arm, shaking him awake.

"Danny, are you okay?"

Danny rubbed his eyes. "Yeah, just dozed off, I guess."

"I'm sorry to take so long," Dr. Gregory said. "This has been one crazy morning. An apartment building caught fire. Several of the tenants have broken bones from having jumped out the windows. I need to attend to them. I don't know when we'll be able to get to you."

"It'll be today, though, won't it, doc?" Danny strove to keep his voice free from desperation.

"I don't know. The entire staff has been working overtime." He looked around the room. "Some of these folks haven't even been treated yet. A few scheduled surgeries have been cancelled already. I'm afraid I can't make any guarantees."

Danny appeared lost.

"Why don't you go to the cafeteria, have a cup of coffee, and check back in three or four hours."

"But doc, you don't understand. I can't stand it much longer. My back--"

"PAGING DR. GREGORY. PAGING DR. GREGORY. REPORT TO THE OPERATING ROOM IMMEDIATELY."

Dr. Gregory started to back away. "I've got to run. Check back in a few hours."

Danny knew it was hopeless so he walked up a steep corridor to the pay phone. It required so much effort he practically dragged his feet. The pain felt like a leaden backpack, slowing him down, making him gasp for air. Speaking to Susan, he could barely hold back the tears.

He waited for Susan at the entrance to the garage. He stood absolutely still, his hands stuffed in his pockets, staring at the hospital. He stood like that for fifteen minutes, so focused he didn't even recognize the pain. His mind was numb. Twice he had prepared himself for surgery. It had been difficult enough being turned away the first time, but now the disappointment came with a sense of embarrassment. How would he explain this to everyone?

Susan slammed on the brakes when she saw Danny. She rolled down the window. "What the hell is going on?" Danny opened the door and got in. "It's a good thing little miss irresponsible had a friend who was willing to babysit," Susan said as she pulled away from the curb. "So you wouldn't have to take a lousy cab."

"There's a lawyer the union uses," Danny said evenly. "Let's go by his office."

They drove downtown in silence, Danny's occasional directions being the only conversation. When he spoke he stared straight ahead, his hands gripping the sides of the bucket seat.

At the lawyer's office, the receptionist chatted on the phone without acknowledging them. When she finally hung up, Danny introduced himself and explained his situation.

"Mr. Dellacourt is very busy today, sir. Without an appointment he won't be able to see you."

"Tell him I'm with the plasterer's union."

She brushed her blonde bangs from her eyes and frowned. "I'm really sorry. He's..."

"Listen to me, honey," Susan interrupted. "You tell your boss he better come out here right now or he's going to lose the biggest case he ever had. Maybe he could even use the money to hire himself some competent help."

The receptionist dropped her pen, stared wide-eyed at Susan, and fled into the back office.

"What a twit," Susan said. "This lawyer better have more on the ball than his staff."

"I sure hope so," Danny said slowly. "At this point I don't know what else to do. All I wanted was to get better." Danny straightened his back, leaned against the wall. "Least I can do is get some money out of this."

"Of course, you're gonna get some money. If anyone deserves it, you do," Susan said, resisting the urge to say, *I told you so.* "The nerve of that hospital—sending you home twice! Unbelievable."

"I need to get on with my life."

They turned their heads as the door opened and a man walked out. "Mr. and Mrs. Mathews, I'm John Dellacourt," he said, shaking their hands and leading them into a glass-enclosed conference room. "I'm awfully sorry about Holly. She's being extra vigilant because she knows how frustrated I am today." He motioned for them to sit across from him. "Went to court this morning for trial and the judge sent us home. 'No courtroom available,' he says. And it's not the first time it's happened. Can you believe it?"

"So," he said, pulling a pen from his jacket pocket and positioning the legal pad in front of him, "what can I do for you folks?"

Have Gavel, Will Travel

The day of Ferdinand Pitt's arrest began with an unsuspecting Ferdinand smiling broadly, his finger firmly pressed on the elevator button. As the elevator ascended, Ferdinand thought of the lucky turn his career had taken since joining the Judge's Company five months ago. With full retirement benefits in tow, nearly a hundred grand per year - he left the bench to become a judge for hire, a rent-a-judge, a gunslinger of the 21st Century, hired by plaintiffs and defendants alike to bring justice to a world where courts had come to a screeching halt, impotent to the onslaught of litigation run amuck.

Ferdinand was still smiling as he hung his Cashmere overcoat and fedora on the hook behind the office door. After sitting back in his Danish recliner, he punched in his assistant's extension. "Marilyn, come here for a moment, will you."

Marilyn was a treasure. A law school graduate who never wished to practice, she found her niche as an administrative assistant to retired judges. For a reasonable salary - in the high five figures she told people who dared ask - she got to rub elbows with the pillars of the judiciary. Well, at least the cracked and battered elbows of former pillars.

"Good morning, Judge," Marilyn said cheerily. Retired five months and people still call me "Judge," Ferdinand thought. Before, when he really was a judge, people called him "Judge" only because he wore a black robe and sat on the bench, high above everyone else. But that kind of forced admiration never satisfied Ferdinand. When you're paid a measly hundred fifty grand a year it's hard to feel like a big shot, especially when half the lawyers who appeared in front of you earned double your salary. It was the young ones who really got to him, the third and fourth year associates who had just cracked the hundred fifty mark. They would look at him with thinly-veiled smirks, thinking: you loser; I'm making more than you and I've been out of law school only three years. Someday, Ferdinand thought, things will be different; someday, you greedy little worms, Ferdinand Pitt will be the envy of you all.

He found revenge because of the Judge's Company. Now Ferdinand was making the big bucks, five fifty an hour - five five zero -

in his pocket. Around the Judge's Company Ferdinand's pay was the subject of continual controversy. The other judges got only five hundred an hour so when word leaked out that Ferdinand made fifty bucks more, the egos went bonkers. All those distinguished jurists, the supposed cream of the legal profession, could not believe that one of their own, especially someone as inconsequential as Ferd-the-Nerd, was worth more money. Chief Judicial Officer Jake Woodworth put them off, protesting Ferdinand's right to privacy. Besides, Jake said, so what if Ferdinand was making more. He was Presiding Judge the last three years and was in heavy demand. I'm not admitting anything, understand, but it would've been worth the extra money to bring him on board.

Every time Ferdinand picked up his paycheck, he thought of all those baby lawyers, making themselves miserable billing the crap out of every file they could get their hands on, while he was having a ball, no stress, and laughing all the way to the bank.

"You've a nine thirty appointment today, then the Tedford versus Marble mediation at ten," Marilyn informed Ferdinand as she handed him a steaming cup of coffee.

"An appointment? Is that so? And who might that be?" Ferdinand sipped his coffee loudly.

"A first-year law student named Neil Darby. He's your nephew, isn't he?"

"Right, right. I'd forgotten he was coming by. My sister Clair wanted me to give the boy some pointers, a bit of career guidance. I've got a lot to say about that, mind you."

Ten minutes later Marilyn ushered Neil into Ferdinand's office. Neil had always been a studious kid, serious about life, stingy with a smile. In fact, Ferdinand could not remember if he'd ever seen his nephew laugh. As Neil entered, Ferdinand was momentarily speechless.

"Hi, Uncle Ferdie, thanks for taking the time to see me." Neil looked nothing like Ferdinand remembered him, a baby-faced boy with stern, severe eyes, all business. Now Neil's neatly cut black hair was gone; in its place a nearly bald, dark pate accented by a four-inch braided tail hanging down his neck. On his right ear hung a gold ring, an inch in diameter. Ferdinand winced.

Neil told Ferdinand he had just started his first year at the California State School of Law and was struggling with his studies. "My father encouraged me to go to law school," he explained. "He wanted me to be like you, Uncle Ferdie."

Ferdinand smiled, flattered that his brother-in-law held him in such high esteem, but at Neil's next words the smile turned to a frown. "At first I protested," Neil said. "What I really wanted was to be a writer."

"A writer?"

"Yeah, you know, novels, short stories. That's what always interested me. But my father insisted I couldn't make a living as a writer; they're all starving, working as waiters and secretaries."

"So you decided your father was right after all." Ferdinand said, trying to get the conversation back on track.

"Well, not quite. What happened was I read *Presumed Innocent* by Scott Turow and I was blown away. And then I realized what I had to do," Neil said, his excitement showing. "To get a novel published I'd have to go to law school."

Ferdinand shook his head, unsure if he were hearing clearly. The dismay he felt at his nephew's career goal showed on his face.

"I'm sorry, Uncle Ferdie," Neil said after regaining his composure. "Sometimes I get carried away. But that's not the reason I'm here. I'd like to learn more about the practice of law and you seemed like the best person to teach me."

"Very well," Ferdinand said, having no clue that Neil was deliberately sucking up to him. For the next ten minutes, Ferdinand lectured Neil about the virtues of gaining trial experience in the district attorney's office, as Ferdinand had, then the monetary benefits of working for a private firm where "you learn to worship at the altar of the billable hour." Although Ferdinand enjoyed making fun of big-firm lawyers, he did envy their money and, especially, the comforts of plush high-rise offices. "You will learn to measure time in six-minute intervals, one-tenth of an hour. You will give up all other pursuits - family, athletic, and" - he raised an eyebrow – "literary."

"The law will be your life," Ferdinand continued. "And you will love the law."

Neil gulped, pulled at his collar, suddenly feeling the room heating up. He had seen how uptight law students got, the worry over grades, being called on in class, the intense competitiveness. Did they have any idea what they were competing for?

Clenching his hands on his lap, Neil looked up at his uncle. "Is that it?" he asked simply.

Ferdinand hesitated. "Is what it?"

"You work all those hours, give up your life, then what? Keep doing that until you drop dead?"

A smile creased Ferdinand's face. He shook his head. "That's just paying your dues," he said. "You pay your dues and then..." - he raised his arms, spread them wide apart - "this."

"This?"

"ADR."

"ADR?"

"Alternative Dispute Resolution, mediations and arbitrations. It's the latest thing. What do you think the Judge's Company does? People get fed up with the court system, all those delays, the congestion, so they pay us to clean up their problems."

Neil scratched his head. "I don't get it. How do you get people to bypass the courts and come to you to settle their disputes?"

Ferdinand smiled. "That's the beauty of it. The court system's such a mess, cases rarely get to trial. So people don't mind paying us four fifty an hour to work things out. It's a great system. This is where the action is, my boy." Lowering his voice, Ferdinand leaned toward Neil. "You know what we call ADR around here?"

"What?"

"A Desert of Riches," he whispered. "Get it," he raised his voice, excited. "There's money to be made as far as you can see. It's endless."

There were two loud knocks on the door then Marilyn walked in. "Everyone's here for the Tedford mediation, Judge. They're waiting for you in Conference Room A."

"I'll be right there," Ferdinand answered as Marilyn left.

Neil stood up. "I'd better be leaving," he said.

"Wait. We haven't finished our little talk. Why don't you sit in on the mediation, I'm sure no one will object. It's one of those sexual harassment cases." He winked at his nephew. "Could be spicy if nothing else."

"Well, I don't know," Neil hesitated. Although he'd had enough of Uncle Ferdie for one day, this ADR business seemed interesting. And sexual harassment - could be a plot line there somewhere. "Okay, I'll stay," he said finally.

"Great," Ferdinand said, picking up the file and walking to the door. "Follow me." He started to put his arm around Neil's shoulders, but seeing the earring again, stopped himself. "Um, this way," he said, opening the door.

On the way to the conference room, they passed two rows of black and white photographs hung neatly on the wall, portraits of the judges of the Judge's Company, fully robed, from their days on the bench. "The rogues gallery," Ferdinand grinned.

As Ferdinand pushed open the door to Conference Room A, he looked with satisfaction at the long shiny table crowded with lawyers and litigants, all waiting for him to share his wisdom.

"Why don't we begin by introducing ourselves, though some of you undoubtedly know each other already. My name is Judge Pitt and I'll be your mediator today," Ferdinand began, sounding like a waiter at a chic restaurant. "This is my nephew, Neil Darby. He's a law student at State and is here as an observer. Does anyone have a serious objection to that?"

Ferdinand looked around the table, everyone shaking their heads back and forth, as he had expected. "Good." Ferdinand stood up and pulled from his pocket a stack of business cards. "Here, let's hand these out." He passed the cards down each side of the table.

When Ferdinand first joined the Judge's Company, he put a lot of thought into attracting business, something he never had to deal with while feeding at the public trough. Ferdinand realized that some mediators and arbitrators traveled on occasion, but no one had focused on traveling to the client as a distinctive feature of the business. He decided to make this idea his niche.

And to promote this feature Ferdinand had figured out the perfect marketing technique: a catchy slogan that lawyers and clients would remember. In the center of the business card now being passed around the table, embossed in gold, was a judge's gavel. Protruding from the sides of the handle were angel wings, also outlined in gold ink. The script beneath the gavel read: "Have Gavel, Will Travel."

When everyone had a card, Ferdinand said, "Let's begin the introductions over here." He pointed to the lawyer on his left.

"Certainly. I'm Gilbert Forest, Snow, Brewster & Chatham, representing the defendant Marble Construction." Forest was forty-five years old with greying side-burns, a thick head of hair which - thanks to a daily dose of Grecian formula - was as dark as his suit. At the Snow firm, Forest was an unquestioned star, a quick study to the firm's notorious tactics of stonewalling on discovery by hiding sensitive documents and overwhelming the opposition with depositions, usually as far out of state as possible.

Next was Martin Payne. "General counsel for Marble," he announced tersely. Payne had been in private practice for sixteen years before joining Marble. He immediately began a campaign to rid the company of all incompetents - a term he used for virtually every employee who crossed his path. Before long, whenever other employees spoke of him, they grimaced, clenched their jaws, and with guarded, conspiratorial voices called him a real "Payne in the ...." One of those employees was sitting to his left.

"And this is Holly Latham, Director of Human Resources," Payne announced with a condescending sneer. Latham nodded, tight-lipped. She wasn't all that happy to be here. If she hadn't approved the plaintiff's firing, none of this would be necessary. Latham knew her days were numbered; as soon as this case settled she was out the door.

Across the table a man said in a loud voice, "Hi, I'm Buck Gaston, plaintiff's attorney." Gaston sat on the edge of his seat with an awkward stiffness, subconsciously trying to appear taller than his five foot seven inches allowed. He had never gotten over being cut from the basketball team at Lowell High because of his size. That was the defining moment in his life; since then, like many short men, Gaston's purpose in life was to prove he could compete with the big guys. At depositions he made it a point to berate the defense counsel, on three occasions grabbing a defense counsel's lapels, threatening to teach him a lesson he'd never forget. His antics became the subject of a well-attended seminar at a convention of the Defense Attorneys Association, where an effective counterattack was devised that substantially changed Gaston's behavior. Now every deposition he attended was videotaped.

Beside him, the woman with long, curly hair said, "And I'm the plaintiff, Jill Tedford." Tedford was thirty-six years old, divorced with a twelve-year old son to raise on her own. She had devoted her energies to Marble for the last nine years, hoping to spend her career there. As the software purchaser; she had introduced several products that had in-creased the company's efficiency threefold, earning her a feature story in the company newsletter. Always meticulous about her appearance, religiously getting haircuts and manicures every Saturday, she had let her-self go when she was fired ten months ago. Now her jeans were faded, her sweatshirts winkled and her hair hung limply over her shoulders.

"Now that we all know each other," Ferdinand addressed the group, "I would like to describe the process we will be going through today. Certainly, the lawyers are familiar with what we'll be doing, so this is mostly for the benefit of the clients. As you know, this is a mediation. You are here voluntarily, presumably because you wish to settle this dispute. It is not my place to tell the defendant what it should pay, or to tell the plaintiff what she should accept. If you want me to evaluate the case for that purpose, I could do so, though I generally discourage it. This is your case and I will never know the facts as well as you. All I can do is act as an intermediary and try to find a middle ground where we can settle the case." After describing the procedures to be followed, he looked at Gaston.

"Let's start with the plaintiff's opening statement," he said.

Gaston stretched his neck higher. In a deep baritone, he began. "This is a sex harassment case in which plaintiff Jill Tedford was fired for refusing the advances of her boss, Mr. Richard Cabeza, who I note is not present here today. Ms. Tedford has testified in deposition that Mr. Cabeza repeatedly asked her on dates; each time she refused. After several months of these rejections, Mr. Cabeza became incensed, telling her, 'You want me, you know you do.' On one occasion, Mr. Cabeza snuck up behind my client while she was in the file room, reached around her and put his hands on her breasts. Because they were alone and she feared for her safety, she said nothing at that time. Immediately after leaving the file room, however, she went to the human resources department where she made a written complaint to Ms. Latham. Two days later Latham told my client that she was a liar and that she was being terminated for making a fraudulent claim."

As Gaston finished describing his client's humiliation and deep depression, the room became quiet. For all of his posturing at depositions, Gaston could tell a great story.

"Okay, let me make sure I've got this down right," Ferdinand said, breaking the tension. Scanning his notes, he then proceeded to repeat Gaston's statement nearly verbatim, omitting only Gaston's theatrics. Neil was fascinated, marveling that Ferdinand got paid five hundred and fifty dollars an hour to imitate a parrot.

It was now Forest's turn. "I'll keep it brief, your honor. Mr. Cabeza and Marble emphatically deny these charges. They are outrageous and totally untrue. Mr. Cabeza is a dedicated family man. In fact, the only reason he's not here today is because he's meeting with his daughter's kindergarten teacher. He is a deacon of his church and a well respected member of the community. The truth is that Ms. Tedford had a crush on

Mr. Cabeza and when he rebuffed her; she sought revenge. That is the only reason we are here."

Forest's indignation came through with every word. He was the defender of Cabeza's honor, and more importantly the finances of his client, who was paying him a cool four hundred ninety an hour.

"There are other facts which we would like to share with your honor in confidence," Forest concluded.

"Yes, of course," Ferdinand said. Glancing at his notes, he again played the parrot and repeated Forest's statement. By the time he finished, two hours alter the mediation had begun, it was time for a break. After the participants had shuffled out of the room, Ferdinand asked Neil for his impressions of the proceedings.

"It's a fascinating case, but ... I don't know. What I don't get is why you repeated what the lawyers said. Everybody heard them the first time."

Ferdinand grinned. "You want the official reason?"

"I guess, yeah."

"The parties have to know that the mediator is paying attention and understands their case. Otherwise, they won't have any confidence in what you say."

That sounded reasonable to Neil. But there was something about his uncle's demeanor that made him wonder. "And what's the unofficial reason?"

"Ah, I knew you wouldn't let me get away with that. You notice how much time I took repeating their statements?"

"I'd say it added a good forty, forty-five minutes to the proceeding."

"Right, and you know what that means, don't you?" Ferdinand reached in his back pocket, pulled out his wallet, laid it on the table. Patting it with his palm, he said, "This is why. The longer it takes the more money we make."

Neil was shocked. "But you're cheating them. Isn't that unethical?"

Ferdinand stiffened, surprised at his nephew's strong reaction. He shook his head, deciding he better take a different approach. "Not at all. That's what they expect. If you don't put in the time, that's when they feel cheated. They want you to take your time to carefully evaluate the case, learn the strengths and weaknesses of each side."

When Neil's shocked expression remained, Ferdinand tried again. "Look. The parties can't vent their hostilities in just a couple of hours. Even if they settle the case, they'd feel unsatisfied, all those conflicting emotions unresolved."

"I suppose," Neil said, unconvinced.

Ferdinand put the wallet back in his pocket. "What the hell," he said, frustrated at his nephew's holier-than-thou attitude. "Everyone does it anyway. People expect us to make some money on these things."

ADR, thought Neil, some alternative to the courts. So much for professional responsibility. All those rules of professional conduct he'd heard about in class must not mean a thing when there's money to be made. Talk about legal fictions. ADR should stand for "A Damn Ripoff." Neil was thinking he had gone to law school for the right reason after all.

Ferdinand decided to caucus first with the plaintiff, while the defense huddled in the small conference room down the hall. Gaston, Tedford and Ferdinand sat at one end of the long conference table with Neil, alone, at the other end. "You've got a tough case," Ferdinand said, shaking his head slowly."

"What do you mean, your honor?" Gaston asked, surprised.

Ferdinand flipped open the plaintiff's mediation brief. "Well, as it says here, the worst thing this Cabeza did was place his hands on the plaintiff's breasts." He paused, looked at Gaston, who sat silently, aghast. "I realize the courts have been pretty strict with sex harassment cases these days, but..." He turned toward Tedford, shrugging his shoulders. "It's not like he forced you to have sex with him." When Tedford tensed and her eyes turned glassy, Ferdinand turned back to Gaston. "What I mean is there was no rape. He didn't threaten to fire her; he didn't cut her salary, job duties, anything." He paused, realizing he had shocked both Gaston and Tedford. "Understand I'm not saying what he did was right," he added, "but I don't see this as a big case."

Beads of sweat formed on Gaston's forehead. Clenching his fists, he leaned forward. "But, your honor; the fact is Marble did fire her. Besides, we're asking for only two hundred and fifty thousand."

"Oh, come on," Ferdinand shot back, grimacing, his voice rising. "You don't expect the company to pay that kind of money for this case. There's no way."

Gaston looked at his client, who was staring at her shoes, clenching her teeth. From his back pocket he pulled out a white handkerchief and wiped his brow. "What do you think we could get?"

Ferdinand shrugged. "I don't know. They've made no offer yet. I'm sure it would cost them twenty five grand, fifty tops, to defend the case, maybe they'd pay that now."

Gaston stood up and faced Ferdinand. "No way, that's not nearly enough. We'd be giving the case away." He looked at his client, who was staring straight ahead, withdrawn. "We're willing to move off the two fifty, but nowhere near fifty."

Ferdinand nodded and he and Neil left together. As they walked down the hall to the defendant's caucus room, Neil asked, "If this is such a lousy case, how are you going to get the defendant to pay even fifty?"

Ferdinand winked. "Watch this," he said, opening the door.

"You said you have some facts you wanted to discuss in confidence?" Ferdinand asked Forest.

Forest coughed, covering his mouth with his fist. "Yes. I didn't want to mention this in front of the plaintiff, because they don't know we have this information. We've done an extensive background check on Ms. Tedford, including hiring a private investigator to check out everything on her resume. We found a number of misrepresentations, outright lying."

"Such as?"

"She claimed she had an Associate of Arts degree from Diablo Valley College. They say she attended for two years but didn't have enough credits for a degree. That's number one. Number two: she claimed she worked for three years at an engineering company, Saturn Consultants. They never heard of her." Forest pounded his fist on the table. "She's a liar, a pathological liar. There's no way a jury will believe her story about Cabeza."

Ferdinand finished writing, looked at Latham. "But you didn't know about that when you fired her, did you?"

Before Latham could say anything, Payne answered. "Doesn't matter. The courts have allowed after-acquired evidence to support a termination."

Ferdinand leaned back in his chair. "Well, that's within the trial judge's discretion, isn't it? You'll never get that in evidence," he said, bluffing. He had never heard of this "after-acquired evidence" business. Sounded like a great idea though.

"But, your honor...," Forest began.

Ferdinand held up his hand. "Let's get down to business. The way I see it, you've got serious exposure in this case. As you know, I've spent a great deal of time talking to the plaintiff, and in my opinion she tells a convincing story. She's going to make one hell of a witness."

"But she's a liar, your honor," Payne said. "Cabeza says she made this whole thing up. She had a crush on him, that's it. He's been with the company fifteen years and there hasn't been even a hint of any harassment in all that time." Payne frowned. "And so what if he did? This is a nothing case." He repeated himself, more loudly. "Nothing! Zip! Zero!" He thrust out his arms, palms down, away from each other. An umpire making the safe sign. "That's it. NOTHING! All he did was grab her boobs. Gimme a break."

The room became silent. Latham looked at the floor, unable to keep the shock off her face. Realizing he might have gone too far, Payne made an apology - of sorts. "Pardon my French, your honor. But you got to admit that at best this is a nuisance case.

"You're wrong, Mr. Payne," Ferdinand pointed his finger at the general counsel. "You've got a thing or two to learn. It is not acceptable in this day and age for a supervisor to touch his subordinate in a sexually offensive way. The law does not allow it. Juries don't allow it. And I would hope Marble Construction didn't allow it. But make no mistake; your company is going to pay for it. You can pay a lot of money when the jury hits you for punitive damages or you can get out of this case, today, at a bargain-basement price. The choice is yours."

Payne rubbed his head; he felt one of his migraines coming on. He couldn't believe his company would have to pay this woman, this lying, hysterical, frigid, sexually repressed woman, any money at all. These sexual harassment cases were nothing but legalized extortion; used to be a guy asks a woman for a date, she'd be flattered. Now she's got a license to sue. What the hell's the world coming to? Payne stopped rubbing his head. Defeated, he asked Ferdinand, "So what's it gonna take to get rid of this thing?"

Ferdinand glanced at Neil, his look telling him to keep quiet. "Now I don't have the plaintiff's authority, but if you can get me a hundred grand, I think I can work on her. It's going to take some time though."

"A hundred thousand dollars for this piece of crap?" Payne shook his head. The anger was building.

Ferdinand stood up. "I can see you want to talk this over among yourselves." He looked at his watch. "It's almost lunchtime now anyhow, why don't we take a break, get back together at one."

Ferdinand and Neil walked out, closing the door behind them. As they walked down the hall they could hear Payne turning his wrath on Forest. "I hire your two-bit law firm that no one ever heard of and you screw this up royally. I'm paying your rent, for Christ's sake, all the fees I've paid you. You never told me the problems with this case. You never told me anything."

Later, after finishing lunch, Ferdinand and Neil returned to the small conference room. Forest had loosened his tie, hung his jacket on the back of his chair. His forehead was moist with sweat. Latham sat in the same seat, her arms folded across her chest. Payne stood on the other side of the room, shouting at someone on the phone.

"Have you had a chance to talk?" Ferdinand asked, looking at Forest. Forest turned to Payne, deferring to his client. Payne swung the chair around and sat down. "One hundred thousand, that's it," Payne told Ferdinand. "Not a penny more. And the offer's off the table after today. I don't want to have to deal with this thing any more."

"Very well, I'll see what I can do," Ferdinand said and waived Neil to go outside. In the hall, he said, "Just hang out in my office a little while, read one of the magazines if you like. I've got to run an errand. I'll get you before I see the plaintiff again."

Neil was confused. "Don't you want to tell them the offer now. They must be getting impatient from all this waiting."

Ferdinand smiled. "You've got a lot to learn, my boy. That's the strategy. The longer they wait, the more anxious they'll be to settle. Just let them stew a while longer."

An hour later Ferdinand retrieved Neil.

"This hasn't been easy," Ferdinand said as he sat down across from Buck Gaston and Jill Tedford. "I've been talking to them for a long time and they feel very strongly about this case. They think Miss Tedford has some credibility problems." As he explained the inaccuracies with the resume, he swallowed, remembering he'd forgotten to get the defense's approval before divulging this confidential information. What the hell, he thought, why'd they mention it if they didn't want the plaintiff to know?

Tedford started shivering. "I never thought they'd check that out," she groaned. "They never cared about those things before. Why the big deal now?"

"Only because that kind of evidence may help them defend the case," Ferdinand told her.

"That's a bunch of crap'" Gaston said. "The trial judge will never let that in. If anything, they were minor misstatements."

Ferdinand raised his eyebrows. "Mr. Gaston, according to the defendant, it was fraud. And Miss Tedford had no right to her job in the first place."

"So because her resume was inaccurate they had a license to harass and fire her? Is that what the law allows?"

"I know it doesn't seem fair, but there is legal support for their position." Ferdinand glanced down at his notes, pretending he was referring to a legal citation that would mean the end of the plaintiff's case.

Tears stared falling down Jill Tedford's cheeks. At first they flowed slowly, one or two at a time, then as she got more worked up she began sobbing. Gaston and Ferdinand stared at her, paralyzed, while Neil hurried to her side with a handkerchief. "Thank you," she whimpered."

After she had regained her composure, she said, "So they won't offer anything at all?"

"I didn't say that," Ferdinand answered. "All I'm saying is they won't come anywhere near the two fifty you'd asked for. They haven't given me a solid number yet, but I think if you say you'll take fifty, they might go for it."

At the end of the conference table, Neil gasped audibly. Everyone turned toward him. "Sorry," he said, afraid he'd made a major mistake. "Must've been something I ate."

"Fifty? That's it?" Tedford asked.

"No way," her lawyer shouted.

Ferdinand held up his hand. "I didn't say they offered fifty. But as I expected, they're looking at the cost of defense. It's a business decision to them. I think I can convince them to fork over fifty, but not unless I can tell them it'll settle the case."

Tedford sighed, closed her eyes. "I don't know if I can go through with this." She looked at Gaston, thinking he must hate her for lying on the resume and not warning him about it. "I know you want more, but if we can get fifty, I think I'd like to take it."

"Jill, you can't," Gaston groaned. "The case is worth a lot more."

She shook her head emphatically. "I'm sorry, but I will take it," Tedford said loudly.

Gaston and Tedford stared at each other, each waiting for the other to give. Alter a few seconds, Gaston relented. "Okay, it's your case," he said, not bothering to hide his disgust.

"Well, let's not get carried away," Ferdinand said, holding his arms out in a gesture of conciliation. "I've got a lot of work to do first. Why don't I go back, see if I can squeeze the fifty out of them."

"If it's one dollar less than fifty thousand," Gaston said, "then we'll go to trial." He looked at Tedford, daring her to contradict him again. He was mad enough as it was; if she takes fifty, his fee'd be less than fourteen thousand. With all the hours he'd put in already, he thought, the case would turn out to be a real loser.

"Sure, okay," Tedford agreed.

In the hall, Neil pulled on his uncle's arm. "Why'd you do that?" he asked. "That was so cruel. You drove that woman to tears."

Ferdinand stopped. "Don't jump to conclusions. You're here to learn, remember? This thing isn't over yet. You'll understand by the time we're finished."

Ferdinand turned into his office and sat down behind his desk Neil looked at him in amazement. "Aren't you going to talk to the defendant?"

"Why? What's to talk about?"

"Then what are we doing here? You could've told her you had a hundred and the case would be settled."

"True, I could have." Ferdinand turned his swivel chair around, gazed out the window at the skyscraper down the street. "And I'd have a defendant who would be very upset he had to pay so much money for this crummy case. Not to mention a defense attorney who would lose face with his client, especially after billing him so much.

"So what if they look bad?"

"So what? I'll tell you so what. So I'll never see another case from Marble Construction or the Snow law firm. I wouldn't be in business very long with unhappy clients." From his top desk drawer, Ferdinand took out a metal nail file. Lifting his feet on the window sill, he started filing his finger nails.

"You know what else? If I had settled this case for a hundred, that woman would've been upset she'd gotten a hundred and fifty thousand less than she'd asked for. That's how she would've looked at it."

Neil bit his lip. This was justice, ADR style, he thought. "So you were doing her a favor?"

Ferdinand laughed, "Now you're catching on. There's a lot of psychology involved in this business. Sometimes I wish I'd been a psychologist 'stead of a judge. This would come a lot easier."

"What're you going to do now?"

"Hang out here for a little while, so both sides will think I'm working on the other." Ferdinand paused, reconsidering. "Or maybe I'll send them home for the day, tell them we're not getting anywhere. Have 'em come back tomorrow." He laughed again, a high-pitched cackle that made Neil look sideways at his uncle. "Yeah, that's it," Ferdinand chuckled. "Bring 'em back tomorrow, bill them a few more hours."

Fifteen minutes later Neil followed Ferdinand back to the plaintiff's room. Jill Tedford looked glum. Gaston purposely ignored her as he busily shuffled through a case file. "I've got some good news," Ferdinand announced, sounding upbeat. "Even I was surprised."

"You got the fifty?" Tedford asked.

"Better. They offered seventy five grand, but that's it. They won't go a penny higher. Shall I tell them we got a deal?"

Tedford's eyes widened and she broke into a broad smile. "That's wonderful," she said, looking at Gaston. "Did you hear that? Judge Pitt got us seventy five thousand."

Gaston grumbled. "Yeah, that's just great." Quickly, Gaston calculated the additional fee: another eight thousand three hundred, still a loss. "Just great," he repeated.

"Let me go down and tell them we got a deal. I'll bring them back here to work out the details." Ferdinand motioned Neil to stay put and hurried down the hall.

"You've been talking to them a long time," Payne said impatiently as soon as Ferdinand walked in.

"It's not been easy," Ferdinand said, "but I think you'll be pleased with the results."

"They'll take the hundred?" Forest asked, surprised that Gaston would give in so easily.

"Better'n that," Ferdinand answered, putting on the same smile he'd just shown the plaintiff. "She'll take seventy five."

"Alright," Payne said, excited now. "How'd you do that?"

"I just told her what you said, laid it all out. She saw the force of reason."

"That's fantastic," Payne said. Then he tapped Forest on the shoulder. "Now maybe I'll pay your bill."

Neil was amazed when everyone convened in Conference Room A, both sides smiling, acting as if they'd pulled something over on the other. Tedford shook Ferdinand's hand. "Thank you so much for your help," she said. Her sincerity made Neil cringe.

Forest also congratulated Ferdinand. "We really appreciate your help," he said. "None of us thought this case would ever settle. Your honor," Forest leaned toward Ferdinand's ear, lowering his voice, "I've got a few more cases I'd like you to work on. They need your magic touch."

"Love to help out," Ferdinand said. "Whatever I can do."

Even Gaston had cracked a smile, figuring Ferdinand had been responsible for his extra fee. Only Latham seemed subdued, her mind preoccupied with planning her job search, which she knew would begin tomorrow.

To Neil, observing everyone from his seat at the end of the table, the whole scene seemed like a Fellini movie.

The party-like atmosphere was broken up when Marilyn rushed into the room. "Judge Pitt, I have to talk to you." She was tense, clenching her teeth, and her voice cracked. Marilyn let go of the door and walked toward the judge. She folded her hands in front of her in a prayer-like gesture. "Judge, there's a man here to see you. It sounds really important." Marilyn darted her eyes around the room, checking to see if anyone was listening. The room became silent. Everyone stared at her.

"Marilyn, nothing is so important it can't wait five minutes," Ferdinand said, getting testy.

Marilyn started to answer when a man's voice said, "Judge Pitt?"

A man in a three-piece suit came into the room. He was at least six foot four, with broad shoulders that seemed to stretch his jacket to the limit. He had a thick black moustache with a patch of grey in the middle and fat red cheeks that glowed from the bright conference room lights.

"What's this all about?" Ferdinand asked, upset with all these intrusions.

"Are you Judge Pitt?" The man asked.

"Yes, I am," Ferdinand snapped.

The man pulled a badge from his jacket pocket, flashed it at Ferdinand. "Detective Dan Blanco, San Francisco Police." Jill Tedford gasped; Neil stood up, his mouth hanging open. Forest and Payne stepped away from Ferdinand. Gaston moved two steps to the side. No one spoke.

"What's this all about?" Ferdinand asked, quietly.

"Judge Pitt," Blanco said gruffly, "you're under arrest for conspiracy to obstruct justice." He put his hand on Ferdinand's shoulder. "You have the right to remain ..."

"That's preposterous," Ferdinand interrupted, shouting, his eyes bulging. "That's the most ridiculous thing I've ever heard. Whatever are you talking about?"

"Come on Judge," Blanco said, stepping forward. "You're too big a boy to be playin' that game. It took us a few months but we got the goods on you. You really liked being the presiding judge all those years, didn't you?" He glared at Ferdinand. "Don't answer until you've been Mirandized. If you like, we can take care of that after our little trip, down to 850 Bryant. You know all about eight fifty, don't you, Judge?" The central police station and lock-up were located at 850 Bryant Street in the same building as the criminal courts, where Ferdinand had cut his teeth as a rookie judge.

Ferdinand frowned, not answering.

"Now will you come peaceably, Judge, or should I put on the cuffs?" Blanco tugged on Ferdinand's arm.

"Of course I'll come. I just wanted to know what these charges were all about."

"Sure thing," Blanco answered. "A little matter of delaying civil trials, backing up the calendar to drive all those civil lit-i-gants to your friends here at the Judge's Company." Blanco talked slowly, making sure everyone in the room could hear him.

As the detective led Ferdinand, his head bowed, out of the room, Neil muttered under his breath, "What a great story!"

What If Holden Caulfield Went to Law School?

I really hate interviews. You have to smile real big, shake the guy's hand like you mean it, and act like you're actually glad to meet him. God, I hate that stuff; it's so damn phony. But if you want to get anywhere these days you had better learn to play the game.

So there I was, sitting in this fancy law office with its outrageous leather chairs and glass coffee tables, waiting to meet Mr. Big Shot Lawyer. Big deal, I thought, this place is no great shakes. Lawyers are strange birds. They think God designed such a messed up world just so lawyers could evolve to fix it. Can you believe that? Most lawyers couldn't fix a flat tire, much less the world. The only reason I went to law school in the first place was because I didn't want all these lawyers walking around thinking they were smarter than me. Now here I was, with my hand out hoping for a job. He probably expects me to kiss his ass. That kind of stuff is real tough to take, but when you're starving you got to put up with crap you normally wouldn't. And I was nothing if not starving. I was sick and tired of eating peanut butter and jelly sandwiches every day. You could say I was desperate.

Anyway, Mr. Big Shot kept me waiting for fifteen minutes. Sitting there on the soft leather couch, I started to get nervous. My palms were sweating and I was feeling queasy. Finally, to take my mind off the interview, I started thumbing through the magazines on the coffee table. There was the usual boring crap: *ABA Journal*, *American Lawyer,* and all the local legal rags. Buried at the bottom, I found a *Sports Illustrated*, and Marvelous Marvin Hagler was on the cover.

I'd been a Marvin fan for years, ever since my father took me down to the old gym in Brockton to watch him spar. Back then, Marvin was knockin' out everyone around, but he got no recognition outside Massachusetts. I already knew he was the best damn middleweight in the world, but the way things stood he would never get a title shot. My father said it was because he refused to sell out to all those sleazy promoters. They wanted to control him and fire the manager who had helped him from the beginning. Marvin told them to stick it and just kept beating everybody in sight. Finally he became champ, and now at long last he makes the cover of *Sports Illustrated*.

I reached for the magazine and then thought, What if Mr. Big Shot sees me reading *Sports Illustrated?* He'll probably take me for some kind of dumb jock. So, like a regular wimp, I put it down and pulled out the *ABA Journal.* I sat on the couch, totally disgusted with myself, and pretended to read the damn thing while I waited for high and mighty Mr. Big Shot to summon me to his goddamn holy presence.

Finally, the door opened and in he walked, looking every bit the fat-cat lawyer. He wore a dark pinstripe suit, and his pot belly hung out all over his belt. Even more disgusting, the guy was completely bald on top and had the most absurd looking comb-over in human history. Did he actually go out in public looking like that? When we shook hands I was surprised to find his palm was sweatier than mine. He introduced himself and led me into his office.

A great big oak desk sprawled between us. I sat in the hard wooden chair in front of the desk while Mr. Big Shot rested comfortably in the soft leather chair below all his framed diplomas and certificates--so there'd be no mistaking what a hot shit he was. My first impulse was to open the window so the wind would mess up his ludicrous comb-over. But like I said, I was hungry. Mr. Big Shot looked at me and then began studying my resume. "Looks like you've done well in school," he said. "Your grades are commendable."

Goddamn right they're commendable, I thought. I worked my butt off in college and law school. I even had to pay my own way, unlike Mr. Big Shot, who probably had rich parents footing every single bill on his road to the bar.

"Let me tell you about our firm. We do a lot of litigation, mostly insurance defense. Our cases range from personal injury to property damage. We expect our associates to bill forty hours a week, and we pay $30,000 a year. Would you be interested in this type of work?"

I barely heard anything beyond "$30,000." It was more money than my father made, and he'd been a janitor at the county courthouse nearly thirty years. Lawyers used to look down on him for pushing a broom, and he always said my becoming a lawyer would be his revenge.

I was so excited I lost track of what Mr. Big Shot was saying. "I'm sorry," I said. "Could you repeat the question?" I felt like an idiot.

He repeated the question and I answered, "Yes. I would be interested in doing litigation in all areas."

"What about insurance defense? Have you thought about that?"

"Yes. I definitely would like to do insurance defense." I almost choked on the words. The last thing in the world I wanted to do was insurance defense. I didn't want to be caught dead defending these big, fat insurance companies from poor people who might have slipped in a grocery store or had something fall on them while shopping at the mall. It just didn't seem right to spend my life helping rich companies get richer and richer. But, hell, this was $30,000. And what if I didn't get any other job offers? My money was sure running low.

"Fine. Tell me what experience you've had."

I told him about all the wonderful jobs I'd ever had, making sure to emphasize those dealing with insurance. I really laid it on thick, selling myself like a regular con-man, and it was clear he was buying.

"You seem to have had some good experience, and your appearance is certainly presentable."

Yeah, presentable—that was me in a nutshell. Then he looked at me without saying anything. I didn't know if he expected a response. He hadn't exactly asked a question. Sometimes these guys will do that. They throw out these vague statements and just stare at you, like they expect you to help them out with their own inability to think straight. Mostly they do this because they have no idea how to conduct a decent interview. They also know you're dying for the job so they get their kicks by giving you a hard time.

After a few seconds he returned to looking at my resume. He seemed to be pleased so far. He was going to make me an offer, I just knew it. My spine was tingling, and I prayed he couldn't hear my stomach gurgling.

He looked up at me, taking a moment before speaking. "Tell me, what does your father do for a living? Is he a lawyer, too?"

I shook my head.

"Well, is he a doctor, banker? What's his profession?" He sounded almost anxious.

I couldn't believe what I was hearing. What did it matter what my father did for a living? The guy was obviously just fishing for a reason to reject me. He was no better than those lawyers my father saw at the courthouse. My head was spinning--$30,000 down the drain. Why did he have to ask me that?

Suddenly the panic faded, and I got really angry. I looked him right in the eye and said, "My father's a janitor and you're a jerk. I'm not ashamed of what my father does for a living, but that should have nothing to do with whether you hire me. I worked my goddamn butt off in college and law school, and that's what counts. And you know what? I don't want to work for a firm that's too lazy to take the time to evaluate my qualifications without regard to my family's social status. Goodbye."

I stormed out of his office and slammed the door behind me. It wasn't until I got home that it hit me what I had done. Now I had no job, no other prospects, and still no money. Things were looking grimmer than ever.

Just then, the phone rang. It was Mr. Big Shot.

"I was very impressed with your performance today," he said. "We like someone who can stand up for himself and who refuses to be treated unfairly. You're just the kind of person we've been looking for. How'd you like to work for us at the starting salary we discussed?"

I thought I was dreaming. He still wanted to hire me—and after all that stuff I said. And I'd be making $30,000! $30,000! $30,000! The figure kept running around my head.

"Are you still there? Did you hear me?"

"Yes, I did hear you. I've just been thinking about what you said." I paused, my mind swirling. Finally, I knew my answer. "I'm sorry. I cannot accept your offer. Thank you and goodbye."

I hung up the phone and walked into the kitchen. I made myself a peanut butter and jelly sandwich, spreading an extra portion on the bread, and turned on the TV. I stared at the screen for a few minutes, then picked up the phone and dialed. "Hey, Dad," I said, smiling. "Are you watching the fight? Hagler is killing this guy."

ESSAYS

Plotting the Legal Mystery[1] and Thriller

The term "legal fiction" is used broadly, encompassing stories in both the mystery and thriller genres as well as literary fiction that feature a lawyer as the protagonist. Mysteries featuring lawyers have been popular for decades. Perry Mason's creator, Erle Stanley Gardner, became one of the bestselling authors of all time. His Perry Mason stories are classic mysteries where the loose ends are neatly tied up and the guilty party always caught and punished. The plots follow a simple formula: an accused man hires Mason to defend him against a serious charge, usually murder; Mason and his private detective Paul Drake conduct a pretrial investigation that raises questions about the client's guilt; then Mason tears apart the prosecution witnesses at trial with the guilty party eventually breaking down on the stand and confessing. Realistic? No, but compelling enough to make Perry Mason a name most Americans still recognize today.

After a few decades of sporadic bestsellers, legal fiction was revitalized by the publication of Scott Turow's *Presumed Innocent* in 1987. Turow's story of a prosecutor charged with murdering his former lover took legal fiction to a higher level. Although Turow's portrayal of realistic characters set *Presumed Innocent* apart from most mystery fiction, his ability to create a compelling plot with these characters made the book a blockbuster page turner. By having the accused murderer Rusty Sabich narrate the story, Turow was able to create tension throughout. The reader is never sure until the end whether Sabich is guilty.

Two years later the suspense legal thriller hit the bestseller lists with publication of John Grisham's *The Firm*. Unlike a mystery, the driving force of a suspense novel is not "whodunit." Although legal thrillers may contain elements of both the mystery and suspense genres, generally in a suspense novel the guilty party is known early on. A suspense novel asks, "How will the protagonist get himself out of this difficult situation?" There is usually a threat on the life of the protagonist,

---

[1] On occasion I have used the term "lawstery" to identify mysteries that feature lawyers or trials.

and often multiple chases with different groups chasing either the protagonist or each other. A heavy sense of paranoia hangs over the suspense novel. In *The Firm*, Grisham raises the stakes to the highest level. Innocent young lawyer Mitch Deere discovers his new firm is controlled by the Mafia. Soon the FBI gets involved and the lawyer does not know who to trust as he runs away from everyone.

Plotting legal mystery and thriller fiction presents different problems for the author. Lawyer authors have differing ideas of how to plot legal fiction. Steve Martini always starts with a puzzle. "You start playing "what if games," he noted in an interview.[2] "What if a character did this, and what if that happened? When you write trial fiction, it sort of takes on a life of its own because of the dynamics of the trial process or the legal process."

But for the late Boston lawyer author George Higgins, plot was not about trials but about character. "The plot is strictly what the character encounters," he said. "First, how the character either gets into, or has already gotten into, an extremely tension-filled, stress-packed, situation at the time that the story begins. And, secondly, what he or she does to get out of it." In response to critics who say he has no plot in his books, Higgins said, "And these are the critics who either haven't heard of, or don't understand, the maxim by which I believe God meant us all to live, which is 'dialogue is character and character is plot.'"

California writer Lia Matera acknowledged that in her first novel she was "bewildered by mystery plotting. There is this old Raymond Chandler line: if you're stuck, have two men with a gun walk into a room. With me it was like, all right, I'm stuck, I'll kill someone else. So I have, I think, five dead bodies in my first book."

When plotting any fiction, the author must make several important decisions that will impact how the plot unfolds. With mysteries, the author's job is to keep the reader guessing. Timing is important. When does the author reveal a certain piece of evidence? If it's revealed too early, the reader may lose interest. If too late, the reader may already have given up and put the book down. With thrillers, the thrill is everything. The author's job is to keep the reader's pulse racing.

---

[2] All quotations from lawyer authors are taken from personal interviews. Many have been anthologized in THEIR WORD IS LAW: Bestselling Lawyer Novelists Talk About Their Craft by Stephen M. Murphy, Berkley 2002.

As we will see, decisions the author makes early in the writing process have a profound impact on how he or she will tell the story.

First vs. Third Person

Choice of point of view affects all types of fiction but in the legal mystery or thriller different considerations arise. First-person legal mysteries often feature the lawyer as narrator. (Of course, Harper Lee successfully used a young girl as the narrator of *To Kill A Mockingbird*, which can be characterized as a legal mystery.) When the narrator is someone other than an attorney, it is helpful to have someone who can describe legal procedures and terms.

In first person, the narrator is present throughout the book. As Martini has stated, "When doing first person, that character, your protagonist, has to be on stage constantly and you've got to be very careful because a reader can get tired of that person unless there is something to keep the reader's attention... for me that's humor. If they keep reading for humor as well as excitement they will stay attached to your character."

With the advent of broad discovery in both civil and criminal litigation, the chances that a lawyer will be surprised at trial are low. When the lawyer serves as narrator, therefore, he or she will generally know what all witnesses will say at trial. Thus, the author of a first person mystery legal thriller must decide how close to reality the plot will be. If it's too realistic, then chances are it will be deadly dull.

To avoid boring the reader by the constant presence of the narrator, the author can use different techniques to expand point of view. For example, the protagonist may bare his soul to a psychiatrist (*Presumed Innocent*), evaluate the evidence with the spirit of his dead wife (Jeremiah Healy's John Francis Cuddy series), or listen to tape recordings of the deceased (Richard North Patterson's *Degree of Guilt*).

First person also means that any clues or information the narrator obtains must be disclosed to the reader. Holding back from the reader information the narrator learns will cause the reader to lose trust in the narrator. There is a compact between reader and author that enables the reader to suspend belief and accept as true what everyone knows to be made up. When this compact is broken by the narrator withholding key information, the reader loses interest.

In third person, the author has more flexibility to develop several aspects of the plot. In addition to showing the lawyer protagonist preparing for trial, the author can also show the opposing lawyer, the police, other bad guys, even the trial judge. These various strands can be woven to develop the plot to a climax at trial. Information can be withheld from the reader that the author reveals only at trial. Alternatively, information can be withheld from the protagonist that the reader knows. For example, the reader may know ahead of time that a particular witness will change her story at trial. The story is propelled by whether the lawyer will uncover the lies, and then how he or she will deal with them.

As with first person, the author writing in third person can use techniques to keep the reader interested. In David Baldacci's *Absolute Power*, a burglar hides in the victim's closet watching her have sex with the President of the United States before she is killed by the Secret Service. (This technique has been used extensively by veteran mystery writer Lawrence Block in his "Burglar in the Closet" series.)

Suspense legal thrillers typically use third person point of view. The author can alternate between scenes of the protagonist running for his life to scenes of the bad guys chasing him. Tension builds as the bad guys close in on the protagonist. Even though the protagonist may not know how close he is to being captured or killed, the reader knows. John Grisham is a master at this technique, which he used to good effect in *The Firm* and *The Pelican Brief*.

Criminal vs. Civil Case

Most legal thrillers focus on criminal rather than civil cases. Criminal cases present clear lines between good guys and bad guys. The public has a general understanding of criminal law so the author does not have to explain what murder or rape is. In contrast, a civil case often involves the alleged violation of complex laws like strict product liability, negligence, or discrimination. The stakes are always high in a criminal case: the liberty or life of the defendant. In a civil case the stakes are usually money, but even a lot of money does not pose as great a risk as in a criminal case.

Thus, in a civil case the author will have to explain the law and make sure the stakes are high enough to engage the reader. There are many ways to do this. The defendant may have more at stake than money: for example, reputation, political ambition, or a love interest. A common civil case featured in legal thrillers is medical malpractice. (Barry Reed's *The Verdict* and *The Deception*, Baine Kerr's *Harmful Intent*, and John

Peak's *Mortal Judgment*). These cases, however, present other plot problems. The author is faced with the daunting task of explaining to the lay reader the complexities not only of civil litigation but also of medicine. In *Mortal Judgment*, the victim died during surgery of disseminated intravascular coagulopathy, a term that may cause the eyes of many readers to gloss over.

Some authors use a civil case only as a springboard to murder. In Phillip Margolin's *The Associate*, a product liability case soon results in multiple murders. One of the risks of following this plot line is losing credibility since the protagonist lawyer will face attempts on his or her life, not exactly a typical experience for most civil lawyers.

High Profile Characters

Many legal thrillers feature high profile characters, either as protagonists or victims. For example, the characters in Richard North Patterson's *Degree of Guilt* are a television broadcaster as the rape victim and accused murderer, a famous novelist as the accused rapist and murder victim, and a former Watergate lawyer as the defense lawyer. In Michael Eberhardt's *Against the Law*, the murder victim is the governor of Hawaii. In Baldacci's *Total Control*, the Chairman of the Federal Reserve Bank is killed in a plane crash.

D.W. Buffa admits that his choice of high-profile characters in *The Legacy*, where the suspects included the President, the Governor of California, and even the KGB, was influenced by television. "A lot of the stories you see on television that move quickly involve people with money, power, or influence in the community. So it's probably a natural thing to put into a story if you want to get other people to pay attention."

One advantage of using high-profile characters is that the reader will immediately recognize that the stakes are high. People in high places have a lot to lose when they are charged with a crime. When high-profile people are murdered, it is easy to expand the list of possible suspects.

Critics have commented on the proliferation of high-profile characters in the legal thriller genre. Many legal thrillers seem to feature the Mafia (Robert Tannenbaum's *Act of Revenge*), the FBI (Barry Reed's *The Indictment*) or both (*The Firm* and William Bernhardt's *Double Jeopardy*), the IRA (Reed's *The Choice*), or the Secret Service (Baldacci's *Absolute Power*).

With low-profile characters (i.e. most people), the lawyer author must take care to sketch them carefully. Because the reader will not immediately identify with the stakes faced by a low-profile character, these characters have to be brought to life with clear personalities, ambitions, and values. For example, Grif Stockley's Gideon Page, a fortyish, balding, self-effacing public defender, has a dog named Woogie, a Columbian wife, and a penchant for timing his urinations. Stockley explained why he chose this unusual characteristic: "The walls of the house he was in were pretty thin and he was kind of embarrassed about the whole thing. That's the way he is, painfully self-conscious about the impression he's making on other people."

Conflicts of Interest

Many legal thrillers rely on conflicts of interest among different characters. Generally the conflicts are due to family relationships. For example, in *Degree of Guilt*, the accused is defended by her former lover and father of her son. In *Against the Law*, the suspected assassin of the Governor of Hawaii is Peter Maikai, who is the godfather of the prosecuting attorney. In Martini's *Compelling Evidence*, attorney Paul Madriani defends his ex-lover, who is accused of murdering her husband. One of the most intriguing conflicts occurs in Phillip Friedman's *Reasonable Doubt*, where the defense lawyer defends his former daughter-in-law accused of brutally murdering his son.

Although these conflicts raise the stakes, giving the attorney a personal involvement in the outcome, they often can strain credulity. At the outset the author will have to present strong evidence showing the attorney's motivation for taking on the case. To ensure the reader accepts the premise, the author may also want to include some legal maneuvering such as motions to disqualify. Even lay readers will wonder if this kind of conflict situation really would be allowed. Friedman acknowledged that "some people did comment on what they felt was the improbability of such representation occurring.... But it seemed to me that the reasons I gave [the defense lawyer] were sufficient."

Realism

One of the elements that distinguishes legal mysteries from detective stories is the adherence to reality. Most real detectives do not act the way Sam Spade or Spenser do, shooting, fighting, flouting the law. Readers do not pick up detective fiction, however, for realist portrayals of the lives of detectives. Unlike detectives, lawyers work in a world proscribed by strict rules and procedures. While the ethical rules of detectives may not be known by lay readers, most readers know that a lawyer cannot take a case where the lawyer's interest conflicts with the client's.

Throughout the writing of a legal mystery or thriller the author will have to make a choice between dramatic effect and reality. Authors differ in which is more important. For George Higgins, accuracy in all aspects of the novel "increases the credibility of the storyteller. It's very important, of course, because when you sit down to write something that's going to be called flat out - a 'novel', everybody who is involved in the enterprise from the beginning -- the writer, the reader, the publisher, the salesman -- knows it's a pack of lies. And the minute you lose that suspension of disbelief, you're finished -- you might as well take up another line of work."

Barry Reed disagrees: "There is nothing more boring than watching a murder trial in real life. So we had to invent a lot of stuff. I always said that doctors don't watch MASH to get tips in surgery. At least, I hope they don't!" Phillip Margolin tries "to make the books as realistic as I can." If given a choice, however, between accuracy and speeding up the story by bending the truth, he'd pick the latter.

Stephen Greenleaf's novel, *Impact*, tells the story of a plane crash case. To explain the litigation process, Greenleaf included actual legal documents such as interrogatories and deposition transcripts. "I felt that you really can't explain any kind of major litigation - which of course, air disaster litigation is - without showing some of the paperwork. As a matter of fact, my editor wanted me to take those pages out. He felt they got in the way of the flow of the narrative, and slowed the reader down, that a lot of people wouldn't read them and would be bored by them and wouldn't understand them. But I felt that ... it was essential to give somebody a taste of what the documents look like."

Legal thrillers tend to stretch reality more than legal mysteries. Margolin effectively implemented the choice between pace and realism in *The Associate*, a legal thriller that features multiple chases scenes, threats on the young lawyer's life, and piles of dead bodies. The pace is fast, though few would consider the plot realistic. Since thrillers involve physical threats, there tends to be more action than a typical lawyer would encounter in a lifetime.

Whatever choice the author makes, it is important to be conscious when the truth is being bent or the story slowed by too strict adherence to reality. The balance between pace and realism will vary with the plot.

Subplots

Most legal fiction has one or more subplots. Jay Brandon uses subplots to keep the action moving. "[O]nce you have one good idea you should wait until you have a second one because it's much better if there are two plots going on. It seems to take up the slack. When your first plot goes on hold, your second one starts up again." Prosecutor Christine McGuire uses the subplot to convey the real life of a prosecutor. "The purpose of the subplot was to show the reader that prosecutors and Kathryn deal with more than one case at a time. Prosecutors never have the luxury of being in trial to the exclusion of everything else."

Subplots can take different forms. The lawyer may be handling two seemingly unrelated cases that intersect at some point, as Clifford Irving did in his novel *Trial*. Irving believed the strength of the book came "from the reader's wondering how the lawyer is going to get out of the mess he's in and resolve the dilemma of the two cases being so stunningly related." In Robert Tanenbaum's *Act of Revenge*, the main plot involves the protagonists' twelve-year old daughter witnessing a shooting in a store. At the same time her father investigates a seemingly unrelated Mob murder and her mother investigates the decades-old apparent suicide of a Mob lawyer. Only in the end do these various plots come together.

In legal mysteries, subplots act as red herrings to distract the reader and enhance the mystery. *Presumed Innocent* has a subplot about the "B" file. For much of the book the reader believes the "B" file may hold the clue to Carolyn Polhemus's murder. What made this subplot so effective is it revealed sordid aspects of key characters' personalities such as the trial judge taking bribes.

Other subplots serve only to expound a theme or develop a character. The main plot of Richard Dooling's *White Man's Grave* chronicles the search for a Peace Corp volunteer who disappeared from his village in Sierra Leone. Meanwhile, his father, an Indianapolis bankruptcy attorney, conducts his own search from home while making regular visits to his doctors for an assortment of questionable ailments. Dooling uses the subplot to poke fun at the American medical system as well as the hypochondriac attorney.

Convergent subplots present a danger of relying on coincidence, a technique that will turn off readers. Here, adherence to reality is important. When the subplots converge for reasons that surprise the reader then credibility is lost. The author has to lay the foundation throughout the book so the reader receives clues periodically. Then when the convergence occurs the reader will be satisfied that the author has been fair.

Trials

Anyone who's read trial transcripts knows that the way people talk can be sleep-inducing. There's no need to include realistic though boring speech patterns in dialogue. Too many "you knows," "sort ofs," "I guesses," and "kind ofs" will turn off readers. The same is true for trials. Trials are slow, tedious, often dull proceedings. Certainly there are moments of high drama and these need to be accentuated in fiction. The challenge then becomes to balance realism with drama. Too far a break from realism may lose the reader; too little drama may bore the reader.

Baine Kerr notes that trial stories in general "are challenging to dramatize because most of the action takes place in rooms: conference rooms, court rooms, etc. And a civil case in particular takes some ingenuity to make things happen in an interesting and visual way."

Ever the advocate for realism in fiction, George Higgins dislikes most trial scenes. "Trials are boring and we both know it. When you watch a television show, if it's artistically and aesthetically and artfully done, you're not going to spend much real time in the courtroom unless it's one of those old Perry Mason epics, which are not trial stories, by any means, they're Perry Mason stories. The courtroom scenes in *Perry Mason* are absolutely preposterous."

Jay Brandon's solution to making the trial interesting was to omit the boring stuff such as jury selection. "One of things that I wanted to do in *Fade the Heat* was to see if I could write trial scenes that were correct by the rules of evidence, because I see so much on television that I just can't even watch because it is so violative of the rules of evidence. So I wanted to be faithful to the rules and yet try to be entertaining at the same time, of course. And I've found that one of the best ways of doing that was to omit a lot of the boring stuff."

On the other hand, Steve Martini found jury selection - known as voir dire - a useful device to portray the feelings and thoughts of the lawyers. "So I had to find ways of trying to make this entertaining to a layman. I literally had to take the voir dire process and dissect it: what it was all about, what would go through the minds of jurors, what were the fears the lawyers would be feeling here, and how easy it is to alienate jurors, how you want to save your peremptories, all of the strategies that go into this process. I want to admit that I did a great deal of research before I wrote that section. And personally, I think it is one of the best sections in the book because there's a lot of humanity."

Lawyers familiar with courtroom procedure may find more drama in a trial scene than would a lay reader. What may be an explosive bit of evidence to the lawyer may go right over the head of a non-lawyer. One technique is to create drama not by what evidence will be presented, but how will it be presented. Will the witness waffle on a key part of the testimony? Will the witness commit perjury and change his or her story? Will the lawyer display extraordinary skill in revealing the witness's lies?

Sheldon Siegel suggests compressing time during trial scenes. "The time for everything is compressed so that while the trial is going on the lawyers are still desperately looking for clues and evidence. And as time goes on, you get a feel for laying things out in a certain order for dramatic purposes."

Legal thrillers usually avoid trial scenes because of the difficulty of depicting action and building paranoia. An exception is Joseph Finder's *High Crimes* which effectively combines thrilling chase scenes with a court martial.

The Ending

Should a legal mystery end before trial, upon reaching a jury verdict, or sometime after the verdict? Of course, there's no set rule. *Presumed Innocent* never went to verdict since the judge dismissed the case during trial. But the story did not end there either since the murderer had to be revealed. Each plot will require a different strategy.

Legal thrillers often end in a series of violent scenes, many deaths, multiple threats on the protagonist's life, and narrow escapes. The bad guys are revealed and thwarted.

The decisions the author made on point of view, type of case, inclusion of subplots, and adherence to realism will dictate the ending. As with all good fiction, the ending of legal fiction should be suspenseful, yet leave the reader satisfied that the author has fairly presented the facts to justify the conclusion.

Touring San Francisco Through Legal Fiction

For an entertaining and informative perspective on San Francisco, readers should pick up one of the many novels written by the city's lawyers. These novels bring readers to parts of San Francisco they might miss on a typical tour, particularly jails and courthouses. Many lawyers may recognize offices used by the fictional lawyers in these books, from luxurious corner offices in Embarcadero Center high-rises to low-rent offices above taquerias in the Mission. Take a tour of the streets of San Francisco with some of the city's best-known lawyer authors as your guides, as they bring the city alive through their protagonists' search for justice.

John Martel

Author of four novels, this former name partner in Farella, Braun & Martel sets his books in San Francisco and the Central Valley. *Billy Strobe* features a lawyer who earned his law degree while serving time at Soledad Prison. Upon his release from prison, Strobe secures a job in a corporate law firm with views "to the north - the Golden Gate Bridge, the Marin Headlands, Mount Tamalpais, and Sausalito - and to the east - the Bay Bridge, the East Bay Hills, and Mount Diablo." But Strobe does not spend all his time in this ivory tower. While investigating a case, he travels through "San Francisco's Tenderloin District" where he passes "Cecil William's Glide Memorial Church on Ellis."

Sheldon Siegel

A corporate securities lawyer at Sheppard, Mullin, Richter & Hampton, Sheldon Siegel has written a series of novels featuring lawyer Mike Daly, an ex-priest who practices with his ex-wife. In *Final Verdict*, Daly defends a man accusing of murdering a venture capitalist from the wealthy suburb of Atherton, south of San Francisco. The victim is found in an alley outside the Basic Needs Adult Theater and Entertainment on Sixth Street.

Siegel takes readers on a tour of the Mission District, the Tenderloin, and even Polk Gulch. Daly meets a cop at Grubstake Number 2, "a funky diner on Pine Street, between Polk and Van Ness....

The smell of burgers and fries wafts through the kitschy icon that's housed in the shell of an old railroad passenger car that was part of the Key Line system that crossed the lower deck of the Bay Bridge and provided service between San Francisco, Oakland and Berkeley until auto traffic put it out of business in the late fifties... It's open until four A.M. and many of us remember when the late Harvey Milk, San Francisco's first openly gay supervisor, held court here in the wee hours as he was building his political coalition."

Lawrence Townsend

Intellectual property litigator Lawrence G. Townsend has written a novel set in Silicon Valley that turns the world of software licensing upside down and inside out. *Secrets of the Wholly Grill: A Novel About Cravings, Barbecue, and Software* is about all those things, but it's also a wicked satire of the heavy-handed tactics of Microsoft. By applying the restrictions on use contained in typical software shrinkwrap licenses to home barbecues, Townsend points out in often hilarious ways the absurd turns such licenses can take.

Townsend's protagonist is Will Swanson, a young associate in a small firm. His defense of an obese man accused of violating the shrinkwrap license for his home barbecue takes him around the Bay Area. To meet a witness he drives "out of San Jose and across the Bay by way of the Dumbarton Bridge. Touching down in the East Bay," he heads north to the UC Berkeley campus. Of course, he also spends some time in San Francisco, "home to the Sisters of Perpetual Indulgence - the few, the proud, the brave - *men* who every year, clad in decidedly irreverent habits, lead the parade in San Francisco's Gay, Bisexual and Transgender Pride Celebration."

D.W. Buffa

San Francisco native D.W. Buffa practiced criminal defense for a decade in Portland, Oregon before returning to the Bay Area. In *The Legacy*, Buffa brings Portland lawyer Joseph Antonelli to San Francisco to defend an African-American medical student accused of murdering United States Senator Jeremy Fullerton during a robbery.

Antonelli's investigation leads him to Nob Hill, which he describes as "the ultimate San Francisco address. The Spreckles, the Stanfords, the Huntingtons: the men who for a while owned a large part of California .... had all lived here, high above the city with a view that had once taken in nearly all the bay. The streets that led up to it were almost impossible to climb, but they never walked when they could ride, anyone who could not afford to ride had no business being there."

Antonelli's business soon involves rides of another sort. "I walked as quickly as I could, forcing myself not to run. I turned on Powell Street, passed the front of the St. Francis, and kept going until I reached Market Street and the rapid transit station."

John Peak

San Jose attorney John Peak's third novel, *Mortal Judgments*, is a legal thriller based on a medical malpractice case. His protagonist is San Francisco defense attorney Vicki Shea, a former physician, who finds herself fighting for her own survival while trying to prevent a multi-million dollar verdict against her client.

A trip through Marin County proves to be particularly frightening. "Vicki didn't think that she'd been at the house very long, but it was after ten o'clock when she went back through Mill Valley and found the entrance to the freeway. Traffic had thinned, so she made good time, breezing past Sausalito, thinking about the case she had just tried .... She had practically forgotten that she was in the car when she came out of the tunnel and headed for the long entrance ramp to the bridge. The windshield burst with a sound like a shell exploding."

Alfredo Vea, Jr.

San Francisco criminal defense attorney Alfredo Vea, Jr.'s novel, *Gods Go Begging*, draws parallels between the Vietnam War and battles among street gangs in San Francisco's Portrero Hill section.

His earlier novel, *The Silver Cloud Café*, also takes readers through some tough sections of the City. Many characters wind up at the Hall of Justice, the building housing San Francisco's criminal courts and jail. "Zeferino climbed the first few steps of the Hall of Justice and paused for a moment before entering the cheerless utilitarian edifice. The pause contained equal parts of pathos and revulsion, and the smallest desire to turn and run away from the problems of the pressurized world with the gray cinder-block building."

REVIEWS

The Education of Oscar Fairfax by Louis Auchincloss
Review Date: 1996

At seventy-eight years of age, Louis Auchincloss still exhibits the same energy that has enabled him to write over fifty books in the past fifty years. During a recent interview to promote his latest novel, *The Education of Oscar Fairfax*, Auchincloss revealed that the most important thing in his life is writing. Unlike some authors, he does not write for money or even to reach the hearts and minds of his readers. "I think the artist does it entirely for himself," he says, "because he has to do it, and for no other reason."

It is not surprising, then, that Auchincloss proclaims, "Fiction is a very serious business to me." So serious, in fact, that he has not read popular lawyer-authors such as Grisham, Turow, and Martini. He draws a strong distinction between novelists and lawyers. One reason he has avoided reading legal thrillers is that "they seem really to have been written by lawyer-hyphen-authors."

Although the protagonist of *The Education of Oscar Fairfax* is a lawyer, no one would characterize this novel as being written by a "lawyer-hyphen-author." There are no murders and not much suspense or action. Rather, the book bears many of the standard Auchincloss trademarks: precise language and a sophisticated style befitting his upper class characters who are constantly struggling with manners, ethics, and morals. A serious business, indeed, but a thoroughly engrossing and enlightening experience nonetheless.

The book traces the formal education of well-bred Easterner Oscar Fairfax through prestigious St. Augustine's School and Yale College. He eventually earns his law degree and joins his father's firm in its Paris branch, where he toys with the idea of writing a book on the artists and writers of the *belle epoch*. As Oscar struggles for meaning in his own life, he confronts morals and ethics in himself and those closest to him.

Throughout his life, Oscar Fairfax involves himself in the lives of others, from a hairdresser's son to a beautiful judge's daughter in Bar Harbor, Maine. Auchincloss views Oscar's distinguishing feature as being the point of the whole book: "his desire to do something, to get into the lives of other people one way or the other." Each time Oscar gets into someone's life the result often is disappointment, occasionally some joy, but never complete satisfaction. Only in the end does Oscar correct the mistakes he has been making his whole life; only then is his education complete.

Although *The Education of Oscar Fairfax*, like all of Auchincloss's books, is peopled by wealthy, highly accomplished characters, Auchincloss bristles at being labeled a chronicler of the upper class. A product of Groton School and Yale College, he explains that he simply writes about what he knows: "My life has been connected both in the law and everything else pretty much with the managerial class, the people who run things, and that's what I write about."

Nevertheless, Auchincloss points out that other writers - Tolstoy, Wharton, and Shakespeare, for example - wrote about the upper class without being labeled as such. He gives as an example *War and Peace*, which nobody thinks of as a class book. "Yet every single character is a member of the very highest and most exclusive Russian society." He concludes: "The fact that I'm branded with that is probably an indication of a fault in my writing."

Many readers would disagree with Auchincloss's own criticism of his work. Although his novels and stories concern the upper class, their themes are universal, dealing with morals and the difficult choices people of all classes must make. His books often deal with morals, Auchincloss explains, because morals play a role in every part of life. "The mere fact that standards of morality are less stringent than they used to be," he says, "doesn't mean that morality isn't there every single second. There's a great deal of talk about amorality and immorality today but that's just a different way of looking at morality."

In *The Education of Oscar Fairfax*, Auchincloss spares no one, including writers, in his exploration of morals. While at Yale, Oscar meets Danny Winslow, a student with ambitions to be a writer. After ingratiating himself with an editor to get published, Winslow then paints a devastating portrait of the editor in his next novel. Fairfax comments in the narrative: "It's true that some writers can rely on their imagination alone, but others can't. Every character of Charlotte Bronte's is directly traceable to a living model."

Auchincloss considers Winslow to be "a completely unscrupulous character." Although he sees nothing wrong with a writer's using "bits and pieces" of real people in fiction, a writer should not hurt somebody. He has regularly used famous people in novels without any problems. In one of his best known novels, *The Rector of Justin*, he modeled the main character after a distinguished jurist. Most readers assumed Auchincloss likened the character on Dr. Endicott Peabody, the famous old head master of Groton School. "In actual fact, the character was closely modeled physically on Judge Learned Hand, a man whom I immensely admired." And in another well-known novel, *The House of The Prophet*, he borrowed a great deal from Walter Lippmann, "whose lawyer I was and whom I admired immensely."

Sexual morals also play a prominent role in Auchincloss's fiction. In *The Education of Oscar Fairfax*, Oscar finds himself swept into an adulterous relationship as a young man in Paris, nearly destroying his marriage. Auchincloss admits that modern writers use adultery far in excess of its actual role in society. The fictional prevalence of adultery, he notes, is like the duel in nineteenth century French fiction: "the role of the duel is out of all proportion to the role of the duel in actual French life. But there's something about a duel that is so exciting and thrilling. As a result, the French writers just couldn't resist it. I think adultery is that way today."

With its exploration of serious moral and ethical issues, *The Education of Oscar Fairfax* is a thought-provoking book, not the easy read you'd want for a long airplane flight. Auchincloss constantly dazzles the reader with his insight, his erudition, and the breadth of his knowledge. Though somewhat overdone, his many references to famous authors such as Henry James, Edith Wharton, Euripides, Racine, and Proust and his sprinkling of Latin and French phrases force the reader to compare his or her own education with that of Oscar Fairfax.

Auchincloss denies writing novels to please his readers. "I don't really care very much if they sell or not sell if I've got the thing right," he says. "If it's right, then I'm very pleased." Readers of *The Education of Oscar Fairfax* will find that they too will be very pleased.

Absolute Power by David Baldacci
Review Date: 1996

David Baldacci's much-publicized first novel, *Absolute Power*, begins explosively: a beautiful young woman, wife of a prominent businessman, engages in sexual foreplay with the drunken President of the United States. Suddenly the President becomes violent, slaps her buttocks, then hits her in the face until blood flows from her lips. Angry, she fights back, grabbing a sharp-pointed letter opener and slashing at his arm. With the President screaming as she threatens to plunge the letter opener into his chest, two Secret Service men burst through the door, guns blazing, and shoot the President's would-be paramour dead.

Such a beginning would be laughable but for Baldacci's clever, though hardly original, plot device. Watching the entire scene through a two-way mirror in a bedroom closet is Luther Whitney, a good-natured burglar whose easy haul was interrupted by the unexpected entrance of the presidential entourage.

As he ponders the precariousness of his own situation, he overhears the President's Chief of Staff, Gloria Russell, plan a massive cover-up. Then when the bedroom is cleared, save for one passed-out presidential carcass, the plot takes another absurd turn: Russell "carefully climbed on top of the slumbering president" and ... well, you know what happened next.

Knowing he's witnessed events that would make Watergate seem like child's play, Whitney scampers out the bedroom window at the first opportunity, grabbing the letter opener on the way. Despite his sixty-six years, Whitney manages to race to his car in time to evade the secret service agents. By now they've realized he witnessed the shooting and took the letter opener, containing the fingerprints of both the President and Christy Sullivan, the victim. With such high stakes, Luther Whitney knows he's a marked man.

Absolute Power is the kind of book you can't stop reading, but you feel guilty the whole time. Many of the plot turns are implausible, but Baldacci keeps you reading at a fast pace. With action that never lets up, *Absolute Power* will probably (and did) make a terrific movie.

But as a novel, the book falls short, especially on characterization. Many characters are one-dimensional, either completely despicable like the President or wholly honorable like homicide detective Seth Frank. Some characters, like protagonist Jack Graham, do exhibit a hint of nuance and complexity. Not enough, unfortunately, especially in the case of Graham, who simply fails to engender much reader empathy.

Graham has lived a charmed life. In high school, "he was a man among boys in virtually every sport offered." In college, he was "first-team all-academic" as a heavyweight wrestler. Naturally, law school was no different: he made law review and graduated "near the top of his class."

Graham does have one little problem though. He's engaged to Jennifer Baldwin, who "possessed instant head-turning beauty to such a degree that the women stared as often as the men." She's also the daughter of Ransome Baldwin, the head of one of the largest development companies in the country. Ransome Baldwin happens to be Graham's major client at Patton, Shaw & Lord, "the capital city's number-one corporate firm." Why is this a problem? Because Graham is not sure he really loves the beautiful Jennifer, or wants to live in a twenty-acre Virginia estate, or skate his way to partner behind her father's huge fees.

Graham finds himself pining for Kate Whitney, Luther's daughter, who dumped him a few years ago. Kate did not approve of Graham's friendship with her thieving father, to whom she has not spoken in years. When Graham runs into Kate (literally) at the Mall, his problem intensifies. He takes her to lunch, but she's cold and distant, immersed in her career as a prosecutor with no interest in a man who's already engaged.

Though we know all along that Graham and Kate will get together, Baldacci manages to maintain reader interest by developing their relationship slowly and convincingly. While Graham chases Kate, everyone else is chasing her father: the White House, homicide detective Seth Frank, Walter Sullivan, husband of the victim, and eventually also Graham.

Sullivan hires an assassin to find and terminate Luther, whom he believes is his wife's killer. Like many of the characters in this novel of the high and mighty and the rich and powerful, Sullivan's assassin is no slouch. He has "a degree in international politics from Dartmouth" and commands a "per-hit fee in excess of one million dollars."

With all these people chasing Luther Whitney, *Absolute Power* contains enough suspense to keep the most jaded reader enthralled. The Secret Service, Seth Frank, and Walter Sullivan's assassin are on a collision course with Luther Whitney and Jack Graham in the middle. You know something terrible will happen; it's just a question of when.

Baldacci's best moments are when he pokes fun at Graham's pompous senior partner, Sandy Lord. During lunch, Lord tries to impress Graham with his candor. He describes himself as "greedy, egocentric, power-hungry." But in Lord's warped view of the world, these are positive traits. "That's who I am," he tells Graham. "I don't try to disguise it or explain it. Every sonofabitch that has ever met me has come away knowing exactly who and what I was. I believe in what I do. There's no bullshit there."

Lord does have some words of wisdom for Graham, words that will ring true for many associates:

> [T]he only security any lawyer has are the clients he controls. They never tell you that in law school and it's the most important lesson you have to learn.... Even doing the work should take a back seat to that. There'll always be bodies to do the work.

Baldacci's portrayal of the Secret Service, however, does not ring true, as he belatedly admits in an Author's Note at the end of the book. *Absolute Power* turns this illustrious group into a bunch of cold-blooded, immoral killers, indistinguishable from Walter Sullivan's hired assassin. Even twelve-year veteran Bill Burton, a hero who once took a bullet for the President, easily succumbs to the blind ideal of protecting the President at all costs, no matter how illegal. His partner, rookie Tim Collin, fares no better. After being seduced by Gloria Russell, he becomes little more than a robot, panting like an obedient dog eager to do the Chief of Staff's bidding.

Despite its faults, *Absolute Power* shows Baldacci to be a writer of some promise, particularly in his humorous and often biting portraits of Washington, D.C. politicos. For a fast and easy read, you won't be disappointed with *Absolute Power*.

Rules of Evidence by Jay Brandon
Review Date: 1992

Despite many reforms in the past four decades, racism still pervades our society. Blacks remain disproportionately poor, undereducated, and imprisoned. During the boom period of the 1980's, blacks experienced the frustration of seeing their white neighbors flourish. But blacks' frustration at their economic or social conditions has been overshadowed in the past decade by their frustration with the legal system. In most major cities blacks frequently charge the police with brutality. On two well-publicized occasions in the 1980's blacks in Miami rioted when a police officer was acquitted of improper conduct in killing a black suspect.

But when Rodney King was beaten by four Los Angeles police officers, blacks had reason to hope that this would be different. The jury would not have to take the word of the black victim that he had been mistreated. The jury would not have to weigh the credibility of white police officers against that of the black suspect. No, this would be different. The beating was recorded on videotape. The shocking evidence was right there for everyone to see. There was no way these white police officers would walk. Justice would finally be served.

So when the jury announced its acquittals it was understandable that blacks - as well as many whites - were outraged. And it was understandable, though certainly not excusable, that blacks expressed their outrage in violent ways. Even with irrefutable evidence the white cops go free. There was just no way a black person could obtain justice in the white legal system. And so there were terrible riots in Los Angeles, urban unrest throughout the country. In a show of uninspiring leadership President Bush blamed the riots on the failure of social reforms of the 1960's. Vice President Quayle took an indirect swipe at the prevalence of maternal families in the black community by attacking the morals of television character Murphy Brown, a white yuppie single mother.

In the midst of all this injustice and dubious theories, it is refreshing to come across a novel like Jay Brandon's *Rules of Evidence*. Brandon, a San Antonio attorney and Edgar nominee (for *Fade the Heat* in 1991), explores racism in an often brutal but realistic way. While he touches on the economic effect of racism on blacks as a whole, he is primarily concerned with the individual, particularly the psyche of his protagonist, a successful black lawyer. Brandon's treatment of the many layers of racism rings much truer than the flip rationalizations of our leaders; one begins to wonder which is fact and which fiction.

Rules of Evidence is told from the perspective of Raymond Boudro, a black criminal defense attorney in San Antonio. In his early forties with numerous trials under his belt, Boudro is considered one of the top defense attorneys in the area.

While defending a black client accused of dealing drugs, Boudro cross-examines arresting police officer Mike Stennett during a suppression hearing. Stennett conducted a full search of Boudro's client after noticing a wad of money in his pocket. Boudro asks Stennett about the role the defendant's race played in the search:

"And a black man with a lot of money just has to be a drug dealer, doesn't he, Officer?"

Stennett wanted to say it. You could see the words in his mouth....

"Not necessarily. He could be a pimp."

Shortly after this hearing a small-time black drug dealer is found beaten to death in an alley on the east side of San Antonio, a predominately black and impoverished neighborhood. The punch was so vicious the victim's nose bone had penetrated his brain. The police make little effort to find the killer until an old man from the neighborhood claims he saw the murder. While at the police station reviewing mug shots, the old man points to Officer Mike Stennett and says "that's him."

Claiming to be impressed with Raymond Boudro's trial skills, Stennett asks Boudro to represent him. At first Boudro balks at defending the man he knows to be racist and to have a reputation for routinely beating up black suspects. Ultimately Boudro decides to accept the case, but for reasons other than proving his client's innocence.

After Boudro's brother-in-law tells him that Stennett is using him, "[g]ettin' the black boy to clean up the white man's mess, like always," Boudro responds: "'If I'd told him to go away, Faruq ... he would've. And I'd be left wondering. And when the case ended I'd still be wondering. Did he get away with it? This way I'll know.'"

Boudro's investigation reveals that Stennett arrested blacks in a far greater proportion than whites. And Stennett was known to beat up black suspects without hesitation. Boudro begins to think Stennett should still be convicted even if he is innocent of this isolated charge.

As Boudro agonizes over his conflicting obligations to his client and his race, his relationship with Stennett becomes increasingly tense.

"White people suck," Stennett said.

Raymond was startled into laughter. "I hate to be the one to break this to you..."

"Yeah, I know. But being white and poor is like being rich and black. Don't do you no good to belong to the club if nobody'll dance with you."

Raymond couldn't let him get by with that. "Poor white boy still has an advantage."

"That's true," Stennett said musingly. "I might could make some money, but you'll always be a nigger."

At trial Boudro astounds prosecutor Becky Shirhart by not objecting to evidence that Stennett routinely called blacks "niggers" and that he frequently beat up black suspects. When she asks Boudro if he intends to use the rules of evidence, he responds that there are no rules. He doesn't care what the jury decides; only the truth matters.

Not all blacks share Boudro's view that Stennett must be punished for his mistreatment of blacks. His own father, the owner of a small grocery store in the east side, thinks highly of Stennett for ridding the streets of the drug dealers who have ravaged his community.

In the end, Boudro makes some surprising decisions which allow him to fulfill his ethical obligation to his client and still maintain his integrity as a black man. At the same time he is forced to come to terms with his own feelings about caucasians and with the delicate balance between blacks and whites in our predominately white society. When he learns that many white police officers disapprove of Stennett's tactics, he gains a greater appreciation of white people.

Despite a contrived climax that makes *Rules of Evidence* an unsatisfactory mystery, the book does succeed in challenging our assumptions about being black in America. Brandon convincingly shows how even a black professional like Boudro must confront racism on a daily basis - in court when the judge assigns him all the indigent black defendants and even at his son's soccer games when other parents attribute his son's athletic skill to his race. The reader admires Boudro - for escaping the lure of drugs that ensnared many of his boyhood friends, and for overcoming his own biases and urge for vengeance to achieve justice, while maintaining his dignity both as a lawyer and a black man.

Perhaps if our nation's leaders had read *Rules of Evidence*, they would have realized the complexity of causes that led to the Los Angeles riots, and have been better prepared to address the solutions.

Loose Among the Lambs by Jay Brandon
Review Date: 1994

A serial child molester is on the loose in San Antonio and citizens are clamoring for his arrest. When an old friend delivers a suspect to District Attorney Mark Blackwell, the favorable publicity boosts Blackwell's chances for re-election. But when the case falls apart, it becomes clear that there is still a wolf "loose among the lambs," and Blackwell suddenly finds himself struggling for his political life. Although Blackwell later files charges against Austin Paley, a prominent attorney with political connections, his troubles are far from over.

Loose Among the Lambs confirms Jay Brandon's reputation as a skilled author of literate legal thrillers, combining suspense with substance. Returning to characters featured in previous novels, particularly *Fade the Heat*, Brandon presents a realistic portrayal of the problems faced by prosecutors in trying to convince a jury to accept a child's word over a respected adult's.

The story is enriched by the political maneuvering caused by Paley's high profile among San Antonio's movers and shakers. Paley is a throw-back to the good old days, when connections and influence were the order of business and even district attorneys were not averse to granting favors. A reporter describes those days to Blackwell: "We had a sort of gentleman's agreement to let certain stories pass. And in return they gave us others. They made us feel we were all in the same club, and you didn't betray fellow club members."

A confidante to politicians, Paley knows where the bodies are buried. He calls in his markers, sending a clear message that he will not go down alone. Blackwell feels the heat, leaving no doubt that by prosecuting Paley, he has put his career in jeopardy.

Although several children have identified Paley as their molester, the evidence is thin. The children give conflicting accounts and because of the passage of time their memories have faded. In some instances parents are reluctant to press charges, fearing the long-term damage to their children from a public prosecution. Reluctantly, Blackwell dismisses three of the four cases against Paley. The heat intensifies. The mayor telephones, arguing Paley's innocence. Blackwell's opponent pulls ahead of him in the polls.

Blackwell's luck gets even worse when his mentor, former district attorney Eliot Quinn, agrees to defend Paley. Quinn's impeccable reputation for integrity lends legitimacy to the defense. Shocked that his former boss would oppose him, Blackwell visits Quinn at his home and learns the secret that binds Quinn to Paley, a terrible secret that changes forever Blackwell's opinion of Quinn and that - if disclosed - would shatter Quinn's reputation forever.

Blackwell's hopes rest with ten-year-old Tommy Algren, a child whose poise and maturity worry Blackwell. Tommy looks like a little adult, a miniature Austin Paley, sitting straight in his chair, his light brown hair carefully combed. He speaks in a detached voice, relating what Paley did to him without shame or embarrassment. His poise is almost too perfect.

WHAT IF HOLDEN CAULFIELD WENT TO LAW SCHOOL?

To convict Paley, Blackwell must gain Tommy's confidence and seduce him in his own way, knowing he will abandon him when the case is over. He gives more of himself to Tommy than he did to his own son, David, taking Tommy to a batting cage to work on his swing, sharing his own childhood battles with bullies. He meets him after school, bypassing Tommy's parents. Soon Blackwell grows so close to Tommy, he feels an urge to hug him, only to hold back for fear of acting inappropriately.

With the help of child psychiatrist Janet McLaren, Blackwell rehearses Tommy's testimony. The case is difficult. Tommy waited several years before reporting the assault; there are no witnesses that Paley was ever alone with him. As with all child molestation cases, the child's credibility will be attacked. In preparing Tommy to testify, Blackwell must be careful to avoid tainting the testimony with suggestions: "Children want desperately to please us," McLaren tells him. "Nothing is as important to them as adult approval."

Like most victims of child molestation, Tommy feels conflicting emotions about his molester. While he fears retaliation by Paley, he occasionally feels affection for him as well, affection for the attention and understanding Paley gave him. And Tommy feels guilty for hurting him. As McLaren tells Blackwell: "'Children hate what happened to them but still love the molester.'"

As Blackwell puts all his energy into the case, he worries about his son's happiness. David is detached, his marriage seemingly loveless. When they get together, Blackwell has difficulty expressing his love for his son. He regrets the way he spent David's childhood, at the office away from David, devoted to his work.

For Blackwell the trial of Austin Paley takes on a larger meaning than simply convicting a child molester, or even winning re-election. As the evidence unfolds, Blackwell learns how little he knew about himself and those closest to him. He is forced to confront his own failures, reevaluate his past, and question his assumptions about others. Ultimately, Blackwell concludes the trial by attacking Tommy's parents - and by implication, himself -for their loose supervision and inattention to Tommy that allowed the molestation to occur. Although Blackwell realizes he too is guilty, he hopes the damage to his own son is not irreversible.

To be sure, *Loose Among the Lambs* does have its faults: the trite district attorney's election, a slow and implausible beginning, and a pat ending. But overall Brandon has written a brilliant book, weaving serious themes with riveting suspense. In portraying the horror of child molestation, Brandon delves deeper, exploring its causes, rooted in how parents treat or mistreat their children. For Mark Blackwell, the trial of Austin Paley has a profound effect, making him regret his past errors in raising his son, yet breathe a sigh of relief at what might have happened. Readers too - no matter their own family experiences - cannot help but be affected by this artful novel.

Defiance County by Jay Brandon
Review Date: 1996

Jay Brandon has written several compelling legal thrillers, most combining a literate style with serious themes such as racism and child molestation. In *Rules of Evidence* and *Loose Among the Lambs*, his thoughtful exploration of these themes overcame occasional lapses in plot. Unfortunately, his latest novel, *Defiance County*, lacks a compelling theme while suffering from frequent lapses in plot.

Despite the title, *Defiance County* has more to do with a small town than the county in which it sits. The book attempts to explore the dark side of small-town life: the petty jealousies, longstanding grudges, and narrow minds. The east Texas town of Galilee thrives because of one person, aging matriarch Alice Beaumont, owner of the Smoothskins panties factory. When Alice's daughter Lorrie and her husband Ronnie are murdered, and her baby granddaughter kidnapped, the town splits apart. Relationships become even more strained when Billy Fletcher, brother of District Attorney Morgan Fletcher and foreman of the Smoothskins factory, is arrested.

Because of the conflict of interest, deputy attorney general Kelsey Hatch is assigned to prosecute the case. Hatch's legal career has been on a downward spin since she compromised a prosecution she viewed as unethical. The assignment to prosecute Billy Fletcher feels, to her, like banishment to Siberia. While driving through Galilee for the first time, Kelsey senses something different about the town: "Kelsey tried to imagine living here. How isolated people must feel. How lonely. The feeling of being alone in the woods must scare some people. Others it would imbue with a sense of power."

As Kelsey conducts her investigation into the murders, she soon realizes how weak the evidence is. Billy Fletcher's fingerprint was found on the gun tied to the murders; a witness saw him arguing with Ronnie a few hours before the bodies were found. Billy and Ronnie disagreed strongly over the direction of the Smoothskins factory, Billy favoring the status quo and Ronnie wishing to sell. Perhaps Billy killed Ronnie in a fit of rage, Kelsey thinks, and Lorrie had the misfortune of witnessing the murder. But that doesn't explain what happened to the baby.

The baby has disappeared without a trace, despite massive search efforts by the townspeople. As Kelsey reconstructs Billy Fletcher's movements the day of the murder for evidence connecting him to the baby, the story drags, since Brandon never offers a plausible reason for Billy to take the baby. When Kelsey does find evidence - recently burned remnants of the baby's clothes - in the woods outside Galilee, it is a pure coincidence. Brandon's purpose soon becomes clear, though forced, as he uses the scene to initiate Kelsey's affair with her investigator, Peter Stiller. The scene soon turns laughable when Kelsey gets attacked by red ants and has to shed her jeans.

Despite the heinousness of the crime, Galilee's sympathies lie with the defendant. Most people don't believe Billy could have killed anyone. The citizens of Galilee are not enamored with the idea that one of their own will be prosecuted by an outsider. Although everyone is upset about the baby, no one's too concerned about

Ronnie's death. He too was an outsider, and dared think about selling the Smoothskins factory.

Despite weak evidence against Billy Fletcher, Kelsey brings the case to trial. Her motivation is questionable: to reclaim her reputation as a competent trial attorney; to show Alice Beaumont (who used her political connections to have Kelsey assigned to the prosecution) that she cannot control her; or perhaps, because she really believes Billy is guilty.

The evidence Kelsey presents, however, will make the reader question why the case is even going to trial. When Billy's defense attorney calls several witnesses to say that Billy was on his way to North Carolina at the time of the murders, we can't help but scoff at Kelsey's weak attempts to discredit them. Without a compelling case against Billy Fletcher, the book fails keep the reader's interest.

The true mystery in *Defiance County* lies under the surface, in the relationships among the citizens of Galilee. As Peter Still tells Kelsey, "This is a small town .... If you only find two connections between some of us, you're still only on the surface." Kelsey gradually learns what he meant: Peter Stiller once had a crush on Lorrie, which may explain his zealous investigation of the case; Judge Linda Saunders and district attorney Morgan Fletcher were once (and may still be) lovers; Morgan Fletcher and his wife are having marital troubles; and Morgan's wife Katherine seems to be hiding a terrible secret. Somehow it all ties into the Smoothskins factory.

In the end, Brandon reveals the murderer using an old-fashioned technique, reminiscent of the Perry Mason stories. Kelsey confronts the murderer and engages in a long monologue describing her theory of the murders and kidnapping. When the murderer sees he's trapped, he confesses and tries to escape. Everything is tied up so neatly - and implausibly.

Despite *Defiance County's* faults, upon finishing the book the reader will feel unsure, cautious, as if a dark foreboding cloud hovers overhead, like the one hiding the deep personal ties of the citizens of Galilee. You realize what these small-town folks know, perhaps even unconsciously: no matter how much things seem to have changed, you can never escape the past.

Brain Storm by Richard Dooling
Review Date: 1998

Richard Dooling thinks hate crime laws are a bad idea. Not that he favors hate crimes, he just views the law's efforts to punish people for their thoughts as preposterous. In his third novel, *Brain Storm*, Dooling takes this theme and runs with it in directions that seem at once outrageously funny, yet disturbingly true. A nominee for the National Book Award for his 1994 novel, *White Man's Grave*, Dooling again displays his exceptional skills as a fiction writer by crafting an entertaining novel while making a serious and thought-provoking point.

The alleged perpetrator of a hate crime in *Brain Storm* is James F. Whitlow, a working-class hothead charged with murder. His victim is Elvin Brawley, a black deaf printer and local artist, who had been hired by Whitlow's wife to tutor their deaf son in sign language.

There is no doubt that Whitlow killed Brawley; the only question is why. Whitlow claims he caught Brawley in bed with Whitlow's wife. Other evidence indicates that after killing Brawley, Whitlow made derogatory comments about Brawley's race and disability. So did Whitlow kill Brawley because he was black? Because he was disabled? Or because he was sleeping with his wife?

The United States Attorney for the Eastern District of Missouri (St. Louis) smells a case with a lot of political mileage and charges Whitlow with a hate crime. The statute in question requires that Whitlow's sentence be enhanced if he intentionally selected his victim because of race or disability. Whitlow's court-appointed lawyer, Joe Watson, is a young associate at a large corporate law firm, whose primary experience has been in the realm of intellectual property violations involving graphic, violent computer games. He was appointed because of a law review article he authored in law school.

The firm is horrified that one of its associates will be defending an accused murderer and asks District Court Judge Whittaker Stang to rescind the appointment on the ground of Watson's inexperience. Judge Stang summarily denies the request and embarrasses Watson's boss in the process, reminding him of a terrible courtroom defeat he suffered years before.

Dooling portrays Judge Stang as a power-hungry jurist intent on abusing his lifetime appointment by humiliating every lawyer who appears before him. The extremes to which Judge Stang abuses his power will bring chuckles to any lawyer who has felt the sting of a federal judge's wrath. Referring to two three-foot stacks of motion papers, Judge Stang tells a full courtroom of lawyers:

> "I can admit to you and to your clients that I do not read any of these papers. Do you know why I can admit it? Not reading them is not a felony. Admitting that I do not read them is not a high crime or misdemeanor."

Concerned only with avoiding impeachment, Judge Stang seemingly knows no other limits. His method of ruling on motions to continue trial hopefully will not be adopted by other judges:

> "I want everybody who is seeking continuance of a trial date for any reason, including, but not limited to, deaths, vacations, missing witnesses, missing lawyers, drunk lawyers, the press of other business, a conflict in another court - any reason. I want all the lawyers seeking continuances to step over to my right...." The judge faced the mass of lawyers on his right and spread his arms like Charlton Heston doing Moses. "All requests for continuances, all the requests for additional time and for leave to file out of time, are hereby denied."

Brain Storm's other characters are no less colorful. Watson hires beautiful Dr. Rachel Palmquist as the defense expert witness to rebut the charge that Whitlow was motivated by hate. Dr. Palmquist studies how certain motives affect or are controlled by specific areas of the brain. She describes her work to Watson as follows:

> "A good brain scientist might ask about the timing, the sequence, the neural hardware required to transmit these two emotions or motives - rage and bigotry.... What if rage caused by marital infidelity is not the same thing as hate inspired by bigotry?"

After his boss's embarrassment in court, Watson finds himself unemployed with one poor client but without the financial support of his firm. He decides to associate Myrna Schweich, a Heineken-guzzling, pot-smoking, foul-mouthed, radical lesbian defense attorney. When this unlikely pair locks horns with the prosecutor, the insults fly in all directions, leaving the reader laughing in tears.

Dooling's writing style is fast-paced and energetic, but never boring. By gradually piling on clues, he keeps the reader guessing until the end why Whitlow killed Brawley. Even then, he makes us wonder if we can ever know why someone acted in a certain way. As Watson tells Judge Stang in response to a question on whether he ever wonders about his own motives:

> "Sometimes I do things, and I don't understand why. Often I have mixed motives, but I can't sort them out, and then at other times I think I have certain motives, but I actually have other motives."

Few books provide as complete a package as *Brain Storm*: wit, wisdom, a compelling mystery, colorful characters, and a powerful and thought-provoking theme. It is a book that stays with you even after you've closed the cover, forcing you to think of hate crime laws in new and perhaps unpopular ways. In short, few readers will remain unchanged after finishing *Brain Storm*. And what more can you ask from a work of fiction?

High Crimes by Joseph Finder
Review Date: 1998

Joseph Finder's *High Crimes* is a legal thriller set in an unusual venue: the military courts of justice. The case involves a top-secret mission in Central America and the My Lai-type massacre of nearly a hundred innocent civilians. Fast-paced, with many intriguing twists, *High Crimes* will keep readers turning the pages until the explosive ending.

The accused, Tom Chapman, has been married for three years to Harvard Law Professor Claire Heller Chapman. Tom, an investment advisor, has been a loving husband and model father to Claire's six-year-old daughter from a prior marriage.

The Chapmans' world shatters after dinner at a Boston seafood restaurant. They are celebrating Claire's recent appellate victory, in which her brilliant advocacy resulted in a rich defendant avoiding conviction for raping a fifteen-year-old girl. While strolling through the mall near the restaurant, the Chapmans are accosted by two men in suits. One says to Tom, "Ronald Kubik, federal agents. We have a warrant for your arrest." Tom tells them they're mistaken, but when they try to cuff him, he knocks them down and runs.

As Tom fights off the federal agents, Claire sees a new side to her husband. His high kicks and sharp punches could only be accomplished by a martial arts expert. Claire "watched in speechless astonishment, a dull, almost vacant state of horror and disbelief."

When Tom escapes, the agents detain Claire and insist that her husband is not who she thinks. His real name, they say, is Ronald Kubik and he's been a fugitive from justice for thirteen years. If not for dumb luck, they never would have caught up to him. There had been a burglary at Claire and Tom's house a few days earlier. The police ran all the fingerprints in the house, including Tom's. A run on the prints led to federal agents being contacted.

Unable to find Tom, the agents begin to tail Claire. Her life becomes uprooted and she begins to wonder about the man she married. She knows little of his family, having met only his father one time at the wedding. Her doubts increase after a private investigator she hired tells her the high school and college Tom claimed to graduate from never heard of him.

Finally, Tom contacts her, insisting she meet him at a remote location in Western Massachusetts. Thinking she shook the federal agents' tail, she drives to Tom. He admits deceiving her about his background but claims he's innocent of the charges. Several American Marines were murdered in an ambush in San Salvador.

Tom's colonel ordered his unit to find and kill the commandos. The unit tracked them to a village outside San Salvador where Tom (Ron) claims he witnessed the mass shooting of eighty seven unarmed civilians. Although he never fired a shot, he was being blamed because he wouldn't cover it up. "They pinned the blame on me," he tells Claire. "They said I'd lost it. I'd flipped out. I'd killed all these people."

Federal agents, of course, followed Claire to Western Massachusetts and arrest Tom. In one of many questionable decisions by Claire, (who does nothing to convince us she deserves her reputation as a nationally renowned trial attorney), she decides to defend her husband.

Recognizing her limitations, Claire enlists the help of a court martial attorney named Charles O. Grimes III. They obtain Tom's military file, which states that he was part of the Turncoat Elimination Program, United States-government-sponsored hit squads whose purpose was to eliminate American traitors and deserters.

Convinced by Tom's denials, (again proving she had no business taking the case), Claire decides to subpoena the chief of staff of the army and launch a broad attack on the military. Grimes disagrees with this strategy, telling her:

> Every civilian who's ever gone into a military general court-martial and tried to attack the foundations of the military has lost his case. No exceptions. The military is a tight, closed fraternity. They take it real serious. Military justice is a deadly-serious business.

The military also assigns Tom a detailed defense counsel, Terry Embry, who's fresh out of law school. Although Claire and Grimes question Embry's loyalty, they decide to keep him on the team. They need his help since, unlike civilian attorneys, he has the power to order military witnesses to appear for an interview.

Things get tense when Claire learns the prosecutor had advance knowledge of defense strategies. Claire and Grimes soon suspect Embry of leaking information, only to discover that Claire's house has been bugged.

For civilian attorneys, as for Claire Chapman, the trial of Ronald Kubik will provide a crash course on military law and procedure. Readers will learn new terms such as Article 32 hearings (from the Uniform Code of Military Justice) and that a speedy trial for a military defendant means within 120 days from confinement. There are also unusual rules for jury selection.

> The members of the jury were selected by the convening authority. It was illegal to stack the court, though it was known to happen from time to time. Members were also supposed to be free to vote their conscience, without guidance from above, or "command influence." Generally, members were supposed to be senior in rank to the accused. If the accused was an enlisted man, not an officer, he had the right to request that at least a third of the jury members be enlisted.

Perhaps the most convincing character is Claire's co-counsel, Grimes, who tells her that a 1996 decision of the Court of Appeals for the Armed Forces allows trial judges to admit polygraph tests as long as they're exculpatory. She makes immediate use of this knowledge by having Tom undergo a polygraph. Her initial elation over the results and the judge's decision to admit them soon turns to regret. The prosecution calls a witness to testify that Tom was specifically trained in the military to beat polygraph tests.

Readers may have a hard time accepting how gullible and naive Harvard Law Professor Chapman appears. Could she really have been married to Tom for three years and never wondered why she hadn't met his family or old friends? Readers may also quibble with Finder's decision to have Claire defend her husband. But this decision drives the plot and, as Finder intended, raises the level of suspense, keeping the reader guessing to the end.

Overall, as a plot-driven novel with gripping suspense, *High Crimes* scores high marks. Finder provides just enough information to keep readers wondering whether Tom is guilty. And, in addition to being entertained, you will learn a thing or two about military justice.

The Pelican Brief by John Grisham
Review Date: 1993

John Grisham made so much money from *The Firm* that he was able to retire from the practice of law and devote himself full-time to writing. *The Firm* showed Grisham to be a writer of some promise so his decision seemed sound. Unfortunately, that promise is not fulfilled in *The Pelican Brief*, a poorly constructed and unsatisfying novel which appears to have been written primarily to capitalize on the success of *The Firm*. It is distressing to see such a promising writer trade literary principles for commercial success.

The Pelican Brief begins with the assassination of two Supreme Court justices on the same day. Elderly Justice Abe Rosenberg, a liberal in the tradition of William Douglas, and his colleague, staunch conservative Justice Glenn Jensen, seemingly have nothing in common. Even though Jensen is found strangled in a gay porno theater, everyone thinks there must be some connection. But the combined forces of the FBI, the CIA, and the White House are unable to find any link to the killings.

The murders go unsolved until Tulane law student Darby Shaw discovers a connection after burying herself for several days in the law library. She puts her theory into a brief - the pelican brief - which finds its way into the hands of the FBI.

All of a sudden people are very interested in Darby Shaw. Her boyfriend, Tulane law professor Thomas Callahan, dies when a bomb meant for Shaw explodes in his car. Shaw realizes the pelican brief was right on target. She knows these people are ruthless so she hides out in New Orleans.

White House Chief of Staff Fletcher Coal dismisses the pelican brief as just a theory, but is concerned that the brief contains a photograph of the president - arm in arm with one of his major campaign contributors - which may hurt his chances for re-election. So the president asks FBI director Denton Voyles to let the matter rest for a week.

Meanwhile Shaw moves around the French Quarter in various disguises. She cuts and dyes her hair but makes the mistake of paying for her hotel room with a credit card. The bad guys easily trace her, but - in one of the more implausible plot twists in a book full of implausible events - Shaw manages to escape the clutches of the assassin, Khamel, a copycat of Carlos the Jackal.

Washington Post reporter Gray Grantham learns of the pelican brief through an informant at the White House. He makes some inquiries of White House officials but comes up with nothing. Early one morning he receives a phone call from a young lawyer who identifies himself only as Garcia. Garcia is scared and tells Grantham he has seen a memo at his firm that concerns the assassinations of the supreme court justices.

Shaw eventually contacts Grantham and together they search for Garcia. Garcia hasn't yet worked up the courage to blow the lid on his firm and refuses to tell Grantham his real name. While Shaw and Grantham search for this mysterious attorney, Shaw continues to run and hide from her own searchers. After a while, with all this hiding, searching and chasing, the plot begins to resemble a slapstick comedy routine with people in different uniforms running mindlessly in circles.

For the first half of the book Grisham withholds from the reader the motive for killing the justices. Although we learn of the pelican brief near the beginning, its contents are not divulged. While many of the characters have read the brief and regularly discuss it, the reader is kept in the dark. This inartful attempt at creating suspense serves only to make the reader feel cheated.

Despite Grisham's considerable commercial success, *The Pelican Brief* shows that Grisham has a long way to go before attaining comparable literary success. The flaws are numerous: the characters are one-dimensional, their motivations either weak or nonexistent, and the plot has enough loose ends to keep a hair dresser busy for years.

If literary flaws were the only negative aspect of *The Pelican Brief*, we could dismiss it as just commercial trash. But the book has a more troubling aspect. Near the end of the book, Grisham introduces more attorneys, the same kind of greedy murderous types that populated *The Firm*. In *The Firm*, a Memphis law firm made bundles of money for its Mafia-controlled partners. Whenever one of the firm's associates suffered a twinge of conscience, the firm promptly had him or her bumped off. The public loved the book, making *The Firm* the best selling novel in the country last year.

In addition to greedy murderous attorneys, *The Pelican Brief* contains a law professor who regularly hits on his students and incompetent or perverted United States Supreme Court justices. Only Darby Shaw, apparently not yet tainted by having actually practiced law, and Garcia, still too young to have been corrupted, are portrayed favorably.

This constant negative portrayal of attorneys becomes particularly grating. A discussion between Shaw and Grantham summarizes what seems to be Grisham's general attitude toward attorneys:

> "If you go to a good law school, finish in the top ten percent, and get a job with a big firm, you'll be earning six figures in a few short years, and it only goes up. It's guaranteed. At the age of thirty-five, you'll be a partner raking in at least two hundred thousand a year. Some earn much more."
>
> "What about the other ninety percent?"
>
> "It's not such a good deal for them. They get the leftovers."
>
> "Most lawyers I know hate it. They'd rather be doing something else."
>
> "But they can't leave it because of the money. Even a lousy lawyer in a small office can earn a hundred thousand a year after ten years of practice, and he may hate it, but where can he go and match the money?"

It is no secret that some lawyers are more concerned with billable hours and making a lot of money than effecting justice. But Grisham goes overboard and actually seems to be pandering to the public's negative opinion of attorneys. Perhaps this is one reason his books sell so well. In overpopulating his books with greedy unethical attorneys, Grisham does a disservice to the majority of lawyers in this country who do not fit Grisham's mold. He reinforces and perpetuates the public's negative attitude toward attorneys. While a novelist should be allowed to portray the legal profession in many lights, Grisham is guilty of excess, an excess which detracts from the literary merit as well as the social value of his work. And in the process, he wastes his considerable talent.

The Rainmaker by John Grisham
Review Date: 1995

John Grisham's sixth novel, *The Rainmaker*, is a fast-paced adventure story with heroes who are all good and villains who are all bad. It is a modern mythical tale where the hero overcomes all obstacles, vanquishes far stronger foes, and rides away in the sunset with the pretty damsel safe in his arms. Even though the plot is predictable - we know all along that the hero will win, - and packed with coincidences, and the writing occasionally uninspired, Grisham makes you root for the hero to the very end.

The unlikely hero of *The Rainmaker* is Rudy Baylor, a third-year student at Memphis Law School. The book begins with Rudy struggling through the final weeks of law school. Although anxious about the bar exam, he worries less than most of his classmates because he already has a job - as an associate at a small insurance defense firm. Rudy's problems begin when his firm merges with Tinley Britt, one of Memphis's largest and most respected firms, known to those not deemed worthy of joining its ranks as "Trent and Brent." When Rudy's job evaporates in the merger, he begins railing against Trent and Brent as he hits the streets in search of work, vowing to get even, which we know that he will.

Grisham uses Rudy's job search to survey law firm stereotypes from the corporate legal factory to the ambulance-chasing, money-grubbing personal injury firm. Desperate, Rudy agrees to work as a paralegal at a respectable plaintiff's firm, only to be laid off after a few weeks. Eventually he lands a job with Bruiser Stone, a sleazy attorney with suspected Mafia ties and heavy investments in local strip joints. Under the guidance of Bruiser and Deck Shifflet, a law school graduate and perennial flunker of the bar exam, Rudy learns the fine art of soliciting cases. He and Deck visit accident victims at St. Peter's Charity Hospital and - amidst the agonized groans of the patients - sign them up to contingency fee contracts.

Rudy's security does not last long, however, as Bruiser skips town with the FBI on his trail, abandoning his law practice and leaving Rudy and Deck in the cold. Showing ingenuity beyond his years, Rudy makes the most of a tough situation by forming his own law firm in partnership with non-lawyer Deck. With little money and a handful of clients, Rudy and Deck are poised to do battle with the bad guys.

But Rudy does have one thing in his favor: a potentially huge insurance bad faith case against Great Benefit Insurance Company. During a visit to a nursing home as part of a law school class, Rudy met Dot Black, whose son Donny Ray is dying of leukemia. Even though Dot had regularly paid the premiums, Great Benefit refused to pay for a bone marrow transplant despite a willing donor in Donny Ray's twin brother. Great Benefit's eighth denial letter to Dot Black peaked Rudy's interest; the letter finishes with the incredible statement, "You must be stupid, stupid, stupid!"

Rudy's suit against Great Benefit takes on David-and-Goliath proportions when Great Benefit hires as its defense attorney the legendary Leo F. Drummond, senior partner at Tinley Britt. Rudy wonders, "What are the odds of the company I hate the most, Great Benefit, retaining the firm I curse every day of my life, Trent & Brent?"

One could ask that same question about many of the plot turns in *The Rainmaker*. What are the odds that the case would be assigned to newly appointed Judge Tyrone Kipler, a former plaintiff's attorney who hates insurance companies? What are the odds that Judge Kipler will actively assist Rudy in litigating the case, ruling in his favor on motions, making suggestions for strategy, and scheduling depositions at Rudy's convenience? And what are the odds that during trial Rudy will receive surprise phone calls from lost witnesses with damaging evidence against Great Benefit? Or from other plaintiff's attorneys who also sued Great Benefit, eagerly offering to provide key documents that Great Benefit withheld from Rudy?

But these are probably unfair questions since Grisham has purposely stacked the deck in Rudy's favor. As myth, *The Rainmaker* does not strive for realism, only to give the hero a way to overcome evil. Nonetheless, Grisham does stretch his readers' acceptance of this myth at the start of the trial. During voir dire defense attorney Drummond angers a prospective juror by accusing him of discussing the case with Rudy:

> Before I can object and before Kipler can call him down, Mr. Billy Porter charges from his seat and pounces on the great Leo F. Drummond.
> "Don't call me a liar, you sonofabitch!" Porter screams as he grabs Drummond by the throat. Drummond falls over the railing, his tasseled loafers flipping through the air. Women scream. Jurors jump from their seats. Porter is on top of Drummond who's grappling and wrestling and kicking and trying to land a punch or two.

In a more realistic (but probably less entertaining) novel, having a prospective juror attack the defense attorney in front of the entire jury would likely justify dismissing the entire panel. But not here. If it's realism you're after, don't bother reading this book.

The Rainmaker does have two major subplots, both loosely involving similar themes exploring the price one pays for love. Rudy helps Miss Birdie, a widow who claims to be a multi-millionaire, re-draft her will to cut out her inattentive children. When the children learn of their mother's apparent wealth, they suddenly become more attentive and loving.

The other subplot involves the damsel in distress, Kelly Riker, recently married to an abusive husband. Rudy meets her at the hospital where she is recovering from a fractured ankle, the result of a well-placed swing of her husband's softball bat. Rudy's battles with courtroom tiger Leo Drummond pale in comparison with his ultimate confrontation with Kelly Riker's husband. Although these subplots help develop Rudy's character, they are so far removed from Rudy's battle with Great Benefit as to seem out of place.

At best Grisham's writing style is workmanlike, enabling him to tell his story clearly and precisely, without nuance or subtlety. For the most part, the style works for this mythical tale. But occasionally Grisham lapses into the worst kind of pedestrian writing. Consider this passage in which Rudy describes his visit to a mall:

> I walk the mall for an hour after I arrive. I watch children ice-skate on an indoor rink. I watch groups of teenagers roam in large packs from one end to

the other. I buy a platter of warmed-over Chinese food and eat it on the promenade above the ice-skaters.

Fortunately, Grisham successfully developed enough empathy for Rudy to overcome these lapses.

That Grisham intended *The Rainmaker* to be myth becomes readily apparent near the end of the book when Rudy and Kelly are watching television. It happens they are watching a *John Wayne* movie! This, it is clear, is not a coincidence. Like John Wayne battling great odds to conquer the Indians, our hero Rudy vanquishes the powerful Great Benefit Insurance Company, the talented trial lawyer Leo Drummond from the hated law firm of Trent and Brent, and the despicable husband of Kelly Riker. His story is the clash of novice against veteran, weak against strong, right against wrong, and ultimately, good against evil.

To his credit, Grisham has never pretended to be a great literary stylist. He writes to entertain: period. He does not aspire to the heights of Hemingway and Faulkner, but rather to those of Zane Grey and Edgar Rice Burroughs. And like the Western gunslinger and the Tarzan stories, *The Rainmaker* is a pure adventure tale, well-told, pleasurable, and - for the most part - satisfying.

Defending Billy Ryan by George Higgins
Review Date: 1993

With at least one novel per year for twenty years, including his latest, *Defending Billy Ryan*, George V. Higgins has established himself as the dean of lawyer authors. Unlike many lawyers who have tried to cash in on the current rage for legal thrillers, George V. Higgins was a writer first, having written fiction and worked as a newspaper reporter before entering Boston College Law School.

His success as a novelist, however, did not come easy. Before publishing *The Friends of Eddie Coyle* in 1972, five years after obtaining his law degree, Higgins had written fourteen unpublished novels. He jokes now that "they were rejected by the most reputable publishers on both sides of the Atlantic."

The decision to go to law school was unconnected to his desire to publish a novel. "They were completely disparate ambitions. I wanted to try cases, and that's the only way they would allow me to do it in Massachusetts." Nevertheless, Higgins does see some similarity in the two professions, and is fond of telling a law school classmate who is now a tort lawyer that "The only difference between the two of us is that admit I make it up."

Higgins has achieved critical success in large part due to his realistic dialogue, described by The New York Times as "impeccable," and by best selling author John Grisham in a recent article as "sharp and colorful." Grisham even calls Higgins "the best at writing about lawyers and the dirty things they do." Higgins attributes his reliance on dialogue to his work as a reporter, first at the Providence Journal and then at Associated Press, where he learned that quotes make the story. "If you can get a good biting one-liner from the principal character in a news event, that's what you want to lead with."

To critics who complain that Higgins's books lack plot, he says, "These are the critics who either haven't heard of, or don't understand, the maxim by which I believe God meant us all to live: 'dialogue is character and character is plot.'" A fine illustration of this maxim is found in Higgins's latest novel, *Defending Billy Ryan*. When Ryan, the Massachusetts Commissioner of Public Works, is indicted on a corruption charge, he has trouble finding a lawyer to defend him. Ryan finds his way to Jeremiah F. Kennedy, the "classiest sleazy criminal lawyer in Boston" and also the protagonist of two previous Higgins novels.

Kennedy's initial impression of Ryan is decidedly unfavorable; he describes Ryan as having "a face that looked like a headman's double-bitted ax, freshly sharpened on both edges for a very special guest - Anne Boleyn, maybe." Despite Ryan's troublesome facial features, Kennedy takes the case. As Kennedy tries what seems like a hopeless case, help comes from an unexpected source, causing Kennedy to reexamine his own perspective on life.

Defending Billy Ryan is not a legal thriller in the tradition of John Grisham or Scott Turow. In fact, the first sentence reveals that Ryan gets acquitted. Revealing the result so early, however, does not make the book less interesting, in Higgins's view, because the story is not about how Billy Ryan got off. As Higgins flatly states, "The story is about how Jerry Kennedy took on this case that nobody else in town wanted because it was hopeless, and won it, and what effect it had on him."

Like another fictional Boston lawyer - Frank Galvin of *The Verdict* - Kennedy is Irish, divorced, drinks a bit too much and has a fledgling law practice. The difference, according to Higgins, is that when Kennedy goes into a courtroom he does what trial lawyers really do. Higgins prides himself on being scrupulously accurate in his writing. "It's very important, of course, because when you sit down to write something that's going to be called flat out - a 'novel', everybody who is involved in the enterprise from the beginning -- the writer, the reader, the publisher, the salesman -- knows it's a pack of lies. And the minute you lose that suspension of disbelief, you're finished."

Higgins admits that Kennedy is his *alter ego*. "If I had not been uncommonly fortunate coming out of law school, I probably would have had a career something like Jerry Kennedy's, except of course for the fact too that I could type."

After getting Billy Ryan acquitted, Kennedy has no idea how he did it. For Higgins this is the lesson of *Billy Ryan*: "Sometimes, quite often in fact, those of us who are engaged most sedulously in the search are furthest removed from the actuality of what we've unearthed."

Defending Billy Ryan contains the same kind of colorful characters that have become Higgins's trademark. Kennedy manages to win Ryan's case only with the assistance of his long-time client Cadillac Teddy, known for stealing only Cadillacs, and his investigator, former state trooper Bad-Eye Mulvey. Even though small-time hoods populate Higgins's novels, he refuses to label them as criminals.

"As a defense lawyer I never once met a person who agreed that he was a criminal." Although some of them would admit committing acts that the law construed to be crimes, "that does not impose upon them the status, in their own eyes, of being criminals. They're still human beings, just like you and me." Higgins enjoys writing about this particular type of human being because "people who are violent and unpredictable and who break codes and laws and all sorts of solemn promises, are more interesting than the people who behave themselves."

Defending Billy Ryan offers a welcome change of pace from the increasingly tired formulas of many legal thrillers. There are no chase scenes, murderous lawyers, or even brilliant legal strategies. Instead, you have Jerry Kennedy trying to scrape together some semblance of a defense for his crooked client. As narrator, Kennedy digresses often, with anecdotes of a former client, a banker, who embezzled from his employer because his wife was cheating on him, and of his first meeting with a Mafia boss at a North End restaurant. He shares his opinions on everything from lawyers who become judges ("a lawyer who becomes a judge believes the explanation is that God noticed his work, saw that it was good, and rewarded him. This is almost never true.") to *LA Law* ("I think it's remarkable that the partners apparently manage to make such good livings while ... getting laid on their office couches with their paying clients.")

Higgins acknowledges that Kennedy has become bitter and, in many respects, mean since his previous report in *Penance for Jerry Kennedy*. "But I think he's had sufficient reason to become bitter and mean. He may come out of it, he may not, I don't know." Whether or not he comes out of it, with his dry wit and acerbic commentary, Jerry Kennedy will undoubtedly tell an entertaining story.

The Pursuit of Justice by Mimi Latt
Review Date: 1998

Much of Mimi Latt's *The Pursuit of Justice* reads like a romance novel, featuring the loves and affairs of the rich and powerful. The protagonist could even be a Danielle Steel creation: Rebecca Morland, a gorgeous 29-year old, who despite her privileged upbringing works as a staff lawyer for a legal clinic serving low income people. Her husband Ryan is a partner with the powerful Los Angeles law firm of Taylor, Dennison & Evans, whose senior partner, Brandon Taylor, comes from an even more privileged pedigree. "As a high-profile lawyer as well as the son and grandson of two former United States senators, Brandon was intent on becoming his party's candidate for the next Senate race."

But like any self-respecting romance novel, there has to be a tragedy and Latt wastes no time by introducing one in the first chapter. During a glitzy political fundraiser aboard a millionaire's yacht, Rebecca's ideal life comes to a sudden end. Somehow her husband walks too close to the edge, falls overboard, and drowns. Because Ryan had been depressed and anxious in the weeks before his death while working on a secret project, police suspect suicide. Their suspicions seem confirmed when Ryan's partner, John Evans, finds a note in Ryan's handwriting that appears to be a partial suicide note. Another reason for Ryan's anxiety also surfaces: the firm discovers large sums of money missing from one of its bank accounts, apparently taken by Ryan.

In a surprising twist, instead of a typical romance-novel heroine, Rebecca Morland proves to be as relentless as the most hardened private eye. Rebecca can't believe Ryan would kill himself, especially since he knew she was pregnant with their first child. Several strange things happen that convince her Ryan was murdered. She discovers a bankbook in Ryan's briefcase in an unfamiliar name. Catherine Dennison, another of Ryan's partners, drops by the house to pay her respects but then abruptly demands Ryan's briefcase. Rebecca returns from Ryan's funeral to find her home ransacked and all the files removed from Ryan's computer. She receives a threatening phone call, telling her to stop suggesting that Ryan was murdered.

Unable to secure the cooperation of the police, who think she's an hysterical grieving widow, Rebecca sets out to find the murderer herself. She questions the security guard, office manager, and bookkeeper at Ryan's firm, tracks down yacht owner Paul Worthington and his wife Diana at their home, then sneaks onto their yacht. She follows John Evans and learns of his shady past, which includes heavy gambling debts. Her efforts bring her into danger as a car tries to bump her off the road. It comes as no surprise that she loses her baby to a miscarriage.

While laying out clues to the mystery of Ryan's death, Latt keeps steady track of her characters romantic lives. The suspects seem distinguished by their desire for or lack of interest in sex. Catherine Dennison, for instance, clawed her way close to the top of the firm through hard work, aggression, and feminine wile. She is prepared to fight John for Ryan's cases, hoping the extra fees will win her the senior partnership when Brandon gets elected to the senate. In an interesting reversal of the cliché of the older man/younger woman affair, Catherine has an affair with a younger man. But she is the one with a voracious sexual appetite, while he longs for more communication and commitment.

Her male counterpart is Maxwell Holmes, a power broker with strong political influence throughout the state. A leering sexually charged man, he uses the aura of his immense power to attract younger women. When his mistress visits him, she always wears the same outfit: a mink coat, high heels, and nothing else.

The intense sexuality of Dennison and Holmes is offset by the asexuality of Brandon Taylor and Paul Worthington. Despite his wealth, power, and prestige, Brandon has never married. Although there are some suggestions that he is attracted to Rebecca, Latt never fully develops his character. The reader wonders why there's no woman in his life, a question never satisfactorily answered.

Similarly, millionaire real estate developer Paul Worthington seemingly has no interest in sex. His wife complains to Catherine, her old college friend, that Paul refuses to make love to her. Like Brandon, he does not appear gay yet has no mistresses. When Paul contemplates challenging Brandon for the senate, we wonder if asexuality is a requirement for that seat.

The senatorial candidates are not the only characters that fall flat. Latt uses a male/female detective team to play good-cop, bad-cop with Rebecca. The female, Detective Nancy Solowski, also a widow, empathizes with Rebecca while her partner, Lt. Glen Walters, dismisses her. As credible as Solowski seems, Walters defies belief. He ignores key evidence, conducts a sloppy investigation, jumps to conclusions, and ignores everything Rebecca tells him. Although we later learn a possible reason for his actions, we have already given up on Walters.

Although Latt never really convinces us Ryan killed himself, she does manage to produce several plausible explanations for his death. In the end, the resolution seems to come more from the romance than the mystery genre. Rebecca solicits the help of Deputy District Attorney Daniel Black, who - despite his name - turns out to be her white knight riding to the rescue. When he first hears about Rebecca's investigation, he reaches the same conclusion as many readers will: "The story you've told me is quite unbelievable."

Despite a plot that plods occasionally and a handful of wooden characters, *Pursuit of Justice* presents a successful blend of the romance and mystery genres. In the end we're left with yet another mystery as Latt hints of a romance between Rebecca and her hero Daniel Black, who she observes is "handsome in a craggy sort of way."

A Certain Justice by John Lescroart
Review Date: 1996

California author John Lescroart is a rarity: a non-lawyer who writes legal thrillers. In fact, the closest he has come to practicing law is working as a word processor for a large law firm. Despite his lack of legal training, Lescroart has written two well-received legal thrillers, *Hard Evidence* and *The 13th Juror*, both featuring sometime lawyer Dismas Hardy.

Lescroart's latest novel, *A Certain Justice*, is a departure from this trend: Hardy makes only a cameo appearance; there are few courtroom scenes and really not much mystery. The book's strength comes from Lescroart's confronting head on the timely theme of race relations, even going so far as having characters refer to Rodney King and OJ Simpson. What sets this novel apart is Lescroart's ability to portray racism from all sides. Although the book depicts a typical angry mob of white men brutally attacking an innocent African-American man, the focus soon shifts to African-Americans and how they too can be racist.

The racial conflict begins with the car-jacking and murder of Michael Mullin by a black man. When charges against the suspect are dropped due to lack of evidence, Mullin's friends and relatives seethe. During a memorial get-together at the Cavern Tavern, they watch on TV as the suspect is released from jail. Fueled by alcohol and anger, they unleash their racism on an unsuspecting black lawyer who happened to park his car in front of the Cavern. The mob storms outside, ties a rope around the lawyer's neck and lynches him.

Only one person tries to stop the lynching: Kevin Shea, a twenty-eight-year-old graduate student and Cavern regular. After fighting through the crowd, Shea lifts up the helpless victim to keep the noose from choking him. But the mob strikes back at Shea, pulling him away. The best he can do is try to hand the victim his pocket knife, give him a chance to cut himself loose.

Unfortunately for Shea, just as he reaches up with the knife, an amateur photographer snaps his picture. The photo eventually winds up on the front pages of newspapers across the country: a white man with a knife and a black man hanging by a rope, the life being squeezed out of him. Ironically, Kevin Shea becomes the ultimate symbol of racism, vilified by the public as much as the white hoods and burning crosses of the Ku Klux Klan. For black leaders, Kevin Shea becomes a priceless bounty: capturing him will guarantee everlasting support from their constituency, and the power and wealth that go with it.

On one level, *A Certain Justice* is a suspenseful chase book, with the police, public, black leaders chasing Kevin Shea as he hides out in San Francisco. With the help of his ex-girlfriend, Melanie, Shea scales rooftops, breaks into apartments, and hides in doorways to escape the massive manhunt directed at him. Like many chase books, however, the escapes are marred by coincidence and the chase prolonged. Lescroart manages to maintain the reader's interest, however, by developing the relationship between Shea and Melanie, who slowly and painfully rekindle their love for each other.

Despite the book's focus on Shea, the real protagonist is Abe Glitsky, homicide investigator for the San Francisco Police Department. The product of a black mother and white, Jewish father, Glitsky provides the perfect vehicle for Lescroart to explore race relations. While all those around him are convinced of Shea's guilt, Glitsky remains open-minded, concerned with doing his job and gathering evidence.

> Actually, on the basis of what he knew, Glitsky didn't think Shea was innocent. But he was uncomfortable with something that smacked of a witchhunt.... Evidently the powers had decided that Kevin Shea was the quintessential white racist, and that feeding him to the maw of the mob was the best answer to the complicated questions they were facing. That this was a fairly typical response didn't make Glitsky hate it any less.

The search for Shea brings United States Senator Loretta Wager, Glitsky's former lover, to San Francisco. Nearing the end of her first term as Senator, Senator Wager was in danger of losing her seat. Anxious to get ahead in "the white men's club that was the Senate," she had compromised her ideals, alienating African-American voters. "She needed the perception that she'd reconnected with her community," Lescroart explains. "And Kevin Shea was the way to do it."

Like Shea and Melanie, Glitsky and Wager reignite their affair. Haunted by memories of his deceased wife, Glitsky submits slowly to Wager's advances, eventually finding himself falling for her again. But something bothers him about Wager's single-minded determination to capture Shea. And when African-American district attorney Chris Locke is shot while driving through the riot area with Wager, the job of interrogating her falls to Glitsky. "Chris was still turned around," she tells him, "still looking behind us to make sure we were clear, and then, I don't know what - all of a sudden his window exploded and there was this man and I see he's pointing a gun at me now."

While the murder of the district attorney provides a diversion from the chase for Kevin Shea, as a mystery it falls flat. Many careful readers will guess the killer early on. And Glitsky's casual attitude toward finding the killer simply does not ring true. Even with the city in turmoil over Shea, the police simply do not put the murder of the district attorney, especially a black district attorney during a race riot, on the back burner.

Some readers may also quarrel with the book's premise of a white mob lynching a black man in liberal San Francisco. Although Lescroart attempts to provide motivation by showing the drunken mob's resentment toward blacks, his efforts fall short of the mark. Nevertheless, with recent court cases teaching us that truth can be stranger than fiction, the premise becomes easier to accept.

Despite these occasional lapses in the plot, Lescroart's fine eye for detail, intelligent style, and clearly drawn characters make *A Certain Justice* a compelling novel. Most notable is Abe Glitsky: half-white, half-black, caught in a struggle over his own racial identity. Glitsky tries hard to be rational, not to give in to prejudice. At the same time, as San Francisco threatens to explode, Glitsky acts pragmatically, sending his three sons out of town to protect them from the violence. Abe Glitsky's struggle parallels that of the people of San Francisco, perhaps people everywhere, in his desperate effort to put aside prejudice and judge people individually, by the facts, and not by the color of their skin.

To share Glitsky's struggle alone makes reading *A Certain Justice* time well spent.

Conflicts of Interest by John Martel
Review Date: 1995

Famed trial lawyer John Martel joined the ranks of lawyer novelists in 1988 with *Partners*, a story of greed and corruption in a large San Francisco law firm. Although the novel focused on the unethical activities of four senior partners in the firm, Martel is quick to point out that he did not intend to condemn large law firms. "I've never known a bad law firm," he says during a recent interview in his San Francisco office. "But in all probability there are unethical partners within law firms who stretch the limits of the law."

In Martel's second novel, *Conflicts of Interest*, the limits of the law are stretched not only by attorneys but also politicians, military officers, and corporate executives. In the context of an explosive product liability case against a federal government contractor, Martel explores the different ethical choices faced by these diverse characters with the insight of a trial veteran, a dizzying series of plot twists, and enough steamy sex scenes to make even Danielle Steel blush.

The book begins with Seth Cameron, a country lawyer from Bakersfield with big city ambitions, speeding down Interstate 5 in a stolen car to make the trial call in a case that could make or break his career. Seth is defending a product liability case against one of California's best trial lawyers. The plaintiff claims severe distress after eating a can of garbanzo beans which included an unadvertised bonus: two and one-half exceptionally ugly potato bugs. It was the half bug that made the plaintiff sick to his stomach. In an innovative and highly amusing (though definitely distasteful) closing argument, Seth destroys the plaintiff's case by swallowing one the offending critters right in front of the gasping jurors.

On the heels of his great victory, Seth's ambition is realized when he is hired by Miller & McGrath, one of San Francisco's largest firms. Soon Seth finds himself working sixteen-hour days, impressing all the partners except one: famous senior partner Anthony Treadwell, who views Seth's hiring as another attempt by the junior partners - "the Young Turkeys," he calls them - to usurp his authority. Treadwell piles work on Seth, hoping to force him to quit. More determined than ever, Seth handles everything Treadwell throws at him, including avoiding summary judgment in a case that was all but lost by the bumbling of an alcoholic, over-the-hill partner.

But when Elena Barton, the beautiful daughter of a U.S. Senator (and the former senior partner of Miller & McGrath), consults Treadwell about her husband's death, a devious scheme forms in Treadwell's mind. Air Force pilot Sam Barton was killed when his X-215A stealth bomber crashed during a routine mission. Since Sam was the third pilot to crash in the same plane, Elena is convinced that a design defect caused the crashes and wants to sue the contractor.

Concerned with the political implications of Miller & McGrath suing a major defense contractor, Treadwell sabotages the firm's calendaring system, allowing the statute of limitations to run. Seth does not discover the problem until one day after the statute apparently ran, when he files the complaint in *Barton v. InterContinental Aerospace*

(ConSpace) in his own name. But as Treadwell had planned, Seth gets blamed for blowing the case and is forced to leave the firm. Unemployed and in disgrace, Seth lands a job with Allyn Friedlander, a Mission Street sole practitioner more concerned with principle than capital.

Down but not out, Seth uncovers new evidence that revives Elena Barton's case. Statements from Sam Barton's colleagues who saw him shortly before the fatal flight suggest that the crash actually occurred the next day. The statute of limitations may not have run after all. The case gives Seth a chance to avenge his failure at Miller & McGrath when ConSpace hires as its defense attorney Anthony Treadwell.

As *Conflicts of Interest* proceeds toward the ultimate showdown between Seth Cameron and Anthony Treadwell, the scene shifts frequently, from a New Mexico Air Force base to the Caicos Islands in the Caribbean, to Washington D.C. and back to San Francisco. Martel inhabits these varied locales with corrupt politicians, greedy corporate executives, and misguided Air Force officers, all plotting to destroy Seth's case. In one hilarious scene, Seth avoids a band of federal goons by sneaking through Finnochio's nightclub while his pursuers gawk at the female impersonators on stage.

A former Air Force pilot himself, Martel drew on that experience to portray the military attitude that the mission was all important. "I tried not to make it as detailed as a Tom Clancy novel," he explains. "But I did want the reader to get some sense of the problems, of that attitude. Just recently we saw that Congress approved 553 million dollars for more B-2 bombers. Where is the peace dividend?"

Conflicts of Interest poses many conflicts for Seth Cameron, who in the midst of the litigation falls in love with his client. Perhaps the attraction resulted from each other's unusual eyes: Elena has "eyes like pale jadestone set in eggshell" and Seth has "guilty .35 millimeter eyes."

Soon they are making love instead of preparing for trial. When Seth visits Elena's apartment to help choose her wardrobe for trial, the inevitable happens: "He entered the room and then he entered her, right there against the wall near the closet while she ripped his shirt open and bit his chest and told him how much she loved him."

Woven throughout *Conflicts of Interest* is Seth's ongoing ambition to succeed in a big firm. Despite the long hours, loss of his personal life, deterioration of his health, and rude treatment he endured at Miller & McGrath, Seth still longs to return to that intellectual sweat shop.

Only when his friend and former colleague at Miller & McGrath commits suicide after being fired, does Seth realize that perhaps his departure from the firm might have been a good thing. When his friend's mother asks him why her handsome, popular boy would kill himself over a partnership in a law firm, Seth answers, "I can't give a reason, ma'am. Not one. I'm sorry."

Winner of over one hundred jury trials, Martel sprinkles his many insights about trying cases throughout *Conflicts of Interest*. He admits writing these sections specifically for lawyers, from whom he received many letters after *Partners*. "I hope there are some things in there that will show lawyers how to behave," he says, then adds, "and certainly how not to behave."

As Seth sets out to prove he can compete with the best trial lawyers, his father warns him: "A trial lawyer lives his life dancing on the edge of contingency. The only two things he knows for sure when he sets foot in a courtroom is that he doesn't know enough and that something will go wrong. He just won't know what or when."

Martel succinctly describes the many roles a plaintiff's trial attorney must play:

> This angst is compounded for the lead-off plaintiff's lawyer, who also must function as his own stage manager (getting the exhibits and witnesses to the courtroom at the right time); director (ensuring that the witnesses know what to say when they get there); psychiatrist (coping with his client's inevitable nervousness while artfully concealing his own); mind reader (the better to pick a favorable jury); and spellbinder, for research shows that eight out of ten jurors never change their mind after the opening statement....

Another bonus in *Conflicts of Interest* is the many references to the country music lyrics of Joe Silverhound, who is described in the copyright page as a "mysterious and reclusive singer-songwriter." What the book does not reveal is that Joe Silverhound is actually John Martel, in yet another role to add to those of trial lawyer and novelist. A native of Modesto, Martel confesses to a life-long love of country music songs, which he describes as telling "a whole story of life, death, love, incest, disappointed love, all the things that are important emotional triggers in our lives and they have to do it in three minutes."

Martel himself has composed dozens of country music songs and still hopes to get some published. He included the Joe Silverhound references because he likes "the idea of combining art forms." In fact, at readings for *Conflicts of Interest* Martel has entertained audiences by singing the Joe Silverhound verses.

In the midst of one of Seth Cameron's many crises, Joe Silverhound sings, "When he's the one, havin' all the fun, The devil takes his time." Lawyers who take the time to read *Conflicts of Interest* will find that the devil is not the only one having fun.

Billy Strobe by John Martel
Incriminating Evidence by Sheldon Siegel
Review Date: 2002

Two San Francisco lawyers have shared bestseller's lists for their legal thrillers. John Martel's *Billy Strobe* features a lawyer who earned his law degree while serving time at Soledad Prison. Sheldon Siegel's *Incriminating Evidence* brings back criminal defense attorney Mike Daley in another high profile murder case.

The two lawyer authors have completely different legal practices. Martel is a veteran trial lawyer with over one hundred trials under his belt and has been named one of the ten best trial lawyers in America. Semi-retired from his firm of Farella, Braun & Martel, he has published four novels since his first, *Partners*, came out in 1988.

Siegel, on the other hand, is a corporate securities lawyer at Sheppard, Mullin, Richter & Hampton who has never tried a case. He burst onto the literary scene last year with publication of *Special Circumstances*, an immediate bestseller that earned Siegel a huge advance from his publisher.

Despite their different backgrounds, both authors' recent bestsellers do share some similarities. Their protagonists have Irish backgrounds, practice in San Francisco, and tell their stories in first person. Both decide to help acquaintances accused of murder and both get so caught up in their cases that their lives are threatened.

Martel's Billy Strobe is a convicted felon as a result of an insider trading scam during his second year of law school. Against all odds, he gets accepted to and graduates from Golden State Law School while serving time at Soledad Prison. In prison he meets Darryl Orton, a stubborn tough convict serving his second sentence at Soledad. Strobe is impressed with Orton the first time he sees him.

> Darryl Orton arrived at Soledad on the first day of spring, with the force of a March wind.... He appeared to be around forty, about six-three and 190 pounds, with straight rust-colored hair cut short. Kind of a Nolte look, but leaner, his face all hard angles with leathery skin drawn tight over prominent cheekbones. He had a nose that had gotten in the way of too many punches and a three-inch scar over his right eye, which I later learned were symbols of survival right here at Soledad, where he had spent a previous four-year hitch for the botched armed robbery of a convenience store when he was in his early twenties.

Orton eventually saves Strobe from being raped, and perhaps murdered. Convinced Orton is innocent, Strobe unexpectedly gets released and becomes determined to help Orton get a new trial. He learns that Deborah Hinton, the woman Orton was accused of killing, worked as CFO of Synoptics Corporation, a software manufacturer. He maneuvers his way into an associate's position at the prestigious firm of Stanton & Snow, the firm representing Synoptics.

At S&S, as the firm is affectionately known, Strobe gets assigned to senior partner Rex Ashton. Martel vividly describes Strobe's first meeting with Ashton:

> Ashton advanced and gave me a handshake that can best be described as, well, competitive. There was no goodwill in his grip. The man reminded me of some of the steel-eyed cons I'd known inside, always sizing you up, control freaks, probing for the weakness we all have buried somewhere. He was also a guy who just missed being good looking and probably resented it.
>
> * * *
>
> "Glad to meet you, Mr. Ashton," I said, telling my first lie of the day. "I'd be obliged for the opportunity to work with you." There went my second.

In *Billy Strobe*, John Martel shows his experience, both as a litigator in a large firm and as a novelist. The writing, particularly in the prison chapters, is tight, assured and convincing. He effectively blends Billy Strobe's past with his quest for the redemption of Darryl Orton.

While pursuing his defense of Orton, Strobe also searches for the truth about his father, an Oklahoma lawyer who killed himself after being convicted of fraud. Strobe's memories of his father fuel his desire to attend and succeed in law school, and later his empathy for those he believes wrongly convicted. To his credit and the author's, Strobe does not pretend he falls into that category. He acknowledges his crime; as he strives to succeed he refuses to allow his mistake to define his life.

The book proceeds along these two plot lines punctuated by Strobe's problems at S&S as he tries to hold onto his job in the face of Ashton's growing hostility. Martel knows big-firm politics and lays it out here with all its warts. Strobe's pursuit of Orton's acquittal leads to murder, arson, and threats to the existence of S&S itself as Strobe probes deep inside Synoptics, the firm's biggest client. The stakes are high and the tension unrelenting.

In *Incriminating Evidence*, the acquaintance Sheldon Siegel's protagonist helps is not a convict but his former partner and current San Francisco District Attorney Prentice Marshall Gates III, who despite his status likes people to call him "Skipper." A leading candidate for state attorney general, Skipper is arrested when police find a dead prostitute in his hotel room after a fundraiser. The prostitute was naked and handcuffed with his mouth, nose, and eyes covered with tape. Perhaps more troubling to the DA, the prostitute was also male.

Skipper insists on his innocence, even as evidence mounts. The victim's blood tests show traces of GHB, a date-rape drug, heroin, and alcohol. His fingerprints on a champagne glass contribute to the police's impression that Skipper killed him during a sexual encounter. When two female prostitutes come forward and claim Skipper used similar bondage techniques with them, the case looks hopeless.

Never very fond of Skipper, Daley sees his chance to make up for past slights when he tells his new client what his defense will cost.

> "And I'm going to need a check for a hundred thousand dollars."
> He's unhappy. "I thought you said it was fifty."

"It was. The price just went up." Rosie and I refer to this as charging the Asshole Premium. We reserve such special treatment for our more difficult clients.

Siegel takes readers on a trip of the Mission District where a prominent businessman mixes philanthropic work on behalf of the Mission Youth Center with heavy investments in a male prostitute web site. Into the mix he throws the mysteriously missing roommate of the deceased, an affair between Skipper's wife and a man he thought was his friend, and a less-than-candid high-society social worker with ties to the shady businessman. Even in San Francisco, the plot seems far-fetched. It's hard to imagine a politician as kinky as Skipper. Well ... maybe not. Thoroughly convincing, however, is Siegel's portrayal of Dan Morris, "political consultant to the stars."

The paunchy, fiftyish redhead is dressed in a charcoal Wilkes Bashford suit with a blinding white shirt and a tie that has a picture of a mule on it. "I'm running a campaign for a Democrat these days," he says through a wide grin. "For the next few months, I have to wear my Democrat wardrobe." He laughs at his own joke. "We're all whores, Mike. You're a lawyer, I'm a consultant. You know what I'm talking about."

Siegel's style is more breezy than Martel's, punctuated by the light humor that has become his trademark. The humor alone, especially the banter between ex-priest Daley and his ex-wife Rosie, makes *Incriminating Evidence* an excellent read.

The Burning Plain by Michael Nava
Review Date: 1998

For many readers, *The Burning Plain* will present a new challenge. The book portrays a way of life unfamiliar - and frequently distasteful - to a large segment of society. On one level, *The Burning Plain* is a classic whodunit, a puzzle with many seemingly disparate and disjointed features. But it is a puzzle with a unique aspect.

The protagonist, Henry Rios, is a Los Angeles criminal defense lawyer. After successfully defending a client accused of assault, he finds himself attracted to his client. He drives by the client's home and fantasizes about starting a relationship. What makes *The Burning Plain* unusual is that the client is a man and, of course, Rios is gay. What makes the book compelling is that Rios's sexual orientation becomes incidental as the reader gets caught up in the plot, the unusual characters, and the strong descriptive writing.

In *The Burning Plain*, Rios becomes embroiled in a case involving a gay serial killer who has murdered three gay men, leaving graphic anti-gay messages at each crime scene. Rios passes through the criminal justice system in several roles, first as acquaintance of a victim, then as suspect, and finally as attorney for the accused. With each new role for Rios, Nava manages to create renewed reader empathy for his protagonist while fashioning a solid and satisfying mystery.

The author, Michael Nava, did not set out to become a mystery writer. In a recent interview to promote *The Burning Plain*, the San Francisco appellate attorney, recently relocated from Los Angeles, confessed to a much different ambition. "I tried to be a poet until I was in my mid-twenties in law school," he says. "Something about going to law school dried up my interest in poetry." He was looking for something that would force him to create a plot and develop characters and "not just write narcissistically about a thinly-veiled me." Because he liked reading mysteries, he decided to write his first book as a mystery, and fortunately, "Publishers kept asking for more."

Nava has adapted so well to the mystery genre that he has won several LAMBDA awards honoring gay literature. While spinning compelling mysteries, Nava also manages to explore serious gay themes: AIDS, gay bashing, gay self-loathing, the tension between a gay man and his lover's parents. Although these are gay issues, Nava's books transcend homosexuality. "The deep underlying theme I'm writing about," he explains, referring to his six-book series of Henry Rios mysteries, "is being different. Standing outside of society and what that looks like to an outsider, how he experiences his life on the outside." According to Nava, Rios "embodies all those virtues that society purports to admire like perseverance and loyalty and compassion." But despite these virtues, Rios remains an outsider - because of his homosexuality.

In addition to Rios, *The Burning Plain* features some intriguing minor characters, including Rios's friend Richie Florentino: "Tall and thin, his long face was framed by a luxuriance of thick, wavy dark hair and he had the square-jawed glamour of a forties movie star, a look he carefully cultivated." Florentino introduces Rios to Alex

Amerian: "His skin was olive-colored, his hair was a toss of damp, black curls and his face had a delicate, Mediterranean masculinity, like the face of an archaic Apollo."

The Burning Plain has a number of sex scenes, which Nava describes with tenderness and restraint. "I'm not interested in writing about sex for its own sake," he says, "and it bores me when I read sex scenes, whether they're straight or gay." His purpose is not to describe a sexual encounter, but to describe a "kind of intimacy or something about a character or to move the plot along. To do that, I don't have to give a blow by blow, no pun intended."

All three suspects in *The Burning Plain* are gay. By making his killer and victims gay, Nava wanted to show how "exposure to hatred turns you into someone who hates." That's the theme of the book, he explains, "the destructive effects of hate." That's why he chose to make the murderer a very conflicted gay man, "someone who responds to the hatred of gay people by internalizing it and acting it out on other gay people."

The title is a reference to *The Burning Plain* in Dante's *Inferno* where sinners are placed in different levels or circles. "The deeper you go," Nava says, "the more serious the sin." Homosexuals are in the 7th circle with the violent since homosexuals are the violent against nature. In Dante's medieval view, says Nava, homosexuality was a sin against nature. "They occupy this plain of burning sand where they run around the perimeter for eternity while fire constantly rains down on them. That's their punishment."

Rios's main antagonist is homicide detective Montezuma Gaitan, who despises Rios for being homosexual and therefore a disgrace to the Latino culture. In many respects their conflict mirrors Nava's own during his childhood. Raised in a poor Catholic family in Sacramento, California, Nava had to struggle with the intense conflict between his own sexuality and Latino cultural values. His family was "very traditional," he says, "and there was very little room to be different." Like Henry Rios in *The Burning Plain*, Nava encountered a great deal of hostility toward and ignorance about homosexuality in Latino culture.

Readers of *The Burning Plain* will encounter gay characters who love, grieve, worry, perform noble deeds, commit horrendous crimes, and die. In these ways, of course, they differ little from heterosexuals. By making the reader care about these characters, Nava has accomplished his objective: to eliminate some of the ignorance, not only among Latinos but among all cultures, and perhaps, if only a little bit, replace the hostility with understanding.

Eyes of a Child by Richard North Patterson
Review Date: 1995

From 1979 to 1985, Richard North Patterson published four novels while working full-time as an attorney, first as an assistant attorney general in Ohio, then as a securities litigator for the Securities Exchange Commission and in private practice. His first novel, *The Lasko Tangent,* won the prestigious Edgar Award from the Mystery Writers of America. Despite this success, for the next eight years Patterson wrote no fiction, concentrating on his law practice with a corporate law firm in San Francisco. In that period, the market for legal thrillers boomed while Turow and Grisham became household names. Sensing that the legal thriller trend might pass him by, Patterson took a three-month sabbatical from his firm to write *Degree of Guilt.*

Coming on the heels of the William Kennedy Smith trial, *Degree of Guilt,* the story of a woman accused of murdering a famous writer she claimed tried to rape her, became an immediate bestseller. Patterson then left his firm to devote himself full-time to fiction. The result is *Eyes of a Child,* an enthralling, though somewhat bloated, book about an attorney on trial for murder.

Eyes of a Child features several characters from *Degree of Guilt.* Fresh from their successful defense of accused murderer Mary Carelli, Christopher Paget and Terri Peralta suddenly find their lives falling apart. Peralta leaves her husband, the despicable Richie Arias, a blood-sucking maggot of the lowest order. Arias has managed to live the easy life by sponging off his wife, who is now Paget's associate, while he pursues several dubious business ventures. When Peralta finally gets fed up with him and walks out, she learns what a scum her husband really is. By portraying himself as the nurturing parent who sacrificed his own career to raise their daughter Elena, Arias manages to win interim custody as well as hefty spousal support.

Distraught over Arias's manipulations, Peralta turns to Paget, who has just decided to run for the United States Senate. When Paget and Peralta consummate the attraction that was simmering in *Degree of Guilt,* Arias springs to the attack. He accuses Paget's sixteen-year old son, Carlo, of molesting Elena while giving her a bath. Then he accepts ten thousand dollars from a tabloid, the Inquisitor, to give them the exclusive story.

In the midst of the divorce proceedings, Paget and Peralta decide to take off to Italy, a most improbable plot twist in an otherwise compelling and authentic book. While developing their relationship in Italy, they learn that Arias is dead, seemingly murdered though there is a question of suicide since he left a note admitting what a despicable life he'd led. Upon their return home, they are questioned several times by the police. Although the accumulation of clues at first creates intrigue, the build-up to Paget being charged with the murder becomes tedious and unnecessary, comprising over one hundred pages.

As bad as their own situations have become, both Paget and Peralta worry more about their children. Because Elena has shown evidence of having been molested, Peralta brings her to a psychologist who explores Peralta's own childhood, growing up with an abusive father. While Peralta strives to understand Elena, she grows closer to her mother, learning more details about how vicious her father really was. At the same time, Paget worries about Carlo's emotional state, especially as the trial draws near and the molestation charges become publicized.

For his defense attorney, Paget turns to another *Degree of Guilt* character, Caroline Masters, the trial judge in the Mary Carelli case who has now returned to private practice. From the beginning Paget tells Masters that he will not take the stand. Although Paget obviously is withholding information, Masters mounts a vigorous defense. A careful, ethical attorney, Masters also spouts some lines that most lawyers have probably said at one time:

> "The reason," she said, "that there are so many of us is that Americans hate every lawyer but their own, and every lawsuit except the one they want to bring. Just as they respect every law but the one they want to break. When a people's social conscience dies, the law thrives; all these lawyer jokes are simply cover for their own complicity."

At times the trial scenes are every bit as enthralling as in *Presumed Innocent*, which shares many plot similarities with *Eyes of a Child*. Patterson vividly describes the usually dull process of jury selection, introducing a cross-section of jurors to reflect different attitudes. The tension, uncertainty, and drama of the trial are skillfully depicted, particularly in Caroline Masters's cross-examination of prosecution witnesses.

An experienced litigator, Patterson knows the nuances of trying a case. For dramatic effect, however, he takes some liberties with trial procedure that will prove distracting to lay readers as well as trial attorneys. For example, Caroline Masters constantly whispers to herself or to Paget during the trial, so much so that one cannot imagine how she does not disrupt the proceeding. Masters and the assistant district attorney, Victor Salinez, also continually bicker in open court. Instead of stating the legal basis for an objection, they give speeches, going far beyond what most trial judges would tolerate. One instance occurs when Salinez questions Jack Slocum, the sleazy reporter for the *Inquisitor*, about a conversation with his editor. Masters rises to object:

> "Move to strike," Caroline said promptly, rising to address Judge Lerner. "This is not only hearsay but double hearsay: Mr. Slocum was not party to his editor's conversation with Mr. Devine or to Mr. Devine's alleged conversation with Mr. Paget. And the likely reason this article didn't run is that no respectable newspaper wants its reporters feeding off the bottom of the journalistic food chain, let alone a garbage trough like the *Inquisitor*. Especially when its ultimate source is an estranged husband embroiled in a custody suit." Her voice turned astringent. "Let alone Ricardo Arias."

While this kind of self-serving speech may be appropriate for *LA Law*, in an otherwise credible legal thriller, it detracts from the book's authenticity.

These quibbles aside, *Eyes of a Child* ensnares the reader early on, so much so that you soon forgive Patterson his verbosity. Even though most careful readers will guess the murderer in the first half of the book, Patterson's clean prose and devious plot twists keep you wondering.

Patterson has been quoted as saying there are three great themes in literature: "parents and children, and how they made their way in this world." With *Eyes of a Child*, he has successfully explored these themes in an intelligent, thought-provoking way.

Protect and Defend by Richard North Patterson
Review Date: 2001

At first blush, abortion would seem an unlikely subject for a suspense novel. In the hands of a lesser novelist, the story would become preachy and didactic. But in the talented hands of Richard North Patterson, the story becomes a compelling tale of secrets, ambition, and power. With its blend of cutthroat courtroom tactics and hardnosed Presidential politics, *Protect and Defend* may be Patterson's best novel yet.

Set a few years in the future after passage of the federal Protection of Minors Act, *Protect and Defend* begins with a case challenging the constitutionality of the Act. Fifteen-year-old Mary Ann Tierney, daughter of attorney and pro-life advocate Martin Tierney, is five months pregnant. Mary Ann learns that the fetus is profoundly brain-damaged. If she delivers, the baby will almost certainly die. The delivery will have to be by classical Caesarean section, a procedure her doctor tells her may leave her infertile. Mary Ann wants an abortion but the clinic refuses since the Protection of Minors Act requires parental consent.

She finds her way to Sarah Dash, a typically overworked and disillusioned associate in a large San Francisco firm. Sarah tells Mary Ann her only hope is to convince a federal judge that the Act is unconstitutional, but she'll have to move fast since she is close to her third trimester.

The story shifts from San Francisco to Washington, D.C. where newly elected President Kerry Kilcannon unexpectedly faces the task of appointing a new Chief Justice of the Supreme Court. After intense lobbying from his female vice-president, he chooses Caroline Masters, a character familiar to Patterson fans from previous books. Currently a Ninth Circuit Justice, Masters must face a skeptical Senate led by Republican majority leader Macdonald Gage. Hopeful of taking his own place in the White House, Gage would like nothing better than to soundly reject Kilcannon's choice. All he needs is some ammunition.

Patterson artfully shifts the story back and forth from the Tierney trial in San Francisco to the Masters nomination proceedings in Washington. With meticulous plotting, Patterson raises the tension with each scene. The conflicts are compelling: the life of a teenage girl versus her probably deformed unborn child; the struggle for power between ambitious politicians of both parties. At the center of the struggle is Caroline Masters.

During her pre-nomination briefings with the White House, Masters reveals that she had a child out of wedlock in her early twenties. Her sister adopted the girl, raising her as her own and Masters as her aunt. She still does not know that Masters is really her mother. Kilcannon's staff tries to convince the President to disqualify her, fearing a backlash from conservatives who would undoubtedly attack Masters for being an unwed mother but also for deceiving her child for nearly thirty years. But Kilcannon persists, sensing in Masters the intelligence and integrity he wants in a Chief Justice. He decides to go through with her nomination at the risk of destroying his own reputation and goodwill.

At the center of everything is abortion. Although Patterson's views are apparent early on, he manages to present both sides of the debate in an engaging and meaningful way. Mary Ann Tierney's fight becomes the cauldron in which swirls the battle over a woman's right to privacy, a minor's right to make decisions that affect her health, a parent's right to protect a potential grandchild, and the rights of the unborn. As this young girl's fight winds its way to Caroline Masters in the Ninth Circuit and then to the Supreme Court, it threatens to ruin those in its path. The tension nearly breaks when powerful people are forced to reconcile their public views on abortion with their own private choices.

Protect and Defend will endure not because it is a masterful suspense novel (which it is), but because its theme is so universal, its conflicts so real, and its characters so compelling. *Protect and Defend* accomplishes what all great literature strives for: it forces readers to question their own beliefs and consider different viewpoints. Perhaps in the process, it will even open a few minds.

Mortal Judgments by John Peak
Review Date: 1999

San Jose attorney John Peak's third novel, *Mortal Judgments*, is a legal thriller based on a medical malpractice case. After ten hours of spinal surgery, a prominent businesswoman begins to ooze blood out of her pores. The Code Blue team is unable to stop the flow of blood and she dies on the operating table. The orthopedic surgeon consults defense attorney Vicki Shea, a former physician who lost her only child to cerebral palsy years earlier. As Vicki gets closer to solving what happened in the operating room, her expert witnesses suddenly die violent deaths. Vicki's own life is then threatened. As trial approaches, Vicki finds herself fighting for her own survival while trying to prevent a multi-million dollar verdict against her client.

Originally the book had a different title, Peak explains in an interview, which was rejected because "some famous novelist" had already used it. "It was not *Bloodlines* - one word, like genealogy, but two words - *Blood Lines* - like an arterial blood line, or a venous blood line that you'd have in a hospital setting. I was also playing on the fact that this woman's progeny - the protagonist's child who died - is so important to her, her blood lines."

In *Mortal Judgments*, the patient dies from a condition called disseminated intravascular coagulopathy (DIC) in which all of the coagulating factors in the blood for some reason get used up. "And when they're used up," Peak says, "you no longer have the clotting mechanism that you need all the time." No one could figure out why this patient got such a terrible outcome. One suggestion, of course, is that the patient was murdered. Peak suggests several possible suspects: the anesthesiologist, the nurse, and even the blood salvage machine.

Although the medicine is complex, Peak manages to maintain suspense by having his characters explain medical jargon in an understandable way. His experience defending medical malpractice cases comes through in his fiction. Whenever he has a jury trial, he says, he has to explain complex medicine to lay people. "I start off in opening statement being as detailed and technical as I can. I know they're not going to get it all. But with any luck they'll get the general backbone of what this is about and then they'll get it again in the evidence as each expert comes up." If the jury or his readers don't get it, he admits, then he hasn't done it right.

Peak was drawn to the character of Vicki Shea by her experience losing a child. After defending several bad baby cases, he realized that the real story rested with the mothers. The mothers often get divorced and have to deal with their loss alone. "If the child survives," he says, "they struggle through getting help where they can, to get by day to day, do all the things they can do. A very high percentage of them wind up not being able to do it. They have to give that baby up, to go to a home."

When Vicki's daughter is diagnosed with cerebral palsy, she is powerless to help. Twenty years later she still struggles to get over her dead child. As Peak explains, "She may be one of the best trial lawyers in the city, but she doesn't think of herself as a success. She says, why am I doing this? Why haven't I arrived?"

As Vicki investigates the case against her client, her life is soon threatened. While driving on the freeway, she nearly crashes when a concrete block drops through her window. Although the reader knows that this near-miss was no accident, Vicki shrugs it off with little concern. Her concern increases, however, when her expert pathologist is found dead of a suspicious cocaine overdose. Somehow Vicki manages to convince a second pathologist to serve as her expert. When Vicki attends a meeting at his office, she quickly learns he'll be no help to her either. Peak describes her discovery in the book: "Then she saw that his head was turned more than his neck, and she knew that his throat had been cut. She could see the wound now, cut so deep it nearly reached the spine."

Although *Mortal Judgments* begins slowly, the pace quickens in the second half of the book. Peak puts Vicki Shea through enough adversity in this one case to make any lawyer quit her profession. But, of course, Vicki perseveres. And even though she doesn't quite win in the end, she does survive, and earns - if not our envy - certainly our respect.

The Choice by Barry Reed
Review Date: 1991

Barry Reed's first novel, *The Verdict*, became a bestseller and hit movie because of its endearing and timeless plot - the underdog lawyer battling huge odds to scrape to victory - and unusual characterization, particularly of Boston attorney Francis X. Galvin. *The Choice*, which begins five years after *The Verdict*, contains many of these same plot elements but with an unusual twist. The bad guys are now Galvin's clients, and his sense of justice struggles with his duty to his clients. The result is a fast-paced but often disjointed story of Galvin's search for truth, in which Galvin discovers the troubling truth not only about his clients but also about himself.

Fans of *The Verdict* hardly will recognize the new Galvin. As originally conceived by Reed and portrayed by Paul Newman in the movie, Galvin was a lawyer on the skids. After his victorious trial against St. Catherine Laboure Hospital (in which he uttered the immortal words: "If you are going to try my case for me, Judge,... I'd appreciate it if you wouldn't lose it") Galvin's life took a turn for the better. He drives a Jaguar and wears custom tailored suits. He has even traded beer with whiskey chasers for soda and bitters.

The most significant change is his legal practice. Instead of the dilapidated office where paint peeled off the walls and the elevator rarely ran, Galvin spends his time in the hallowed quarters of the Brahmin law firm of Hovington, Sturdevant, Holmes & Hall "where echoes of Oliver Wendell Holmes, Louis Brandeis, three Governors, two United States Senators, ten Superior Court justices still reverberated within the corridors." His clients are the rich and powerful - a banker accused of laundering money, a businessman involved in insider trading - who are willing and able to pay the firm's outrageous fees.

Reed never satisfactorily explains why Galvin decided to sell out and join the establishment. Galvin himself does not question his decision until the middle of the book when he learns that his clients have not been completely honest with him. In a speech to a law school graduating class, he admits, "Not long ago I was a drunk, a sleazy ambulance chaser, working funeral parlors and hanging around courthouses, like a jackal waiting for some probate judge to throw a few legal scraps my way. I was a man searching, for a lost soul. My own! ... I'm not so sure I ever found it."

Galvin's dilemma begins when he receives a surprise visit from young sole practitioner Tina Alvarez, who wants to refer him a product liability case. Children of her clients, a group of Portuguese families from Fall River, suffered devastating birth defects when, during pregnancy, their mothers ingested Lyosin - a new wonder drug in preventing coronary atherosclerosis.

After meeting the families, Galvin decides to take the case but later reverses his decision when he learns that his firm represents Universal Multi-Tech, the British-based manufacturer of Lyosin, and Gammett Industries, its New Jersey distributor. Rather than completely abandon the families, Galvin convinces his mentor Moe Katz, miraculously recovered from the stroke that left him comatose at the end of *The Verdict*, to assist Alvarez.

Despite Galvin's divided loyalties, his team of Hovington associates holds nothing back in defense of their clients, bombarding the plaintiffs with motions and discovery requests. As the plaintiffs' expenses mount, Moe Katz is forced to mortgage his home. A defense victory appears certain until Galvin's suspicions are aroused by the death of Universal's London postal carrier. In a remarkable role reversal, he assumes a false identity to investigate his own clients. When he learns that Universal and Gammett altered documents, committed perjury and perhaps even murder, he is forced to make "the choice."

To keep the plot moving - and it does move: from Boston to New Jersey to London - Reed sacrifices authenticity. Lawyers change sides as if they were playing a pickup basketball game. A successful plaintiff's medical malpractice attorney, Reed well knows that the conflicts of interest in *The Choice* would never be allowed. Nevertheless, he uses the conflicts of interest and the procedural inaccuracies - such as having a summary judgment hearing on the first day of trial - to enhance the drama of the plot.

As Galvin agonizes over his choice, the plot tends to meander, taking some strange and unlikely turns. Galvin's romantic interest, the alluring Dr. Sabrina Bok-Sahn, Universal's director of medical research, disappears for an extended period. The IRA makes a sudden appearance when a ship explodes off the English coast. And Moe Katz unexpectedly receives tape recordings that could assure the plaintiffs of victory.

Despite these flaws as well as the predictability of Galvin's choice, *The Choice* has many engaging moments. Reed displays his considerable legal talent and medical knowledge in Galvin's hard-hitting cross-examination of the plaintiffs' expert Dr. Rafael Meideros. The proceedings in England before the Master of the Queen's Remembrances are fascinating and add a distinctive flavor to the story. Though less dramatic than *The Verdict*, *The Choice* does present an intriguing portrayal of the complexities, as well as the inequities, of our civil justice system.

The Indictment by Barry Reed
Review Date: 1994

Boston lawyer Barry Reed published the blockbuster novel, *The Verdict*, in 1980, long before legal thrillers became mainstays on the bestseller lists. *The Verdict* enjoyed widespread popularity due to the movie starring Paul Newman as protagonist Frank Galvin, a lawyer on the skids with a potentially huge malpractice case against a Catholic hospital. Reed concedes that without Newman, "I probably would have sold twenty thousand copies and that would have been the end of it. I would have been writing poetry or love letters here and there."

Nevertheless, Reed still waited a decade before writing his next novel, *The Choice*, featuring a recycled Frank Galvin as a well-heeled defense lawyer for a powerful multi-national drug company. Although less well-known than *The Verdict*, *The Choice* still sold - according to Reed - over six hundred thousand copies in paperback. The movie option for *The Choice* was sold to Orion Pictures, but has been dormant due to Orion's financial problems.

The Indictment is Reed's third novel, and the first to feature a criminal case. Although predominately a medical malpractice attorney, Reed believed "the idea of cause of death and time of death - as in the O.J. Simpson case - would be very interesting to the reader." His studies of pathology in civil wrongful death cases enabled him to write a riveting opening chapter in which the county medical examiner conducts a meticulous autopsy of the murder victim, describing each finding and conclusion in detail.

The book also introduces a new protagonist, Dan Sheridan, another Irish Boston attorney, though very different from Frank Galvin. Sheridan is senior partner of Sheridan & Buckley, a two-lawyer criminal defense and personal injury firm. Unlike Galvin, Sheridan enjoys a solid reputation and drinks in moderation. Reed decided not to use Galvin for two reasons. "Frank Galvin's getting pretty old; he's like an aging fastball pitcher," he explains. "He was fairly old in *The Verdict* and that was fourteen years ago." Reed had a much more practical reason, however: "My contract with Orion for the movie of *The Choice* wouldn't let me use the same character."

The Indictment begins with the discovery of the body of Angela Williams, an exotic, dark-skinned beauty with a $25,000 per month apartment and an international travel itinerary. The body is found near the highway north of Boston, just before midnight on April 3rd. The autopsy by county medical examiner, Dr. Bernard McCafferty, is inconclusive. McCafferty finds no indication of the cause of death. He does determine, however, that Williams died around 8:30 that night and that she had nothing to eat for several hours before her death, findings that contradict the story told by the last person to see her alive, prominent cardiovascular surgeon Christopher Dillard.

When the police question Dillard, he claims he ate a gourmet dinner with Williams and was with her until 10:00 o'clock the night of her death. Convinced that Dillard is guilty and anxious to advance his own political career, District Attorney Neil

Harrington castigates McCafferty for failing to determine the cause of death, telling him he bungled the autopsy. He brings in a prominent pathologist from New York who finds evidence that Williams was strangled. Even though McCafferty questions the reliability of this new evidence, he decides to go along as payment to Harrington for saving his career years before when McCafferty's drinking problems nearly ended his career.

As Harrington and his assistant, Mayan d'Ortega, prepare to bring the case before the grand jury, Dillard retains Sheridan, hoping to avoid an indictment and save his career. Although Dillard swears he is innocent - he claims Williams's empty stomach resulted from bulimia - Sheridan has his doubts, especially after a shady Irish contractor offers him $200,000 to get Dillard off. Even when Dillard passes a lie detector test, Sheridan still presses Dillard for the truth. While drinking in a bar with his partner and Dillard, he says: "You tell me you snuffed Williams or had her killed, I give you back your retainer and we walk out of here right now. We won't even pick up the bill."

Unknown to Sheridan, the FBI believes Williams was a courier in an international drug trade aiding terrorist organizations. Suspecting Sheridan and Dillard of conspiracy and racketeering, the FBI obtains a court order allowing electronic surveillance and wiretaps of their phones. The fun begins when Sheridan discovers the wiretap through a source at the district attorney's office. Trying to force Sheridan into unethical activity, an FBI agent poses as a crooked client, only to have Sheridan pretend to be the most ethical attorney in town. He throws the crooked client out of his office, then proceeds to accept pro bono cases and turn down a lucrative settlement offer from an insurance company executive seeking a kickback.

The height of absurdity occurs after agent Sheila O'Brien poses as a legal secretary and is hired by Sheridan & Buckley. When she learns from the office staff that Sheridan mysteriously disappears on Wednesday afternoons, she follows him, hoping to catch him in the midst of some serious impropriety. She is shocked and embarrassed to find that Sheridan spends his mysterious Wednesdays playing catcher for a semi-pro baseball team.

While stating he has "utmost respect for the FBI," Reed still portrays the Bureau as unethical, narrow-minded bunglers, much like the agents depicted in John Grisham's novels, which Reed claims not to have read. "Back to the days of J. Edgar Hoover," he says, "they cut a few corners." When an agent once asked Reed for information on a client, he "wouldn't give them any information one way or the other."

As in *The Choice*, the IRA plays a dominant role, as the FBI suspects Dillard and Williams of funding IRA activities. Reed portrays the IRA characters sympathetically, outwitting the FBI at every turn. "Some people call the IRA freedom fighters, others call them terrorists," he says. "The line is very thin."

By focusing on grand jury proceedings rather than trials, *The Indictment* provides a fresh departure from the typical legal thriller. Even without the drama of cross-examination, the grand jury scenes move quickly. The suspense builds as the jury considers whether to indict Dillard; at the same time, the police uncover evidence pointing to a different suspect, one just as prominent as Dillard.

As the book reaches a climax, the flaws in Reed's characters become exposed. They are forced to choose between doing the honorable thing or pursuing their self-interest. The ending neatly brings together the personal crises facing several characters, from the county medical examiner to the deputy district attorney.

Criminal defense attorneys may take issue with many of Sheridan's tactics, such as forcing his client to take a lie detector test or surreptitiously obtaining confidential information from the district attorney's office. Although Reed has been criticized before for taking liberties with legal situations, he makes no apologies. "You have to have a little panache, so I had to invent a lot of stuff." Like movies, Reed explains, a novel has to move. Reed warns lawyers, however, not to read his books to learn trial tactics. "I always said that doctors don't watch MASH to get tips on surgery," he says, laughing. "At least, I hope they don't!"

The Deception by Barry Reed
Review Date: 1997

In Barry Reed's novel, *The Deception*, he returns to some of the same plot elements that made his first novel, *The Verdict*, so successful: a comatose victim bringing a high-stakes medical malpractice case against a Catholic hospital in Boston. Instead of down-and-out Frank Galvin as the plaintiff's attorney, *The Deception* features Dan Sheridan, a 46 year old baseball-playing trial horse with a mixed civil and criminal practice. Sheridan faces many of the same obstacles as Galvin: a prominent defendant, uncooperative witnesses, and a biased judge.

The Deception blends the high stakes of a civil case (one based on Reed's own practice) with the moral underpinnings of a crime. As in his previous novels, Reed effectively portrays the disparity in vast resources, machinations, and cutthroat tactics of the defense. Nevertheless, despite some promising moments early on, *The Deception* ultimately proves unsatisfactory in large part because of its thin plot line.

Donna DiTullio is a rising teenage tennis star burdened with a domineering father and bouts of major depression. Her psychiatrist is Dr. Robert Sexton, nationally renowned nephew of the Cardinal of Boston, who runs St. Anne's Hospital where Sexton is chief of the psychiatry department.

Near the end of an extended hospitalization, Donna seems upbeat, anxious to leave the hospital and renew her career. Sexton holds a group session with Donna and two other patients near his office on the fifth floor. At a break Donna wanders to the Atrium and leans over a railing to gaze at the lobby five floors below. Sexton walks toward his office when he suddenly screams as Donna topples over the railing, landing on the lobby floor. She survives but has extensive brain damage. Sexton was the only one to see her fall.

Donna's parents retain Sheridan, whom Reed introduced in *The Indictment*, in which Sheridan defended a physician accused of murdering his beautiful mistress. This time Sheridan sues the physician, Sexton, as well as St. Anne's Hospital for carelessly leaving a suicidal patient alone in a dangerous location.

This simple premise drives the plot. Sheridan goes up against Mayan d'Ortega, a former assistant district attorney, now in private practice for an insurance defense firm. D'Ortega is "a stunning amber-skinned woman ... statuesque, jet black shoulder-length hair, almost an Oriental visage." As Sheridan knows from a prior case, d'Ortega is also a tough competitor. Since Sheridan beat her before, she is determined to even the score.

In an effort to dig up dirt on Sexton, Sheridan's investigation takes some unusual turns. He decides to check out Sexton's background as far back as high school in New York, learning only that Sexton was an exceptional student. His persistence eventually pays off when he uncovers evidence that Sexton's girlfriend during medical school was murdered while jogging in Central Park. Sexton told the police he was attending class at the time of the murder. Sheridan's suspicions are aroused, however, when he learns that the girlfriend was pregnant at the time of her murder. Coincidently, or perhaps not, Donna DiTullio also was pregnant at the time of her tragic fall.

Both sides engage in questionable tactics. The defense lobbies the judge to rule in its favor on a pre-trial motion, then solicits a key witness to Donna's fall, who also happens to be one of Sexton's patients, to entrap Sheridan. With a hidden wire tape-recording their conversation, she tries to seduce Sheridan and induce him to suborn perjury. Despite some ethical lapses of his own, Sheridan refuses to take the bait.

He has no qualms, however, about hiring an investigator to burglarize Sexton's home. While jogging just before trial, Sheridan nearly gets shot by a sniper. He suspects Sexton and sends his investigator to find the gun in Sexton's home. The trail leads to shady criminal elements.

For the first half of the book, *The Deception* reads like a mundane medical malpractice case, in fact, one with obvious liability. Nevertheless, Reed manages to build tension by showing the defense's devious strategy to force Sheridan into a settlement. The defense knows that the value of the case will drop dramatically if Donna dies. When she is transferred from St. Anne's Hospital to a state facility in Western Massachusetts, Sheridan suspects this strategy immediately. He turns down a $300,000 settlement offer, saying he will take only policy limits of $20 million. Then he takes control of Donna's medical care, saving her life, and even improving her condition to the point where she can communicate by blinking her eyes.

By introducing criminal elements, Reed takes *The Deception* beyond a simple malpractice case. Unfortunately, the plot then seems forced, and the characters lose their credibility. At the beginning of the book, both Sexton and Sheridan are well-drawn, convincing characters. By the end, as the story nears resolution, their actions become outrageous, defying belief. One gets the impression Reed was writing with an eye toward the movie: a condensed Hollywood finish full of action, shock, betrayal.

Despite his failings, Sheridan impresses the reader with his honorable intentions. At the beginning of the case a witness put him down by saying: "'You and your kind never build, never try to improve or create.... You're like jackals, feeding and living off the misery of others.'" Even with the lure of $20 million, Sheridan remains focused on helping his client. Instead of living off Donna DiTullio's misery, he alleviates her misery.

Though his final tactics may be not only "deceptive" but also criminal, we forgive him for this. Strange as it seems Sheridan reminds us of lawyers, real and fictional, from another time. In this age of lawyer bashing, Sheridan is a rarity: a fictional lawyer motivated by something other than greed.

Religious Conviction by Grif Stockley
Review Date: 1995

Arkansas attorney Grif Stockley has achieved critical and commercial success with three novels featuring an unlikely hero: Gideon Page, a fortyish, balding, self-effacing criminal defense attorney. All three novels are set in Eastern Arkansas, tackling serious themes with humor, insight, and suspense. Perhaps Page's most endearing quality is his honesty, a trait he shares with Stockley who admits that "Gideon Page is a lot like me."

In Stockley's latest novel, *Religious Conviction*, recently released in paperback, Page is trying to build his private practice after leaving the public defender's office. He is scrounging for clients when Chet Bracken, Arkansas's top criminal defense attorney, asks for his assistance. Bracken represents Leigh Wallace, the beautiful and temperamental daughter of a fundamentalist minister, who is accused of murdering her husband, Art. Leigh's father, the Reverend Shane Norman, is the founder of Christian Life Church, one of the largest nondenominational churches in the South.

Though Page is flattered that Bracken asks for his help, he worries he is not equal to the task. "I have the same mixture of dread and awe for Bracken that is supposed to be reserved for God... This is my chance to prove how good I am in the sight of the master, and I already feel my stomach begin to churn." Page's stomach churns even more when he learns that Bracken is a member of Christian Life Church, is dying of cancer, and has done little preparation for trial.

Bracken tells Page that Art Wallace was involved in a pornographic video business and owed two hundred thousand dollars to a San Francisco distributor who had been threatening him. When Page asks why the police don't have this information, Bracken says that Leigh is concerned about her father's reputation. But Page has his doubts, believing Reverend Norman to be a better suspect: "The son of a bitch still hasn't checked out Norman's alibi," he muses. "What has Norman got on him? Chet must have confessed to some crime and had to cut some deal." Despite his doubts, Page agrees to fly to San Francisco to check out the distributor.

Even though the trip to San Francisco is clearly a wild goose chase, Page's culture shock lends a humorous twist to the plot. He visits Reggie's Bar, a Finocchio-like transvestite bar, where he finds himself drawn to one of the dancers. "She has a little cleavage (possibly pushed up, but maybe hormones), and as she dances by the table in front of me, I feel the faint stirring of lust. What the hell is going on? I know she isn't for real."

Unable to obtain any useful information in San Francisco, Page returns to Arkansas convinced he will have to take charge of the case for Leigh to have any chance at acquittal. But to his surprise, Leigh Wallace is evasive and uncooperative, seemingly uninterested in his help. He is convinced she is protecting her father. "'I think you know your father killed Art but you won't admit it,'" .... "'Daddy didn't kill Art!' she says shrilly. I don't believe her."

The dramatic tension in *Religious Conviction* comes not with determining Leigh's guilt or innocence, but with Page's ongoing battles with religion. A committed agnostic, Page gets upset when his girlfriend, Rainey, encourages his teenage daughter, Sarah, to join Christian Life. He tells Rainey: "You can believe God took one of Adam's ribs and made a woman out of it; you can believe that after six days of making a world God needed a rest, so he called the next day Sunday. The trouble with people like you is that you think it's perfectly wonderful to pick and choose your beliefs."

Like Stockley's other novels, *Religious Conviction* is distinguished from most legal thrillers by the emphasis on Page's family life. Instead of the typical divorced, bitter alcoholic protagonist, Page is a widower with a troubled teenage daughter and a dog named Woogie. He struggles to raise his daughter, making the same mistakes many fathers make but growing in the process. Whether exploring the serious issues of family life or Arkansas's fascination with fundamentalism, Stockley never gets heavy handed, breaking the tension with humorous details such as Page's salivating over large-breasted women.

Religious Conviction does have its flaws, most notably Stockley's tendency toward redundancy and continual digressions, which often get in the way of the plot. But if you're looking for a different kind of legal thriller with fully realized characters and meaningful themes, *Religious Conviction* will prove more than satisfying.

The Burden of Proof by Scott Turow
Review Date: 1990

In his second novel, *The Burden of Proof*, Scott Turow draws on his experiences as a prosecutor for the U. S. Attorney's office and defense attorney for securities brokers to produce a thoughtful portrayal of the many personal and professional conflicts faced by attorneys. Alejandro "Sandy" Stern, Rusty Sabich's defense attorney in *Presumed Innocent*, confronts great personal tragedy when his wife Clara commits suicide. Stern later finds himself delicately balancing the interests of his major client and his family when the client faces potential criminal charges. Turow's presentation of Stern's story, like Stern's attempts to avoid conflicts, meets with mixed results.

Turow deserves credit for taking an unpopular position and portraying a lawyer as a human being. He writes compassionately of Stern's emotional turmoil following his wife's suicide. Stern struggles to find an explanation to his wife's action, and in the process questions his own choices in life. Stern spent little time with his family and mistook his wife's resignation to his absences as approval. While she raised their three children, he became so engrossed in his work that he missed all signs of her discontent.

Stern's work continues to intrude on his wife even in death. As the family prepares to leave for her funeral, two FBI agents appear at his house to serve a grand jury subpoena on Dixon Hartnell, Stern's brother-in-law and owner of Maison Dixon brokerage, one of Stern's major clients. In the midst of his own personal struggle Stern is thus thrust headlong into defending Dixon from potential criminal charges.

The plot alternates between Stern's investigation of these two seemingly unrelated events. The clues to Clara's suicide come slowly - mysterious pills hidden in her dresser; a medical bill from a lab for an unknown test; $875,000 missing from her personal bank account. Stern concludes that Clara was having an affair with a neighbor to whom she gave the money. He does not disclose his conclusions to his three children, only to learn later that at least two of them knew far more about Clara's activities than he did.

Stern's conflicts intensify when John, his son-in-law and a Maison Dixon employee, is subpoenaed to testify against Dixon. Stern tries to explain to Dixon why he cannot represent John. "I cannot represent someone whose best interests may lie in testifying against you.... It would be a hopeless conflict of interests." Instead, Stern decides to refer John to lawyers he is familiar with. "Lawyers who would talk to Stern, who would do their best to moderate the danger of John's testimony. This was very delicate." Delicate also are Stern's ethical dilemmas when he learns his client is hiding evidence, when he is subpoenaed as a witness against his client, and when he finds himself attracted to his opponent, a pregnant assistant U. S. Attorney. Lawyers especially will appreciate Turow's skill in presenting the various nuances of these conflicts.

Turow describes Stern's reappraisal of his life compassionately, and effectively employs flashbacks to describe Clara's character as well as her relationship with Stern.

The reader cannot help but empathize with Sandy Stern, to feel his pain, and share his grief. Unlike the protagonist in *Presumed Innocent*, who fights accusations of murder brought by others, Stern is engaged in an internal struggle in which the accusations that he caused his wife's death come from within.

Unfortunately, however, the strength of *The Burden of Proof* is also its primary weakness. Turow became so enamored with explicating Stern's character that he ignored the elements of suspense that made *Presumed Innocent* so successful. The plot barely progresses for several hundred pages, as Stern ponders each new item of information. Stern's representation of Dixon Hartnell consists primarily of determining the nature of the government's case. He sifts through subpoenaed documents and questions Dixon and his employees. His primary focus, however, is obtaining information about the potential charges against Dixon from the Assistant U.S. Attorney, Sonny Klonsky. To accomplish this, he ingratiates himself with her. Ultimately, Stern becomes attracted to Sonny. He realizes she possesses qualities Clara lacked - an easygoing manner, unassuming honesty, and a willingness to express her feelings. Sonny provides information about Dixon's suspected RICO violations only after she and Stern expose themselves, symbolically and literally, while sharing a hot tub.

The nature of family relationships pervades *The Burden of Proof*. Turow explores in detail Stern's feelings for each of his children, his distaste for his son-in-law, and his love of his sister. Stern's tentative and clumsy efforts to date are tinged with a sense of guilt about Clara. Turow's descriptions are vivid and touching. He evidences keen insight into the often contradictory bonds and discord of families. The book reaches a thrilling climax when the two plots cross and Stern learns that his family has not been honest with him.

Despite making cogent observations of family life, Turow is guilty of excess. Every conceivable marital and family conflict is thrown in: Stern's distance from his son Peter, blind love for his daughter Kate, disdain for his son-in-law, and growing affection for his lawyer daughter Marta. Marriages are crumbling all around Stern: his neighbors Nate and Fiona Cawley, Dixon and Stern's sister Sylvia, Sonny and her husband the poet. In the midst of this discord, the pregnancies of Kate and Sonny provide hope for a happier future. After awhile, the story borders on becoming a sophisticated soap opera.

Readers expecting another *Presumed Innocent* undoubtedly will be disappointed by *The Burden of Proof*. The suspense is minimal and takes far too long to build. By the time we learn why Clara committed suicide or whether Dixon was guilty we don't really care. Despite these shortcomings, however, Turow manages to explore many themes intelligently with lively and engaging prose. He displays genuine talent in portraying the complex emotions and varying motivations of his characters. When Turow combines these commendable qualities with the suspense of *Presumed Innocent*, he surely will become known, not as an attorney who writes novels, but as a novelist who happens to practice law.

Pleading Guilty by Scott Turow
Review Date: 1993

The disappearance of senior partner Bert Kamin, along with $5.6 million from a client trust account, creates an understandable stir at Gage & Griswell, the high-powered corporate firm featured in Scott Turow's *Pleading Guilty*. The three partners on the Management Oversight Committee decide to enlist fellow partner and former beat cop Mack Malloy to find the money, and if all goes well even Mr. Kamin.

Malloy proves to be one of Turow's most intriguing creations, combining a sharp wit with irreverent observations on his own life and those around him. In a series of dictated memoranda to the Committee, Malloy reports on his progress while lamenting his own failures in life: a wife who left him for another woman and a son he calls the Loathsome Child: "The PDR doesn't list half the drugs he takes. Nineteen years old. And he doesn't flush the toilet." Malloy's biting wit targets even the Committee to whom he is supposedly reporting. He describes one member as "a pale little guy with a mustache like one of those round brushes that comes with your electric shaver." As Malloy looks at another member, he wonders "how I ever ended up working for anybody in a bow tie."

On the surface Malloy fits the cliché of many legal thrillers - another divorced, Irish attorney with a drinking problem. But Turow makes him a complex character, ethically ambiguous and haunted by the demons of his past. Torn by his sense of duty and his own selfish needs, Malloy's decisions on what to do about Bert Kamin and the money are fueled by his past failures.

Prominent in that decision are Malloy's feelings toward Jake Eiger, his ex-brother-in-law and general counsel of the firm's largest client, TransNational Airlines. Malloy owes his partnership to Eiger, who passed the bar exam only because Malloy used his inside position with the bar association to alter Eiger's grade. Malloy still resents Eiger for involving him in that incident, but especially because of his easy life: "I envied him ... that his father was rich and that Jake was easy with people."

Malloy's resentments and failures add suspense to his search, making the reader wonder what Malloy will do when he finds the money. After breaking into Bert Kamin's apartment, Malloy finds some surprises: credit cards in the name of Kam Roberts and a body in the refrigerator. The trail leads to a cheap motel where Malloy tangles with his former partner on the police force, Pigeyes, who years earlier got caught stealing drug money, thanks to Malloy's finking on him. Now assigned to the financial crimes unit and still bent on revenge, Pigeyes suspects Malloy of being involved with Kam Roberts in a gambling fix.

The tension builds as Malloy stays a few steps ahead of Pigeyes, eventually tracking the money to a bank in the tiny Central American country of Pico Luan. Finding the connection between the money and Bert Kamin, however, proves far more difficult.

By tracing Kamin's betting activities, Malloy discovers a scheme to shave points off college basketball games. He soon learns the scheme's bizarre connection to

Gage & Griswell, and why the police and Mafia are interested in Bert Kamin. Eventually Malloy calls on his grateful client, Toots, an eighty three year old lawyer with a questionable practice, to put the puzzle together.

Fueled by the complex character of Mack Malloy, yet intricately plotted, *Pleading Guilty* satisfies on many levels. Despite some gratuitous sex scenes, including repeated references to self-gratification, *Pleading Guilty* is a thoughtful story of how the past shapes our future and how greed, that most basic of human weaknesses, makes us do things we never thought possible. As Malloy struggles with these issues, his transformation proves fascinating. Although most readers will have anticipated Malloy's ultimate decision, Turow's polished style keeps the story flowing.

In the end the pieces fit together perfectly and the significance of Malloy's earlier comment becomes clear: "Money's why the clients hire us - to help them make more or keep what they have. God knows, it's what we want from them. It is what we all have in common."

Personal Injuries by Scott Turow
Review Date: 2000

Despite the astounding success of his first novel, *Presumed Innocent*, Scott Turow has never succumbed to the easy and lucrative lure of formulaic writing, a fate that has befallen many of his fellow lawyer authors. Of Turow's novels, only *Presumed Innocent* has been made into a full-feature film. His novels are dense, nuanced character studies. Suspense takes a back seat to atmosphere and complex motivations. Unlike plot-driven novels, they are not easily adaptable to the big screen.

Personal Injuries, his fifth novel, fits this mold. The novel begins with the arrest of 43 year old attorney Robbie Feaver for tax evasion. Feaver has managed to turn a fledgling personal injury practice into a lucrative enterprise thanks to well-placed payoffs to several members of the Kindle County bench. Now the ride is over and the United States Attorney wants to use Feaver to take down the crooked judges.

Feaver may be Turow's greatest literary creation. He is anything but one-dimensional. Just when we are ready to dismiss him as sleazy and greedy, he surprises us by tenderly caring for his terminally-ill wife and visiting his aged and ill mother at a nursing home. When he cries at the hospital bed of a prospective client, he comes across as caring even when we know he is being mostly manipulative.

Turow contrasts Feaver with FBI agent Evon Miller, nearly equal to Feaver on the complexity scale. Miller has been assigned to work undercover as Feaver's paralegal while he sets up the crooked judges. She is single, athletic, a former Olympic athlete. As she shadows Feaver, she reacts to him much as the reader might. At first disdainful, at times fascinated, always wondering, Who is the real Robbie Feaver? Slowly Turow brings out Miller's background, her insecurities, loyalties, budding lesbianism. The effect is like two completely different flowers - Feaver and Miller - slowly blooming before our eyes. Only we never know if the final product will be a rose or an unsightly weed.

In a rare moment of apparent sincerity, Feaver explains to Miller what drives him:

> "Look, I love the spotlight. I dig the bucks. I adore getting the chance to strut around on my victory lap down Marshall Avenue whenever I win a case. But hell," he said, "you actually think I drop to these judges *just* for myself? Get real. I can't bear to come back to these people and say, I lost, you lost, fuck hope, it's only pain, and it's only going to get worse. I can't do that. That's why it's a play. They need it. And I need it."

The plot of *Personal Injuries* appears simple: Feaver agrees to obtain evidence against the Kindle County bench in exchange for a lenient sentence. He will then be able to care for his wife in her last days. The subterfuge is elaborately planned: cases are manufactured with fictitious plaintiffs and defendants, defended by a fictitious law firm run by another FBI agent. The complexity of Feaver's character drives the plot: Is he leveling with the FBI? Is he hiding information? Could he, perhaps, be double-crossing them?

Turow masterfully sets the stage and draws us to his characters. In the first third of the book, we are completely intrigued. But then the momentum slows. Turow continues to explicate his characters, almost to the point of overkill. The book starts to seem bloated. The plot barely progresses. Then in the last third, *Personal Injuries* takes off. Tensions mount as Feaver gets closer to the judges and the plot takes surprising turns. Feaver's character continues to change as he is faced with tougher decisions.

Overall, *Personal Injuries* proves to be an immensely satisfying and powerful novel. In many ways, particularly in the last third, it rivals the suspense of *Presumed Innocent*. Only the bloated middle prevents *Personal Injuries* from surpassing *Presumed Innocent* as Turow's most noteworthy creation.

Mackerel by Moonlight by William F. Weld
Review Date: 1999

Former Massachusetts governor William Weld has enjoyed a distinguished career. A Republican in a state known as a Democratic stronghold, he won two elections as governor, earning a reputation as a bold and innovative leader. As United States Attorney, he targeted political corruption and succeeded in cleaning up Boston's political landscape. Recently, he testified against the impeachment of President Clinton before the House Judiciary Committee, one of the few Republicans to do so.

His career appeared headed for a different path when President Clinton nominated him as Ambassador to Mexico. But Weld found his confirmation blocked by more conservative members of his own party. Showing his trademark fighting spirit, Weld resigned the Massachusetts governorship to lobby for his confirmation.

Thwarted at every turn, he became a politician without an office, a candidate without a race. Like many lawyers who have experienced setbacks in their careers and have time on their hands, Weld turned to writing. Although his experiences would have provided fascinating material for a memoir, Weld chose the safer fictional form.

His novel, with the peculiar title of *Mackerel by Moonlight*, features a protagonist much like Weld. Terry Mullally is a New York prosecutor who moves to Boston and, against all odds, defeats an etablished incumbent to win the race for district attorney. Despite Mullally's surface similarity to Weld, *Mackerel by Moonlight* turns out to be more than a thinly disguised memoir.

Written in a breezy style, this fast-paced novel surprises in many respects. *Mackerel by Moonlight* is sprinkled with political insight: from a candidate's strategy for manipulating the media to Mother Mullally's Helpful Hints on running the DA's office (e.g. "Never mind who gets the credit" and "Take pleasure in doing little things well.") The book contains much humor, witty observations, and political jokes. What it lacks is a cohesive and credible plot.

The twenty chapters, each with its own title, consist of vignettes that are interesting by themselves but do not build on each other to create a fully developed plot. What plot there is follows two paths: Terry Mullally's campaign for district attorney interspersed throughout with flashbacks to his life in New York. In the end, the two paths do cross, though unconvincingly. That Mullally wins the election comes as no surprise. But when Mullally's New York past comes back to haunt him in the end, it seems forced, an afterthought.

Orphaned at a young age, Mullally finds himself befriended by local cops who take him hunting and fishing. He distinguishes himself enough in school and college to gain admission to Fordham Law School. From there he joins the Brooklyn U.S. Attorney's Office where he stays for seven years before leaving in a cloud of suspicion.

He moves to Boston where he joins the firm of Warfield & Coles. "It was far from the best firm in town, but it was Harvard-Yankee 'cold roast Boston' all the way." Invited to a Beacon Hill Dinner Party, Mullally suffers through his snobby hostess who comments, "We've got a live one here: an honest-to-goodness red-blooded two-toilet lace-curtain Irishman in our midst!"

The dinner party proves to have a bright side. Mullally meets Emma Gallaudette, a local real estate attorney from a prominent North Shore family, who puts him at ease while setting him on fire. Her husband, Elijah Low, has been in Thailand and Hong Kong for the past three months involved in some murky mergers and acquisitions business with the Asian government. Despite her marital status, she seems interested. After a few dates, Mullally decides to sweep her off her feet by taking her fishing and camping at the Quabbin reservoir. He breaks the lock on the boathouse to borrow a canoe, then treats Emma to a half-pint of Dewar's scotch.

Despite being a newcomer to Boston, Mullally decides to run for district attorney. Although Weld makes a weak case for Mullally's candidacy, he brilliantly evokes the machinations of Boston politics. The legendary sharp wit of Boston Irish pols is displayed during a breakfast at the James Michael Curley Center in South Boston. Mullally realizes he has to make a good showing at this gathering of the state's most powerful politicians including the governor and mayor. Noting that only the district attorney seems to be absent, Mullally tells the crowd: "I'm awfully sorry not to see District Attorney Gross here .... I'm sure the reason is because he has been getting out and palling around recently with a whole new group of people he hasn't seen in eleven years.... They're called *voters*."

As Mullally's campaign progresses, Weld reveals more of the case that caused him to leave New York. Operation Submarine was an investigation of police corruption, particularly police who were shaking down homosexual bars and sex clubs. The mastermind was Joe Ballaster, one of the cops who had befriended Mullally after his father's death. Rather than disclose his relationship with a suspect, Mullally gives Ballaster total immunity, then - using an illegal intelligence wire - convicts six cops. His campaign manager proves to be an adept spin doctor and spins this story into an epic tale of Mullally as a hero prosecutor.

Mullally's career continues upward after his election as district attorney and he considers a run for the United States Senate. The seat is held by Republican Harold Dellenback, the state's junior senator. During a Senate hearing into Mullally's conduct, Dellenback steals a centuries-old line by stating, "Your record, sir, resembles a rotting mackerel by moonlight: it shines and it stinks."

A lot happens in the last part of the book. Important events seem rushed, not receiving the attention they deserve. Mullally's true character is revealed, his relationship with Emma Gallaudette changes direction, and his old cop friends from New York tell Mullally secrets that change him forever.

For a first-time novelist, Weld has done a creditable job. Much of *Mackerel by Moonlight* does indeed shine; the rest - while not stinking - could still smell a whole lot better.

INTERVIEWS

THE LAWYERS

HERB BROWN

After reviewing cases involving child sexual abuse as an Associate Justice on the Ohio Supreme Court, Herb Brown wrote *Presumption of Guilt*. His first published novel tells how the criminal justice system can go awry when a child is sexually abused. After Charles King's mother finds bloody underpants in his closet, his teenage male babysitter is charged with the crime. As Charles's parents, his psychiatrist, and the prosecutor push for a conviction, the best interests of Charles are forgotten and the truth ignored.

Before winning election to the Ohio Supreme Court in 1987, Justice Brown was in private practice as a civil defense attorney for twenty-five years. A graduate of the University of Michigan Law School, he has also served as Lake Lands Commissioner and Ohio State Bar Examiner.

This interview took place in 1992.

FICTION: *Presumption of Guilt* (1992); *Shadows of Doubt* (1994); *Rage?* (1997)
PLAYS: *Power of God* (2002); *You're My Boy* (2006)

MURPHY: Presumption of Guilt, *your first novel, reflects empathy with persons accused of child molestation. It's a rather different perspective than we generally see in the media. Why did you choose to write from this perspective?*
BROWN: In Ohio a litigant has an automatic right to the court of appeals and then our Supreme Court hears cases of great public and general interest. I was seeing a number of these cases where all we see is the record. You don't see the people. It's difficult to tell where the truth lies. What also struck me is that the legal system itself, in a criminal case where the child is the key witness, is almost a form of unintentional child abuse. I was more interested in looking at the system and that process through the eyes of the child than evaluating who was guilty or where the sympathies lie. That was my main motivation.

MURPHY: *Is your interest in child molestation derived solely from your work as a Justice on the Ohio Supreme Court?*
BROWN: There's nothing biographical. was one case that we had that was very close that interested me. I did take from that some of the cross-examination of the psychiatrist. But it's just an imagined thing, a composite. I did want to stay away, too, from something that I thought would be more trite, like the school teacher, or what you see in so many of these cases - a relative - being the accused person.

MURPHY: *Despite trying to stay away from that, there are innuendos in the novel that the father or the school teacher is the guilty party.*
BROWN: I used that for suspense. You could think it might go that way. Actually, I have read that half of the child abuse cases that come to court are in the context of custody fights. Which means to me that there's a lot of abuse that's not reported. That also means that kids are being used as pawns to some extent, because I'm sure that half of the child abuse in this country doesn't occur in situations where there's a custody fight for the kid.

MURPHY: *Earlier you mentioned the psychiatrist. Your portrayal of the psychiatrist, Dr. Hartenfells, is decidedly uncomplimentary.*
BROWN: I think she's competent. The little boy has physical symptoms so she's not misreading her tests and her charts. What she is doing, though, is coming in with a pre-conceived notion and fitting her findings to fit her notion of who the perpetrator is. And I think that's a very real risk the people who work in this field face.

MURPHY: *Do you propose any solutions to that problem?*
BROWN: No, I don't really. I was just trying to tell a story. You know, as I've gone around people have suggested things. One suggestion might be to have a recording of the interviewing process, but I really haven't given a lot of thought to that.

MURPHY: *Part One of the book is narrated by Charles King, the victim. It's noteworthy because your language, of course, is the language of an eight-year old child. What difficulties did this point of view pose for you in your writing?*
BROWN: From a literary standpoint I wanted to do that to stretch myself. I wanted to look at suburbia through the eyes of a kid. I think abuse comes in many forms. This pushing of kids that you see so much of in suburbia interested me. I really wanted to do the whole novel through the eyes of the child, but I realized that the court system would be basically a blur to a small child. So I had to shift the point of view to get in the mechanics of the trial.

MURPHY: *Then in Part Two you changed to the prosecutor's point of view.*
BROWN: Yeah, kind of alternating. Some of the child's point of view comes back, but I switched to the point of view of the prosecutor to flesh out the court proceedings.

MURPHY: *In narrating the first part of the book, Charles never reveals how his underwear got bloody. And then we find out later, in a dream sequence, what happened. Was it difficult for you -- writing from Charles's point of view, not to reveal the truth?*
BROWN: The first go-round, I had that revealed in the second chapter. It was interesting. In selling the book, my agent multiple-submitted it. One publisher, who didn't make an offer because I had no track record, said this can be a terrific novel, but you've got to withhold what really happened until late in the novel, and if the author would try that we would sure like to look at it. Well, not having sold a novel in twelve or thirteen years, I was not about to ignore that in the face of a firm offer. While I was waiting for the editor at Donald I. Fine to get back to me, I did that on my own. I liked the idea and then the editor at Fine did too, so that's how that came about.

MURPHY: *Charles keeps a vocabulary notebook. Was this a technique just to make the language a little more adult?*

BROWN: It really wasn't. I read a thing called "The Gifted Child Monthly", which is sort of advice to people with gifted children on how to get the most out of them. I think that might have been in there. I wanted Charles to be kind of quirky in his language. Very, very childish in some things, but also having this intelligence for a kid his age and using words that you wouldn't expect, not always properly, --you know, things like "jammies" and all. You might even associate that with a younger child.

MURPHY: *Did you do any research such as speaking to children to get more background for the character?*

BROWN: I read a lot of stuff in child development, but basically, I drew that out of my imagination.

MURPHY: *After doing all the reading you've done on child abuse and writing the novel, have you given any thought to ways the courts could better handle these cases?*

BROWN: It's tough because the court has to deal with it. Most adults, at least in my experience, are petrified of going into court, sitting facing a jury. The jury is evaluating whether the person is telling the truth or not? It's a very traumatic experience and I think it's even much tougher for a child, particularly when there're so many consequences riding on it. I think there could be more use of alternate means, like using closed-circuit television. Where children are involved, the courtrooms could be made a little less intimidating. We ought to look into assigning a guardian ad litem or have someone there for the child - even in criminal trials. One of the problems is that the prosecutor is really interested in getting a conviction; defense counsel is really interested in getting his client off. I'm not saying they're cruel to the child -- but what the process is doing to the child is of secondary interest. But I think it's difficult. I don't think there is any pat solution. It's necessary to raise the consciousness of judges, lawyers, people who work in the system. And if anything came out of this novel, I hope it would be that.

MURPHY: *Have you gotten much feedback on the novel from attorneys who are working in this area?*

BROWN: Not a lot. Basically, they say they like the story. But along the lines that your question suggests, as to what can be done, not a lot. A couple have said that we ought to look into the guardian ad litem approach.

MURPHY: *Just take the parents out of the picture entirely?*

BROWN: Of course, parents would have to be involved. You couldn't cut them out. But a child is totally dependent upon adults for support, whether it's a teacher, a parent, whatever. That also makes the child vulnerable when certain behavior is needed to gain approval. And hopefully the psychologist or psychiatrist would fit that role. But I think there is a danger there that the psychologist or psychiatrist who sees a lot of child abuse can get involved in an agenda that may differ from the child's. The real problem here is that nobody heard Charles. And nobody really gave him the opportunity, without threatening him, to tell what really happened, and when he tried, he wasn't heard. So, it seems to me that a guardian ad litem, or somebody like that, might serve the purpose of giving the child someone who could hear him or her when the case gets into court.

MURPHY: *You say Charles was not heard, but Charles did lie to people.*
BROWN: He did lie, but he tried to weasel out of it. The irony there is that the recantation is part of what victims go through when they want to avoid court. So the therapist here just reads confirmation of the abuse into that. But he did try to recant.

MURPHY: *Do you find fault with children in this setting for not being truthful?*
BROWN: No, I don't really. I think the children are vulnerable because of the support system involving adults. But my belief is that if you put enough pressure on anyone - child or adult - under given circumstances the person will lie. I don't see children as a lot different. Most of the time they're probably telling the truth, but the pressures of the system can be so great that they will alter the truth, or that they will lie, or they can be manipulated. That's a danger but it can happen. And I'm uneasy with the simplistic notion of "children don't lie, children always tell the truth" or, "these children lie, they're always manipulated." It's a gray area. You just can't make a judgment like that.

MURPHY: *According to the cover of* Presumption of Guilt, *you had some assistance from Tim O'Brien, the acclaimed author of* "The Things They Carried." *What help did Mr. O'Brien give you?*
BROWN: For about eight years I've been going to the Breadloaf Writer's Conference in Vermont, and I've been working with Tim. It's a series of workshops and readings and things, but you also can work with a writer. They have about twelve on the staff and another twenty on associate staff. You get to pick one person who looks at fifty pages of your manuscript and you go over that in detail with him. And that's basically what I did with Tim on this book. Because of that I changed the beginning. He thought it was a slow beginning and it should open up right with the trial. I thought about it and thought of a way to do that.

MURPHY: *Tell me about your private practice. What kind of cases did you work on?*
BROWN: I was a civil trial lawyer -- about half was defending products liability cases. The biggest case I was in - although I was the local counsel; the lead chair was a lawyer from New York - involved Robert Guccioni who publishes *Penthouse*. He sued Larry Flynt of *Hustler* for libel out here and we got a thirty-nine million dollar verdict.

MURPHY: *You were in private practice for twenty-five years. How did you get interested in writing?*
BROWN: The first novel I wrote, which I haven't looked at for a long time and I'm sure it's really terrible, -- came out of a personal injury case I lost. The injuries were horrible. The little girl was a quadriplegic. I've never seen any novel get into the nitty-gritty of a civil case. I wanted to do that. I think I got too enamored with detail and what actually might interest lawyers practicing in that field, but I don't think it had much general interest. And then I found that novel writing is something you've got to just learn by doing. You write, and then you start reading more carefully to see how others do it and you pick up and see things you've not done well, and it's a self-educating process.

INTERVIEWS-Herb Brown

MURPHY: *I know you're working on another novel, what's that all about?*

BROWN: It has to do with a thirty seven-year old woman lawyer, who is adopted and, because of a genetic disease, the confidential file is broken into. She ends up with a half sister who she defends on a charge of murder. I'm interested in women of about that age who have been in practice and have been successful. Maybe they've gone into the practice for fairly idealistic reasons, value-shaping reasons, and get in a big law firm and see that it's a business. So she's facing that sort of a semi-crisis, and then it does involve a murder trial.

DW BUFFA

San Francisco native D.W. Buffa practiced criminal defense for a decade in Portland, Oregon before returning to the Bay Area. For the first ten years of his life he lived in Napa where his father was the high school football coach.

In Portland he began writing a series of mysteries featuring attorney Joseph Antonelli. For his latest book, *The Legacy*, Buffa brings Antonelli to San Francisco to defend an African-American medical student accused of murdering United States Senator Jeremy Fullerton during a robbery. His cousin's partner Albert Craven is acquainted with the defendant's mother and asks for Antonelli's help. Craven is not a typical high-profile attorney:

> After four miserable marriages, the practice of law was one of the few remaining things for which he permitted himself any serious enthusiasm. Carrying a caseload that would have exhausted the energies and taxed the talents of a lawyer half his age, Albert Craven worked relentlessly.... Craven practiced what in the trade was called office law. In his entire career he had appeared in court only twice, and on both occasions had become physically ill.

It turns out that Fullerton was having an affair with the daughter of powerful financier Lawrence Goldman. Shortly before Fullerton's death, his wife confronted her husband's mistress: "Tell me, what do you think is worse - a man who sleeps with a woman because it's the only way he can get to her father's money, or a woman who sleeps with a man because it's the only way she can get close to the power she so desperately needs?" The mistress's reply caused a scandal: "What's worse is a woman who won't give up a man who doesn't want her anymore."

Now a full-time writer, Buffa has received three post-graduate degrees. In addition to a bachelor's degree from Michigan State, he has earned Masters and Doctorate degrees in political philosophy and international relations from the University of Chicago. His law degree is from Wayne State University.

This interview took place in 2003.

FICTION: *The Defense* (1997); *The Prosecution* (1999); *The Judgment* (2001); *The Legacy* (2002); *Star Witness* (2003); *Breach of Trust* (2004); *Trial by Fire* (2005)

NONFICTION: *Taking Control: Politics in the Information Age* (with Morley Winograd) (1996)

MURPHY: The Legacy *is about a Portland, Oregon lawyer, Joseph Antonelli, who comes to San Francisco at the request of his cousin to defend a murder suspect. In the first chapter you spend quite a bit of time trying to explain why a Portland, Oregon lawyer would be defending a high profile murder case in San Francisco. Did you think readers might have a hard time accepting that premise?*

BUFFA: No, actually I didn't. As you know, lawyers, especially criminal defense lawyers who achieve a certain degree of notoriety, end up taking cases all over the country. The main reason for the attention given to movement from Portland to San Francisco in that first chapter is to explain some of the family background that connects Antonelli with the City. His cousin Bobby Medlin turns out also to be a lawyer but a tax lawyer at a large firm in San Francisco. I also wanted to set up the location of the book because it was at least my attempt to have *The Legacy* be as much about San Francisco as about any particular character.

MURPHY: *As a San Francisco lawyer, I thought there would be plenty of high profile criminal defense lawyers here who would love to take a case involving the murder of a US Senator.*

BUFFA: You're probably right. But I had to set it up in a way so that there was hopefully some tension involving that fact itself as to why nobody wanted to touch this case. It turns everybody's afraid of offending some fairly powerful people. And it was also of course another way to get Antonelli into this thing in a way that adds or helps some element of the mystery of it.

MURPHY: *In* The Legacy *you have a high profile victim and a number of high profile suspects, including the President of the United States. Do you think it's important in the legal thriller genre to have high profile characters such as these?*

BUFFA: No. I think it is useful once in a while. My first three books are set in Portland and also involve Antonelli as the main character as well as the narrator. In the second book, *The Prosecution*, there were some people who might be considered somewhat high profile only in the sense that one of them was a I think a chief deputy district attorney in Portland but nothing as high profile as what is the case in *The Legacy*.

MURPHY: *I've read a lot of legal thrillers and suspense novels. It seems that the majority have either high profile victims or suspects. What element do you think that adds to this genre?*

BUFFA: I'm probably the last person to ask that because I confess I don't read much contemporary fiction. Most of what I read are from authors who have been dead for awhile. I think it is probably a function, frankly, of television. A lot of the stories you see on television that move quickly along involve people with money, power, or influence in the community. So it's probably a natural thing for people to put into a story if they want to get other people to pay attention to it.

MURPHY: *In* The Legacy *you set out some potential suspects including not only the President, but the Governor of California, the victim's wife, and even the KGB. As you plot a book of this type, how do you decide where to lay the evidence in terms of the types of suspects?*

BUFFA: I did want this to be as much a political thriller as a legal thriller. I wanted to deal in some measure with the tension that exists between the various political forces in this country. I also wanted to bring in something about the demise of the Soviet Union. There was, curiously enough, a story that appeared in the newspaper maybe five years ago about a Soviet operative who worked out of the consulate in San Francisco and carried on some interesting operations. And in a way, the former KGB agent that you're talking about, Bagonovich in the novel,is in some loose sense based on that kind of thing. But I wanted to get into political intrigue at the highest level as opposed to writing something about, for example, what was going on in the politics of some local community.

MURPHY: *Andrei Bogdonovich is one of the more fascinating characters, a former diplomat and KGB agent who eventually gets blown up in his office building, which turns out to be a key event in developing the plot. When you write a key event in the plot, how difficult is it not to give away too much of the mystery but at the same time give away enough to make the reader feel convinced?*
BUFFA: I think that's very difficult. It's a fine line between giving away too much, in which case everything is obvious, and therefore it loses whatever suspense it's got, to giving away so little that in the end it looks altogether too cute. One of the things I don't like is to read something where all of a sudden on the last page twenty seven different things are explained that really don't seem to have any connection with what went on before. The best approach to this, or certainly the best effect, is at least at the end to make it appear that everything that happened was inevitable, but you still couldn't be quite certain until the very end of it. And that is difficult. You're right.

MURPHY: *I haven't read your other books, I confess. Are they all mysteries?*
BUFFA: Yeah, somebody's always getting killed in these books. Stop me before I kill again. In The Defense, which is the first novel, there are a couple of murders and in fact there are two trials. But in each book I try to deal with a different issue or at least have the central idea of each book different from book to book. The first book was in a certain way about revenge, but also about the question whether it's better - if you're a lawyer - to follow the rules, use them in the way you're trained to, and achieve a result which everybody understands is unjust. Or is it better, as Antonelli does in the second case in The Defense, to actually break the rules in order to ensure a result that is just. The second book, The Prosecution, is essentially about lying and tries to take up the question as to those situations in which it's not only permissible to lie, but almost obligatory. The Judgment was about something altogether different. That had to do with madness, or understanding of it. And again, The Legacy is an attempt to write something about political power and the way it's used.

MURPHY: *It seems to be about secrets as well. Not only did the Senator have some very deep secrets but so did Goldman, and of course Bogdonovich. I found that element to go throughout the book.*
BUFFA: I think right at the end, Antonelli makes the remark that he knows everybody's secrets and he tells everybody's lies. Sure. Although I don't know that that's so different from the other books. Wherever there's a murder you're going to have at least some people that are lying and people who have secrets. And I suppose the more interesting thing about reading this sort of thing is to try to discover what sort of secrets people have and how they try to keep them.

MURPHY: *I found it interesting at the very beginning, when talking about the city of San Francisco one character comments that everybody knows everybody else and you can't really keep secrets. And then we find that there are a lot of secrets.*
BUFFA: Yeah. Sure.

MURPHY: *You use characters' names that seem to have a relationship to their function: Goldman is a rich financier, Craven's a lawyer who may have that attribute.*
BUFFA: I don't know if he does or not. I confess I thought about that with respect to Craven. As far as I'm aware you're the first person to pick up on that. Maybe it's because we're both lawyers.

MURPHY: *Or perhaps Craven's four miserable marriages.*
BUFFA: When you write this sort of thing I suppose it's normal, but there are certain characters that you end up really liking. Others you don't like so much, but Craven was one of my favorites. I liked just about everything about Craven. As you know, people who aren't in the business don't always comprehend that there are a lot of lawyers who never go to court. And there are some lawyers for whom going to court would be worse than death. It just scares the heck out of them. And Craven is one of those people who is extraordinarily bright, an exceptionally good attorney, but he doesn't have the stomach for going to court. I think there's a reference early on to the fact that he had gone to court twice and both times become physically ill. I knew people who got physically ill going to court. And I could never say why they would.

MURPHY: *The accused in* The Legacy, *Jamaal Washington, is an interesting character in that on one level he fits the stereotypical image many readers may have of a young black man. On another level, he is a pre-med student at Cal, very bright, and not someone you'd think would be a murderer, particularly a murderer involved in a robbery.*
BUFFA: I wanted to break the stereotype. I also wanted to create some tension between what people too often anticipate when they hear somebody's age and their race, and the difficulties they have overcoming that when confronted with the fact that in his case he's not only bright - I think he's gifted - coming from a very difficult background who ends up becoming a pre-med student at Cal working his own way through.

MURPHY: *Did you start writing much before* The Defense *came out in 1997?*
BUFFA: I was a writer with some failures much before I began practicing law. I should explain I came to law sort of late. That's in part explained by the fact that I went to law school once, dropped out, and then years later went back. And the only reason I didn't drop out a second time is that you can't do that. I mean you can't quit something twice. But I had started writing years ago and wrote a couple of non-fiction things that were published. An old friend of mine and I wrote a nonfiction thing called Take Control: Politics for the Information Age which got published by Henry Holt in New York. Because of that, I became aquainted with an editor at Henry Holt who, to make a long story short, ended up being the fellow who decided that *The Defense* was something that they wanted to publish.

MURPHY: *So had you written much before that?*
BUFFA: Yeah. I probably wrote maybe three or four really bad novels before I wrote *The Defense.* I would write these long novels that were perfectly useless and would send it out to somebody and would get a rejection back. I figured, "Well, that's that," and I started on the next one. I did that for four or five years. I wasn't very smart about it. When *The Defense* was submitted to Henry Holt, by the way, Jack McCraig who is my

editor there, gave it to his then-brand-new young assistant with the remark that the transition from nonfiction to fiction is almost impossible. She took that to mean, read a page or two if you want, but then send a formal rejection letter. Fortunately for me, she started reading it and she kept reading it. She liked it and then Jack read it and that's how it got published.

But his comment about the transition from nonfiction to fiction, which at first I didn't understand, I think I now understand. I went back and read some of the fiction I had attempted and it's just dreadful. I went back and read some of the nonfiction I had written, and it's not too bad. The difference is that, as every editor will at some point scribble on a manuscript page, in nonfiction, you can tell the reader what's happened. In fiction, you've got to show the reader what's going on. A simple example: if you're writing, as I used to, about politics in a nonfiction sense, you can say Smith lost the election to Jones and retired from active political life. If you're writing that in the form of a novel, you describe how he got the news, how he had to go down to the ballroom to make a concession speech, how gracious he was, how when he came back to his hotel suite, he kicked in the door, took a bottle out and drank for three straight days. So that's the difference. But I was very lucky in getting *The Defense* published in the first place and even more lucky to have an editor at that point spend a lot of time on it.

MURPHY: I *assume your early unpublished novels did not involve the law.*
BUFFA: No. Well, that's not true. The first one I wrote, if I remember, was basically a political novel. Then I tried one that had a lawyer in it. There's a tendency - because you're writing about something that you feel or that you know or that you've got some experience with - to let your enthusiasm get away from you. You're so enthusiastic about what it is that it comes across as a little gushing and there isn't a sufficient detachment from the writing and what you're trying to describe. At least I think that's what happened to me.

MURPHY: *Were you influenced at all by the success of other lawyer authors to focus on the legal thriller genre?*
BUFFA: No. I have read only two. I read Scott Turow's *Presumed Innocent* when it came out. And then some years later, I read Grisham's *The Firm* because you couldn't go anyplace without seeing somebody sitting in an airport reading it. No, it wasn't that. I just ended up liking to write and, because I had been practicing criminal defense law, I decided that instead of trying to write about political things, I ought to try to write about something more immediate. I suppose in that sense, you're right. Aware of what others had done, I thought that I might have a chance at it. Having said that, the biggest mistake I made, and the big mistake that I finally had to get over, was trying to write something I thought other people would find marketable. That sounds a little convoluted. What I'm trying to say is that I kept trying to think of what will somebody in a publishing house see in what I'm writing that will make them think this is something that they would want to publish. Which is absolutely the worse thing to ever let cross your mind because you're not going to have any chance at doing something the right way unless you write what you want and write it as if you're writing a description of something to somebody whose judgment you trust. Then I thought if people like it, great; and if they don't, well, you can't help that.

MURPHY: *It's a difficult situation though, isn't it? Because a lot of rejection letters say something like, "Well written, but I don't think I could sell it."*

BUFFA: Oh, I wasn't good enough to get such nice-sounding rejections. I sometimes wouldn't get anything. I never was able to get an agent. I'd send chapters off to agents. Once in a while, you get a postcard back and once in a while you get a nice but short and firm note. But no, I got published before I ever found an agent and didn't get an agent until before my third book. I don't think I ever would have gotten published if it hadn't been for that nonfiction book and the fact that this fellow at Henry Holt had liked the work. And because of him I was able to send something directly to an editor and know that he was going to take a look at it.

MURPHY: *From your comments about law school, it sounds like you didn't particularly enjoy practicing.*

BUFFA: Oh no, that's not quite true. I didn't like law school for a variety of not very good reasons. I didn't like it the first time around and I was only in for maybe five months. I found it, as most people do that first year, deadly dull. The idea that you're going to spend the rest of your life doing that kind of work was really more than I wanted to think about at that point. Then, some years later, I came back to it really for two reasons: one, I decided that practicing law might not be all that bad and two, the things that I found dull were at least concrete and specific and there was something to be said about mastering that kind of discipline. I liked practicing law. At least I liked that part of it that involved being in court. I did almost nothing but criminal defense work. Most of that, at least for the first four or five years, was indigent defense work. I loved going to trial. I loved arguing a case to a jury. It really concentrates the mind when you're doing that. I didn't much like dealing with clients all the time. In part, because there's a sameness about it and it becomes depressing. After awhile you realize the system is really fouled up. Not much is done for people who make those first few early mistakes and one thing builds on another and pretty soon they're in trouble and they're never going to get out of it.

MURPHY: *But you quit practicing, as I understand it, after at least the first few novels were successful.*

BUFFA: That's not exactly the timing. I was still practicing law in Oregon. I went through a divorce, decided I wanted to get out of Oregon and went to Colorado. And ended up for about a year and a half practicing mainly corporate law in Colorado. At that point, while I was just outside of Denver, this friend of mine and I wrote the nonfiction book, *Taking Contro: Politics for the Information Agel*. My co-author, a fellow named Morley Winograd, went on to be the domestic policy advisor to Al Gore when Gore was Vice President. But before that happened, we found some people who thought the ideas in the book were sufficiently interesting that they raised some money and we set up a think tank called The Institute for the New California and that's what brought me out to California at first, to run that. And about a year after that started up, *The Defense* came out. But I stayed with the Institute for about three years.

MURPHY: *I know you've got another book coming out soon. Can you give me a little bit of a preview on that plot?*

WHAT IF HOLDEN CAULFIELD WENT TO LAW SCHOOL?

BUFFA: *Star Witness* is my trashy Hollywood novel. *Star Witness* is set in Hollywood/Los Angeles. This probably plays into what you were raising earlier about so many of these thrillers involve high profile characters. But I wanted to write a novel about not simply about the movie industry, but the way in which it influences much of American life. So the book opens with the murder victim being found. The victim's name is Mary Margaret Flanders who is one of the best known movie stars in the world. I wanted to call the book *The Naked Dead Body Found Floating Face Down in the Pool*. She's found floating in the swimming pool of her huge Spanish-style house in Beverly Hills and the only person who could possibly have done it - it appears - is her husband who is probably the most powerful guy in Hollywood - Director, Producer named Stanley Roth. Roth has a movie studio that he has created called Blues.

Antonelli agrees to take the case in part because more than he would like to admit, he's attracted to the whole idea of celebrity. So that's what the book is about. In the course of representing Roth, Antonelli becomes fairly well acquainted with some of the more hopefully interesting people in the movie industry structure. He finds Roth to be an unforgettable character in that Roth, who has been enormously successful, has contempt for his past success. Hr wants to make a movie as good as, or better than, *Citizen Kane*. He spent years studying the script trying to figure out how you can make a better movie than Orson Wells did. Besides, as he tells Antonelli at one point, if you're going to do Citizen Kane now, the William Randolph Hearst character would have to be somebody that runs, not exactly a media empire, but somebody who has power to decide what people in America see. He tells Antonelli, "So a movie like Citizen Kane would have to be about me, Stanley Roth." He's been writing this script for years and tells Antonelli his theory of what happened is that somebody kills Mary Margaret Flanders, his wife, in order to frame him for it. The only way they can stop him from making this movie, that's going to expose all of Hollywood and everything that goes on in it, is to have him convicted of a murder. Then no one will take anything seriously that he's done. And it goes on from there.

MURPHY: *What influenced you to write?*
BUFFA: I've always liked it. But what really did it is I went to graduate school. I'm one of those people who spends half a lifetime writing a doctoral dissertation; it was on some political things. I ended up, as a result of that, with a couple of books that were published by the University of Michigan Press. I found that I really liked the writing, but I didn't want to spend the rest of my life doing the kind of painstaking detailed field research you have to do for that sort of thing. I also discovered when you're writing nonfiction the line between nonfiction and fiction isn't quite as clear as a lot of people would like to think. And so I decided I would like to just write. And as I was telling you earlier, I wrote a number of things that were perfectly dreadful and nothing happened with them but I kept it up. So, that's sort of why I did it and I don't regret it at all.

MURPHY: *It's an interesting contrast because most of the criminal defense lawyers I know hate to write.*
BUFFA: You know I read something, I think it was Clancy when his last book came out. Somebody asked him about this sort of thing and he said, "Oh, I hate it. I hate it. It's work." No, I love the work. When I'm finished with a book and start the next one,

I think I'm going to lose interest. But what really keeps you going, what you're really concentrating on, is the thing you're doing now. It's like when you practice law: if you're the defendant in a criminal case, it's the only case you're ever going to care about. If you're a witness brought in to testify, you're going to be nervous and you're going to worry about it. But that's the only thing you're probably going to think about in terms of being involved in a trial. But if you're the judge, the prosecutor, the criminal defense attorney, or in a civil case, the one of the lawyers on each side, the only thing you can think about is the case that is going on. When you're in trial, you can't think about anything except what's going on right that minute. But the moment that trial is over, or shortly after that, you've got other things to do. The judge has got another hearing, another case, the prosecutor has got to get ready for the trial he may be starting tomorrow or the day after that. The plaintiff's attorney has a number of cases that are lined up for trial and you move on to the next one. So writing for me at least is somewhat like that. You concentrate everything you've got on the one you're working on and when that one's done and gone, you're on to the next thing. But I guess I do understand that some people would hate doing this. On the other hand, I'm not certain why anybody would want to read something written by somebody who didn't like what they did.

MURPHY: *That would seem to show through the writing. There are a lot of lawyers, and I suppose non-lawyers, who like the fame of being an author but don't like the process.*
BUFFA: Somebody made that remark. It was a neat formulation: they didn't like writing, but they liked having written. That's cute, but that's not somebody I'm likely to read.

ALAFAIR BURKE

Former prosecutor Alafair Burke's second Samantha Kincaid mystery, *Missing Justice*, finds Samantha on the trail of a missing judge. Was Judge Clarissa Easterbrook the victim of a disgruntled litigant? Could she have been on the take, doling out favors to powerful politicians intent on enhancing their own influence on Portland, Oregon's powerful Metro Council?

As she fights special interests and battles her ex-husband who represents a key witness, Kincaid begins to view the whole legal system with suspicion. She even goes so far as to join forces with the defense to uncover the truth, a decision that incurs the wrath of her superiors. But Kincaid suspects a double standard. "If I had a dollar for every time a pissed-off man told me *I* was being emotional," she says, "I wouldn't have to deal with angry men any more. Apparently rage is only an emotion when combined with estrogen."

In her first-person narration, Kincaid offers the reader acerbic commentary on the characters as well as tips on trial tactics. In either instance, she holds nothing back. "I recognized Susan Kerr from the press briefing. As I took in her powder-blue suit, French twist, and full face of makeup, a few bars of that Stephen Sondheim song about ladies who lunch came to mind. She had that great dewy skin I always envy, beautiful dark hair and eyes, and had probably even had some work done, but she looked seriously uptight."

After her opponent asks a question he later regrets at a pretrial hearing, Kincaid comments, "A tip to defense attorneys: Don't ever ask a cop a question that begins with *why*. It's an invitation for a subjective opinion and a quick way to sink your client."

A graduate of Stanford Law School, Alafair Burke worked as a deputy district attorney in Portland before joining the faculty of Hofstra School of Law where she teaches criminal law. Her father is famed mystery writer James Lee Burke, best known for his Dave Robicheaux stories set in Louisiana.

This interview took place in 2004.

FICTION: *Judgment Calls* (2003); *Missing Justice* (2004); *Close Case* (2005)

MURPHY: *Your main character, Samantha Kincaid, is a deputy district attorney in Portland, Oregon. You had a similar job and I wonder how much of your own experiences you put into the books.*
BURKE: I was a prosecutor in Portland and I chose to base the story there and to have a crime novel around the role of a prosecutor. And I did use the atmosphere of a district attorney's office from what I saw was the relationship between a prosecutor and police officers, other lawyers, and judges based on my own perspective. But clearly it's fictionalized. If I had as many jerks in my office as Samantha has I don't think I would've lasted as long. But I try to make it realistic.

INTERVIEWS-Alafair Burke

MURPHY: *My impression of Samantha is that she has somewhat of an edge in terms of the way men treat her in the workplace. There are a lot of times she comments, that you wouldn't say that if I was a man or if I had a penis.*

BURKE: She's definitely a little touchy about whether she's being treated equally. She tries to deal with things she doesn't approve of with a sense of humor so she doesn't come across as lecturing. But then she gets upset with herself when she's not quite prepared with the perfect come-back.

MURPHY: *I like the way when she seems on edge, she backs up, thinks about it herself, and analyzes whether she behaved the right way.*

BURKE: Right. One unusual thing about Samantha as a protagonist in crime fiction is that she's really pretty healthy and normal. It's not unusual to find protagonists in mystery novels whose parents abused them or whose mothers were prostitutes and who were crime victims themselves. Samantha actually had a pretty loving and healthy upbringing and she deals with the kind of normal things people deal with: balancing your family and work, trying to see your friends on the side. She has to deal with unusual things because of her job. You see her trying to deal with her own flaws in a regular accessible way.

MURPHY: *She's got the ex-husband she has conflicts with, higher-ups in the DA's office she sometimes butts heads with. I've heard some people say you've got to have an unusual character in mystery fiction to sell. Yet you've managed to be successful with a normal character. I wonder if that concerned you while formulating her character as to whether it would sell.*

BURKE: No, almost what makes her unusual is she's normal. She doesn't have a lot of demons; she's a likeable woman who's in this unusual job, at least for lay readers. I think that's what people find interesting about her; she seems like the girlfriend-type of person who has to deal with these tough situations.

MURPHY: *In* Missing Justice, *the tough situation is the disappearance of an administrative law judge, who eventually is found murdered. I like the way you set it up; first there's suspense in terms of whether she was killed; you get a lot of mileage out of that. Then when the body's found, there's an immediate suspect with a lot of misdirection. Why did you decide to make the victim a judge, a prominent member of the community?*

BURKE: One of the things I was trying to develop in *Missing Justice* is the fact that victims lose their privacy in death. The assumption is when someone's murdered they must've done something, or there must be some secret in their lives because random abductions and murders are somewhat atypical statistically. So a judge conceivably could have something going on in their case load that could make them a target. But in the end the police start looking at the usual suspects: they look at her husband; they scrutinize her marriage, what she was up to at work, all of her friendships. One of the things Samantha deals with is she thinks she's being rational in joining the police in their natural suspicions. At the same time she feels guilty that she's not respecting the victim in death by turning over all of her secrets.

MURPHY: *One thing I found unusual about Samantha in the way she handled the prosecution of Melvin Jackson. During the course of the preliminary hearing, she really joined forces with the defense* *lawyer in trying to ferret out the truth. Is that an aspect of her character - that she is so principled that she would go against her own interest - that you wanted to emphasize?*

BURKE: Yeah, I think that's completely accurate. One of the most defining things about Samantha's character is her commitment to herself and her own notions of what justice is. So she's willing to cross the lines of what's required of her; she's willing to put herself in danger, in fact, to do the things she thinks are morally right. So you see her in the preliminary hearing when she thinks Jackson is being railroaded by the investigation, she starts giving the defense hints to the defense attorney, telling him who to subpoena. Then eventually she comes to regret it because she starts to think Jackson is guilty and she helped get him off. She's constantly doubting she's doing the right thing, but the importance of doing the right thing is always first in her mind.

MURPHY: *One of the tensions in the book is her relationship with her father in the sense that he's not completely open about his past, at least for most of the book. I wondered why you inserted this into the plot.*

BURKE: Part of it is a plot device since the father's story folds together at the end. Also I thought, as part of explaining Samantha's character. In her romantic relationships, Samantha is immature and really has unrealistic expectations of what a relationship should look like. She wants to know why her father left law enforcement and he's not forthcoming with her. It becomes clear that she always thought he sacrificed for her mother, that he'd done it all for his family. She looks back and remembers it was the only time her parents ever fought. They were so perfect: "Why can't I have a relationship like that?" And her father points out that in fact her parents fought quite a bit. When you actually find out why her father left law enforcement, you realize that perhaps they were much more flawed people than Samantha ever admits to herself. That sort of self-discovery - of realizing that the people who raised her were themselves flawed - shows some growth on her part. She realizes that people are less than perfect. Part of why she's so intolerant of others is because she expects everybody to be absolutely perfect all the time. So having to realize her own father was flawed was part of her development in the second book.

MURPHY: *One aspect of the book that seems to permeate is the effect of politics on the prosecutor, which is not an uncommon theme. But you have an unusual aspect of politics that relates to Portland.*

BURKE: Portland is my favorite city in the country. I attribute Portland's uniqueness to this SMART growth plan where there's an urban growth boundary where people are not allowed to develop beyond the metropolitan area. So you don't see the suburban sprawl you see in a lot of places, and that becomes an aspect of the book. Samantha starts to notice too many coincidences in terms of connections between her victim, Judge Easterbook, and the people who are involved in this high-stakes development plan for the city. Samantha has to start looking into who exactly the players were, and coming up with a plan and how they may have become corrupted and their connections to the victim.

MURPHY: *Besides corruption of public officials, you also hit on other social issues such as racism and sexism. I wonder if you had a prevailing theme you were trying to express in this book.*

BURKE: One of the things I like writing about a prosecutor is fleshing out the discretion a lot of prosecutors have. A lot of people who don't understand this get the impression that the police do all of the investigative work, and once they've caught their man, the case goes to a jury, and the jury decides whether to convict. People don't understand how much power prosecutors have on whether to issue the charges at all, at what level to issue them, whether to plead the case out or go to trial, and that they basically steer the case to its resolution. I try to flesh that out through Samantha, who sees herself as a buffer between a potentially unfair system and the defendant. She takes very seriously the discretion that she enjoys. So you see part of why she's willing to cross the line during the preliminary hearing. She feels that the police wouldn't have been so quick to assume he was guilty if he hadn't been a poor black man living in public housing.

MURPHY: *One of the aspects of writing legal thrillers that a lot of authors have problems with is making the procedural aspects of trial interesting. You present mostly the preliminary hearing. Were you conscious of the need to make it interesting?*
BURKE: I'm a big mystery novel buff. I'm actually not a big reader of things called legal thrillers because to me that's sort of an oxymoron. When I read these books that are ninety percent trial scenes, it's not easy for me to sit there and listen to people object and not have much character or plot development outside of the courtroom. You rarely have Perry-Mason moments in trial where something completely unexpected happens. So I try to take Samantha out of the courtroom. That's what's interesting about having a prosecutor as a character: you can have her meeting with the police officers, talking to other lawyers, being an active part of the investigation. I try not to have it too courtroom-centered but enough of it so people who love legal thrillers will like those scenes. But enough story happens outside the courtroom because of course that's how the real criminal justice system works.

MURPHY: *How important is it to you to make your book realistic?*
BURKE: It's important. I'm on the faculty at Hofstra Law School and I think if I ever had anything too far fetched in the books my students would call me on it, not to mention my colleagues. Obviously it's fictionalized and the primary concern is the quality of the novel, not the truth of the law. But I try to avoid things that are just completely unbelievable. The law as depicted in the book is plausible and realistic.

MURPHY: *I've read some of your father's work. I noticed a real difference in style and I wondered if that was conscious.*
BURKE: I don't know if it was conscious so much as a reflection of differences in who we are as people. He's a man of his generation, raised in the South with a literary background. I'm a woman in my middle 30's who spent most of my life on the West Coast and I'm a lawyer. So I think it's inevitable that our voices are going to be different; it would in fact be surprising if they were the same. The one thing people have said is a similarity is in the moral commitment of the protagonist. So in some sense Samantha Kincaid could be the daughter of Dave Robicheaux, just not Cajun. They both tend to be so committed to doing what they believe is right. They're willing to tip people off and get in trouble and be endangered physically.

WHAT IF HOLDEN CAULFIELD WENT TO LAW SCHOOL?

MURPHY: *Your father's writing is very flowery, almost poetic. I noticed there's really an absence of that in your book: it's straightforward, clean, clear prose. Were you tempted to be more poetic in your writing?*

BURKE: No, I like to think my dialogue is sort of witty. I actually go out of my way not to describe the rain coming off the trees in the Pacific Northwest because that's when people would be tempted to compare my writing to my father's and I guess I fear how I would come out in that comparison. So I kind of do my own thing and leave the poetry to him.

MURPHY: *Did you grow up wanting to write?*

BURKE: I did as a little kid. Like a lot of people, what I wanted to do changed every year or maybe every month. When I was really young I did a lot of creative writing. As I got older in high school I was interested in politics and was active politically and civically. I also stayed within the arts though I didn't really write all that much as a teenager. Then of course I decided to be a lawyer. Even as a lawyer I always thought it was important to write well and in an interesting way. I actually had judges say, "I've never enjoyed reading a brief before ...." So I prided myself on staying away from the dry writing that people associate with law. But I was always a big reader of mysteries. Like a lot of people, I had in my mind that one of these days I should write a book. And here I am still doing it.

MURPHY: *Do you think it was leaving the DA's office that was the impetus to start writing the first book?*

BURKE: Yes. I had moved to New York and I really missed Portland and the DA's office. I was spending way too much time reading books while taking the summer off. I finally had some time on my hands and missed what I considered my home town, Portland. Writing about a fictional DA's office was sort of a way to visit the place that I missed. I've always been envious of people who could write prolifically while in practice. I certainly could not have done it. I'm writing now while I'm teaching but I don't think teaching drains you mentally and physically the way practice did.

MURPHY: *You decided to write in the first person, which I've been told is difficult for a first novelist.*

BURKE: Oh, is that right? I wish someone had told me that. I thought it would be easier. What makes it easier is you find a voice and you get to stay with it. You get to develop the character more easily because you have this running internal monologue. What's difficult about it at times is bringing out the facts that the protagonist doesn't know about. So you have to think a little more about how it is your character is going to find out what she needs to find out.

I always think of it as a challenge between the writer and the reader where the writer is supposed to set out all the clues and challenge the reader to figure it out. The perfect mystery novel in my mind is where you get to the critical moment and you say, "Ah, I should've known that," but of course you didn't. When you're writing in the first person you have to leave those clues along the way and sometimes not have the protagonist figure them because otherwise the reader would.

MURPHY: *Your ending of* Missing Justice *seemed like a traditional mystery ending because you had the murderer telling the protagonist how the murder was done.*

BURKE: Quite a bit of it. She does get a sense of what happened; at the same time she says the murderer is doing what they do when they confess they tell part of the story and shift the blame to someone else. Subsequently other people come forward and contribute their side of the story and in the end Samantha senses the truth is somewhere in the middle.

STEPHEN L. CARTER

Stephen L. Carter's first novel, *The Emperor of Ocean Park*, combines the suspense of a mystery with the complex characterizations of a family saga. The book traces the lives of an upper class African-American family after the death of the family patriarch. At the funeral of Judge Oliver Garland, an old family friend asks his son Talcott about the judge's "arrangements." The friend, a notorious gangster who caused Judge Garland to lose his bid for a U.S. Supreme Court seat, means information, not funeral or financial arrangements. What information he wants is unclear to Talcott, who spends most of the book searching for the arrangements. Talcott soon learns that the gangster is not the only person intent on learning about them.

As narrator, Talcott intersperses plot with history, both of his family and the country.

> Ours is an old family, which, among people of our color, is a reference less to social than to legal status. Ancestors of ours were free and earning a living when most members of the darker nation were in chains. Not all of our ancestors were free, of course, but some, and the family does not dwell on the others: we have buried that bit of historical memory as effectively as the rest of America has buried the larger crime. And, like good Americans, we not only forgive the crime of chattel slavery but celebrate the criminals.

The Emperor of Ocean Park generated intense media scrutiny, in part because of Carter's $4.2 million advance. But the reader soon learns the reason for such a high advance. Carter has created a book of wide scope, with complex characters and an intricate plot, told in an intelligent and engaging style. As Ward Just stated in The New York Times Book Review: "[A] hidden world is brought to life, a world with its own language and modes of behavior and domestic economy and myths and legends."

Stephen L. Carter is a professor at Yale Law School where he teaches Constitutional law; contracts; intellectual property; law, secrets, and lying; and law and religion. He received his bachelor's degree from Stanford University and his law degree from Yale. Before joining the Yale faculty in 1982, he clerked for U.S. Supreme Court Justice Thurgood Marshall and spent a few years in private practice with a Washington, D.C. law firm.

This interview took place in 2002.

NONFICTION:
Reflections of an Affirmative Action Baby (1991); *The Culture of Disbelief* (1993); *The Confirmation Mess* (1994); *Integrity* (1996); *The Dissent of the Governed: A Meditation on Law, Religion, and Loyalty* (1998); *Civility: Manners, Morals, and the Etiquette of Democracy* (1998); *God's Name in Vain* (2000)

FICTION: *The Emperor of Ocean Park* (2002)

INTERVIEWS-Stephen L. Carter

MURPHY: *Your first novel,* The Emperor of Ocean Park, *was released to pretty much positive reviews. I've read some articles that indicated you had been contemplating writing a novel for a long time and I'm wondering what the impetus was, after writing so many nonfiction books, to actually finalize a book of fiction.*

CARTER: The answer is I don't know. It's also a true answer because *The Emperor of Ocean Park* is kind of a mid-point on a road that began fifteen to twenty years ago when a lot of these characters began to come into my mind. I can't say quite where they came from, but I began to have characters floating around, characters I felt had interesting stories to tell. I admit I spent a long time looking for a vehicle for them. I have actual drafts of so many false starts. I couldn't call them a first draft of this novel because they are on such far different subjects. Yet many of the main characters are recognizably the same, with even the same names as the ones in this book. I think I wanted to do it for a long time and I finally hit upon a story that I thought was worthy of the characters and one I actually wanted to do. But I can't tell you where the story came from or why it happened that way. And when it happened, it became a compulsion and then I had to finish it.

MURPHY: *One thing that struck me initially reading the book was how well developed the characters are. You go into great detail about their histories and idiosyncrasies and it seemed obvious that you'd spent a lot of time thinking about these people. Did you actually do a character study for each one before putting the novel together?*

CARTER: I don't enjoy the kind of fiction that has cardboard stereotyped characters. I like fiction where the characters are well developed. I like what used to be called character-driven fiction. Most of the fiction that I read is probably character driven fiction. So the characters seem to be polished and well rounded in a sense. I am glad to hear that because the characters to me are the important part. The characters and their stories are more interesting and important than the larger story in which they fit. I don't mean the larger story is an afterthought, but I mean that the characters are what I really care about most.

MURPHY: *Did you have a writer that you tried to model your own fiction after who was particularly adept at characterization?*

CARTER: The short answer is no. I have never thought that authors' fiction or nonfiction ought to be imitated. I think we all need to find our own voices. But there are many authors I admire who do wonderful character studies. You can go back as far as you want. To pull one book out of the air, James Baldwin's book *Go Tell It to the Mountain* is one of the great character studies in twentieth century fiction. But there are a lot of authors that have done great character studies. You can go back to the 19th or early 20th Century and think of people like Thomas Hardy. Or you can go into this century and think of contemporary writers like Tony Morrison and John Updike and E.L. Doctorow and Tom Wolf and other people who really want to give us enough of the character that we care about what happens to the character as much as about, in the page-turning sense, what happens next.

MURPHY: *Tell me about the writing process. You indicated you did write some character sketches or starts on novels with the same or similar characters. I'm wondering how long it took you to complete the book once you decided on the plot and what kind of routine you had.*

WHAT IF HOLDEN CAULFIELD WENT TO LAW SCHOOL?

CARTER: When I started writing *The Emperor of Ocean Park*, I wrote in much the same way as my nonfiction books, because I had never written a novel before and I didn't know how it was done. So I wrote a novel and I assumed that - like my nonfiction books - I would just stick to the outline. Of course it didn't turn out that way. Many other novelists say the same thing: that the characters, if they're all real and well rounded, really do take over the story. They become the story of these characters. And that was a new and interesting process. The story of course went on in interesting directions. Once I got started, it took me about four years to write *The Emperor of Ocean Park*, but it wasn't four years of constant writing. I'm a law professor, I have a full-time job, I do my legal scholarship. As a matter of fact, I wrote two nonfiction books while I was writing *The Emperor of Ocean Park*. I also did not want to slight my family so I did a lot of the writing after 10 o'clock at night - between ten and one or ten and two in the morning and occasionally on weekends. That's why it took me so long to do it. Until the end. The last month or six weeks of writing it, I finally realized I might actually be able to finish this thing, I wrote pretty much around the clock. But other than that, it really was something I had to squeeze in. It was something I loved doing. Something I felt compelled to do in certain ways and yet still something for which I was not willing to push aside other work or the obligations I have to my family.

MURPHY: *Did you have the book sold before you finished it or was it only after you completed the novel?*
CARTER: No. The book was not sold before I finished it. My agent didn't look at it and the publishers didn't see it until I was finished.

MURPHY: *I have talked to a number of authors of nonfiction and one of the difficulties they have with fiction is writing dialogue. I didn't detect that you had a problem with that. Did you work particularly hard at it?*
CARTER: I guess I worked hard on my dialogue. I also don't think I have a very good ear for it. But maybe it came out pretty well. The hardest thing for me about the transition from nonfiction to fiction was not dialogue. It was not having the protection of footnotes. As a scholar I am accustomed to having footnotes and the practical way of footnotes protects the author. If I write a nonfiction book or a scholarly article and somebody calls me and says, "Carter, you're a fool." Usually the dispute is actually one of fact and I can say I have this source. If we argue, our argument is over the source. Now my source may be wrong. Or I may have the wrong source. But my ego is not on the line. It's not as invested in it. I want to know what's right. Many times in my nonfiction work, if I'm wrong, I've issued corrections, or have changed my mind in later work. I think that's a scholar's shield. If I'm right I stick to my point. Well, with fiction there're no footnotes. So if somebody says, "Carter, you're a fool. This scene is utterly implausible." That's not a question of some source. That's not a dispute over what really happened. That's an argument against my imagination. So in that sense I feel a lot more vulnerable. And that was one of the really hard things. The other hard thing about writing fiction is I wrote in the first person but in a voice that's very unlike my own. And that was very difficult to do, to sustain the voice of Talcott Garland my narrator. He has some surface similarities to me - he a law professor after all. He is black and his wife is black and he lives in New England, but that about exhausts the similarities. But he's a person who is skeptical of the world. He is more cynical than he

lets on. He is depressive. There are many things about him that I hope are not the way I am. Now you have to talk to my friends to see if I really am that way. But I like to think I have a greater generosity of spirit, a broader view of nature and human possibility than he does. I hope.

MURPHY: *I think he makes an engaging narrator. I was struck by how erudite Talcott was. He does have cynical observations, but he seems to back them up with at least his own view of the facts. One aspect of fiction that a lot of writers are asked is whether it's true factually, but I'm not going to ask you that. I am going to ask you if you consciously avoided putting in the book factual events as sort of a preemptive strike against that kind of reaction to the book.*

CARTER: It depends on what you mean by actual events. I tried very hard not to pattern it on the events of my life for example, and with minor exceptions, I think I succeeded with that. But there are some actual historical events that are referred to in the book. One small example: the narrator's father - the judge whose death sets off the chain of events that draws the plot of the book - is a black conservative judge whose nomination for the Supreme Court in my fiction was rejected in 1986. It was after that bitter confirmation fight in my book that Antonin Scalia was unanimously confirmed later in 1986 out of a sense of general relief. Now of course we really know that Scalia was confirmed in 1986 just on his merits. There wasn't any bitter confirmation fight that involved some other previous justice, but nevertheless that was a little way that I shoved the truth rudely around a bit in order to fit the needs of the fiction. I have a kind of aversion to doing that because I'm a scholar. I feel uneasy about twisting history to fit neatly in a narrative, which is probably why in the author's note I try to lay out, as fairly as I can for the reader, the time and place in the book where I changed history to fit the story.

MURPHY: *People often refer to fiction writers as professional liars. That would seem to me to be completely contrary to the image you want as a nonfiction writer where you have to back up everything you say with factual information. So I could see where that would cause you some difficulty. Do you think that inhibited your creative process at all?*

CARTER: I don't know the answer to that. My temptation is to say that it's all just writing. That is to say that all writing, fiction or nonfiction, imaginary or objectively true, involves a process of communication between author and reader and also involves a pact. The pact says that the reader will go along with the author if the author promises to be consistent and coherent within whatever universe, fictional or nonfictional, that the reader is being invited into. And that can be as true of nonfiction as it can be of fiction. For example, I have been lately reading Norman Kanter's really wonderful book about the black plague and what it did in Europe. Well, that's nonfiction. Kanter's an eminent historian. But part of the appeal of the book is that precisely that you sit there and he's telling a story and you agree as a reader to say, "Okay, I'll sit back and let you tell me as long as I feel you're being fair and consistent." So I think in that sense the nonfiction writer's pact and the fiction writer's pact with the reader are pretty similar.

MURPHY: The Emperor of Ocean Park *really goes in two different directions. A few reviewers have commented one part is a family saga and the other part is a thriller. Did you envision the book going in both directions when you started it or is this something that came about in the writing?*

WHAT IF HOLDEN CAULFIELD WENT TO LAW SCHOOL?

CARTER: It's a hard question to answer. I didn't envision the book in a particular way. I wanted to tell the story of this family, this old African American family that had been professional college educated for generations. There're families like that around. I wanted to tell the story of this family and I wanted to make it a readable book. But I think it could be thought of in a lot of different ways. A family saga, yes. A thriller, sure. But it could be a mystery. It could be felt as a love story. There are a lot of different ways to think about it. I wasn't trying to write to a particular genre. I was trying to find a way to make the story of this family an interesting story. And so when people break it down and say it has a little bit of this and little bit of that, they're doubtless right. And if they stuck with it, they could probably break it down a little more and find more different books in it as well.

MURPHY: *Did you do any particular study or analysis of thrillers or mysteries in order to make the mystery element of the book come off?*
CARTER: No, not really. I don't read that many mysteries and thrillers myself. I was trying to offer the reader something plausible. I was trying to find a way to reward the reader for his or her perseverance. To make it an interesting story with a pay-off at the end that the reader would find useful and plausible. But at the same time, to talk about this family in a story put into a package that you would find appealing. And I didn't set out to write a thriller. In fact, I didn't set out to write a mystery. I set out years ago just thinking that I had to find a way to tell the story of the family. And when I hit upon the current story, I was thinking more mystery than thriller. But as I began work on it, it became clear that some aspects of it left itself to a little bit of the page turning variety. After a while I did begin to write to that a little bit, although less than it may appear because a lot of the aspects that the people find thrilling, I didn't so much consciously invent as just felt made sense in the context of the relationship between the characters.

MURPHY: *The New York Times gave you a mixed review. Michiko Kakutani liked the family saga, but didn't like the thriller aspect and she said in her review that "The thriller is a contrived, implausible needlessly baroque melodrama, which reads as if it were written for serial publication, with nearly every chapter ending on a hokey cliffhanger and portentous foreshadowings of what fresh hell is yet to come." I wonder what your reaction is to that statement.*
CARTER: None. Did you see the review in the Sunday Times or just that review?

MURPHY: *I have the one by Ward Just which is much more positive.*
CARTER: I've written a lot of books. And they've all collected some good reviews and some bad ones. And I think if you start to worry about bad reviews then you need to stop writing.

MURPHY: *I noticed that many chapters do end with sort of a bombshell, the discovery of the murder, or the allegation of murder and some new evidence. It seemed to me you were consciously trying to create a thriller, not that there's anything wrong with that. But I'm wondering if that's what you were trying to do.*
CARTER: As I was saying before, I tried more consciously to shape some parts of it that way, but less than you'd think. A lot of it still happened kind of naturally. A lot of it didn't require contrivance because the story, for the most part, was so clear in my mind. It was simply a matter of deciding how to set the story out and that includes a lot of the

twists and turns that take place in the course of the story. There're probably a few places in the book where I was reaching a bit. But I think not so many because I really did not add many - if any - of the plot elements to try to say, "Oh, this will make it more thrilling." Most of the story as you see it laid down, the basic story, is pretty much as it came from when I sat down and started writing. A lot of the architecture had to be worked out. But the main architecture to be worked out didn't so much revolve around the thrills, but on the mystery. It was a matter of deciding which clues would go where. Things like that were by far the harder work, the work that took more, "How will I do this?" The thriller aspects came pretty naturally as they say.

MURPHY: *Getting back to the historical events, you make a point in your author's note to say - as many fiction writers do - that this book is not based on actual people. Yet the reviewers obviously make parallels between Oliver Garland and Clarence Thomas and a few others. I'm wondering, given that Thomas is a Yale graduate, if you know him and followed closely his nomination proceedings. How much of the details of that are you familiar with?*

CARTER: If the question is have I ever met Clarence Thomas, the answer is no. A lot of reviewers think, oh well, this must be Clarence Thomas meets Robert Bork or something like that. But this is a matter of how short-sighted we are in a way. Or how short our historical memory is. When people think of scandals, in the Supreme Court nomination context, they think of Thomas and Bork. The reason they think of those is because they were televised. But every constitutional scholar and historian could tell you that there were dozens of nominations where scandals arose long before they were on television. There were dozens of hotly contested nominations and people didn't follow them as much. And so for me in envisioning these characters, the idea of Oliver Garland as a judge came to me long before I ever heard of these contested nominations. The idea that a conservative black judge would have risen in the Reagan era had a certain appeal. I thought he would be a better character if he could be a bitter old man in a sense and it was a matter of hunting around for what made him a bitter old man. The idea that he had tried for the purple, as they used to say, and not made it was an idea that had come to me actually before these nomination fights. Obviously these nomination fights give it more currency with readers, but we had a lot of these fights before that. As a matter of fact, I really think, and I argued this in a book I wrote about the confirmation process, that the most bitterly contested confirmation battle we had was Thurgood Marshall's in 1967. The reason that people don't remember it that way is that it wasn't on television. Contesting something in the newspapers and contesting something on television are very different in terms of the way they lie in memory later on.

MURPHY: *Your book covers an area of black life about which there is not a whole lot of fiction: the black middle upper class. Did you have in mind a particular readership that would be interested in this aspect of American life that people don't hear about? Did you think it would be appealing for all Americans to know more about this side of black America that people don't hear about?*

CARTER: I didn't set out to tell the story of a particular substratum of African America. I set out to tell the story of this family and my view of the family that when I was writing is that its problems, its tensions and its joys and disappointments are mostly universal, at least in the Western experience. So I felt it would appeal to a lot of different people. At the same time, it is certainly true that we don't read much in popular literature and we don't see much in the media about black professionals and about the middle class. As a matter of fact, if you see film for example, it's really odd that a lot of movies now do have sort of salty middle class black characters. You'll see them as a judge or a district attorney or an air force officer or a surgeon, a school principal, or whatever it may be. But the characters tend to exist in a contextual vacuum. We don't know anything about their background, about the world that spawned them. And what's striking about the experience of black Americans is how many of these black professionals come from parents who are black professionals and grandparents who were professionals and so on. That's a story often missed. A lot of them also are marvelous success stories who came from more difficult beginnings and that's a very important story that we like telling and we should. Horatio Alger has always fascinated us and should. But it's always the case that in black America there are many families that have been professionally educated and pretty well off financially for many generations and that's also an interesting story. Now, I myself don't come from that background, but we weren't poor. I have college-educated parents. I kind lived in the fringes of that world a little bit although it was not really quite my world. But I think it is useful to think about that world for more than one reason. For one thing, when we realize that there was within black America for a very long time this substrata, this culture, that was able to build an ethic of professional achievement and nurture that over time in the worst days of segregation. That suggests something to be applauded in what these families achieved. At the same time, also in the book I try several times to draw the very sharp contrast between these success stories and the many people of color that the society leaves further and further behind with each passing day, and in my judgment cares less and less about with each passing day.

MURPHY: *It seemed to me that the way that Oliver Garland was treated in the nomination process was a bit extreme in that the alleged reason for his demise was his association with a shady character who happened to be his college roommate. And I'm wondering if you think that if Oliver Garland were Caucasian, rather than African American, if the same result would have occurred.*

CARTER: I think that's a great question but it's too complicated of a question to demand of an author. That is, that is a question more for the reader to think about. If readers want to be stimulated to think along those lines, so much the better. There's a lot of places in the book where I try to be provocative in raising questions that I hope readers will think about more. But I'm not trying to answer them, I'm just trying to raise them. I said in an interview about some of my nonfiction work years ago, that I'm more interested in provoking than persuading. It doesn't so much matter to me if people think I'm right. What matters to me is they think I'm wrong in an interesting way. And so for me as a scholar, the argument is as important as the conclusion. I care about argument. I care about the back and forth, the give and take. And so a lot of the questions I raise in the book I raise so that people will think about them and talk about them, not so they will agree with me about them.

MURPHY: *That is an interesting point because as I was reading the book my thought was you're not hammering the reader with this point but it's out there for the reader to grasp if the reader desires and I really appreciated that in your writing. I know you're working on the second book and I'm wondering if you're able to share any of the plot of that book.*

CARTER: I prefer to share very little about the book. It's not a matter of anybody's strictures but my own. The first book, *The Emperor of Ocean Park*, I see as character-driven fiction. That is, what produced it was these characters bouncing around in my head in the sense they have stories to tell. So with the second book, which is about half done at this point, again I have some characters who have some stories to tell. Some of them were characters in the first book. Some of the characters didn't make it into the first book. I don't think of it as a sequel to the first book though I still hope it will have some of the aspects of mystery and thriller, some of the aspects of political and social commentary, some of the aspects being a window into a world a lot of readers are unfamiliar with that I think people have found in the first book and enjoyed. I hope it will have those things; we'll have to wait and see how people feel when it's finished. I'm the worst person to judge because I never dreamed the first book would generate the kind of enthusiasm that is has.

MURPHY: *I have a stylistic question. In reading the dialogue I noticed that rarely is there a statement by a character and then another statement by the character that would go on for a page or two. Typically it seemed to me your dialogue was a statement by a character followed by exposition by the narrator and then a response to that statement which is a style that I thought Scott Turow used very well. And I'm wondering if you consciously developed that style or even gave it any thought.*
CARTER: The first person narrator has been a matter of some debate in literature for a very long time. I think it was Ernest Hemingway, I am told, who said that any fool can write a first person novel. And maybe that's true. Hemingway, quite famously did very little exposition in his books. It was all action and some description and dialogue and yet managed to do wonderful character studies with that style of punchy writing. But most people who have done character studies in the first person haven't done that. Most have been much more discursive, I think is the word for it. And I suppose I'm more in that tradition. I mentioned Thomas Hardy before and Thomas Hardy I think would be an example of someone who was maybe more discursive that way. It's not so much a style I selected as a style I fell into. As I worked on the book it became what was comfortable, but it was particularly comfortable given the voice of the narrator. The narrator is someone who is self analytical to a fault and is also analytical to the rest of the world to a fault. It constantly is searching for meanings, reflecting, wondering, obsessing about meaning. He's a semiotician by training; he mentions that to us several times. He studied Semiotics before he went to law school and so he cares about language. He cares about not only how we communicate but the actual tools. What do these words and symbols actually signify? He cares about that deeply. So he broods on that. He cares about it to the point of worrying about it and he worries about it a lot. So it seemed to be correct that he would be constantly analyzing and thinking about what other people would say. And so it goes with his personality.

MURPHY: *Now that you've finished the book, have been on a book tour, gotten reviews, and have been interviewed and are half way through a second book, is there any part of* The Emperor of Ocean Park, *in hindsight, that you wish you had done differently?*
CARTER: Oh, of course. You know, it's funny because I recently saw an interview with the actor Allen Rickman whose work I really admire. He was on a talk show and the host was showing tapes of some of his films and Allen Rickman kept saying, "Stop, I don't want to see it." And it became clear he wasn't joking, that somehow when a fan

saw the film, a fan would say, "Look at this film." When he saw it, he would think, "Oh, I could have done that better." And I feel that way about everything I write. *The Emperor of Ocean Park*, my nonfiction, everything I write, I feel I could have done better. And yet you can't worry about that too much or you'll never get anything done. One of the best pieces of advice about writing I ever got was from one of my first term law professors at Yale Law School back in 1976, who said to me, "There's no piece of writing you can't improve if you spend a little more time on it. The discipline is making yourself stop." And so whether I'm writing a novel or a nonfiction book or an article or an essay or a book review or notes for a lecture I'm going to deliver that day, the discipline is stopping. The discipline is saying, "I'm going to stop this and go on to something else." I tend to be a perfectionist about my work, but I try not to let that make me the kind of person who won't let go of it. I try to let go. I love writing, I love the act of putting words together and I don't worry much about what I'm writing. I'm the kind of writer who always has a dozen things going on at once and if one thing gets boring I work on another one. It's very important because it helps me to finish things. Rather than obsess about one paragraph or one page, that I'm quite capable of doing, I go on to something else then I go back to what I was working on before and finish it or try to finish it and go on to something else yet. And I enjoy that too.

JAMES DUFFY aka HAUGHTON MURPHY

James Duffy, a former partner with the Wall Street firm of Cravath, Swaine & Moore, left the practice of law to write murder mysteries under the pseudonym of Haughton Murphy. His book, Murder Saves Face features series protagonist Reuben Frost, also a retired Wall Street lawyer, investigating the murder of a young associate at Chase & Ward, his former firm.

Frost's investigation of possible suspects includes a partner at Chase & Ward, who had risen quickly through the ranks. Duffy describes Chase & Ward as a "meritocracy. Every partner, by instinct in some cases, out of principle in others, had realized since the earliest days of Charles Chase that advancement within the firm must depend on ability; that it would sink into mediocrity if nepotism or other irrelevancies entered the advancement process and the brightest law school graduates shunned it because of a lack of commitment to merit. This is not to say that those who formed the traditional, WASP backbone of the firm did not rejoice when one of their own showed the ability to compete fairly and squarely with his peers."

James Duffy is a graduate of Princeton University and Harvard Law School. He has served as Treasurer of The Mystery Writers of America.

This interview took place in 1992.

FICTION (as Haughton Murphy): *Murder for Lunch* (1986); *Murder Takes a Partner* (1987); *Murders and Acquisitions* (1988); *Murder Keeps a Secret* (1989); *Murder Times Two* (1990); *Murder Saves Face* (1991); *A Very Venetian Murder* (1992)

FICTION (as James Duffy): *Dog Bites Man: City Shocked* (2001)

MURPHY: *You quit the practice of law to write a series of murder mysteries about a lawyer named Reuben Frost who is retired and in his seventies. Elderly protagonists typically are found more in English mysteries rather than American. Why did you choose a protagonist of this age?*
DUFFY: I thought it was getting out of the mold a little bit and doing something a little more unusual than what is normally done. And it also gave me a chance to focus on a segment of the population that isn't the center of attention very often.

MURPHY: *What led, initially, to your decision to stop practicing law and begin writing these novels?*
DUFFY: I started writing while I was still practicing. I've written seven, the first three while I was still at Cravath. It seemed to me that if I was going to continue writing, that I really had to make a choice between the practice and writing - there just wasn't time to do both.

WHAT IF HOLDEN CAULFIELD WENT TO LAW SCHOOL?

MURPHY: *What attracted you to fiction in the first place? Murder mysteries are something you usually don't associate with a partner at Cravath?*

DUFFY: (Laughter). This all started - I guess it must be 10 or 12 years ago now - when my wife and I considered writing a murder mystery together. We thought it would be something that would be fun to do. We started and both realized right away that this was a sure way to the divorce court. After that, I decided to continue on my own and tried intermittently to work on a plot. I then finally put it together and began writing. It started in the first instance as a puzzle or an amusing thing to do and then it grew. All of a sudden I was looking at a series and it had become something that was not just a little hobby but was taking up a lot of time.

MURPHY: *The tone of your books is much like an English-style puzzle, more so than a hard-boiled Raymond Chandler story. Why did you choose this style?*

DUFFY: I think it was something that I was more comfortable with. I would be reasonably uncomfortable writing terribly violent, hard- boiled stuff and it doesn't interest me that much. And, frankly, I don't think I would be very good at it. This style just seemed to be something that I felt I would be more comfortable with.

MURPHY: *Does your style reflect your own reading habits? Do you read a lot of Agatha Christie and other English authors?*

DUFFY: certainly have in times past. But I don't read them exclusively nor do I read only soft-boiled mysteries. I'm a fairly selective reader of mysteries.

MURPHY: *Your most recent Reuben Frost mystery,* Murder Saves Face, *involves the murder of a beautiful, young associate, Juliana Merriman. You've inserted a lot of issues in the book, from sexual harassment of an associate by a partner to the immorality of investment bankers in the 80's. Do you generally try to weave these types of themes into your murder mysteries?*

DUFFY: I'm not sure I set out to do that deliberately. But if they arise in the context of the plot, I try to deal with them or try to treat them the way they would appear in a contemporary setting or the setting I'm talking about.

MURPHY: *You start off* Murder Saves Face *with the body of Juliana Merriman being found in the law firm library. And then you discuss her activities before the murder and Reuben Frost's investigation after the murder. Is this the kind of format you follow in creating your plots - that is - start with the murder, then go backwards, then forwards?*

DUFFY: No, I think it varies from book to book. In this particular novel, I had gone to visit the new offices of my old law firm and two separate partners - my former partners - got me aside and said you've got to come and see something. They both showed me the sliding shelves in the firm library and they said, "Surely you can do something with that!" That's how it began. So in that case I really started with the setting. We're going to open them up and there will be a body. Then we took it from there. So in that case you're right - that was the sequence that I followed but it's not always that way.

MURPHY: *Your books always involve the upper class, either as lawyers' clients or suspects in the murder. Why this emphasis on the rich?*

DUFFY: There's more chance for satire and poking a little fun at things with the kind of people I'm talking about. That's really a good part of it. It offers a chance for some social commentary.

MURPHY: *There's also a bit of the art world involved in your books and I understand you served on the Cultural Affairs Commission in New York City. Do your books reflect your interest in art?*
DUFFY: I suppose they do. I'm a collector of a minor sort. I've always been interested in contemporary art and try to keep up with it. Again, there are a lot of things there that one can poke a little fun at and I've done some of that - not a great deal but some.

MURPHY: *You make mention in* Murder Saves Face *of Louis Auchincloss. I couldn't help but see similarities between your books and his, which also involve the upper class and the legal profession. Was he an influence to you?*
DUFFY: No. I've read a good number of his books but I would not call him an influence.

MURPHY: *Are you conscious of being compared to him by your readers?*
DUFFY: No, not really. I know there have been some reviewers who have, from time-to-time, mentioned us together. But, I think it's because the surface similarity of both of us being lawyers.

MURPHY: *Also in* Murder Saves Face*, you mention the English writer, Michael Gilbert, whose* Smallbone Deceased *was written in 1950. It seemed particularly unusual to me that you would plug another writer in your own novel. Why did you mention Gilbert?*
DUFFY: Just because I think he's one of the real masters of the mystery story and was one of the first lawyers - at least contemporary lawyers - to write mysteries. It was just kind of a homage to him, if you will.

MURPHY: *The book mentions that the circumstances of Juliana Merriman's body being found in the law firm bear some similarity to* Smallbone Deceased*. Did you borrow any other aspects of that book for* Murder Saves Face*?*
DUFFY: No, I don't think so. There's a big surprise when Smallbone's body was found in a will box in the office of a tiny firm in London, just as there's a surprise when Merriman's body is found in the library. But no, I don't think there are other similarities, at least that I'm aware of.

MURPHY: *What is it about the murder mystery genre that particularly appeals to you?*
DUFFY: It has the appeal of being a very structured kind of writing. I don't have the guts to sit down and start a book unless I pretty much have the plot outlined. I wouldn't want to start writing, get half way through and find myself up a tree that I couldn't get back down. So the idea of having a structured book is appealing. By having a series and series character like Reuben and his wife, Cynthia, they are well connected in New York and around the country - you can really poke your finger in anything and manage to comment on a lot of things that way.

MURPHY: *Reuben is retired from his legal practice and is now in his 70's. How many murders can a retired Wall Street lawyer encounter in his lifetime?*

DUFFY: In real life, probably not very many. In a mystery series of fiction, quite a few. I don't think you can look at it by saying, well, gee, this is pretty improbable that you would run across seven murders in a short span of time (laughter). But I think that's just an aspect of fiction that you've got to accept.

MURPHY: *You mentioned Cynthia Frost, Reuben's wife. She is, of course, a major character in all the books, discussing the evidence with him, analyzing it. Does she play the role of someone like the fool in Shakespeare - to ask questions that the reader would be asking?*
DUFFY: She does ask questions and she can turn the evidence over in a different way than the people who are so bound up in it that they may lose sight of some detail. A friend of mine, who I think has read all the books, said a couple of books back, "I finally figured out how to read your books and that's to pay attention to what Cynthia says." There's some truth to that.

MURPHY: *Was Reuben's practice at all similar to yours when you were with Cravath?*
DUFFY: Yes, the practice was similar. He was a corporate lawyer and I was a corporate lawyer so, yes, there is similarity there.

MURPHY: *When did you retire?*
DUFFY: I retired at the end of 1988.

MURPHY: *Were you involved in all of the mergers and acquisitions of the 80's?*
DUFFY: I was around in that period but I never was particularly involved in hostile takeovers. The mergers and acquisitions I worked on were mostly back at an earlier time when you didn't have the hostile game in the 80's.

MURPHY: *Did the atmosphere in the 80's contribute to your decision to stop practicing?*
DUFFY: No. I had a very good time practicing. I practiced for almost 30 years. I enjoyed it very much. But it just seemed like a good idea - if I was going to do something else, to do it - rather than wait around until I was in my mid-60's. I was very lucky. I was able to do it, so why not? It really had nothing to do with any great dissatisfaction with the legal practice. It was a very difficult decision, in fact.

MURPHY: *Have you written any fiction in addition to the mystery novels?*
DUFFY: No, so far it's only been the mystery novels. Whether that will change or not, time will tell. I finished one which will be out in May and I'm really kind of thinking about what I do next - whether I go on with the series, or maybe start a new series or maybe try a novel that's not a mystery. At this point, I can't tell you because I don't know.

MURPHY: *What is the new one called?*
DUFFY: The new one is called *A Very Venetian Murder*. It is the first one that has not been set in New York. It's set in Venice. Reuben and Cynthia are on vacation and come across another murder.

MURPHY: *Do you have any idea what the sales of your books have been?*

DUFFY: I think they've been modest. I mean, these are not wild bestsellers - there's no question on that. But they've all been in paperback and they come out in paperback a year after the hardback, so *Murder For Lunch* first came out in February or March of 1987, and so on. *Murder Saves Face* just came out in paperback. And they've done reasonably well. But, again, we're not talking about any sort of mega-hit here.

MURPHY: *As someone named Murphy, I have to ask you why you chose the pseudonym of Haughton Murphy?*
DUFFY: Right. Murphy is my wife's maiden name and Haughton is a family name of an old friend from college that struck me as being an amusing first name.

MURPHY: *Did you need a pseudonym because you wanted to keep your writing a secret?*
DUFFY: No, it wasn't so much a matter of keeping it secret but it was a matter of kind of keeping it separate. If I had it to do over again, I wouldn't bother.

MURPHY: *I've read that Charles Alan Wright, the Texas lawyer, claims credit for exposing you as James Duffy. Is there any truth to that?*
DUFFY: I'm not sure it's entirely true. I mean, he was one of the first, certainly, but I've forgotten just how the sequence ran. Jim Stewart of the Wall Street Journal identified me about the same time, so it was no big deal. And, as I say, if I had it to do over again, I would not use a pseudonym. It's hard enough to establish one identity, let alone two.

MICHAEL FREDRICKSON

Michael Fredrickson's second novel, *Witness for the Dead*, borrows its plot from real-life headlines from the 1990s. Whitey Bulger, brother of former Massachusetts Senate President William Bulger, was reputed to be a leader of the Irish mob. Many people thought he avoided prosecution because of his family. In fact, as the Boston Globe later revealed, Whitey Bulger was hired as an informant by the FBI to turn on high-level members of the Mafia. In exchange for turning in his Italian colleagues, Bulger gained control of organized crime. Although Bulger claimed he kept the drug-dealers out of his native South Boston, it turned out he was the biggest drug dealer of all.

A graduate of Macalester College in St. Paul, Fredrickson also attended Oxford University as a Rhodes Scholar and the University of Toronto as a graduate student in English literature. He has worked as an English professor, subsistence farmer, auto mechanic, lumberjack, folk musician, and singing telegrapher. With this diverse background, he then decided to attend Harvard Law School from which he graduated magna cum laude in 1982. After five years as an associate in a large Boston law firm, he became general counsel to the Massachusetts Board of Bar Overseers.

This interview took place in 2001.

FICTION: *A Cinderella Affidavit* (1999); *Witness for the Dead* (2001); *A Defense for the Dead* (2004)

MURPHY: Witness for the Dead *is based on a quite notorious true story involving Whitey Bulger. Were you concerned in writing this novel that the truth would be even more compelling than anything you could make up?*
FREDRICKSON: To some extent yes. I remember when I first began to follow the story; I kept thinking it was like something out of a Pat O'Brien movie from the thirties, the good brother and the bad brother. Who'd believe it? The truth was harder to believe than anything I could make up. But, as you probably noticed from reading the book, I strayed quite a bit from the center of the story. I was more interested in a different angle: the reward and having some amateurs figure out how to find the guy.

MURPHY: *The book seemed to take two different directions. First, the court sequence around Arthur Patch, the witness informant, and getting him to testify. He never did actually testify against Larry the Rabbit. And then you change directions to chasing down Tommy Crimmins, the Whitey Bulger figure. Why did you structure the book in that way?*
FREDRICKSON: The first third of the book is a set up for the latter two thirds, in one sense. The squeeze that Arthur finds himself in tells provokes him into using the one little piece of information he really has, which is that this guy's a snitch. He recalls

an episode that seems to confirm a rumor to that effect, and as a result the US attorney lets him out of his fix. But the lawyer he's assigned is in a fix of his own. The lawyer uses Arthur's information in such a way that the secret comes out. And that's what sets off the train of events that leads to the hunt. That was how I envisaged the book coming out. I wanted to use the true-life story to get to the other one.

MURPHY: *The key bit of information, of course, is that the FBI had been using Tommy Crimmins as an informant for years and letting him get away with a lot of other crimes of his own, including murder. One thing that occurred to me is that Martin Flukes, the FBI agent who tipped off Crimmins that he was going to be indicted, never suffered any repercussions for doing that. Nothing seems to happen to him once it came out that he had actually tipped off Crimmins. Did I miss something?*
FREDRICKSON: No. I don't think so. The local FBI has no interest in seeing that something happens to Flukes because they're involved in it themselves, not necessarily in the tip-off, but they have a good deal of concern about how much of their own involvement is going to disturb their own careers. Similar things happened in the true-life story with an FBI agent who has now been accused of tipping off Bulger. The agent has been indicted for that--plus obstruction of justice and what not – and no one really quite knows what he did or who he talked to. I suppose the short answer is that Flukes' fate just didn't interest me very much. I guess your question poses a fair comment.

MURPHY: *Did you do a lot of research into the actual case in preparation for writing the book?*
FREDRICKSON: Not that much. Just newspapers. I didn't want to get too closely tied into it. I did the same thing with the first book. I wanted to take the structure of the situation and tell a different story. I didn't tell the Whitey Bulger story. I don't know very much about Whitey Bulger. I know he has a brother who resembles a character who is the governor in my book -- a powerful politician here. He was also a character for my first book - the district attorney. At the end of *A Cinderella Affidavit* he becomes governor, so he was a natural to use again, this time as the gangster's brother. It was an intriguing bit of information but it wasn't the story I wanted to tell. What I wanted mostly was the story about Arthur and Dani on the one hand and about Mavis and Tommy on the other -- and then of course Jimmy Morrissey and his own problems. Jimmy Morrissey also is a minor character in the first novel.

MURPHY: *He is the lawyer for Arthur Patch who's got ethical problems of his own.*
FREDRICKSON: Who lives by his wits, not his ethics.

MURPHY: *I'm assuming he is the composite of various people you've encountered in your ethical duties.*
FREDRICKSON: I wouldn't even go that far. He's somebody I made up. I've known a number of lawyers who have gotten in trouble by drafting wills in which they, or someone they know, some relative, stands to inherit under the thing. That is a fairly common kind of ethical misconduct. As is, of course, the shifting of funds from one account to another to stay out of the poor house. Those are fairly common sorts of serious misconduct I see in my work.

MURPHY: *What was it about the search for Tommy Crimmins, really the quest for the reward, that intrigued you enough to make it the focus of your book?*

WHAT IF HOLDEN CAULFIELD WENT TO LAW SCHOOL?

FREDRICKSON: That these were amateurs. That they really don't know they were doing. You've got the FBI, allegedly anyway, mounting this manhunt – the fugitive is now on the Ten Most Wanted list – and they can use television and all kinds of media. So I invented two sets of amateurs who are going to sit down and try to find him. So you ask yourself: How would I go about doing this? What would I do? I would want to throw some kind of hook into this story. Some way to figure out how you attract this guy. And I made up a story. I did know that Bulger had fled with his girlfriend. That seemed to me to be a big mistake. So I had to invent a girlfriend find a way to exploit that mistake. That's what made the book interesting to me. You have all these characters converge at some point in the future.

MURPHY: *And really the weak link in terms of Tommy Crimmins was his girlfriend's love of greyhounds. Did you do much research into the world of greyhound racing?*
FREDRICKSON: Yes. Actually when I was thinking about how I would go about finding this, I happened to spot a story in a newspaper somewhere about the decline of greyhound racing. With off-track betting, lotteries, and more and more casinos everywhere, it's become kind of a shabby business these days. The story mentioned that people were rescuing greyhounds and trying to outlaw racing. I knew of a senior partner from a very prominent downtown firm here, who had three or four of these dogs. So I called him up and I said what's this all about. And he gave me an earful, told me about this local group and how they're all hooked together. So I called the local group and they sent me a packet of stuff, including all the web sites. I started getting on the web sites and running it down. It's like another world there. You could spend years running this stuff down. You don't have to make up too much crazy stuff. It's there. Not that I mean to malign the people that save greyhounds, but many of them have a cutesy kind of new-age slant on the world. I asked myself, what would this Mavis do? If she were hooked into these people, she would have to establish contact. What else is she gonna do with herself with this guy on the run all the time? So that was the idea. That was how I wanted to use the dogs.

MURPHY: *Having known about the Bulger story, I was really intrigued by these two brothers at opposite ends of the spectrum. Has anybody done a true story/biography or some nonfiction work about them?*
FREDRICKSON: I know that there are nonfiction treatments of the whole Whitey story, but I never read them. I didn't dare read them. For one thing, they were kind of intimidating. But Dick Lehr and Gerry O'Neill were Globe reporters who wrote a book called *Black Mass*, a very successful book about the scandal itself. Another reporter named Ralph Ranalli has a book called *Deadly Alliance* coming out -- it's about the FBI itself. And of course, George V. Higgins, a dean of Boston writers, did a rendering of this problem in his last novel.

MURPHY: *You have a chapter in the book – Chapter 11 - in which you use a* Boston Globe *newspaper article verbatim. I'm not sure you copied it, but the whole chapter is a newspaper article revealing the scandal.*
FREDRICKSON: I made the article up.

MURPHY: *I'm just wondering why you decided to use that technique instead of more fictional techniques in disclosing what really was a dramatic moment in revealing to the public this FBI scam.*

FREDRICKSON: I did it actually in the first book too. I wanted to cover a lot ground in a few pages. And I wanted to get through the set-up. And this permitted me to cover a lot of ground fairly quickly and get to the point where the FBI is pressured into doing something to get past this embarrassing public predicament. What is it going to be? It's going to be the posting of the reward which then becomes the engine for the rest of the novel. So I think it was a device to cover a lot of ground in a few short pages and to talk about what had happened.

MURPHY: *You have the search being conducted independently by Dani and Arthur Patch, as well as the lawyer Jimmy Morrissey. I found it curious that you have a team that is composed of a former Assistant US Attorney and a witness she had previously subpoenaed to testify. From you're position as General Counsel of the Board of Bar Overseers, is there any kind of ethical problem that arises from that kind of partnership?*

FREDRICKSON: That's interesting. It's not a legal representation so it wouldn't necessarily implicate the conflict of interest rules for Dani. There are certain confidences that she's unable to use and she confronts that immediately. It bothers her. Whenever Arthur seems to suggest a less straightforward route, she is all over him. So it certainly was a looming issue for me. But it's more an issue about confidences and her need to keep them, and I think she does.

MURPHY: *Wasn't there an issue still pending on appeal regarding Arthur Patch as a witness?*

FREDRICKSON: I suppose there is, but she's not involved in it.

MURPHY: *But she had been. The US Attorney's office still was. It occurred to me that was a big problem.*

FREDRICKSON: You may be right. Putting aside the rules governing Assistant US Attorneys, which I am certainly no expert on, I look at the classical rules of professional conduct and ask which rules would be implicated other than the rules respecting client confidences, I can't think of anything.

MURPHY: *What occurred to me was the appearance of a conflict of interest, whether there was an actual one or not it appeared unseemly to me.*

FREDRICKSON: What she does is a little unseemly. It would be unseemly for her to have a current representation of a client and to be going into business with somebody like Arthur, given his role. Someone out there will no doubt correct me if I'm wrong about this.. It's a situation in which the lawyer goes into a venture that has nothing to do with the practice of law or lobbying or anything like that and she is not using information from the previous representation. But somebody could land on it, if they knew about it, which is one of the reasons she stays out of the spotlight in the end.

MURPHY: *Arthur Patch is an interesting character: the owner of a Sicilian restaurant, from a Polish background and grew up in South Boston. How did you come about with that mix? It's certainly not a stereotype in any sense.*

FREDRICKSON: That's good because I felt I was sort of skating close to line with Larry the Rabbit – maybe over it. I wanted to portray Larry as a cartoon villain in a sense, and to contrast him to Tommy who is a much more seriously evil person. And so when I conceived Arthur and Dani I wanted people with more flesh and blood who were less tied to their ethnicity.

MURPHY: *I don't know if you've had a chance to read many of the legal thrillers out there, but a lot of them feature the FBI and the Mafia, even since* The Firm *which seemed to be the ultimate FBI-Mafia book. Have you noticed a trend of lawyers being drawn to that kind of scenario?*

FREDRICKSON: In fiction? To be honest with you, I don't read too much lawyer fiction. But maybe I ought to leave the topic alone. I promise my next book will have anything to do with it – well maybe the FBI a little bit, but no Mafia. That's why I've never seen *The Sopranos*. People always tell me, "You've got to watch *The Sopranos*." They described it to me and I said I can't watch *that*. I know I'll either be intimidated by it or I'll start picking it up. So I left it alone just like I leave the legal thrillers alone.

MURPHY: *Your first book,* A Cinderella Affidavit, *is also based on a true story. Can you tell me a little about that story?*

FREDRICKSON: In that story, some policemen were raiding a crack house in Dorchester. There was a no-knock warrant. There was a steel reinforced door and drugs were sold out of a hole in the door. They were battering down the door with a sledge hammer - don't ask me why - and someone fired a gun through the door and killed the police officer. And when they finally battered their way through the door, they found the room empty. There were back stairs down to a room below, which was sort of a back-room operation for the crack house. And there they found four people and a gun beneath a mattress. They arrested everyone and took the gun and eventually three people in the room turned on the fourth and said he was the person who had worked in the room all this time. They also claimed he was only one who worked upstairs and had come running down with the gun after the shooting. So he was charged with the murder. The defense counsel gets the search warrant affidavit sworn by the police officer who was in charge of the raid. The affidavit uses information provided by a confidential informant who had been in the room the day before the shooting. He describes the occupant of the room and the description doesn't fit the defendant. So the defense counsel said, "That's my witness. I want him. Produce him." The police say, "No, he's confidential." The judge says, "Not anymore he's not. Produce him." But they can't because he doesn't exist. They made him up.

MURPHY: *Are you telling me the plot line or the real story?*

FREDRICKSON: I'm telling you both at the moment. The police then faked a search for the informant and said they couldn't find him. The judge didn't believe them and dismissed the case. Now, this was a major cop-killing case. To have a judge dismiss the case over an apparent technicality like the inability to find an informant . . . ? The press was all over this judge. Within a day, the police were back in court admitting that there was no informant. If you do criminal work, you know this is not that unusual an occurrence – to have a fake informant. It's common enough in Boston that they have a term for it - a Cinderella affidavit. Because it's fantasy. And in fact this particular informant had been used in like fifty different cases, each one interlocking. You know how you establish the credibility of your informant by referring to cases that he worked on before? If you went and followed the daisy chain back, there were fifty warrants issued on the word of this fictitious informant.

And when I read that story, I thought this is a great dilemma for that policeman whose partner and good friend has just been killed in front of him. He sees himself faced with the choice of watching the guy he's convinced killed his partner walk out of the jail because the judge has dismissed the case, or fessing up to perjury and obstruction of justice and doing time -- which is what actually happened to the Boston policeman involved.

And so that was the germ of the story. I thought that was a great story. You've not only got this murder trial, you've got this cop who started out as kind of a stick villain for me and became a much more human character. So then I had to look for some very complicated plot so that I could also write about what it's like to practice in a large Boston law firm.

Maybe that explains the odd structure of both books. In each case I've taken true-story ideas that I wanted to work into the book, then created a plot as a kind of a chine on which to hang the skeletal work for the rest of the book. Now I'm seventy-five pages into the third and it's going to be very different. It's not based on anything real.

MURPHY: *Completely made up.*
FREDRICKSON: Completely made up. With Jimmy Morrissey occupying a major role.

MURPHY: *You've had a varied work history before law school. You've been an English professor, a subsistence farmer, a car mechanic, a lumberjack, folk musician, singing telegrapher. With that background, what made you want to go to law school?*
FREDRICKSON: Actually, I went to college in 1963 as a pre-law student. So I've come full circle. I grew up in the Midwest and went to college to be a gung-ho pre-law student and I got seduced away into literature, poetry and all that good stuff. From there I went to Oxford for a couple of years to read English. More graduate school in Toronto. Then I was an English Professor. And by now I was 27 years old and I don't think I had ever done anything in my life except go to school or teach. This was the early '70s. Seemed to me the next thing to do would be to be a farmer. So I became a hippie farmer for a while. And I did a number of jobs to support that. I worked as a mechanic, a terrible mechanic (you have to start when you're 14 or forget it) I cut pulp wood and timber out of my wood lot. I did construction and I was a bookkeeper, did some extension teaching. I did that for about five years. Then in '77 I split up with my then-wife and went back to Minneapolis. I had always wanted to play music so I played bars and coffee houses. I sang and played guitar. One night I got into a discussion with by brother about what ever happened to singing telegrams. So we started a singing telegram business. As they say in the anti-trust business, it's a business with low entry barriers. A telephone and a car and a little chutzpah and you can do it. I delivered about 2000 singing telegrams in Minneapolis and Detroit and Cincinnati for two years. Then my brother took over the business.

That's when I went to law school because I realized that I was 34 and I was not going be able to spend my life being a singing telegrapher. And law school kind of came back around for me. It all seemed like a natural progression at the time. So I went to law school, then clerked for the DC Circuit.

MURPHY: *And now with the Board, do you actually litigate attorney discipline cases?*
FREDRICKSON: Rarely. I advise the board itself. Run its hearing system and when it wishes to be represented, I go up and argue its position before the Supreme Judicial Court. The bar discipline piece is the biggest piece of what I do and I really enjoy that. It's a perfect job. My clients are these twelve volunteer board members. Eight of them are lawyers, four aren't. They are very busy people. It takes them two to three years to figure out what's going on then they rotate off at four years. They're terrific people. I have no discovery ever. I only practice in the Supreme Court. What more could you ask?

It's government work, so it doesn't pay me a fortune but at least I have a little more energy at the end of the day. I just realized I didn't want to turn seventy and wonder if I could have done written that novel I always thought about writing. That was really the impetus to start writing for me.

MURPHY: *With your background as an English Professor I would think that would have been in the back of your mind for a long time.*
FREDRICKSON: Thirty-five years. When I was fifteen years old I would fantasize about writing books. The Cinderella Affidavit case had happened in the late 80s and it stuck in my head as a good idea. So when I turned fifty I said I'm going to find out. I'm going to set aside time, I'm going to try to do it, give it a few months anyway. And in all candor I fully expected that I would hate it, couldn't do it, or lack the discipline or whatever it was. But at least I would put this thing to rest so that I would know. I wouldn't look back at seventy and wonder.

And it was awful for a long time. Everything I wrote looked like crap. I didn't show anybody. Even my wife didn't see it for a couple of months. And it became very seductive, just like a mistress you stole away to. It's really fun.

MURPHY: *You do it every day now?*
FREDRICKSON: Not quite. I do it when I can. I do it evenings. I found that it is a little harder to find the time now. When I started, my son was three, I'd put him to bed, then I'd have some time. But he stays up later now, he's busy on the weekends, so that's harder. My wife has been very supportive but the novelty of having an author in the house has worn off. So I do it catch-as-catch-can. But it's still great. You get in there and you spend time with these characters that just do what they're gonna do. I don't know how to explain it. I'm sure you've heard this from other people. People talk about how their characters have lives of their own and minds of their own. It's really true.

For example: A writer friend and I get together and read each other's stuff. I'm working on *Witness For the Dead* and I'm three fourths of the way through. Something's bothering me about it. I can't put my finger on what it is, it's just bothering me. And he's reading it and he turns to me and says, "You're not going to kill BLANK off, are you?" And in that instant I knew what it was. Because that's what I was gonna do. I was gonna kill her off. And that's what had been bothering me. It didn't feel right. As you can imagine, at that point I had to change the whole plot. I mean the whole ending of the book. How was I going to get her out of this mess? And so I had to do some serious thinking about how to do that. I like how it ends. I think it's a good way for her to get out of it. It strings a bunch of things together.

MURPHY: *You do give the reader a hint that she might have been shot.*
FREDRICKSON: Yeah. And then I have her bump into Jimmy. Jimmy physically bump into everybody, including Tommy. And so that's how I got out of that mess.

With the first book I had the same problem. From the beginning, I had mapped out where I thought the book was going to go and how it was going to end. I was half-way through it and realized that ending just didn't work. The way the characters had developed just didn't fit that ending anymore. I didn't know what to do and I was kind of treading water. One day I was at some conference on alcoholism in the profession. There was this boring speaker up there and I had this epiphany on how to end the book. I started scribbling madly away – do this, fix that, change this. How I could make it consistent with the way my characters were now and the way the story should work, while making the ending a little less predictable. So I tore into that. I'm not kidding, it's just intoxicating to get times like that.

MURPHY: *One last question: Has Whitey Bulger ever been located?*
FREDRICKSON: Nope. Spotted every once in a while. But nobody ever found him. They've upped the reward to a million dollars now.

MURPHY: *Who's paying that?*
FREDRICKSON: The FBI.

BAINE KERR

Before Baine Kerr attended law school, he studied creative writing, worked as a reporter, and published a collection of short stories, one of which was included in the Best American Short Stories series. When the writing life proved financially challenging, he followed his father into the law. Baine now practices in Boulder, Colorado where he represents plaintiffs primarily in medical malpractice cases.

For the plot of his first novel, Kerr turned to his own cases, writing a polished and suspenseful book that bears the imprint of an experienced novelist. *Harmful Intent* traces the prosecution of a medical malpractice case for failure to diagnose breast cancer. In less skilled hands, the plot could have become pedantic and predictable. But Kerr creates compelling characters, starting with plaintiff's attorney Perry Moss, who had soured on malpractice cases.

> After fifteen years of his doing little else, malpractice cases remained too hard to win; they cost too much; and winning meant too little. Settlements were confidential, the client was still as maimed or dead, and the practice and malpractice of medicine would proceed unedified.

When Terry Winters consults Moss complaining of mistreatment by Moss's old adversary Dr. Wallace Bondurant, Moss decides to take another shot at a malpractice case. Winters is accompanied by her precocious twelve-year-old daughter, Emmy, who is also Bondurant's patient. Moss instantly takes a liking to both Terry and Emmy. As he digs deeper into the case, his motivation alternates between empathy for his client and enmity for the defendant. The case seems solid until strange things start to happen. His expert melts down at his deposition; then his client disappears just before trial.

Kerr's mastery of litigation tactics and complex medical issues shines throughout *Harmful Intent*. Through Moss's arguments to the jury, Kerr explains in simple terms the concept of legal causation.

> In breast cancer, Moss told his juries, there is a magic day. There is a day when a woman goes to sleep with a treatable illness and wakes up with incurable cancer. The outcome of a cancer case should turn on a fundamentally simple calculation: Did the doctor's negligence in failing to find detectable cancer happen while the patient's magic day still lay ahead of her? If so, the doctor is responsible for all the harm the cancer will cause.

Kerr also presents the defense arguments in a humorous way, exposing their fallacies. "In closing, Moss would ridicule it all as the Three Dog Defense: Bondurant doesn't have a dog. But if he did have a dog he wouldn't bite anyone. But if he did bite someone he must have been crazy."

A graduate of Stanford University, Kerr earned a Masters Degree in creative writing and then his law degree from the University of Denver. He is a partner at the Boulder, Colorado firm of Hutchinson Black and Cook, LLC.

This interview took place in 2003.

FICTION: *Jumping-Off Place and Other Stories* (1981); *Harmful Intent* (1999); *Wrongful Death* (2002)

MURPHY: Harmful Intent *is a legal thriller relating to a medical malpractice case involving breast cancer. Did you encounter any difficulties in trying to dramatize a civil case since most legal thrillers involve criminal cases?*
KERR: Yes. I think that is a major challenge. A lot of thought. I don't think I came up with a unique approach to meeting that challenge. Legal thrillers in general are challenging to dramatize because most of the action takes place in rooms: conference rooms, court rooms, etc. And a civil case in particular takes some ingenuity to make things happen in an interesting and visual way.

MURPHY: *What techniques did you use in the novel to explain complicated medicine to the lay reader and still maintain the drama of the story?*
KERR: That was another challenge, another potential obstacle to a dramatic narrative in addition to just the lawsuit which is a long, drawn-out, tedious, and boring affair. With both those issues, one technique is to have a client who is very naive in the ways of the court system who constantly needs to have things explained both medically and in terms of what's going on in the litigation. So the lawyer can explain to the client and educate the reader. And similarly in medicine, medical experts can explain medicine to the lawyer. The other way to do it was to set up the protagonist, attorney Peter Moss, as experienced in these kinds of cases. He approaches them in a certain way; therefore going through his strategic thinking allows for exposition of what medical issues are important and how they can be communicated to a jury.

MURPHY: *The case itself, in terms of the failure to diagnose breast cancer, seemed, from my perspective having done some malpractice cases, to be a clear liability case at the outset. Were you concerned in writing the book that you would lose some readers who might think, what's the drama here? What did you do to try to avoid losing those readers?*
KERR: It definitely was a clear liability case. The suspense never depended upon it being a whodunit. It was obvious who did it. The suspense I was hoping to generate was through an examination or a mystery about motive. Why would a doctor, who presumably knows what he's doing, have let this much time elapse? Sort of a whydunit, not a whodunit or a what-happened in terms of motivating the suspense. I wanted the case to be one that would, with the litigation, get better except not as good as the early settlement offer indicated. And that's by Colorado standards, which is a highly tort-reformed state. But I wanted motivation always to be the source of suspense. Why are they offering to settle so early and at fairly high levels? What motivated Bondurant?

The protagonist's wife Sally is sort of the intuitive side that questions his analysis and tells him he has to take his analysis deeper. You've got to understand this man. You've got to understand his family, she even intuits at one point. So motive is really what that was all about. The case did look like a winner at the outset, but as we know, those who prosecute these cases, your own client is as important as the defendant's culpability. And that's where the case starts going south. With the heroine of the book, Terry Winters, who is a difficult client in every sense of the word. And a flaky client in certain senses, except in the context of what she was facing which is the imminent loss of her life and leaving a daughter behind.

MURPHY: *She's the ultimate difficult client in that she disappears right before the trial.*
KERR: Yeah, and that's not good in the real practice of law.

MURPHY: *Even though it is a clear liability case, the defense attorneys still fight it as if there's no liability. I think you do a great job summarizing the defenses: the Judgment Call Defense, a.k.a. Hindsight Is 20/20, a.k.a. Medicine Is An Art Not A Science, the Low Index of Suspicion Defense, the Respectable Minority Defense, the Phantom-Phone-Call Defense. You really made a compelling examination of the realities of prosecuting one of these cases.*
KERR: That was definitely a goal. As all of us who practice in this area know, the reality is not something that the lay public understands very well and not something that TV educates them on. You see the Phantom-Phone-Call Defense over and over again: something is completely undocumented and uncharted. A critical conversation that is either frankly suborned perjury by the opposing counsel, or a massaged and reconstructed memory that is far from anything that actually happened. That's basically when the doctor supposedly is talking to the patient and tells the patient to come back or get a second opinion or whatever it is. It's not documented anywhere but is clearly recalled, five or ten thousand patients later. These are very hard-fought cases. There are tremendous advantages on the physician side in that physicians are quite rightly held in high esteem, although maybe not quite as high as in the past. The defenses, like those that you mentioned, can work even in a case that seems open and shut.

MURPHY: *In this case Peter Moss hires a documents examiner who discovers that handwritten notes have been added to the typed chart a few years after the events documented. A similar thing occurred in* The Verdict, *probably the most famous med mal legal thriller because it became a hit movie. Were you influenced at all by* The Verdict *in any of the plot ideas in* Harmful Intent?
KERR: I don't think so, although I think it's a terrific movie. I've seen it three times. At least one of those times was in the last five years. At the time it came out I was sort of offended by it because no ethical lawyer behaves in the way Frank Galvin does. He got a settlement offer that he never disclosed to the client. I was a young lawyer at that time and saw that as a terrible way for the profession to be portrayed. But I've gotten over that. And I really like the movie. The alteration of records did not come in any conscious way from *The Verdict* but really from the realities of the practice. I mean it just happens. I probably don't have a year go by without encountering altered records somewhere.

MURPHY: *Other than obviously different colored inks, how do you figure that out?*

KERR: I had a case that made me adopt the practice of always subpoenaing the original records at the very outset, and not relying on photocopies. A young woman had shortness of breath and chest pain, was evaluated, sent home and later wound up in the hospital with a massive pulmonary embolism tested for, and was comatose. Obviously a huge damages case. The family physician who had first seen her and dismissed her shortness of breath and chest pain as anxiety was in the hospital and saw that she was in ICU. He went back, pulled the chart, added six entries, which were mostly data of tests that he never gave. Then he actually used white-out on the abnormal values in the chart. I just got photocopies in that case and never knew this until seeing the original chart. It was so obvious with thick gobs of white-out all over it. But getting the original chart and looking at it with a high suspicion for the possibility of alteration is now standard in every one of these cases. In that case, the problem for that doctor was he wasn't aware that his clinic had faxed over a page of the chart on a request from the ER. So there was an unaltered page in the hospital record which made proof of alteration very easy. In *Harmful Intent* the documents examiners lab is where this all comes out. That was a chapter I enjoyed writing very much. And it's pretty close to some of the things you go through in cases where there may be alteration.

MURPHY: *Getting back to the motive of Bondurant not to treat this cancer, I wonder if you went through a checklist of different types of motives to evaluate which one a reader would find most credible. It seemed it had to be something criminal and I wonder if there's anything else you thought of that you discarded as a motive.*
KERR: That's a very interesting question. And it kind of gets back to your opening question about the challenge of writing about a civil lawsuit. I did write about a civil lawsuit that was actually a Trojan horse for criminal conduct. Motive is theoretically irrelevant in most civil lawsuits. A medical malpractice motive is irrelevant; it's just what was the care, what are the standards, did the care meet the standard, not why did the care fail to meet the standard. But clearly the reader of fiction - and actually juries - almost always needs to know more.

The way I started this book was to first arrive at characters - the lawyer Peter Moss and the client Terry Winters. Then the overall structure of medical negligence in that she had a neglected breast cancer that had been let go so long it was likely to be terminal at some point. And then I just started writing the case pretty much along the chronological lines of how a lawsuit proceeds without knowing what the motive or the negligence would be. I probably got through seventy five pages of manuscript with that question always in the back of my mind before it all came together with the motive that in fact is the one in the book. I won't give it away but it seemed just the right one because it brought together all of the themes and characters: the relationship between mother and daughter, when you're leaving your daughter and losing your life to ensure that she is as strong and protected as she can be. Later, the holes in Moss's own family life that he was trying to patch up. I can't remember now what motives were discarded. I think I toyed with some sort of HMO - economics of medicine issues - which I think could be perfectly well-written and has been written about to a certain extent. So I picked a motive for these particular characters.

WHAT IF HOLDEN CAULFIELD WENT TO LAW SCHOOL?

MURPHY: *One of the ways that Peter Moss gets clued into Bondurant's motive is because Bondurant's daughter actually comes to him and reveals key information. In reading the book, something occurred to me that you hear about in writing fiction that the protagonist is supposed to be the one who generates whatever the success is. In this case, even though Moss really did an incredible job on the case, the ultimate discovery of the motive was sort of fortuitous. I wondered if that concerned you in resolving the plot and in revealing the motive.*

KERR: That's another great question, Steve. I actually gave a lot of thought to that and the initial version of the book, which remains the one I like best, was a hundred pages longer and those hundred pages were all from the point of view of the client Terry Winter. And they expanded greatly on her spiritual quest in Mexico as she knew that her life was ending. That was too much for the editors. It took away too much from the focus of the legal and courtroom drama in their view although I tried to keep a fair amount of that there. But my idea was that there were two protagonists here. And there were two investigations that would both drive the plot and drive the suspense. There was the lawyer's factual investigation and the client's spiritual investigation. And they would both converge really with the same point of understanding and at the same place and time. That was the return of the client and her daughter to the lawyer just in time for the trial.

The trial would be the synthesis of those two investigations: the mother and the daughter, in their journey to Mexico to confront what happened and why and how to gain strength from it, which is the spiritual quest; they come to an understanding about their foe that is actually coincident with the lawyer piecing that together from the evidence he has. It's relatively simultaneous but the full breadth was really revealed by the daughter herself when she took the stand. That was the idea anyway. I was also playing off the journey of the hero-quest story. That was more fully worked out in the portion of the book that did not make it to publication. But that is going off to a series of quests and tests and coming to enlightenment and then returning with restored powers.

MURPHY: *That would be Terry of course.*

KERR: That would be Terry. That's the Joseph Campbell myth basically. And she returns with the strength to slay the foe and to fortify her daughter and as it turns out, her lawyer through the process.

MURPHY: *I have a question on the structure of the book. You divide it into four parts: the case, the client, the trial and the judgment. It's obvious why the trial and judgment would be at the end. I just wondered if you considered putting other parts in that I've seen in other books, for example the plaintiff's attorney, the defense attorney, the defendant , and maybe changing the order. What led you to decide to structure it in this way?*

KERR: This structure grew out of what I was just describing: the two different levels that were proceeding on a factual plane and a spiritual plane at the same time. That's the case and the client. That's where that came from. As published, the client part was a little different than as initially envisioned. The case was really about Moss's putting together the winning case, which culminated in the revelation of the diagram that had been obscured by the alteration of the document by the doctor years later. That was the final nail in the structure of the case that the lawyer was building against the doctor.

The client is where things go south and everything that Moss has built is threatened - even to the point of document alteration as you mentioned being turned against him. And then the trial and the judgment as you say are pretty self evident.

The case and the client I chose, rather than the plaintiff's attorney and the defense attorney and so on, because I really wanted to write about these twin protagonists. I wanted the reality of a lawsuit like this to be seen through the eyes of the lawyer and also through the eyes of the client because they are really utterly different experiences, I believe. And I think you would probably agree from your cases. They're two different realities in fact.

MURPHY: *Not only does the client Terry literally go south to Mexico, but the plaintiff's expert goes south in his deposition.*
KERR: Yeah. That's almost a direct description of an expert who went south on me.

MURPHY: *I noticed that you have the expert living in Manchester, New Hampshire which struck a chord with me because I lived there for a year.*
KERR: Well, I guess I can say without further identification, that the real deposition of that expert happened in New Hampshire. So I'll never forget it. Writing that chapter was a way to try to exorcize that from my memory.

MURPHY: *In the book you describe a lot of the strategies of the plaintiff's lawyer Peter Moss in prosecuting the case. In your own practice, do you ever hear from defense lawyers that they've read your book to try to figure out how your strategy is in that particular case?*
KERR: I have heard that. They don't tell me what they glean from doing that, but several of them have said that they've read the book. A couple have said that the reason for doing so is to get inside how the plaintiff's case is put together by me.

MURPHY: *In your second novel,* Wrongful Death, *you go in a different direction by bringing the Bosnian conflict into a medical malpractice case. I know you've had some experience in Bosnia. Did you get to use that in writing the book?*
KERR: Oh, yeah. I had the wonderful experience of a sabbatical year in Europe in 1997-1998 and I spent part of that year in Bosnia and the rest of it in The Hague. I was a member of the Press Corps of the International Tribunal for the former Yugoslavia. The work in Bosnia was elections work. And that was just a hyper-stimulating experience, provocative, a really transforming experience that I knew I wanted to write about it. That was the motivator for the book. To set a book in the States - because I didn't think I could probably sell the book otherwise - that tried to convey the meaning of what I learned that year. That was the whole idea of the book.

MURPHY: *You've also written short stories, one of which was included in* Best American Short Stories. *I'm sure you encountered some different problems or issues in writing the long-form novel than with the short story. What kind of problems did you have and how did you overcome them?*
KERR: I wrote really nothing but short fiction for about twenty years or more. And I have a collection of stories that was published a long time ago by University of Missouri Press. I thought of myself as a short story writer. But my stories were always a little voluble and digressive and they were always spilling over; they were anything but the

Raymond Carver minimalist style of story. What I now see with the novel is a much more natural form for me. The stories were kind of novels that were being constrained into a short story form, although many of them really wouldn't have had the breadth of concept to sustain a novel. But that was still the impulse each time. So going on at greater length in the novel form is really a much more natural form for me, I realize now. I probably should have been focusing on it much earlier, although short stories are much easier to do when you are practicing law at the same time.

MURPHY: *Were you a writer before you became a lawyer?*
KERR: Yes, I was. I've actually been through writing programs at Stanford as an undergraduate and the University of Denver. Then I was a freelance writer, a newspaper and magazine journalist, and a magazine editor with an aspiration to be a literary fiction writer of short fiction. And that's where the short fiction came from. As anyone knows who wants to make a life of writing literary short fiction you know you can't do it and make a living. So law school was not an afterthought, but the economic need was what got me there rather than wanting to be a lawyer above all else.

MURPHY: *One final question. I did an internet search of your name and I came up with some references to Baine Kerr and President George H.W. Bush. I assume there's only one Baine Kerr in the world, unless it's your father.*
KERR: It's my father, in fact.

MURPHY: *Was he an advisor to former President Bush?*
KERR: He's a lawyer and was both his business and personal lawyer for many years and is a close confidante of his.

PHILLIP MARGOLIN

Oregon criminal defense attorney Phillip Margolin has written eight bestselling legal thrillers set in the wet streets of Portland, Oregon. His latest, *The Associate*, starts as a typical civil case but soon turns into a multiple homicide. Prominent plaintiffs attorney Aaron Flynn has sued Geller Pharmaceuticals for product liability on behalf of children born with terrible birth defects. Their mothers took the drug Insufort, known as the Son of Thalidomide.

Daniel Ames, a first-year associate at Portland's largest firm, is assigned the menial task of reviewing documents to sift out privileged communications before producing them to Flynn. Unlike his silver-spooned colleagues, Ames's path to legal success was not an easy one.

> Daniel had made it through Portland State and U. of O. law school the hard way, earning every cent of his tuition and knowing that there was no safety net to catch him if he failed. He took pride in earning a spot in Oregon's best law firm without Ivy League credentials or family connections, but he could not shake the feeling that his hold on success was tenuous.... His mother waitressed when she was sober and serviced long-haul drivers when she was too drunk to hold a job.

One privileged document seems to have slipped by Ames's scrutiny, a study by Dr. Sergey Kaidanov claiming Insufort caused birth defects in rhesus monkeys. At first Ames is skeptical, confident the study is false and his firm's client has been truthful. The plaintiffs, he believes, are overreaching. He tells a colleague, "Americans can't accept the fact that shit happens. You get cancer, so you blame overhead power lines; you run someone over, so you blame your car." But of course things are not as they seem and Ames soon finds himself immersed in a conspiracy bigger than he ever imagined. Bodies start falling and soon bullets are flying his way.

A native of New York State, Margolin graduated from The American University in Washington, D.C. and from New York University School of Law. From 1972 to 1996, he was in private practice in Portland, Oregon specializing in criminal defense at the trial and appellate levels.

His first novel, *Heartstone*, was nominated for an Edgar Award for best original paperback by the Mystery Writers of America in 1978. Among his other literary honors is a nomination for an Oregon Book Award for his seventh novel, *Wild Justice*. His short story, *The Jailhouse Lawyer*, was selected for the anthology *1999, The Best American Mystery Stories*.

WHAT IF HOLDEN CAULFIELD WENT TO LAW SCHOOL?

This interview took place in 2002.

FICTION: *Heartstone* (1978), *The Last Innocent Man* (1981), *Gone, But Not Forgotten* (1993), *After Dark* (1995), *The Burning Man* (1996), *The Undertaker's Widow* (1998), *Wild Justice* (2000), and *The Associate* (2001); *Ties That Bind* (2003); *Sleeping Beauty* (2004); *Lost Lake* (2005); *Proof Positive* (2006)

MURPHY: The Associate *seemed like a departure for you in that it focuses primarily on a civil case whereas your other books reflect more your background as a criminal lawyer.*
MARGOLIN: A little bit. I mean the civil case gets the whole thing going, but I've got plenty of murders. There's a murder charge so I don't think it's that different except for the fact that I use a civil case as a set-up.

MURPHY: *It is a springboard to the murders, of which there are plenty. Did you have to do a lot of extra research or consultations to get down the nuances of civil procedure?*
MARGOLIN: Definitely, because my practice was almost exclusively criminal. In twenty five years of practice I had three civil cases. So I talked to some friends at the big law firms in town. I actually interviewed about seven associates, one from one of the big firms and six from another one. That was really interesting. I used that as the research to set up what an associate goes through at a big firm. Some of it is embellished for dramatic purposes. Then I talked to two attorneys in town - Jonathan Hoffman and Mike Williams - who do these big cases. Mike is a plaintiff's attorney and was involved in the breast implant and Dalkon Shield cases. Jonathan Hoffman is a defense attorney who defends those types of cases. So I spent a lot of time talking to them about how you do these cases, what are the expenses involved and all the other information I needed.

MURPHY: *The one thing that jumped out at me as a plaintiff's lawyer was procedural - I don't think any non-lawyer would probably get it. That was when* The Associate, *Daniel Ames, personally delivered documents to the plaintiff's attorney's office. I thought that was a bit unusual. I've never heard of that being done.*
MARGOLIN: Ever heard of literary license?

MURPHY: *Yeah. And I can understand why you did that. But as a lawyer, certain things jump out at you that wouldn't jump out at a lay person.*
MARGOLIN: There's a difference between writing a book and actually doing cases. Most real cases are sort of dull. They may be interesting for the lawyer because of all the legal issues and procedural stuff. For a reader, it would be pretty dull. So you have to spice them up a little bit and change things to prevent the reader from falling asleep.

MURPHY: *Did you do any reading on product liability cases, specifically the drug cases, that you mention in the book?*
MARGOLIN: A couple of books on junk science. That was sort of what got me started with this in the first place. Some of these cases where people brought outrageous suits. And the two that really got me interested were the Dalkon Shield

cases, which were for real, and then this breast implant thing, where there's a serious question about whether there's any causal connection between the types of injuries that the women were suing for and the product. And what shocked me was the manufacturer was willing to make a multibillion dollar settlement, then sometime after that the first studies started coming out from the New England Journal of Medicine showing that there's no causal connection. I was just astonished that a big company could be buffaloed into making this type of a settlement offer when there's not a shred of evidence that they were liable for anything. So that got my brain going about this book. I started reading a number of books about junk science and some of the claims that have been made and have been successful when they were total hooey. So I did research that, but when I do research it's to obtain just enough information so I can write the book. I don't try to become an expert in the area like I would if I was asked to try the case.

MURPHY: *In terms of the structure of* The Associate, *you start with a prologue set in New York where an Arizona attorney sees a photograph and then has a very intense emotional reaction to it. Then that attorney doesn't appear until halfway through the rest of the book. I'm curious why you decided to structure it that way, with about half the book focused on the Insufort lawsuit and Daniel Ames, and then in the middle - all of the sudden - we go to Arizona with flashbacks of murders that happened years before.*

MARGOLIN: What I like to do in a lot of the books - because that's the type of book I like to read - is to have a number of things going on that do not appear to have anything to do with each other. Sometimes I'll have two or three different story lines that appear to be totally unconnected, and then I like to bring them together. And I think readers enjoy that. You start off reading about this guy going into an art gallery in Soho who has a very strong reaction to this photograph he sees and then sort of disappears. So you say, "What's that for? What does that have to do with anything?" And it's the type of thing that I think keeps the reader interested. You say, "It's got to have something to do with something, but what is it?" So it's a good tool to use to make the book more interesting to the reader.

MURPHY: *The scenes in Arizona seem to make a dramatic shift in the tone of the book. In some ways I liked it because you get on one level and then a different one and you get drawn into these other characters. What was it about the murders in Arizona - the rich business man and this other lawyer's wives - that drew you to that as a plot device?*

MARGOLIN: It's almost a stand-alone story. In fact in 1995 or '96, I was invited to be the main participant in Holland in a month-long celebration of thrillers and mysteries. They do this every year and they usually invite one writer from around the world to be the centerpiece for the month. Robert Ludlum did it one year and also Dick Francis and Elizabeth George. So I was absolutely thrilled that they asked me. One of the conditions is that you're supposed to write a novella. It is translated into Dutch and they give it out to anybody who buys a certain number of books, whether they are mysteries or not. You can buy dictionaries in these bookstores in Holland and you get a free copy of this novella. So the novella that I wrote is very similar to this back story and I really liked it. I just had so much fun writing it. It stood alone. And I was thinking, boy, I hate to use this on such a small audience because the story is so good. And then my wife gave me the idea for the plot device involving the photograph and I got interested in the junk science and all of the sudden a light bulb went off in my head. And I said, I could use the guts of that novella as the back story for this new book. And so that's how the Arizona stuff got into the book.

MURPHY: *What brought you to writing thriller books? Is it simply to entertain the reader? Your books do have a lot of action and your style seems to be spare with a lot of short chapters, very fast moving.*

MARGOLIN: I started writing as a hobby. Because I couldn't figure out how anyone could write a novel. But I started reading about one to three books a week when I was in elementary school. And I love reading. I mean reading for me is almost my biggest hobby. I do a lot of other stuff, but I always have a book with me. And I read everything, but I do like thrillers. The first book I published was a legal thriller - *Heartstone* - back in 1978 when I was in my early 30's. I was very comfortable writing a legal thriller because I had a full-time criminal law practice and it was something I was really familiar with. So over the years, all of my books have been legal thrillers involving criminal stuff just because I feel comfortable with it. Also I can make each book different within the confines of the genre. I've had a lot of flexibility. - *Heartstone*'s almost like a historical novel, *Gone, But Not Forgotten* and *Wild Justice* were really scary serial killer books. *After Dark* was a bizarre love story. And I've been able to play around with different themes in the context of the legal thriller.

As far as being spare, I can't stand filler. I don't like books that have forty pages of description. I appreciate them, but it's not my favorite type of thing. So I try to write the type of book that I would want to read. I like books that really move like a bandit. So I intentionally make the books move fast. I mean, if there's stuff that's interfering with the flow, I just take it out. So, my main idea when you read one of my books is that you should feel like you're on a roller coaster. On page one, the roller coaster starts going and it doesn't stop. In fact, when I wrote *The Associate*, the editor said that I should keep in my mind an image of Daniel Ames - who is the hero - running down the highway at night with headlights on him, looking over his shoulder. And that's the type of pacing that he wanted me to keep in the book. And I really tried to do that and I hope it succeeded.

MURPHY: *It seems that with a thriller the challenge is to keep the pace going, but also to make it realistic. Do you think in this book you've gone overboard in terms of putting pace before realism?*

MARGOLIN: I try to tell a good story that will keep you entertained. I think pace is more important than realism. I try to make the books as realistic as I can, but if I have to choose between keeping the story going really fast or bending the truth a little, I'll pick the latter.

I've got a sort of funny anecdote. My second book, *The Last Innocent Man*, was made into a movie and filmed in Portland. And I had a little acting part in it. I was the jury foreman in the big trial, which meant I was on the set during the trial sequences. The director also wanted me to be a technical consultant, which I told them I'd love to do to make sure that the trial scenes were realistic. The very first trial scene they filmed, Ed Harris - who was the star - is cross examining a witness in the witness box and he gets up and walks across the floor to the witness box. I immediately wrote a note because at that time it was improper in Oregon courts for lawyers to stand up and approach a witness when they were cross examining. You have to question from your seat. The only time you could actually get close to the witness was when you'd say to the judge, "Your honor, may I approach the witness?" It was usually to hand them something or for some technical reason. So I wrote a note to the director which I passed through some people saying, "This is not how we do it Oregon and Ed Harris should be sitting." The assistant director came back during a break and said that the director really appreciated my note, but they were making a movie and if everyone was sitting down, the audience would fall asleep. So that's sort of my feeling about the books. I do want to try to keep it realistic, but I don't want my readers to fall asleep.

MURPHY: *How do you plan out the characters? Do you write character studies before you write out the plot?*

MARGOLIN: No. I'm more plot driven than character driven. So what I really concentrate on are plots. And the plots for me are the most fun thing because I look at writing like problem solving. I used to be a serious chess player and I do crossword puzzles. In my law practice I looked at it as problem solving. I spend a lot of time trying to think of the idea. Sometimes it'll take me a couple of years before I'll start writing a plot for the book. And once I've got the plot pretty much in my head, I won't start writing until I know the ending. I have to know who the bad guy is and how he's going to get caught. Otherwise I won't write the book. I get upset when I read a book that's great and then the ending is really stupid. I try hard to get endings where everything is tied up. Once I've got that, then I do an outline. I call it a talking outline. I sit in front of my word processor and I write the outline as if someone said, "So, what's your next book about?" I say, "Oh, in the first chapter John and Mary meet, in chapter two this happens." It takes me about a month to three months to write the outline. The outline for *Wild Justice* was about sixty eight pages and for *The Associate* about twenty eight. The one I just finished was a twenty two page outline. So they're usually between twenty and forty pages. Then after I've got that outline, I start writing the book. That's when I start developing the characters. When I'm actually writing the book, I'll start thinking, Who's my main character? I've already got the characters worked out when I write the plot, but I sort out the details - what do they do when they're not practicing law, what do they look like - during the first draft.

MURPHY: *How important is the setting in Portland to your books?*

MARGOLIN: I always joke that the reason I use Portland as a setting is because I'm lazy. I could just look out my window. In *The Associate* there's a scene where the two main characters have a cup of coffee at Starbucks in Pioneer Square. Right now I'm looking out at Pioneer Square at a Starbucks. I also love Portland; I think Portland is the best place to live. And since I write mysteries, it's great because it rains a lot. So I get this moody black, dark rainy atmosphere all the time. I don't have to make that up. I don't have to use literary license because it's always raining. It's where I live and nobody else sets their books in Portland. I think I'm the only guy who does it consistently. We have other mystery writers in Oregon, but a lot of them set their books out on the coast or other places so Portland is sort of my bailiwick.

MURPHY: *You've definitely been identified as a Portland writer.*

WHAT IF HOLDEN CAULFIELD WENT TO LAW SCHOOL?

MARGOLIN: All of the books are set mostly in Portland. *Heartstone*, my first one, is largely based on a real case, so I call it Portsmouth. But everybody knows it's Portland. Actually, when *Heartstone* made the New York Times best seller list, the Times listed the book as set in New Hampshire. I never bothered to correct them. I thought maybe people in New Hampshire will start reading the book too.

MURPHY: *With* The Associate *did you have any particular theme or agenda in writing the book other than obviously to entertain? Because there are a lot of comments made by characters about product liability suits generally in terms of people blaming others for their problems.*
MARGOLIN: No, I didn't. And my agenda is to provide people with a book that will get them from Portland to New York on a plane without them noticing that they're up in the air. If you'll notice, I try to give both sides of the argument, the pros and cons, for plaintiffs lawyers and defense attorneys in these big cases at various stages of the book. But no, there's no agenda whatsoever. I think very small.

MURPHY: *Maybe because I'm a plaintiffs lawyer, I'm particularly sensitive about these things. Aaron Flynn seemed like the caricature of the plaintiff's personal injury lawyer. I got the sense reading the book that you consulted a lot more with defense lawyers than plaintiffs lawyers.*
MARGOLIN: No. And as I said I didn't have an agenda. What I do is I try to figure out what kind of character do I need to make this book go. For example, my big breakthrough book was *Gone, But Not Forgotten* and that had a main character as a woman even though I'm a man. And then the next book, two out of three of the main characters were women. So, I've gone to book tours and people would ask, "Are you making your main characters women because you're pandering to women audiences?" And my answer was always, "No." Because I'm trying to figure out who would be the best person, a man or a woman, to make the book go the best way. For instance, *Gone, But Not Forgotten* originally had a man attorney as a main character. Then I realized if I had a woman character the relationship to the serial killer would be much more intense. So I just made her a woman. Then in *The Burning Man* I decided I wanted to have a man main character and I had a man main character in *The Undertaker's Widow*. But then I switched back to a woman for *Wild Justice* and then my new book's got a woman. So when I pick a person out, it's just because that is the person I feel will make the book go and that's the personality that I feel will make the book go. But I'm not real deep, if you're looking for symbolism or anything like that. I just like to write a fun, exciting, interesting book.

MURPHY: *I read* Gone, But Not Forgotten *when it came out. It was a little different from* The Associate *in the sense that I found it very gruesome. The murders just seemed very gruesome to me.*
MARGOLIN: Yeah. *Wild Justice* is really the same way. I wanted to write a serial killer book. And when you're writing serial killer books you're going to get more gore. In *Wild Justice*, I think I had twenty one murders. I did a body count. I thought this is the all-time record for dead bodies. In *The Associate* there aren't as many murders because it's not necessary to the plot. But it's less gory because I'm not getting into that genre. So I like to use the legal thriller genre but I like to write different types of books. *The Associate* is just a really different kind of book from *Gone, But Not Forgotten* and *Wild Justice*. And that's intentional.

MURPHY: *The trial scenes in* The Associate *are limited too. You have a bail hearing and the cross examination of the prosecution witness, Dr. April Fairweather. It seemed to me that if you wanted to sit down and write your dream cross examination, that would be it. Is that how that came about?*

MARGOLIN: No. It's actually based loosely on a real transcript from a real case which I learned about. I said, "This is so fantastic." And actually the cross went a lot like it did in the book. But with thirty homicide cases and I don't know how many trials, I have a lot of experience in setting up crosses. So anything that's in my books I've actually done in real life. I argued before the US Supreme Court and I did twelve death penalty cases and big drug conspiracy cases in Federal Court. So if it's in the book, I've done it. But it would be a dream cross. When I was writing this cross, obviously I tried to set it up the way I wanted it to come out.

MURPHY: *Some lawyer authors tell me that they don't write courtroom scenes because it's all been done and it's impossible to make it fresh. Have you found that to be a problem?*

MARGOLIN: I think courtroom scenes are fabulous. And every one's different because each case is different. When I was starting out, I used to do lots of drunk driving cases, which were pretty similar. But every single time you do a case there are different human beings involved. I always give the example of tough-guy detective novels like Mike Hammer or Sam Spade. Every single one of those is identical if you just said, "What it's about?" Tough-guy detective who drinks hard, down on his luck, he's sitting in his little office when a busty blonde comes in and wants him to find her sister. So if you look at them they're all the same, so why bother writing another tough-guy detective? But every author who writes one of those is writing from their own perspective with their own background and their own unique ideas. And so there are similarities with every courtroom scene but the facts - the plot of your novel - are going to make them different. And I like to have courtroom scenes if they work. I don't like to stuff them in there just to have a courtroom scene. But if they work, I think they're really dramatic.

MURPHY: *What's your next book about?*

MARGOLIN: It's different too. It's about a conspiracy that started back in the '70s and continues through the present day. And it's lots of fun. Lots of murders.

MURPHY: *Have you got a working title?*

MARGOLIN: Oh yeah. The working title is *The Courthouse Athletic Club*. And it's the nickname that the members of the conspiracy pick for themselves because they are lawyers and policemen and judges. Again it's the first time I've ever had a conspiracy in a novel - a big conspiracy - so I thought that would be something fun to do.

MURPHY: *Earlier you mentioned you do a lot of reading. Do you read legal fiction?*

MARGOLIN: Some. I just finished a biography of Marcel Proust and now I'm reading Carl Hiaasen, so anything I can get my hands on. I just love reading. And I do read Steve Martini, Bill Bernhardt. I really liked Scott Turow's last one - *Personal Injuries*; I thought that was brilliant. So I do read some of the competition. I'm friendly with some of the competition too - Lisa Scottoline. Bill Bernhardt is a really nice guy. I had a couple of short stories in anthologies that he's done. In fact, *Natural Suspect* is out right now. It's a collaborative novel. Michael Palmer's in there; he writes medical thrillers.

But most of the writers are legal thriller writers. We each got a chapter. It was fun. You get sent the chapters that everyone's written before and you can't collaborate and ask how do you want the plot to go. You just do whatever you want to do. It came out really well.

MURPHY: *Do you identify who wrote which chapter?*
MARGOLIN: No. They have a contest. You know Bill Bernhardt wrote the first chapter, but you have to guess who wrote the rest. If you get them all right, you get a poster with everybody's signature on it or something. It was fun. So I had a good time with that. But I do read other legal thriller writers, but not exclusively.

MURPHY: *You started writing, I think you said, in 1978?*
MARGOLIN: Yeah. I started writing in law school. I worked my way through NYU law school at night my last two years. I went through it three years like everybody else by taking summer courses and a heavy load at night. My last semester I had just a couple of classes, and since I had a job already I only had to get Ds. So I had this free summer. I didn't have to work because my wife was working. I decided to spend the time writing a novel because I couldn't figure out how you did it. I would read these books and say, "How do you write 400 pages?" So that's why I really started - in my mid-twenties. I wrote two really bad novels. Were never published - never will be. And then I sold this short story in 1974/75 and that's what gave me self confidence to write a book that would be a little more serious. I got a lucky break and *Heartstone* was published in '78. And then I published another book in '81 - *The Last Innocent Man*. Then I had a twelve-year gap.

My law practice got really exciting. I always wanted to be a lawyer; I didn't want to be a writer. The writing thing is a hobby that ate my practice. I wanted to be a criminal defense lawyer from the time I was in seventh grade. And that's the only thing I was ever interested in. The same year I had my first book published, I argued before the US Supreme Court and I started doing heavy duty murder cases. That was much more interesting to me than writing books. So I stopped for a long time then I got this idea at a dinner party for *Gone, But Not Forgotten* in '91 or '92. That became - again much to my shock and my surprise - a huge international best seller. It was on the New York Times list for nine or ten weeks and then all the other books were on the Times list after that.

MURPHY: *Why do you think that one hit it big whereas the others didn't before that?*
MARGOLIN: One of the big reasons is being at the right place at the right time. When I wrote *Heartstone* and *The Last Innocent Man*, there was no legal thriller genre. There were murder mysteries and no murder mystery writers made the NY Times list at that time.

MURPHY: *That was before* Presumed Innocent.
MARGOLIN: Right. And *Presumed Innocent* came out and then Grisham wrote *The Firm* and all of the sudden everybody and his brother wanted to read legal thrillers and all of the publishers were dying to get them. I was one of those guys. When the genre hit I had this book ready and I wasn't thinking about breaking into the genre. I just got a good idea for my book and sent it in. My agent shocked the hell out of me by auctioning it. It's a really good book, but if medical thrillers were in at that time, it

probably would have sold, but I don't know whether it would've become such a huge best seller. There was a huge appetite on the part of the public in the early '90s and the late '80s for legal thrillers. So that's why I think it broke out. My first two books were re-issued after *Gone* became such a big hit and they were both on the Times list for over a month. And *Heartstone* was nominated for an Edgar back in 1978 but it didn't sell anywhere near bestseller numbers and neither did *The Last Innocent Man*. So I think it was just being at the right place at the right time.

MURPHY: *So now you're writing full time?*
MARGOLIN: Yeah. I always say this because people lawyer-bash and I hate lawyer bashing because I think it's a really great profession. I love it. And what happened, though, was when *Gone, But Not Forgotten* became such a big hit, I was doing mostly death penalty murder cases and federal drug conspiracy stuff where you were in court a couple of weeks to a couple of months and your prep time is pretty similar and you gotta be around. You can't be running around on book tours. I didn't know what a book tour was cause I hadn't done one for the first books because they weren't big enough. So it started to slowly dawn on me that I was going to be out of town for like a month to month and a half at a time. The first time I did a book tour, the judges and the DAs were really supportive. They let me set over stuff. The tour wasn't a solid month and a half like I do now, but I realized that you can do that one time, ask the DAs to be nice. But I couldn't keep on saying, "I know there's this big murder case we have to try, but I want to go sell some books." I had been a lawyer for twenty five years and I never had a chance to write full time. My first five novels I wrote with a full-time practice, raising two kids so I thought, Well, let's see what it's like to be a full time writer. So I kept all my cases but I didn't take new ones. It took me a couple of years to wind down and by '96 I didn't have any more clients and I just started to write full time. I'm really enjoying that as much as I did my law practice.

MURPHY: *So you still go to an office every day to write?*
MARGOLIN: Yeah, I'm sitting in my law office right now; I just don't have any cases. Nobody likes me.

BRAD MELTZER

Many lawyer authors manage to write novels while maintaining their law practice. Few, though, manage to write a novel during law school, and even fewer to sell it to a publisher. Brad Meltzer is one of those few.

While studying at Columbia Law School, Meltzer got the urge to write a novel about the Supreme Court. He convinced one of his professors to give him credit for writing the novel. When it turned out to be a national bestseller, Meltzer never looked back to the practice of law and has been writing full-time ever since.

His latest novel, *The Millionaires*, features two protagonists who are not lawyers. Brothers Oliver and Charlie Caruso work at an exclusive private bank where they discover a fool-proof way to steal $3 million. After Oliver enlists an unwitting assistant to help steal the money, he stands by impatiently watching the computer screen.

> It takes Mary a total of ten seconds to type in the account number and hit *Send*. Ten seconds. Ten seconds to change my life. It's what my dad was always chasing, but never found. Finally ... a way out.... The cursor glides to the *Send* button and I start saying my goodbyes. I could still stop it, but ..

The book shows what happens when the theft does not prove to be as easy as they thought. The brothers are forced to run from the Secret Service and others interested in recovering the money, perhaps for their own uses.

After growing up in New York, Brad Meltzer moved with his family to Miami. A graduate of the University of Michigan and Columbia Law School, he lives in Washington, D.C. with his wife, who is also a lawyer.

This interview took place in 2001.

FICTION: *The Tenth Justice* (1997); *Dead Even* (1998); *The First Counsel* (2001); *The Millionaires* (2002); *The Zero Game (2004)*; *The Book of Fate* (2006)

MURPHY: *It seems to me* The Millionaires *is somewhat of a departure from your other books. Even though there is a lawyer in* The Millionaires*, the lawyer is not the protagonist and really not the central character. Were you trying to get away from lawyers in this book?*
MELTZER: I've never wanted to get away from lawyers. I'm proud to say I write legal thrillers, but I think I'm one of the few legal thriller writers who's never written a courtroom scene. And it's simply because it doesn't interest me whatsoever. We've seen it ten thousand times. It goes something like this: *Your honor, I object ... Ladies and*

gentlemen of the jury ... Where were you on the night of February 18th? Those things have been done ad nauseam. Unless you can add something new, which some can, I tend to go to places where lawyers have never been.

With *The Millionaires* I found that one of the recent trends in the law was private investigators who are also attorneys. I definitely was excited to pursue that. They know the law, so they know how to stretch the law. I think the Joey character in the book is one of my favorite characters I've ever written. She's one of the few characters I think about as a serious character. But she is definitely not the center of the book. I thought she was going to be the star and then I just realized that she wasn't. It was better for her not to be the center of the book, which is why the anti - protagonist became the protagonist.

MURPHY: *Your protagonists are brothers Oliver and Charlie Caruso, both likeable characters. I wondered if you chose to focus the book on two brothers who really complement each other in that one is an artist type, the other is a numbers/business type. Was that contrast what made you decide to focus on them?*

MELTZER: The contrast for me was trying to pick heroes who don't necessarily always do the right thing. I've tried in every single book to make it different for the reader. The worst thing I can be as a writer is the kind of writer who every year pumps out the same book with the same plot with the same paint-by-numbers characters who have the same lantern jaw, and take down the FBI and the CIA and the President of the United States all in a day's work and then go and get the girl. People know when authors get into that and readers are very smart. Readers are smarter than the authors they read. And they know when the author is kind of churning out the same book all the time. So I always try to do something different. For *First Counsel*, I tried writing in a different point of view, doing first person for the first time. In this one, I tried the multi-point of view and I also tried to take heroes who, as I said, were not necessarily always doing the right thing. And that was a very conscious choice.

To get back to the question, there is no question Oliver and Charlie started first as characters before they started as plot devices. And I spend months, literally, writing their lifestyles. I love the idea Oliver was going to be this kind of hard-numbers-thinking kind of person and Charlie was going to be the id to his super-ego. But obviously every novel is about a journey. If the characters don't become different people by the end, then I always feel, what's the point of the book? If you don't learn something, if you don't become something, either bigger, better or lesser, what's the point? As you read the book, Charlie and Oliver almost become each other. And it's a very conscious choice on my part. In fact, I can narrow it right to a certain scene where you actually see them switch places. But I think that that contrast is what makes readers care about characters. The characters butt heads because of who they are, not because of the situation they're in.

MURPHY: *Do you think you run a risk of the reader losing interest or losing empathy with the character if you have a character who really does some bad things? I notice you made it a point to give some strong motivation for both Oliver and Charlie to take the money in that their mother had a lot of medical expenses that needed to be paid off and you find out later that Charlie has a serious health* *condition himself. Were you conscious of the need to balance their motives in terms of doing what is really a pretty serious crime?*

MELTZER: Yes. There's no question the hard part of writing Charlie and Oliver was figuring out how to make the reader really root for them. And I was very conscious about trying to make them likable. I wanted to like them. I like Charlie and Oliver as people. I like what they stand for. I think they are very honest, even though in the beginning they start out as thieves. And do they do the right thing in the book? Sometimes yes, sometimes no. But I think that's the fun of it. And I think everyone at one point in time has hit that moment where they say, "You know, I can get away with this, but should I do it?" Sometimes you choose right and sometimes you choose wrong. And to me that's also what *The Millionaires* is about: that choice. Sometimes making the wrong choice in a single moment of anger -- which is really where it comes from for Oliver -- that you wish you could take back. For most of us, we do that. The consequences may be important, they may not be important. But in this case, clearly, they have devastating effects for the characters.

MURPHY: *You mentioned you consciously are not writing trial scenes because a lot of lawyers are doing that and it gets pretty stale. You did have in this book the Secret Service as being real bad guys. And that has been done, of course, in David Baldacci's* Absolute Power. *And there've been a number of others. Did you have any concern that that plot device would also seem stale?*

MELTZER: The funny thing is I don't read anyone else's books. I don't. The truth is I stay away from the genre completely. I know what's out there. Of course I know that *Absolute Power* had Secret Service Agents in it. It's a choice; on some level you need the bad guy. Now you have a choice of bad guys: You have the FBI, and you have the Secret Service, the more interesting bad guys. There's not a question in my mind. If I said line up all your bad guys who are FBI agents, line up all your bad guys that are Secret Service agents, there's going to be some overlap. That's like saying no one can write about the Supreme Court after *The Tenth Justice*. But obviously we're going to all approach it a different way. To be fair, every writer is totally different, and will have a different take on it. I think the hard part of writing a courtroom scene is that it's hard to be different because there are things that are always true. And my Secret Service agents may be different than another person's Secret Service agents. But the form of closing arguments, even though they can be written with flair and can be done differently, is always the same. And the objections are always the same, even if they are for different reasons. So I'm trying to break out of a little bit of that mold.

MURPHY: *Let me digress a little bit and ask you about your legal background. Have you ever actually practiced law after law school?*

MELTZER: Define practice. I was lucky in the sense that *The Tenth Justice* sold while I was a second year law student. I will be the first to say I got lucky. The first book I ever wrote got twenty-four rejection letters and it's still sitting on my shelf published by Kinko's. It's called *Fraternity*. Then I wrote *The Tenth Justice* when I was still in law school. It sold while I was a second year law student with 30K worth of loans plus undergrad loans. I would have had upwards of 60 to100K when I graduated. I got lucky. They called me up one day and said, "Hey, I want to buy your book. " And there are better writers than me who never get a shot. As my agent once said to me, it takes one person to say yes. And luckily we found that person. So, there's no question when it came to the choice of practicing law versus writing, I chose writing. But I am not a self-hating lawyer. I like the law. Intellectually, I find it stimulating. I still wind up devouring any kind of case I can get my eyes on. But the bottom line is, I'm passionate about writing and I think you should always follow your passion. So that's always where I go on that and that's the only reason why I've avoided practice. And God bless the people who can practice and write at the same time. I just couldn't do it and get a book out. It would just take me forever.

MURPHY: *So you finished law school and have been writing ever since?*
MELTZER: Yes. Finished law school, took the bar. I'm a realist. I realized that you're as good as your last book. You always want to put your best work out there so I took that Bar exam. I studied hard; I always realized at any point I may be back to practicing.

MURPHY: *It sounds like you've had a long ambition to be a writer.*
MELTZER: It sounds like it, but in reality, I never thought I would be a writer. I grew up in a very normal middle class family. I used to think that when you graduated high school you went to work. I didn't think you went to college. That wasn't my background. When my Dad was forty years old, he lost his job and decided he was going to start over from scratch. He was going to have the great do-over of life. And he picked up my family and my mother and my sister and myself, and moved to Florida. He had no job, no place to live. We lived with my grandmother. He had no idea what he was going to do. He was going to start over from scratch. He had twelve hundred dollars to his name. He put us in the car and off we went to Florida.

When we got there, I had no idea what was going on. I was in the middle of starting high school. And my parents did an amazing thing. My parents lied about my address so that I could go to the wealthiest nearby public school. And so for four years, I gave a fake address. I wasn't zoned for that school. But because of that lie, I got to go to the wealthy school. And at this wealthy public high school, every one there talked about this thing called *college* and this thing called the *SATs*. I had no idea what the SATs were, but because I was going to this school, you follow what everyone else is doing. It's kind of like wearing Britney Spears outfits. I mean, you do it because other people are doing it. People seemed like they were studying for college, so I was going to study and try and go to college. And I just literally stumbled into that.

So I always say if we didn't move to Florida, I don't know what I'd be doing today. I certainly don't think I'd be writing. When I was in high school, my ninth grade English teacher said, "You should do this writing thing, you're pretty good at it." I still never thought it was a real job because that wasn't my background. Real jobs get dirt under your fingernails, they put calluses on your hands. They don't come from talking to your imaginary friends while you're at a computer.

I went to Boston after college. I had a job offer to work at a magazine, doing marketing of all things. They said, "If you love it, you stay. If you hate it, you leave and go to law school with some money in your pocket." I thought that was a good deal. I had some loans to pay off, so I went to Boston, where I knew almost nobody. And the week I got there, my boss left the job. The whole reason I went to Boston was to work with him. I had no idea what I was going to do. I thought I wrecked my life. And I did what all of us would do in a situation where you think you wrecked your life. I said *I'm going to write a novel*. I said *I have one year of my life before I go to law school* -- everyone must have one novel in them. So I'm going to take my shot. And I literally started writing. I never thought about it before. I didn't think about it when I graduated. And I borrowed a computer and I just started clicking away. That's how I started writing.

MURPHY: *And that was* Fraternity.
MELTZER: That was *Fraternity*. That was my first book, and I found an agent with that, and fell in love with the process. And every day, I realized I cared more about the book than I did about the job. And at that point, I started law school. They were sending out the manuscript at that point. It took me a year to write it. And by the summer of my first year we had twenty four rejections. Now when you get twenty four rejection letters, the copy shop doesn't want to photocopy your manuscript anymore. It just gets ugly. But I said, if they don't like that book, I'll write another; if they don't like that book, I'll write another. Because the truth was, I just loved to write. And that was when writing became something that I really wanted to do.

MURPHY: *Did you get any positive comments in the rejection letters?*
MELTZER: You get the complete mix. You get, "Meltzer is great at this and bad at this," and you get "Meltzer is bad at this and great at this." And now, of course, it means, you're either bad at two things or you're good at two things. But on some level you hope for the best. You believe in your heart that what you wrote is good and you move on to your next thing. And my first novel was not a thriller. It wasn't about lawyers because I didn't know anything about lawyers at the time. I was a fresh-out-of-college kid. So it wasn't until I got to law school that I felt, "Now I have something to write about." I didn't go to law school for plot ideas, it just happened along the way.

MURPHY: *It's amazing that most people have a hard enough time just getting their studies done in law school, and yet you managed to get your studies done and write a whole novel.*
MELTZER: I've been lucky. If you want to study Spanish to be an international lawyer, they'll give you credit for it at Columbia Law School. If you want to become an entertainment lawyer, they'll give you credit to watch Woody Allen movies all day. But if you want to write legal thrillers, they'll give you nothing. They told me that I had to find a professor to give me independent study credit if I wanted to do such a thing. And I looked around and found a man named Professor Kellis Parker. And Kellis Parker taught a class called "Jazz and the Law." Right there, I knew, "This was my guy." And Kellis Parker, who sadly passed away last year, gave me sometimes two, at the most three, credits a semester to write my novel. And what happened was, it was enough that I could take one less class each semester. And the truth was, I did more work for those three credits than I did for any other class because I was spending all my time on writing a hundred pages a semester.

MURPHY: *You had more fun at it, I bet.*
MELTZER: I had much more fun at it. And I was the guy in the back of the class who would wave his hand and say to the professor, "Hypothetically, you have a guy who goes to law school and when he's there he suddenly wants to write a book. And he

wants to know *"Can he deduct his law school tuition for research?"* And a couple of my friends in that course are laughing. I'm sitting there saying, "Listen, I got free legal advice." These professors are standing in front of me, I might as well take the free legal advice.

MURPHY: *Let me get back to* The Millionaires. *Your comment about taxes is sort of a good one because this book does cover a lot of high tech financial transactions. What kind of research did you do to be so detailed and precise in your descriptions of these transactions?*

MELTZER: Any subject, I tackle very seriously. I want to take readers into a world they've never been before. In *The Millionaires* I wanted to show: *If you really want to steal money, if you really want to hide money, how do you do it?* And it's one of those things we've seen for years in movies: *Oh, I'm going to launder the money.* But it's something no one understands. They just put it in there because the script calls for it. And I wanted to teach people how you really hide money. And so I spoke to private investigators, to the top government financial investigators at FinCEN, at the Secret Service, at the Federal Reserve, at all the top financial places. The amazing thing is - with all this Bin Laden stuff, and all the assets we're chasing if you take care of Bin Laden -- does that really end it all? Because if his money is still available and if he can still hide it, doesn't it mean that this thing keeps growing? And the truth is, of course it does. And it's so easy to hide today.

Now, these top financial people can't talk to anyone. But back then [while researching *The Millionaires*], I spent two years researching with these people who were explaining to me how you hide money, teaching me you've got to find the stutterers. And the stutterers are the guys who are the first listings in the phone book (like AAAAA Attorneys). It's an amazing thing. You never think about it. These people are right in front of your face. Open up a phone book. You'll see them there. Most are ambulance chasers -- some of them, I should say, don't subscribe to the same ethical standards I think the rest of the Bar should. And I remember calling one up -- it was AAAA-whatever attorneys -- and I said, "Hi, I'm looking for a lawyer." He said, "You got one." And I said, "Okay, what's your name?" And he says, "I said...you got one." I said, "Well, I want to know your name." He says, "Tell me what you need." And it was very clear that this guy was exactly the kind of guy that Tony Soprano hires. And he's hiding right in plain sight in your phone book. You want to know where terrorists hide their money? Check your phone book.

The investigators also taught me that you should check your in-flight magazine next time you're on the airplane. In the back of those magazines, you'll always see classified ads for off-shore money: *Put your money off-shore. Stick it to the IRS. Call us here at this 800 number.* Where are they hiding? In plain sight. And no one realizes they're there. And I just think that in today's age, when money has become ones and zeros on a computer screen, I felt like there was a lot of fun to be had there -- a lot of legal and illegal fun. I wanted to tear apart that world and show people what it's like, how people really move money in this day and age.

MURPHY: *As the book goes on and the brothers discover where the money went and how it multiplied, they spend a lot of time looking at computer screens. It would seem difficult to make that* *interesting to the reader and yet I think you did make it interesting in a number of different ways. Were you conscious of the problem of trying to make high tech crime interesting?*

MELTZER: Absolutely. I was terrified of it. The last thing I ever want to do, and every good and bad movie has it, is where the character is sitting in front of this computer screen going, "I'm almost in, I'm almost in..." and they're clicking the computer furiously. There is nothing more boring to anyone than watching that. It is as fake and boring as can be. So I did it in the only way I know how, which is to do it realistically. I found playing around with wealth on these web sites was a fun way to do it. I like the idea that where the money is hidden in the book, is a place that we all know and have the potential to see. It's on one of the most popular websites in the world -- and it's right in front of your face. So it all rides on: do you have a good idea at the end of the day? Is there something visually you can see on that computer screen? The brothers see actual people's faces on the screen, something visual. It's not ones and zeros, it's not just code, it's not some silly computer program. I hope that helps the reader walk through it.

MURPHY: *At the end you have Disney as the focus. From reading the scenes of chases through Disney World, where the brothers see Pluto, Donald Duck, and Mickey, it seemed to me you had a lot of fun writing that.*

MELTZER: I loved writing about that. I wrote about the Supreme Court and then I wrote about the White House. And I said, "How do you top that?" You top it in the only place that's bigger, which is Disney World. And I will tell you that after researching the White House and the Supreme Court, the only place that has better security is Disney World. They're better at keeping their secrets than the White House and the Supreme Court combined. I grew up in Florida and I love Disney World and I just thought, *there's a lot of fun to be had playing around with Donald Duck and the locale.* And when I found out that there are secret tunnels that run below Disney World, I said to myself, "That's the place I want to go. I want to go into the secret tunnels under Disney World and take my readers there." What you see in those tunnels -- the layout, where the door is, the locale -- that's real.

MURPHY: *They let you go there?*

MELTZER: They did. It was very hard actually to get through. It was harder to get into Disney World than it was for the White House. And they eventually were very helpful; but, rightfully so, they're nervous. They have a business to worry about. People in the White House leave after four to eight years, maximum. So the White House will let you in because they're not going to be there very long. In Disney World, people are there for life. They're true believers. They take that stuff very seriously. It's their business; it's their livelihood. It took a lot of finagling and begging and pleading to get in there. Eventually they said yes, but it took some time.

MURPHY: *The plot goes from New York to Florida - like your family - and there's a constant chase going on. I found it interesting the way you parallel the chase of the Caruso brothers running away from the secret service with the secret service just watching their mother and seeing what she does. When you first envisioned the book, did you consider it to be a chase type book?*

MELTZER: I wanted the book to start with a chase. I'd never written a chase book before. I thought, *let's see if you can keep this sucker running the entire time.* Usually my books are paced over a couple of weeks, a couple of months. *Tenth Justice*, I think, takes something like six months. This whole book starts and finishes in thirteen or fourteen days. I've never tried to do it that quickly before. *Boom boom boom, let's go, let's move, let's see it all.* I was very conscious of that. But I try not to think callously about *How can I mesmerize the reader?* as much as I try to think of *What's realistic?* What's realistic? What would actually happen next? Fiction is always best when it has one foot in reality. And I can make up the craziest plots I want. I can put knives in the back of everyone's heads; I can have blood shooting everywhere. But that's not scary. The action is not scary. What's scary is what can really happen.

When I spoke to the Secret Service, they said, "This is what we do. This is exactly how we do it. These are the toys we use to do it." And that's what happens in the book. And that's why in *The Millionaires,* the Secret Service do what they do. It's not for any other reason than that's exactly how the investigation would normally take place. I'm much more conscious of that than trying to figure out what's the most manipulative thing I can do right now to my readers. Readers know when they are being manipulated. Readers are smart. Today, we have access to so much information. We have the internet, and magazines, and newspapers, and televisions, and movies. We have the best BS meters than any generation in the whole existence of time. And when you have a good BS meter, it's much harder to fool a reader. So I don't try to fool them. I try to show them, *Here's what really happens. Here's real life.* You want to see the underground tunnels of Disney World? Here's what it's like. You want to see how the Secret Service actually does their investigations? Here's what it's like. You want to see how to really hide money -- more money than you've ever had in your life -- and how simple it is, and how you can do it from your house? Here's how you would do it. And that makes it be far more scary than any other crazy plot you can come up with.

MURPHY: *At some point in a thriller or chase book you need to develop suspense. There must be certain times where you wonder: Am I really suspending belief here? Is the reader really going to buy this? Do you think in this book there are any plot devices that you skirted the edge there?*
MELTZER: I'll be very honest. I was very nervous about the big secret at the end of the book. Any time a book hinges on *what's the big secret that we're waiting to discover,* if the big pay-off is no good, the book falls apart. If the pay-off is good, then it stays together. So I came up with the big secret and went to the head of FinCEN, which is the government's financial crime enforcement network, and which basically does all of the government's financial investigations. And I went to the head and said, "Here's what I've come up with. Here's the idea I have. Here's how it'll be done and here's how they would do it." And he looked me straight in the eye and said, "That's the next level of financial crime. That's it. That's the next crime. That's the next big thing. No one knows how to do it yet, but that's what's coming next." And it was one of those moments where the hair on your arms stands up, because you think, *oh my gosh, I'm onto something.* And that's when I said, "Okay, now we've got something." So I literally took the idea, went to a computer specialist, and said, "Design how it would work." I went to bank security people and I said, "How would you do this in your system?" I went to the head of security at a big bank here in DC and I said, "What's the best way to steal money?" That was how I got all those answers. It wasn't me sitting around in a room

just trying to think of the craziest thing. It was me trying to give it a little breath of reality.

MURPHY: *There was one item in the plot that I had a hard time buying, frankly. To avoid ruining the plot, I won't mention it specifically. But it involves the brothers essentially being duped. Did you worry whether it was realistic for these really two bright guys to seem so gullible?*
MELTZER: It's a very fair question. I think the only reason it works in the book - I hope - is because Charlie knows the truth. The reader at that moment is Charlie. And the point of view for the reader is Charlie's point of view. And I think you can only do something like that - let your character be dumb for a moment - if someone else is going to call him on it. Because if Oliver is just going to be dumb and no one's going to say a word, then the reader's going to say, *doesn't the author know?* But if you can have another character say exactly what the reader is thinking, then the reader knows you're in on the joke. That's what it came down to. I put the clues right out there. They're there for you to see. It's just a function of, *is the surprise going to be the surprise I think it is?* And I personally think that's the only way, the only fair way, to play the game. I think that every novel is a game between the reader and the writer. Can I fool you long enough or surprise you, or are you going to guess it before I do? When I read a book, or I see a film, or I see something that has kind of a mystery ending, I see it as a game between me and the author, and I'm going to try and solve it before they give me the answer. And I will. There's nothing worse than when you get to the end of that mystery, and they say, it was the butler who did it, and you never even met the butler before, and you feel like you couldn't guess *that*. But that's not even a fair game. The writer's not playing fair. He didn't give me the clues, he didn't put them out there. If I read the book again I still wouldn't get any closer to solving it.

In all of the books from *The Tenth Justice* to *The Millionaires*, the clues are there. And one thing I'm proud to say is that I've never tried to pull it out of nowhere. Even the big surprise at the end of this one is there if you want to see it. It was always meant to be there. It's obviously meant to be a shock; on some level you'd really have to be thinking to guess it. And I have one friend who said he guessed it. And that means that I'm playing fair.

MURPHY: *Let me get back to the lawyer/investigator Joey Ann Lamont. You have her doing things like trash diving, planting bugs in the mother's house, following the Secret Service. She even breaks into the Secret Service agent's car to plant a bug. What was it about her legal background that you think gave her some credibility in doing these things?*
MELTZER: Let me break it down one by one. In terms of breaking into the Secret Service's car, that has nothing to do with her legal side of things. Because it's illegal and she knows it, yet she still does it. That's part of her character. Dumpster diving, however, is part of her legal side. She knows that in the State of New York - - it may not be true in California - - when you put your trash outside, it's no longer your own. Every investigator told me that's the first place they'd go. They go right for your trash. It's the easiest piece of information you put out there about yourself. Do you have to be a lawyer to know that? Of course not. But I like the fact that she does. I like the fact that she knows exactly how far she can go. When she gets on the phone with someone, and has to BS a little bit, I like the fact that she knows what cut-outs are. And cut-outs

are real. And it's really used by the investigative industry. If I go to ATT and I illegally get information, I can't use that information. But if someone else gets information illegally and I don't know how they got it, but they suddenly give it to me, it becomes a little cleaner. The CIA has used this for years. There have been stories about how they use it with "black" agents and "white" agents. The black agents get the dirty stuff, and then the white agents are the lawyers who suddenly say, "Oh my gosh, where did this come from? It's all clean."

MURPHY: *What happened to the fruit of the poisonous tree?*
MELTZER: Yeah. The fruit of the poisonous tree, sadly, is becoming a dead tree. And it's still obviously legalese. It's absolute legal fiction -- that's what the characters are doing and what these people are doing. But I did like the fact that Joey's conscious of it. I like the fact that she knows. You know, on some level, does she know it's illegal? Of course. So is it the fruit of the poisonous tree? Absolutely. But she's smart enough to push the law just enough to skirt it. Even if she's doing it illegally, I like the idea that there's someone who's conscious of it. Most characters do what they want to do -- which is what Joey does -- but Joey knows what she's doing. She's very self aware of which law she's breaking. And her assistant Noreen as well. She's also out of law school and knows when Joey's breaking into that door. She says, "You can't go in there. Don't do that. You don't have authority to go that far." And that's always the fun of the character.

MURPHY: *You mentioned Joey's assistant Noreen. You use an interesting device with her. Most mystery or PI stories have the investigator doing searches using an internal monologue about what they see and what they find. But you use the device of having Joey talk on a headphone with Noreen so that you get actual dialogue instead of interior dialogue. Why did you chose this device over the traditional one?*
MELTZER: I hadn't seen it before, so I really liked it. I thought, *what's the fastest way to move information?* You don't want to have to find something, take it back to a lab, then look it up on your computer, then bring it back, and start over again. You want to move faster. So I thought, *what's the fastest way to move* It's like having someone at home in the Batcave running numbers, and you're free running around as the information keeps coming back. What I didn't realize consciously until I started doing it, is that it also allows me to write a lot of dialogue. I will always use dialogue rather than a passive description of something. Even if it's internal dialogue. I love writing dialogue. I love hearing people speak. I love getting the voice just right. And you hear it resonate in your head. And that was something that I didn't plan on consciously; but obviously, that was good for me as a writer because it helps me get the story across in a much easier way.

MURPHY: *I thought that worked really well.*
MELTZER: Well, thank you. I wish I was shrewd enough to think consciously about that one. I was actually thinking of how to move it fast, and lucked in to that. I really thought it worked once I started it, but I had no plan of it working until I started it.

WHAT IF HOLDEN CAULFIELD WENT TO LAW SCHOOL?

MURPHY: *You use two different points of view in this book. You tell the story from the first person point of view of Oliver and the third person point of view of various other characters. I don't think I've seen that done quite as much as you did it and I'm wondering why you chose that technique.*

MELTZER: I chose it simply because I've never seen it before. I didn't know of anyone who ever did this. I thought I was breaking ground that no one had ever broken. The first editor I ever had once told me you can't mix points of view. It was the unwritten rule: *do not mix points of view.* And I thought, "Who makes these rules? Who are these people who say I can't do that?" I said, *No one's ever done this so I'm going to try it. Let's see what happens. Let's see how it works.*

I will say that this book was originally written with *three* points of view. All the chapters were alternating between Charlie and Oliver in first person, and the third person ones happened in third person. The problem was, as I was getting through the book, I found it very hard to switch perspective when the two people were standing right next to each other. If Charlie's on the right and Oliver's on the left, and I suddenly jump from left to right, and then a chapter later, I'm right to left, it's too confusing. You're still in the same room and you just feel like you have changed who "I" is. And it wasn't working. So I said *forget it, it's all Oliver in first person. Let's make it easier for the reader.* I had to rewrite those alternate chapters to make sure Charlie's point of view still stayed, but in a very different way. It was the hardest thing I had to do creatively. It was the only time I've ever leapt out on a branch and then run back because it wasn't working. It was one of the few times I said *that doesn't work.* But I still liked this first person/third person thing. And I thought: no one had ever done it in the history of the world. Then someone said to me, "James Patterson does that once in a while." And I thought, *Are you kidding me? I've never read a Patterson book; no one ever told me that.* [laughter]

MURPHY: *If you just stayed in first person, there would be no way to portray the surveillance of the mother and Joey's actions.*

MELTZER: *First Counsel* was written all in first person. And I learned a very important lesson about point of view in that book, which is: the only way to scare a reader with a first person book is through paranoia or direct threat right in the room. But you don't want to bring the villain in every chapter because eventually, it's not scary anymore. So from purely a professional point of view, in terms of callously looking and saying, *How does this plot work?* - you'd have to work a lot on paranoia. Most thrillers have a moment with the villain standing over the shoulder of the hero and the hero doesn't know that the villain is behind him. That's a very scary moment because the reader knows something the character doesn't. The problem with first person is it's very hard to do that because everything is seen through the first person's eyes.

My agent once warned me that the only writer who can pull a good first person book off is one who realizes there is a way to make the reader see something that the first person character does not. And it was the best piece of advice anyone ever gave me. If you look back to a book like *To Kill A Mockingbird* -- that eight year old little girl sees things that *we* know, and we know that *she* doesn't know. And that's why Harper Lee is a genius. It's an amazing thing to do. So it took me a very long time to figure out *how do you do that? How do you make sure that there is something that the first person character just saw but almost doesn't realize he just saw?* It took a while. After *First Counsel*, I said, "Now I can do it both ways." I don't think I could have written *The Millionaires* until I wrote *First Counsel*.

MURPHY: *Do you think the quality of your writing has improved with each book?*
MELTZER: I hope so. If not, I'm not doing my job. I actually see, very much, the trap of wanting to write a book a year. And I could write a book a year. I could write a book every year and put out a new thriller every January. But if I did, it would be garbage. It just wouldn't have the depth of character. It wouldn't have the sense of realism, because I couldn't do all the research I'd want to do. The characters would be just a hair too black and white. I mean, God bless the people who can do it. And there are a lot of writers who do it and do it well. I'm amazed. It just takes me longer. I need to sit with these characters; I need to sleep with them; I need to be in the shower with them; and I need to just let them percolate in my brain for at least six months before I can even get started on a book. I need to understand them as people.

And I will say that when I started writing, I didn't understand that point. It made no sense to me. The first thriller I wrote - *The Tenth Justice* - was pure instinct. *Fraternity* was a much more literary tale, so it was just me telling the story I understood. So when I wrote *Tenth Justice*, it was all instinct. I didn't think about how to scare anyone. I didn't think about how to do anything. I just said, *Let's just do it, it'll be fun and scary, and let's go.* I just picked up everything and ran. And when I wrote *Dead Even*, it was a much harder book to write because I spent the entire time wondering how not to make it like *Tenth Justice*. The last thing I wanted to do was to put out the same book. When I got to *First Counsel*, I said, let's try changing the point of view. Let's try something different. I felt my instinct come back again. And it had a kind of new breath to it. And I realized at that moment that you always have to change, because if you don't change, you stagnate and you're just going through the motions. I want every book to feel like it's my own -- like you can hear me in your head, and you hear the voices that are from the same author - but at the same time, that no book reminds you of the one before it. And it just takes me longer to do that, so I hope that's okay.

MURPHY: *One last question. What's next?*
MELTZER: I am not writing now. I have no idea. I mean, I'm dabbling a little bit in research. I'm checking out a couple of different things. *The Millionaires* came out one year after *The First Counsel*. It still took me over two years to write, but it was because *First Counsel* got delayed by eight months. It took everything I could to get this book out. I knew I had to push myself to do it.

MURPHY: *When did you actually finish the writing?*
MELTZER: I think the final was done in September or October.

MURPHY: *That's fast, isn't it? The book's going to be released next month?*
MELTZER: What happened was, I was three-fourths finished with the book. I usually need an extra month, then I can get it done. So I had to have a draft for them really eight months ago. I said to them, "Here's the book, read it. If you think it's good and in good shape, we'll go forward. If not, then we'll wait." And they just really wanted to go forward. And that's when they said "*We should really run.*" So I was determined to finish

as quick as I could. I certainly finished the early draft -- maybe the third or fourth draft -- eight months ago. But the final i's and t's were done in September. At best, that was six months after I handed in a full draft that people could read. So it's been written for awhile, but I can't start a book until I'm completely done with the one before it. I just mentally can't get into the characters' heads. I can't think about it while I'm still worrying about what else to do to make Charlie and Oliver come to life.

JOHN JAY OSBORN, Jr.

John Jay Osborn, Jr. achieved success as a writer of legal fiction long before today's lawyer authors appeared on bestseller lists. The 30th anniversary edition of his first novel, *The Paper Chase*, was recently released. The book details the tense relationship between first-year Harvard law student Hart and his contracts professor Kingsfield. Like many characters in the novel, Hart and Kinsfield have no first names. *The Paper Chase* was made into a successful movie starring John Houseman and Timothy Bottoms and Houseman later starred in the hit television series.

Hart becomes fixated on his contracts professor. He dates Kingsfield's daughter Susan, confessing the effect her father has on him.

> "I sit in that damn class. For days I sit there. Then I read his books in the library, and I abstract the cases he's chosen. I know everything about him. The stripe of his ties. How many suits he has. He's like the air or the wind. He's everywhere. You can say you don't care, but he's there anyway, pounding his mind into mine. He screws around with my life."

The first year of Harvard Law School changes Hart before he realizes it. But Susan has been around law students most of her life and bluntly tells Hart how he's changed. "Something's happened to your mind. I thought it might be me, but it isn't. It's you, your mind.... You were fresh before, you weren't like other people in Cambridge."

A direct descendant of John Jay, the first Chief Justice of the United States Supreme Court, Osborn graduated from Harvard University and Harvard Law School. He now teaches contract law at the University of San Francisco School of Law, which he calls "a wonderful law school." In addition to practicing contract and estate law, he has written teleplays for various programs including *The Paper Chase* and *LA Law*.

This interview took place in 2003.

FICTION: *The Paper Chase* (1973); *The Only Thing I've Done Wrong* (1977); *The Associates* (1979); *The Man Who Owned New York* (1981)

NONFICTION: *The California Coast – A Traveler's Companion* (2003)

MURPHY: *As I understand it, you started writing* The Paper Chase *during your third year in law school. I was wondering how you were able to sift through all the events and characters you must have encountered during your time in law school to decide which ones to put into the book.*

WHAT IF HOLDEN CAULFIELD WENT TO LAW SCHOOL?

OSBORN: I had two very lucky breaks. One was from the beginning I knew where the book was going; I knew what the ending was, which is just a tremendous help if you're writing a novel. Then everything is lined up to make that point meaningful. The ending of the book was where the student, Hart, says to Kingsfield, "I want you to know your course really meant something to me." And Kingsfield says, "What was your name?" The whole book is going to that point and everything is designed to make that point have a lot of reverberation. That was just a gift. I don't know how I knew that, but I knew that from the very beginning.

And the other great gift was that I had Lon Fuller for contract law. Fuller was not the model for Kingsfield; he was a perfect gentleman. But he was also a genius in contract law. And I worked for him after that class as his research assistant. So I knew him really pretty well. And he was interested in reciprocity and he saw contract law as a form of reciprocity. Lon Fuller is the guy who developed the reliance interest. There wasn't any reliance interest in contract law until Fuller invented it. The way Fuller outlined the reliance interest was as a form of reciprocity. He believed that there was an ethical and moral basis to reciprocity. Thinking about the work Fuller had done, I set up *The Paper Chase* so that the teacher is teaching contract law, i.e. reciprocity. But the class itself is being taught in a way that completely undermines the subject. The class is at loggerheads with the subject in the sense of the way the class is being taught.

MURPHY: *There's no give and take with the professor. The professor has all the control.*
OSBORN: Exactly. There's no fundamental reciprocity. Fuller would say that just you and I having this interaction has a certain reciprocity. Each of us assumes certain things about the other one, about what this is going to be about and how it is going to turn out. There's a certain implied reciprocity in everything we're doing here which allows us to do this. Well, there was no reciprocity in the contracts classroom. You asked how did I sift through it all. I had these two landmark concepts to guide me through the book.

MURPHY: *The book does progress toward the culmination of the relationship between Hart and Kingsfield. But there's really not any plot; it's more development of the character of the students and their perception of Kingsfield and how that may or may not change.*
OSBORN: You're absolutely right; there is no plot in the traditional sense. Things happen but there is no traditional plot. A book that could end on that ephemeral a note - a student just telling a professor he enjoyed the class and his professor responding and that the whole book could be about that moment - it's amazing to me how successful the book is. But you're right, there is no plot; it's very episodic. At least on the surface it's episodic.

MURPHY: *One thing that I found very interesting was that you rarely give first names to your characters. The study group Hart was in had Andersen, Bell, O'Connor, Ford, then Brooks. And Brooks is the only one with a first name. My guess is there's a reason you gave Kevin Brooks a first name and not the others.*
OSBORN: Right. And the reason is that Kevin Brooks is the most vulnerable.

MURPHY: *Most vulnerable to being influenced by Kingsfield?*

OSBORN: Most vulnerable to failing. Most vulnerable to not being able to cut it. He's the most susceptible to failure.

MURPHY: *In fact he does fail in the end. What was it in the character of Kevin Brooks that led to his failure?*
OSBORN: It's a good question. Kevin Brooks should not have been in law school. External things got him to go to law school. It's not coming from within him.

MURPHY: *It's his wife's father's money that got him there.*
OSBORN: Exactly. And he shouldn't be there. A lot of people shouldn't be in law school. He's a human guy in the wrong place. He doesn't have the personality or the skills needed to survive in law school. There's nothing unique about him that makes him fail. I mean millions of people shouldn't be in law school and he's one.

MURPHY: *You use a lot of different personality types in the study group and they criticize each other, they complain, they act behind each other's backs.*
OSBORN: They all represent different personality types that I ran into at Harvard law school. Bell just becomes obsessed about one course and one outline. He totally loses perspective.

MURPHY: *He's got an 800-page outline.*
OSBORN: Yeah. He just loses it. He hones in on this one thing and he can't help himself. That becomes his whole reason for existing. And then you contrast him with students like Andersen who are completely rational. They're like thinking machines. They've got it all plotted out so they're going to get the highest possible grade point average and everything goes into that calculation. And what's wrong with O'Connor? Nothing really. He's trying to make it work but these people are lunatics.

MURPHY: *The book makes the point that it's the school that makes them lunatics, rather than coming in that way.*
OSBORN: That's right.

MURPHY: *Even Hart has several moments of lunacy. One was when he goes out on the icy lake and risks not only himself but Susan as well. What was it that drove him to that kind of extreme?*
OSBORN: First of all, Hart is from Minnesota. There are a couple of things that go into that lake scene. In Minnesota that lake would be hard as iron. He doesn't realize it's not the same in Massachusetts. I mean Minnesota is thirty degrees colder than Massachusetts. So there's that. That actually went into my thinking. Then he's with Susan and Susan provokes the irrational, the individualistic, the inner Hart. That provokes him into doing something which she perceives to be against his best interests, as being irrational, as being risk taking. It's like she's getting that inner Hart out.

MURPHY: *And it's a constant struggle for her to do that.*
OSBORN: Yeah. I don't think it's enough. Look, in the abstract it's very hard for people to change. It's almost impossible for guys to change. And the guys I know who have changed have only done so because women with tremendous influence over them have hit them over the head, just forced them to change.

WHAT IF HOLDEN CAULFIELD WENT TO LAW SCHOOL?

MURPHY: *That lake scene seemed symbolic in a way, in that Hart is walking on thin ice. And that's how he's going through law school: on the edge all the time.*

OSBORN: Yeah. Gosh. You know, you're a really good reader. That's absolutely right. That's the metaphor for the scene. He's walking on thin ice in the sense that he will lose his soul to the law school. That's the thin ice. That's the message Susan is giving him.

MURPHY: *Then he'll become a robot.*

OSBORN: Exactly. He'll sell his soul. He'll sell his individuality. And that's what attracted Susan to him in the first place because he didn't seem to be that kind of a robot. That's it.

MURPHY: *The other scene that I found curious was when Hart and his friend were in a sandwich shop in Cambridge. There was an Indian couple who had just ordered a hamburger and some guy comes by and steals the hamburger from their table. And Hart goes chasing after them. It seemed odd that there would be an Indian couple eating beef, especially when you make an allusion to the Hindus.*

OSBORN: This scene is a really interesting scene because most of the novel is invented. That scene is exactly as it happened in real life when I was in college. My college roommate who was and is a wonderful guy was a philosophy major. He was from Minneapolis. And he was a star hockey player. He was a short guy, but solid as a rock. That scene happened exactly the way it's portrayed in the book. I don't know why the Indian couple were eating hamburger, but they were. Hart was kind of a combination of me and this roommate. It struck me as so profound about the character of the guy. You wouldn't think Hart would be violent. I never would have thought my roommate would be involved in anything like this. He went out there and he was curious. He wanted to know what's the story with the hamburger. Why would you take it and then insult them? When this guy hit my roommate, my roommate just flipped. I mean he would have killed the guy except these people mistook him for the aggressor and pulled him off.

MURPHY: *There's obviously a reason you put it in the book. It does illustrate Hart's deteriorating psyche.*

OSBORN: Yeah, I know. I don't know what it says. It just seemed right. It was just real.

MURPHY: *You have another very unusual scene where Kevin Brooks goes to his tutor's house where there's a beer-bellied guy with a bunch of girls that he's groping, sort of a pre-orgy scene. I wondered why you chose that kind of setting for Brooks to be visiting with a tutor.*

OSBORN: This relates to your question of why the other scene is in there. There was a myth in the administration department that "We've got everything under control." Of course, the tutor was like the rightest guy in law school. He'll have everything under control. It's not like the law school is ever checking any of this out though. They're doing it all on paper. They're doing things like having these tutoring programs. And the reality is that they're not working. Kevin starts out going down to this guy's office in the basement of the law school and even that's pretty grungy. And now the tutor is living this absurd life.

MURPHY: *It's not as it seems.*

OSBORN: Exactly. And from the law school's point of view on paper, they've hooked up the smartest student with the student who needs the most help. No problem, everything's going to work out fine.

MURPHY: *You give Harvard Law School, and particularly Langdell Hall, almost a mythical quality. Particularly when Hart and Ford sneak into the Treasure Room of the library to find Kingsfield's papers and his original notes. It's almost like they're on a quest for the Holy Grail.*

OSBORN: Hart is looking for the essence of contract law. He wants to go beyond what the cases say. He wants to go beyond the rules. He wants to go one step beyond. He wants in essence to get to where Fuller was and really see the beauty of the whole system and get to the ethical dilemmas that matter. And once he gets to the ethical dilemmas, he'll realize that the class is not following what it should be and he'll ultimately revolt, which he does.

MURPHY: *He takes quite a course. He goes through many sleepless nights working on a research paper for Kingsfield which does not even count toward his grade. He's not getting paid and he can't finish it anyway. He's really becoming a mess.*

OSBORN: Yeah. No doubt about it.

MURPHY: *At the end when Hart and Susan are sitting on the rocks and Hart throws his grades transcript into the water, I thought at that point you'd give him a first name. Did it ever occur to you to do that?*

OSBORN: I worked very closely on the movie and was also the chief writer for the TV show. We got much more sophisticated on this first-name issue. I didn't write every teleplay. Some of the other writers would want to know what's the story about the name. We began to use his first name - James - when he was vulnerable. Then you might get his whole name. And then everywhere else we would just use his last name. The other thing is in my study group, everybody used everybody's last name. The reason they did is because that's how they're called on in class. And you can see that what's happening in that the class is actually affecting their lives.

MURPHY: *I understand Harvard Law School first admitted female students in the 1950s. You have very few, if any, female law students in the book, very few female characters at all in fact. I wondered if that concerned you as you were writing the book, that maybe it's just too much from the male point of view, other than the fact that that was probably the reality.*

OSBORN: That was the reality to me when I went. Harvard Law School was just starting to change. There were about maybe 15-20% women. Now I think more than 50% of their students are women. I didn't have any women in my study group. I gave a talk at the California Lawyers for the Arts and I got attacked for that. I didn't realize I was walking into that attack. She said if you were writing the book today, would you change anything. And I thought she meant would I go back and change the original *Paper Chase* and I said no. Then I got attacked for the book not having any women in it and for being sexist. But it's true to the reality of the law school thirty years ago. And this is a thirty-year-old book.

WHAT IF HOLDEN CAULFIELD WENT TO LAW SCHOOL?

MURPHY: *Even with the few female law students, did the professors treat the women in the same disrespectful, demanding way as the men?*
OSBORN: They treated them worse.

MURPHY: *Maybe if you had depicted them that way you'd also get some flack.*
OSBORN: The women tended to keep their heads down. They were no dummies. I could have had a woman. It just so happened that I didn't have a woman in my study group. If I had had one, I'd probably have put one in the book.

MURPHY: *You started writing the book in your third year, but when did the idea for a book actually occur to you?*
OSBORN: It occurred to me at the beginning of my third year. Because, remember, this was in the era of the protests against the Vietnamese war. And for the very first time, there were huge protests at Harvard in '69 and '70. For the first time Harvard law students were saying, "Hey, wait a minute, I'm not sure everything is as great as it's cracked up to be around here." And I was certainly thinking that. But they were thinking it everywhere else and other important books at law schools got written in this milieu. So I was thinking very hard about whether this law school is a good place to be.

MURPHY: *And you were able to keep your focus on your studies while having those thoughts as well?*
OSBORN: First of all, there's not as much to do in your third year of law school. In the second semester of my third year, through a great deal of luck, I got to take an English course working individually with a professor. And because of that, I got credit for writing *The Paper Chase*.

MURPHY: *No kidding? That's great!*
OSBORN: Very very lucky. And I got an A.

MURPHY: *What percentage of your career since law school have you been actually practicing versus writing?*
OSBORN: I've always either been teaching or practicing at least part of the time. I've never stopped being a lawyer.

MURPHY: *Have you ever stopped being a writer?*
OSBORN: A little bit on and off, yeah. I have a funny feeling about this stuff. I am a lawyer. Do you know what I mean? You know, I'm fifty seven years old. To pretend I'm a writer, that just doesn't feel right to me.

MURPHY: *Yet you've written four novels.*
OSBORN: Yeah, but I am actually a lawyer. I can go out and write your estate plan.

MURPHY: *Why did you stop writing?*
OSBORN: I was doing TV. I don't know how many pilots I did, but I cranked out a lot of pilots. And then I got tired. I got tired of going down to LA and I got tired of doing television pilots. So that was that. In that period of time the whole legal fiction genre has taken off. But it's not really legal fiction. You see, there's a real difference.

Those are disguised detective stories starring lawyers as detectives. That is not real legal fiction. It's not about legal institutions, it's not about real legal problems, it almost invariably has a criminal law background, because it's really a detective story. I mean Louis Auchincloss writes real legal fiction.

MURPHY: *Do you have any more writing projects, either screen plays or books?*

OSBORN: I'm trying to write a novel right now about a senior partner in a fairly large San Francisco law firm. He's sort of a King Lear character. And it's about him reassessing his life and his relationship with the law firm.

MURPHY: *About six years or so after The Paper Chase came out, Scott Turow published One L, a nonfictional account of the first year of Harvard Law School. What did you think of that book in terms of realistically portraying the Law School?*

OSBORN: I didn't like it very much, but it's a nonfiction book and as much as I had problems with Harvard Law School, there's also a romance to it that is very important, that I found completely missing from *One L*. And maybe that's because it was a nonfiction book. Do you know what I'm saying? There's something romantic about Hart's quest. There's something romantic about him wanting to find the treasure room, find Kingsfield's notes. There's an element of quest. He wants to go further. He's not just reactive. He's pushing to take it to a higher level. And I think it's that quality that made *The Paper Chase* so successful.

SHELDON SIEGEL

At first glance San Francisco corporate securities lawyer Sheldon Siegel seems an unlikely candidate to write a bestselling legal thriller. An accounting major in college, Siegel admits to never trying a case. Somehow he learned enough in his nearly two decades of practice to write a first novel that attracted the first agent he contacted and a two-book deal from Bantam for $850,000. And all while commuting to work on the ferry from Marin County.

That book, *Special Circumstances*, features a protagonist much different than Siegel. Criminal defense attorney, Mike Daley, is defined by what he isn't rather than what he is. He's an ex-priest, ex-public defender, ex-husband, and ex-partner at a prominent San Francisco law firm. He is also the close friend of Joel Friedman, who is accused of murdering a senior partner and beautiful female associate in the fictional firm of Simpson & Gates. Police suspect Friedman because he was found holding the murder weapon and his fingerprints were on the victim's computer keyboard. Distinguished for its biting sense of humor, hilarious portraits of big-firm lawyers, and quick pace, Special Circumstances brings a ray of hope to a genre that has risked becoming stale and uninspired due to over saturation. The opening sentence sets the tone: "For the last 20 years or so, being a partner in a big corporate law firm has been like having a license to print money."

A graduate of the University of Illinois and Boalt Hall School of Law, Siegel is with Sheppard, Mullin, Richter & Hampton in San Francisco. Before joining Sheppard, Mullin, he worked at Petit & Martin and was in the 101 California Street office during the shooting on July 1, 1993. Siegel lives in Marin County with his wife, Linda, a technical trainer at Lucasfilm, and their twin eight-year-old sons.

This interview took place in 2001.

FICTION: *Special Circumstances* (2000); *Incriminating Evidence* (2001); *Criminal Intent* (2003); *Final Verdict* (2003); *The Confession* (2004)

MURPHY: *Your success with* Special Circumstances *has made you the envy of many lawyers. A lot of reviewers like the humor. And that immediately struck me as setting your book apart from the dozens of legal thrillers I've read. How did it come about that you decided to inject so much humor into the book?*
SIEGEL: I worked very hard at trying to create a voice for this book, the voice of Mike Daley. And I wanted that voice to have humanity and a sense of humor. I wouldn't say many lawyer books lack humor, but they are certainly very serious at least in tone. This particular book is about a very serious matter. It's about a murder trial but

there is a protagonist who has a little bit of humor in his soul and I thought that was important to bring out.

MURPHY: *Did you come by the humor naturally or is it something that you had to work at?*
SIEGEL: Mike Daley's voice sounds very much like mine. My wife would confirm this. I wanted to write a book that sounds like me. I thought it would be easier to get into character every day if I wrote a book in a voice that sounded a lot like my own. I also wrote about San Francisco so that I could write about things I knew.

MURPHY: *I understand that Mike Daley was not your original narrator. My guess is that your original narrator was Joel Freidman.*
SIEGEL: That's true. This book actually had two other narrative voices before I got to Mike. Joel - the corporate and securities lawyer who looks, walks and talks a lot like me - was the first person I tried as the narrator. And I found after writing fifty pages that that didn't work because Joel is the defendant and the defendant typically spends a lot of time in jail. So much of the book would have been situated in the Hall of Justice in the jail cell and that didn't work. I tried it a second time in the third person and I didn't like the way the book sounded. I didn't think the humor came through as well in the third person. So the third time through I decided the criminal defense attorney would be a better narrator. So I took the same voice that I was originally using for Joel and grafted it onto Mike.

MURPHY: *And then you made Mike different than Joel in many respects. Joel was more like you: he's Jewish, the father of twins, and trained in the Yeshiva whereas Mike is known by what he used to be rather than what he is. He's an ex-priest, an ex-public defender, and ex-partner at a big firm. I found it interesting that most of the reviews refer to what he wasn't rather than what he was.*
SIEGEL: That's true. Mike has a lot of history. He is an ex-public defender. He is an ex-priest. He is an ex-husband. And as the book begins, he is an ex-partner in a big law firm. Hopefully I've given Mike enough history to last for several books. He will be back in the second installment next year. But Mike is a lot different than I am in many respects and Joel is lot more similar at least in background. But I found Mike was a more interesting character and he's also the right character to tell this particular story. Mike is a good criminal defense attorney. He was a very good public defender. And he does wisecrack, although a lot of it is internal. But when push comes to shove he knows what he's doing. He has certainly evolved into a much broader, fuller character than I originally thought he would. When I started writing the book, I thought he was going to be actually a pretty minor character. Mike's ex-wife and law partner Rosie evolved completely out of thin air because I needed someone for Mike to talk to. And I needed to give Mike someone in the office since the book is written in first person. I discovered in first person that if your protagonist doesn't have someone to talk to or react with, the story doesn't move forward. So Rosie also evolved a great deal over time and she sounds a whole lot like my wife, but Linda and I get along much better than Mike and Rosie do.

MURPHY: *You obviously had to make some choices in terms of Mike's background. One of them having him be an ex-priest. What did that background add to Mike Daley as a narrator?*
SIEGEL: For one thing I've known a couple of ex-priests and they are very nice people. They've read the book. And they have a lot of history, a lot of background. Mike Daley is fundamentally a good person with a good heart who tries to do the right

thing. He's also clueless about money and business. He doesn't always necessarily say the right thing. Most public defenders I've met are people trying to do the right thing for people who are down on their luck. It fits together with the type of character I'm trying to write: someone who had empathy, someone who had a heart, someone who really does very much try to do the right thing. This is a book about a guy who tries to help out his friend. And I think it just fit.

MURPHY: *Why have Mike having an ongoing sexual relationship with his ex-wife as opposed to having a girlfriend or fiancée or even a wife?*
SIEGEL: That's actually a good question. I brought in Rosie originally so Mike would have someone to talk to and I was trying to decide what kind of baggage I could attach to that relationship. And I thought about doing it any number of different ways. I thought of giving him a law partner, maybe an older person, an older man or an older woman, sort of a mentor type and that didn't work particularly well. So I thought, well, if we could add more baggage to him -- he's an ex-priest, he's an ex-public defender, let's put him into practice with his ex-wife, sort of out of desperation just to fill out the fact that he's a guy who's a bit down on his luck. I also wanted a tension there that I think is natural. They get along well most of the time, but when they try to live together they just can't put the pieces together. The reaction to that relationship has been very positive for the most part. A number of people have said Mike and Rosie's relationship is almost identical to their relationships with their ex-spouses. So I kind of stumbled upon it, but it worked. In this book, I was trying to hit him from every side because these books are really about Mike's reactions to the circumstances that surround him.

MURPHY: *I think that's true. There is a spark between them. Sometimes it's a good spark, sometimes it's a nasty spark, but there's always something going on when Mike and Rosie are together.*
SIEGEL: Rosie too is very good at what she does. And they do egg each other on. In the best of all worlds they probably never would have gotten married, they simply would have remained public defenders and worked on cases together. When you factor in marriage, children and money and all those other issues, I think it was probably more than they could handle easily.

MURPHY: *When I was reading* Special Circumstances, *I was in court against an Oakland lawyer whose name is Mike Daley. Afterwards, I asked him about this book and he said I know Sheldon and he borrowed my name. Have you consciously used the names of actual lawyers in the book?*
SIEGEL: Oh no. Mike Daley was a name I stumbled upon. I needed an Irish sounding name. I had picked the name Michael because it's sort of an everyman-sounding name. The name Daly came about because I'm from Chicago and the most famous Irishman in Chicago was Mayor Daley. So that's where Mike Daley came from. The other names in the book I pulled pretty much out of thin air. You've probably talked to other authors who are selective about what names sound like. I certainly didn't use any real names. Although the lawyers in the book bear characteristics of a lot of people I've met over the years, they're again pulled out of thin air. Except for perhaps Joel, who looks and walks and talks just like me, down to the twin sons.

MURPHY: *Let me ask you about the plot. Your book is a murder mystery and the victims are Bob Holmes, partner in Simpson and Gates and his beautiful young associate Diane Kennedy. How did* *you decide in what way to lay out the clues, both throughout the pre-trial and the trial to keep the reader engaged?*

SIEGEL: That's an interesting process and it's one that I'm not trained to do very well. As you know, I studied accounting in college and I'm a corporate securities lawyer so my formal training for how to write novels has come as I've gone along. I know the beginning of the book, and I know the ending. I know who did it and how and why. And although this book is considered a legal thriller, I think it really lays out in some respects more as a mystery. And mysteries have a structure. There's a murder, there's an investigation, there's a resolution. In a trial book like this one there's also a trial. So I knew the four pieces. The tricky part was laying it out in a manner where you didn't find out too much during the investigation phase, because if you did there would be nothing to talk about at the trial. And that's where I think most attorney authors take perhaps more liberties, because theoretically under California discovery rules you should find out most of everything during the investigation phase and you should find out very little that's new within the trial. In this case and in many legal thrillers, the time for everything is compressed so that while the trial is going on the lawyers are still desperately looking for clues and evidence. And as time goes on, you get a feel for laying things out in a certain order for dramatic purposes. In this case, I am told by my criminal defense attorney friends also is pretty realistic in terms of how a trial might go. The other thing that I think was realistic about the trial is that nothing ever quite goes the way you plan it. Things happen and everything then gets pushed aside so you approach things a little differently.

MURPHY: *There is a balance you have to make as an author between two things: making the book - particularly a trial book - realistic, and making sure it's dramatic. At points in writing* Special Circumstances, *did you find that you were maybe taking a little too much license to make something dramatic opposed to making it realistic?*

SIEGEL: I think I kept it within the bounds plausibility. We all take liberties because real-life murder trials take a very long time. There's a lot of minutia that really is not very dramatic and so you try to arrange your plot to get through those issues as quickly as you can. But it is a tough one. It's probably the toughest part of writing a trial book: selecting which of the characters you should have go through cross examination and which you should just summarize in two paragraphs to keep the story moving.

MURPHY: *One device you use that I've seen in many novels is you have a suspect disappear: the client Vince Russo. Frankly, that's one of the only parts of the book I found contrived. I wonder if you could explain why you did that.*

SIEGEL: In mysteries there is often one wild card. And in this book Vince Russo is the wild card. It was by no grand design and I was again trying to remain within the realm of the plausible there. But I would agree with you he does tend to come and go when it's convenient. But his actions within the book are certainly within the realm of what I've seen out in the real world. I think it's probably fair to say that that particular character is maybe the biggest stretch in the book.

MURPHY: *You admit that you're not a trial lawyer, and I wonder how you went about writing trial scenes that were realistic.*

WHAT IF HOLDEN CAULFIELD WENT TO LAW SCHOOL?

SIEGEL: I am not a trial lawyer. I am a corporate and securities lawyer. I've never handled a criminal matter. And I went about writing trial scenes by reading a lot of other fiction, by studying Court TV and the Simpson case and other readily available things that are out there in the public domain. And to be honest, I watch all the TV shows that do trials. I was actually very flattered because one of the critics said that my trial scenes were as good as *Law and Order*. And I think that's a good show. I tried to come up with something that was realistic and something that was dramatic and I pulled it pretty much out of thin air based upon my experience and what I see in popular culture. In some respects that may have helped me because I am writing books at a level that is directed toward people like me who really don't necessarily know the elaborate ins and outs of criminal procedure. Maybe that made the book move along a little bit more quickly. I can tell you for sure that in this book and in the sequel and hopefully in the Mike Daley books down the road, the cases will probably never turn on very esoteric elaborate legal issues because I don't have enough experience in criminal law and criminal procedure to really do that very well.

MURPHY: *You have another plot device where the characters go to the Bahamas. It seems to me -- maybe I've read too many of these books -- that a lot of legal thrillers are situated in the Caribbean. I wonder why you went there.*
SIEGEL: All authors want a vacation. The next book is going to be in Hawaii. Actually that part of the plot line is based upon some personal experience I've had over the years representing investors. I have dealt with bankers in the Bahamas. Interestingly, I must confess, I've never been to the Bahamas, but I got enough travel brochures and did enough research that I'm told that the scenes down there read pretty accurately. But you're right; it is another very common device that I've seen in a lot of books where they end up offshore in the Caribbean. I'd kind of like to do a book in Tahiti some day.

MURPHY: *The attorneys in Simpson & Gates are very distinctive: the managing partner Chuckles Stern and one of the senior partners Arthur Patton are arrogant and condescending. All archetypes, but very distinctive because they're seen through Mike Daley's eyes. How did you decide what types of characters - among the many that one encounters in a big corporate law firm - to put in the book?*
SIEGEL: The hardest part was cutting back the number of lawyers in the firm to something that was manageable. I actually had two or three more caricatures from big law firms. We will see some of them perhaps in the second or third book. But I was trying to find a balance two or three of the types you seem to see in every big law firm, for that matter, every big institution of any size. And I thought typically you find an Art Patton who is the big evil nasty litigator who runs the place. The Bob Holmes character is the corporate gorilla who has the big book of business and drives everybody crazy. Every big firm seems to have somebody who counts the money. I'm finding that people in big law firms all think it's about their firm. And there are ongoing discussions about which firm in town I'm harpooning. The reality of it is it's all of them. I've been working in big law firms for seventeen years and I think I've accumulated every war story. And in one manner or another - with a little bit of exaggeration - they all found their way into the book.

MURPHY: *It's your way of getting even.*
SIEGEL: Maybe.

INTERVIEWS-Sheldon Siegel

MURPHY: *Are you in a position where you can talk about your second book?*
SIEGEL: I can tell you a little bit about it. It's another Mike Daley story. Mike and Rosie will be back and a prominent politician in San Francisco is accused of murder and asks Mike and Rosie to help him out. I can't tell you too much more.

MURPHY: *So Mike Daley is going to be a series character?*
SIEGEL: Mike's coming back. I had not really thought about a series until about two-thirds of the way through the first book. I discovered that criminal defense attorneys are good protagonists for series. Like Perry Mason, they can just get another case in another year. I've started on the third one so there's going to be at least two more of them.

MURPHY: *I've read the press clippings and I know that you had always wanted to write a book before you turned forty. How did you come to decide to write a murder mystery - legal thriller as opposed to perhaps a literary novel as some lawyers do?*
SIEGEL: I like the genre. When I first got the idea for this book, which was probably ten years ago -- Scott Turow has just come out with *Presumed Innocent* and John Grisham had just come out with *The Firm*. When I read *Presumed Innocent* in 1988 on my honeymoon, somewhere in the back of my mind I filed away the idea that if I ever write a book, I'd like to write one like this. Not that I had spent any time in a courtroom, but it just seemed like a genre you could play with. And I filed that away for another seven or eight years before I started writing this book. And when I started writing, I did decide very affirmatively that I would write about San Francisco so I didn't have to do a lot of research about other places. And I would write about a big law firm because that's what I know the most about. And I would write in present day San Francisco because then I again don't have to do a lot of research on time and place other than to fill in Mike Daley's background. And I decided to write a book that sounded a lot like my own voice so that I wouldn't have to think a lot about what the characters sounded like. And all those pieces came together.

MURPHY: *Some of the press reports indicate that you really decided to write after the 101 California massacre at Pettit and Martin. Is that what happened?*
SIEGEL: That really is true. I was an attorney at the Pettit firm for about ten years. In 1993 there was this horrible event at the firm. When we closed the firm in 1995 most of us from the San Francisco office moved to the Sheppard Mullin firm where I am now. It was kind of a fresh start and a new perspective. I thought it was time that I started writing the book that I had always been promising myself that I was going to write. I think the events at the Pettit firm changed a lot of people's lives. Some more so than others. It was just one of those profound events. It's kind of like having kids or getting married or moving away from home for the first time. It's just something that you mark time by and it changes you. And I thought a lot about the things that I wanted to try before I got too old to try them. And I realized I was never going to be a professional baseball player. But one of those things I had wanted to do for -- really since high school-- was to write a novel. And I have no logical explanation for that at all.

LAWRENCE G. TOWNSEND

San Francisco intellectual property litigator Lawrence G. Townsend has written a first novel that turns the world of software licensing upside down and inside out. *Secrets of the Wholly Grill: A Novel About Cravings, Barbecue, and Software* is about all those things, but it's also a wicked satire of the heavy-handed tactics of Microsoft. By applying the restrictions on use contained in typical software shrink-wrap licenses to home barbecues, Townsend points out in often hilarious ways the absurd turns such licenses can take.

Insurance salesman Lenny Milton receives a free frozen sirloin tip in the mail. At over 300 pounds, Milton is always receptive to a free meal. But there's a catch. The shrink-wrap license for the steak provides that it can only be grilled on a ThinkSoft laser barbecue grill using only ThinkSoft's own barbecue sauce. When Milton fails to follow the restrictions, terrible things happen. He turns to plaintiffs attorney Edwin G. Ostermeyer, famous for his television commercials if not for his successes in court. Ostermeyer assigns the case to his young associate, Will Swanson, who proves no match for seasoned defense attorney Thurston Crushjoy.

With the help of technology reporter Persi Valentino, Swanson begins to build a case that will make the tobacco litigation pale by comparison.

Townsend's satire hits the target with his depictions of not only attorneys but also unlikely subjects such as law firm receptionists. Because Edwin Ostermeyer has trouble retaining a receptionist, he calls them all "New Receptionist." When his latest reports he has no calls, she is "absorbed in a game of solitaire on her computer screen, oblivious to the call she had just missed. Her hair resembled spikes of cotton candy, in three rigid rows of bright pink.... 'I guess I missed that one,' she said. 'But I'm doing a lot of things at once.' She shuffled an envelope from one side of her station to another and straightened the telephone console."

Townsend reserves his hardest hits, however, for the software industry. To enforce its shrink-wrap license on the Wholly Grill ("whole e-grill" or "wholly electronic"), ThinkSoft sends out enforcers called SMEL units, for Society of Manufacturers for the Enforcement of Licenses. After catching a couple using their Wholly Grill at an outdoor market, one SMEL agent tells them:

> "You agreed to K-Nine enforcement under paragraph seven, and you assumed the risk of all injuries arising from misuse of the system under paragraph eight.... This is a serious violation of paragraph four, which prohibits any commercial use of the Wholly Grill. By law you will be required to turn over your illegal profits to SMEL or be sued. The sooner you

cooperate in allowing me to shut down the unlawful enterprise, the better off you'll be!"

Full of sharp humor and insight, *Secrets of the Wholly Grill* will become the standard by which all high tech satire will be judged.

A graduate of the University of California at Santa Barbara, where he majored in English, and the University of San Francisco School of Law, Townsend serves as Of Counsel to Owen, Wickersham & Erickson in San Francisco.

This interview took place in 2002.

FICTION: *Secrets of the Wholly Grill: A Novel About Cravings, Barbecue, and Software* (2002)

MURPHY: *Your first novel* Secrets of the Wholly Grill *is - to say the least - an unusual book. I wondered how you pitched it to an agent. What did you tell the agent to entice her to take this book?*
TOWNSEND: Actually, I found my agent through an introduction by another writer who had read the book. She was told that it's different than the usual legal thriller. It's definitely satire that borders on farce, it's a lot fun to read, and she should take a look at it. Fortunately, she had a wonderful sense of humor and she loved the book.

MURPHY: *What was the genesis for the idea of the book?*
TOWNSEND: Truth is stranger than fiction sometimes. A dear friend of mine actually signed me up for a writing course and told me that you had to have a work in progress in order to be in the course. I said I had no work in progress, but thanks very much. She said, "Well, you love to write. In fact, you've written and published some articles recently on the subject of shrink wrap licenses." Which was true. Several years ago I had done that. And she said, "Why don't you write a novel about a shrink wrap license?" And taking the bait, I said, "Oh, you mean like making it a little more crazy than it currently reads?" And just taking it one step further, she said, "How about a shrink wrap around a barbecue?" I said, "That sounds like a great idea." So she dared me and I double dared myself very shrewdly. I took the idea and I wrote a first chapter. I had a first chapter by the first course and things started to unfold from there.

MURPHY: *The title* - Secrets of the Wholly Grill - *is that your title?*
TOWNSEND: Actually it is my title, but the original title when the publisher bought it was *A License to Grill* which is a fun title. And they said we love the title *License to Grill*, but there's a cookbook out there named *License to Grill*. Now as a trademark lawyer, I'll tell you - and they know this too - that's not a legal problem because they're two different channels and they're very unrelated. But because everything gets searched online or electronically these days, it creates enough inconvenience to have two titles come up named *License to Grill*. In the old days, it wasn't electronics. You would just walk into a bookstore, you'd never wander over to the cookbook section looking for a novel. There's no problem here. Anyway, they asked me to come up with an alternative title. So I came up with that title.

WHAT IF HOLDEN CAULFIELD WENT TO LAW SCHOOL?

MURPHY: *You start off with Lenny Milton, a 340 pound insurance salesman, who gets a free steak in the mail, then buys the barbecue system to cook the meat. In terms of plotting out the book and developing the characters, what went into your decision to make Lenny such an obese individual?*

TOWNSEND: Certainly we had to have somebody who was likely to buy ThinkSoft software, was already somewhat of an addict of software, and just couldn't resist buying the latest upgrade. And of course we just had fun with that. Instead of having software we had somebody who not only buys lots of software but likes to eat. ThinkSoft gets into the food business. Sure enough it now has consumers who cannot resist buying the latest software upgrade but also can't resist the barbecue which turns out to be highly addictive. So in order to make that more visual and to make the story work, we wanted to make clear that Lenny has a predisposition to either food or software in this situation.

MURPHY: *You have some of the best firm names I've ever heard. Kilgore, Crushjoy, Clubman and Powell. And another defense firm was called Barr, Block, Milkit and Cave.*

TOWNSEND: It just so happens to be an insurance defense firm. That's right.

MURPHY: *The main character is a young lawyer named Will Swanson who lands a job with Edwin Ostermeyer, a high profile plaintiff's attorney who is described as "humility challenged." You obviously didn't limit your satire just to the software industry. You take on lawyers actually in several different ways. When you conceived the book, did you intend this to be a sort of global satire?*

TOWNSEND: I couldn't resist hitting any target that would present itself. It's true, it is a broader satire than the software industry. You find as you start to write a novel that you need to expand and have other subject matter, plot and subplot. More characters get introduced, although there's not a huge number of characters in this book. As the writing process proceeds, you see where another character will enhance a particular area. But as far as the scope of the subject matter: Yes, I definitely found that I had more to say than what goes on in the software industry. I obviously know a fair amount about what goes on in the legal trade so there was room for a broader satire to address some of the characters we encounter in the legal world.

MURPHY: *Tell me about the writing process. When did you start writing it and how long did it take you?*

TOWNSEND: It took a little over three years to write it. There're different ways to approach it. Some writers can sit down and flush out a complete outline of each chapter and have it in sequence. I don't write that way. I have lots of ideas as big blocks that I think in. Basically the first draft is the outline. That's the way I work. And then once I have that draft, which is really the outline, then I can start reorganizing and flushing it out and refining it.

MURPHY: *Had you tried your hand at fiction before this novel?*

TOWNSEND: Actually, I had written what we'll call an experimental novel twenty five years ago, before I went to law school. I did not have as a goal publication for that, although I dabbled with the idea. It was really just experimental fiction. But it was a great experience in that I'd given a lot of thought and time to the writing process. So it made it a little easier at picking this up twenty five years later.

MURPHY: *So there must have been something more than just getting into this class that inspired you to want to write fiction after twenty five years.*
TOWNSEND: Well, sure. I've always loved writing; always loved fiction. Not surprisingly, I was an English major in college and I've always been the one called upon to write skits for groups I belong to. So I've always had some hand in it. But this is of course a much more ambitious project than anything I've undertaken before.

MURPHY: *Did you have any help in plotting the novel?*
TOWNSEND: I took this course I mentioned earlier and that was helpful with plotting - some of the do's and the don'ts. Very helpful in terms of using point of view as a device for telling the story. For example, in this story we have Will Swanson who's the young coming-of-age lawyer and he doesn't even emerge until like the third chapter. In the first half of the book, the point of view shifts among several characters. But the second half is entirely his point of view.

MURPHY: *Was that purposeful?*
TOWNSEND: It's a combination of you see what works - having done it unconsciously - and then you consciously make that work in a way that makes sense.

MURPHY: *Did you start out with the idea of writing a courtroom scene in the book?*
TOWNSEND: Again, being a lawyer that was a natural outcome. That's something I found myself gravitated towards. But, yeah, there was no question it was going to end up in court and there would be some kind of courtroom drama.

MURPHY: *You've got a defense lawyer named Thurston Crushjoy, who is every plaintiffs lawyer's worst nightmare. You take some great shots at the expert doctor Elizabeth Stone in terms of her selling her testimony. The only characters you don't hit too hard are Will Swanson and Persi Valentino, the reporter. Were you conscious in the writing process that these two characters would stand apart from everyone else?*
TOWNSEND: That's a good question. I naturally wrote it that way. Someone described it early on that Will Swanson was the eye of the storm. I think that made it funnier. He really acts as the straight man. In this particular story, it seemed to work to keep somebody who had one foot in reality since there's so much craziness going on. Persi Valentino is an alter ego of Will. So, yes, she's a little more out there and a bolder character than he is. She's very sane, but she's just a little more bold in her approach.

MURPHY: *So bold that she actually goes under cover inside the ThinkSoft company and steals secrets. You have her discover electronic truth serum where people who come in contact with it will broadcast their own security breaches. You have other innovative ideas such as SMEL units where agents just go out and track down people who are illegally using their barbecues. Did you ever think as you were going through the book that maybe you were pushing it too far?*
TOWNSEND: The beauty of writing about high technology and the software industry is it's pretty hard to be far-fetched. And that's what was really fun. It turns out that a lot of the things in there are really not that far-fetched. This electronic truth serum where people are caused electronically to disclose their own security violations I would agree would otherwise sound pretty far-fetched. But just a week or so ago, there was a story about how they were able to implant chips in monkeys' brains so the monkeys can

move the cursors on a screen just by thinking where they want the cursor to move. And they're going to be using this kind of technology for quadriplegics. I couldn't help but think that that particular feature, which someone might describe as too far-fetched, turns out not very far-fetched at all. We encounter this kind of thing all the time with technology. It just constantly amazing what's coming down the pipe.

MURPHY: *Are there any parts of* Secrets of the Wholly Grill *that you thought may get you in trouble - either legally or public relations wise - in terms of your criticism of the industry?*
TOWNSEND: I can only hope legally, because nothing could bring more attention to the book than to be sued by Microsoft. But again, being a lawyer, I think I know where the lines are and know of course there's a great deal of latitude. Putting aside any legal tussles, I don't think any of the commentary between the lines in the book will get me into any trouble. I hope that it raises some questions and causes people to talk about it. Maybe it might ruffle some feathers; it's possible. But I think the light tone serves a purpose of diminishing the chances of somebody taking this too personally or misinterpreting what I'm trying to do, which is to raise questions and have some fun while we do it.

MURPHY: *The whole concept of the book is a very ambitious one and I wonder what you found to be the most difficult part of the writing process?*
TOWNSEND: The first draft is always the most difficult. I think that other writers find that too. I actually enjoy the revision process. I think some don't. I really enjoy the details and the revision process. But the subject matter of this book involved things that were very familiar to me. I'm writing another book now and I'm getting into things that are beyond my day to day experiences. I am doing a little research and that is always a little more challenging, but very doable. But this book involved nothing but material that was very very familiar to me.

MURPHY: *Except in your legal practice, of course, you're not creating characters, devising plots, and writing dialogue. Which of those did you find the most difficult?*
TOWNSEND: The dialogue came very easily and I've gotten good response on the dialogue. The courtroom scene, of course, is question and answer. That's something that's very familiar to lawyers and I think that's probably no surprise. There is a love scene in there. Some people gravitate to writing that more so than I. Of course, as somebody said, you can tell what a writer doesn't want to write about by the number of tricks he uses. I used a few tricks in the love scene. But it seemed to work very well so I'm happy about that. On another related subject, the book itself really could be described as an amicus brief for consumer rights in the software area. So the logic of setting up this book is, I think, highly related to that of writing a brief. As lawyers must, you have to state the issues first, and then you have to proceed to a discussion. You get what the issue is on the first page when Lenny Milton goes out and finds marinated sirloin tip under a shrink wrap license. You have to ask yourself: 1) what's going on here? and 2) how can they do that? And we then tell the story, the expository that proceeds throughout the book. And we even have exhibit A attached to the novel and that is the Wholly Grill.

MURPHY: *What was your intended audience for this book? Did you have a readership in mind?*

TOWNSEND: I was really seeking the broadest possible readership. I know a lot about intellectual property and software and that kind of subject matter, but I didn't want to just be writing for lawyers. We know the general reading public is interested in what lawyers do because they're popular on television and in books. I know they're interested in what goes on in technology. That's in the papers every day. But it seemed to me that no one had really written a book that reached out to the average reader - the non lawyer - and presented issues that are day to day issues for IP lawyers and technology people.

MURPHY: *The book is scary at one level in the sense that - you obviously have Microsoft in mind - software companies can assume so much control over people's lives. It's frightening. Was part of your purpose in writing the book to send a message to this effect?*
TOWNSEND: Certainly for dramatic effect - to tell a good story - I wanted to present it that way. It clearly is a dark comedy. There's some light humor but there's also, as you allude to, there's quite a bit of dark comedy and that's part of it. I'm not saying that this is real. I think that it should be pause for thought as to how much power a large company can have, especially with technology advancing as quickly as it is. Again, it's not too far-fetched when you think about it.

MURPHY: *There's a section in the book where quote verbatim a pamphlet called the Life and History of Santa Tostada, in which a nun steals a secret formula that will kill some bugs that are destroying their corn fields. I'm wondering whether that was an original for the book or something you borrowed elsewhere. And why did you insert that several-page item in the middle of the novel?*
TOWNSEND: I certainly have set up some extremes here. On the one hand, you have ThinkSoft that claims to own everything it's ever created and claims to own your own thoughts. On the other end of the spectrum, we have a mythical figure, Santa Tostada, who Persi describes as the patron saint of the public domain, which is just the opposite of being proprietary. And that particular example of course is quoted right when the SMEL police are descending on the picnic about to effect a bust of Lenny Milton for not abiding to the terms of his Wholly Grill end user license agreement. And so we had some fun, but also, I think, we are posing some questions about the nature and the abuses of what Persi Valentino calls proprietary fever running rampant. On the other side, you have public domain. Santa Tostada certainly comes across as a heroine in taking information from these mercenaries that was in the public domain but they treated it as though it wasn't. So again we're just raising some questions and having some fun with it.

MURPHY: *You indicate you've written on shrink wrap licenses. I assume those were technical legal articles.*
TOWNSEND: Right. They were for legal publications, yes.

MURPHY: *Your practice of course is intellectual property. But I'm wondering what sort of practice areas do you have that relate directly to what you wrote about in the novel?*
TOWNSEND: I've certainly done a fair amount of software licensing agreements including various shrink wrap licenses, but also ones that are vendor to vendor, vendor to vendee software licenses. I do copyright litigation in California and this particular story revolves primarily around trade secrets but it has lots of flavor of copyright issues in it. Of course, shrink wrap licenses are typically used in the copyright area, but they always have boilerplates about trade secrets also being protected. Needless to say,

there's lots of fun with names in the novel. In fact, I do a lot of trademark work and it's just natural for a trademark lawyer to want to play with names I think. It's very much a part of what we encounter day to day.

MURPHY: *Your biography on your website indicates that you are a fourth generation intellectual property lawyer. And you related to the old Townsend & Townsend firm?*
TOWNSEND: Correct.

MURPHY: *What's the relationship?*
TOWNSEND: My father, my uncle, my grandfather and my great grandfather all worked there. And my great grandfather started working there in the 1860s. He was - if there's a distinction - a patent attorney, not a lawyer, which is to say he could do everything but go to court. These days all of that stuff is highly licensed but he was in what was a new profession being a patent attorney. That meant he could not only prosecute patents but back then he could give any kind of legal advice short of going to court for a client. In other words, he could do license agreements and counsel clients on legal matters relating to patents as well.

MURPHY: *Did you go into law knowing that you were predestined for intellectual property?*
TOWNSEND: Not really. There are more lawyers in my family than you'd care to know. My grandfather on my mother's side started the Bronson firm. And then on my father's side - the Townsend firm - so there nothing but lawyers. All of my cousins, my brothers and sisters said, "Not for me." I was the only one that was curious enough - maybe crazy enough - to say I have to find out what this is all about. I just have to do this. So I gravitated to law. But it was not clear in going to law school that I would end up in IP. I was open to doing lots of things.

MURPHY: *You got out of law school in 1979, at a time when software was just a baby really. Things have dramatically changed in the technology area since then. Has that affected the way you practice?*
TOWNSEND: Actually, in the first ten years of my practice, I always did some IP but I also did lots of other things. I was based in Marin County with my partner, Lynn Duryee, who is now a Superior Court judge. In fact, she's the one who coaxed me to write the book. She's a very dear friend. Certainly things have changed a lot even in Marin County, which then was a pretty small place on the map as far as legal practice was concerned.

MURPHY: *You mentioned that you are writing another novel. Does that involve the high tech industry at all?*
TOWNSEND: Yes. Actually I'm writing something that addresses the biotech industry which is in fact headed toward where we've seen the electronics industry. And the two are very related of course. I think more and more we'll be giving lots of thought to what goes on in the biotech area.

MURPHY: *Are you dealing with things like the human genome?*
TOWNSEND: Yes, very much and again raising some serious questions. But if we can present them in a way that keeps them light and interesting, I think it will be an interesting topic.

M. DIANE VOGT

Florida lawyer M. Diane Vogt has published a series of legal suspense novels with United States District Court Judge Willa Carson as the protagonist. Married to a Tampa restaurateur, Judge Carson enjoys dining at her husband's restaurant, eating Cuban sandwiches, and drinking Ybor Gold beer.

But she's also an avid runner. While training for the Gasparilla Distance Classic, she eats with abandon, savoring the Gasparilla Goldbrick, "golden vanilla ice cream, coated with butter toffee chocolate sauce that hardens into a sort of classy Eskimo Pie with crushed pecans on top." It's served in a pirate ship-shaped dish with a chocolate coin wrapped in gold foil on the side. "The coin is embossed with the face of the legendary Jose Gaspar, for whom the month's festivities were named, on one side and his pirate ship on the other."

Vogt's novel *Gasparilla Gold* features huge parties, parades with floats that rival Mardi Gras, jewelry theft, bank fraud, and murder. In addition to investigating the apparent murder of her secretary's husband during Tampa's Gasparilla Pirate Festival, Judge Carson must also deal with personal matters. Her stepfather, she learns, has remarried, and his wife is younger than Judge Carson. And worst of all, the new wife is already pregnant.

A member of both the Florida and Michigan bars, Diane Vogt practices medical products liability defense in jurisdictions around the country. Vogt graduated from Oakland University in 1974 and Wayne State University Law School in 1980. Active in the Mystery Writers of America, she currently serves as a member of the Edgar award committee selecting the best original paperback novel of 2002 and was recently elected a member of the Florida Chapter's Board of Directors. She is also a principal in PeopleWealth, providing retention services to improve job satisfaction for lawyers.

This interview took place in 2003.

FICTION: *Silicone Solution* (1999), *Justice Denied* (2000), *Gasparilla Gold* (2002), *Six Bills* (2003); *Marital Privilege* (2004)

NONFICTION: *Keeping Good Lawyers: Best Practices to Create Career Satisfaction* (2000); *The Little Book of Bathroom Crime Puzzles* (2006)

MURPHY: *Willa Carson is a Federal District Judge, married, no children. What characteristics of Willa Carson interested you so much to build a series around her?*
VOGT: Willa has been described by reviewers as "one of the most original and likable characters to come along in years." I believe there are several reasons why. First, she's a judge and there aren't that many novels featuring a main character that's a judge. The

only other one that I know of is Margaret Maron's Judge Deborah Knott series, which is very different from Willa Carson. So that was one thing, that it was a different line of work for a protagonist in a mystery series. Willa has a lot of eccentricities which people find either interesting or amusing. And I wrote Willa to be heroic. She has heroic characteristics. She's the kind of person who is going to help people who are less fortunate than herself, or put herself in danger to assist someone who needs help or someone who's in trouble. She has somewhat of a privileged lifestyle which wasn't given to her, which she worked for and that makes her interesting as well.

MURPHY: *As a judge, she would be held to a higher standard of behavior I think than a lawyer or any other lay person in terms of her moral code. And I found that in reading the book she generally holds up well to that higher standard except there were a couple of instances that I thought were out of character. One was when she went to Margaret Wheaton's house and basically absconded with evidence. I found that hard to accept from a federal district judge.*

VOGT: I hate to say the fact that Willa is a federal judge has been something of a blessing and a curse for me as a writer. I made her a federal judge because I wanted her to have a lifetime appointment. And I wanted her to be able to keep her job unless she did something sufficient to get herself impeached. And that was because – I agree with you – every judge that I know personally is very hard working, very ethical, very conscientious. Judges would never be involved in investigating murder at all and they certainly wouldn't be doing it in the way that Willa Carson does in my books. So if Willa was a state court judge, she would be subject to reelection and her unconventional activities would be a problem. It would be a very big problem. The legal community would never stand for that. I know a lot of eccentric federal court judges, and you probably do too, and I'm not saying that they do anything similar to what Willa does, because they don't, but in order to write the books, you have to take some literary license. I'm not writing nonfiction here. So every once in a while Willa definitely does things that judges would not do but her activities do advance the plot. She always does them for the right reasons and thinks she's doing the right thing.

MURPHY: *In* Gasparilla Gold, *her long time secretary, Margaret Wheaton, is suspected of murdering her husband who has ALS and is dying anyway. Willa was very close both to the victim and the suspect and it gets her into a lot of predicaments which I think make it very interesting. Was euthanasia a theme that was a motivating factor in your decision to have this in the plot?*

VOGT: Actually it was. As a writer, and you probably know this, Steve, different things spark your imagination and you pick things, an issue, a subject or a topic that would make a good story for a novel. And one of the things that happened at the time I was conceiving this book, *Gasparilla Gold*, was that there were quite a few news stories about Jack Kevorkian, as well as stories about assisted suicide among the elderly. I learned the sad truth that often an elderly couple, particularly a childless couple or a couple whose children have grown and left home, and really are in reasonably good health except one will have a terminal illness. Among this group, there's an alarming rise in assisted suicide, of one spouse taking the life of the other. There was something about that and about the typical characteristics of the couple and the way suicide occurs that I thought was a very interesting thing and something that we need to know about, something that we need to raise awareness of. Generally speaking it's the husbands who more often assist the wives in suicide because the husbands just seem unable to cope. There are sociological issues that are going on here too. But I don't think most people are aware of that and I think most people don't realize the extent to which this is really a social issue that needs to be addressed.

MURPHY: *It's interesting to have a murder mystery where at least the initial suspect is accused of killing someone for good reasons and then of course later suspects come in who have less laudable motives.*
VOGT: Exactly. And of course in real life, a motive for killing someone may be anything. Our society is divided as to whether it's okay to kill somebody for good reasons and the book explores that issue.

MURPHY: Gasparilla Gold *also focuses a lot on family life. Willa's husband George and her father Jim Harper and his new wife, Susanne Harper, and it seemed like that was a very important part of who Willa was. Her relationship to both her husband and her father.*
VOGT: Well that's right. The book starts out with her step-father having announced to her that he has in fact already remarried and his second wife is substantially younger than Willa herself. And Willa is having trouble coping with that. Again, that's something that happens a fair amount in Florida, older men marrying younger women and the other way around, but it's more often older men /younger women. Then their children and families cope with that with varying degrees of success. There are a lot of typical things that happen, but there are also a lot of unusual things that occur. Sometimes those relationships are excellent ones and sometimes they're not. But I thought it was worth exploring. I thought it was fun to write about.

MURPHY: *And I thought that it worked, the way you had them develop the relationship. Toward the end of the book they were seeing more eye to eye than at the beginning.*
VOGT: Right. I think it would have been easy to write the relationship and its conflicts in kind of a clichéd way, the new wife as a trophy wife and she's an air head and she's not very bright. That kind of caricature of the second wife would be relatively easy to write; it's done all the time. But I thought it was more interesting and more difficult to create believable characters where the second wife is a pretty smart cookie. She's pretty established and she's a strong character in her own way. She just happens to be younger than her husband. And that's not a crime. Or even necessarily a bad thing. And that's what Willa finds out.

MURPHY: Gasparilla Gold *starts with the body being found after the parade then you have to flash back for a while. You basically bypass the time of the murder and cover events after the murder. I'm wondering if that was difficult in terms of structuring the book.*
VOGT: Yes. The structure of a novel is always a deliberate choice, particularly writing a mystery. And so I made some very definite decisions about that. Then of course I had to figure out creatively a way to make it work once I decided that's what I was going to do.

MURPHY: *Tell me about the Gasparilla Pirate festival. It sounds a lot like Mardi Gras.*
VOGT: Gasparilla is an event that has been going on here in Tampa, Florida for about a hundred years, believe it or not. And it has grown over the years. It started out as an opportunity for civic-minded folk to get together and raise awareness of the area and

raise money for charity and just have a big party. They used to hold it around the same time as the state fair. And so it was just an opportunity for a party really.

MURPHY: *Gasparilla Gold seemed to deal with the past on a few levels. I thought it was a nice parallel between having the pirate festival - which as you say is over a hundred years old - at a time when at least two characters - Armstrong Yates and Gil Kelley - have their own pasts come back and haunt them. I wondered if you were consciously trying to draw this parallel.*
VOGT: Well, yes. One of the things I'm always trying to do is encourage people to challenge their assumptions. To look at things maybe in a different way, not to get too comfortable in the way they think about things. Not to get in a rut about everything. Try to see things the way they are instead of how we think they are without analyzing them. But also a theme in my books always is what I call the Karmic theory. You know, "who you are is a result of choices you've made in the past; things you've done before have formed your life and shaped you and brought you to where you are today." You know somebody said no Karmic debt goes unpaid. I was thinking about that a lot as I was writing the book. And the past is a very important indicator of what is going to happen in the future.

MURPHY: *That's an interesting comment about the choices you make determine what your life is like. I noticed you also authored a nonfiction book called* Keeping Good Lawyers. *Is that theme a part of that book?*
VOGT: Well it is. You know *Keeping Good Lawyers* is a nonfiction law office management book and also a book for individual lawyers to assist in improving their job satisfaction. It is very much a theme in that book as well that you can make choices that will make you happy but you have to make those choices. If you make other choices, you're going to end up with different results. And so yes, we talk about that a lot.

MURPHY: *So is there a list of these choices that we should know about?*
VOGT: Well you already know about them and you know what they are. You've seen this happen a number of times. Say a young lawyer who decides that he's going to borrow a hundred thousand dollars to get through school because he wants a nice car and to attend school in relative comfort. Then he goes away with a hundred thousand dollars worth of debt. Well, that means some choices, doesn't it?

MURPHY: *Then you have to work for a big firm and get a big salary.*
VOGT: And you have to work very hard for a long time. Then you find yourself with the golden handcuffs and not so happy about it. All lawyers who've practiced for any length of time know lots of people like that and some of us even did those things. So you know what those choices are. It's hardest to look at your current situation and say not only what choices did I make to get me here, but what choices can I make to get me where I want to go? And that's what we talk about a lot in *Keeping Good Lawyers.*

MURPHY: *What kind of law do you practice?*
VOGT: I do medical products liability defense. I've done that pretty much exclusively for the past ten years.

MURPHY: *Is there a lot of that litigation in Florida?*

VOGT: Yes there is. And around the country. Most medical products are miraculous frankly, and they save an awful lot of lives. It's not often that litigation against medical device manufacturers is warranted. It happens. And it's a good thing that the litigation is not successful very often because medical products are good for everybody. And so you want to have them, you have them work. And when you need them you want them to be there and do their job.

MURPHY: *It sounds like your practice was the genesis of your first novel* Silicone Solution.
VOGT: That's exactly right. I defended breast implant manufacturers and I wrote *Silicone Solution* about breast implant litigation.

MURPHY: *What motivated you to start writing fiction?*
VOGT: I think many lawyers are writers first. The practice of law is very often written work. I've been a litigator my entire career. So I've done a lot of written work because a lot of litigation is briefs and memorandums, things of that nature. So it always went hand in hand as far as I'm concerned and I have always considered myself a writer as well as a lawyer. I started writing fiction probably about 1985. I fooled around with it for a long time before I actually completed *Silicone Solution*. But I really put my mind to finishing *Silicone Solution* and getting it published about 1994.

MURPHY: *Willa Carson is the protagonist in all of your books. Is there another fiction series?*
VOGT: I'm almost finished with the out-of-series book called *Think No Evil*. The next book that will be coming out is called *Six Bills* and then *Think No Evil* will follow that.

MURPHY: *Is that going to be another series with a different protagonist?*
VOGT: It depends on the publisher. It's written as an independent stand alone and if they want it to be a series, it might end up going that direction.

MURPHY: *And who's the protagonist in that one?*
VOGT: Her name is Cyrene Newton. She's named after a Greek Goddess who was allegedly the daughter of a shepherd. And in the myth, Apollo comes upon her father's grazing land and observes Cyrene wrestling a lion and he's so impressed with her courage that he takes her back to the coast of North Africa in what is now Libya and names a city after her.

SUSAN WOLFE

Susan Wolfe's first novel, *The Last Billable Hour*, won an Edgar Award from the Mystery Writers of America for Best First Mystery Novel by an American Author. The plot involves the murder of a partner at Tweedmore & Slyde, a high tech Silicon Valley law firm.

Wolfe received her bachelor's degree in English Literature at the University of Chicago and her law degree from Stanford Law School. For four years she was associated with Wilson, Sonsini, Goodrich & Rosati in Palo Alto where she practiced trade secret, real estate and securities fraud litigation.

This interview took place in 1989.

FICTION: *The Last Billable Hour* (1989); *The Promised Hand* (2000)

NONFICTION: *From the Ground Up: Building Silicon Valley* (co-author 2002)

MURPHY: *What was the inspiration for* The Last Billable Hour?
WOLFE: I had a friend who was writing a murder mystery. She asked me to work on a murder mystery of my own so that we could get together once a month and try to talk out some of the problems that came up. That was how I started writing a book. I was pretty immersed in the legal environment and so it just made sense to work with that. I was also facing the possibility that I might not be able to go ahead with my original goal of full partnership because I felt that I didn't have enough time for other things that were important in my life. And I think ultimately I wrote the particular book I wrote, because I was trying to express why partnership might not work for me.

MURPHY: *You mean problems working all those billable hours and stopping the rest of your life?*
WOLFE: Yes. I was so immersed in what I was doing, not only in terms of the time that I was in the office, but the fact that I carried it home all the time. I felt the other parts of my life had really shrunk after four years and I wasn't sure that was something I was prepared to do for the rest of my life.

MURPHY: *Did you use any of your cases at Wilson, Sonsini as the basis for any of the plot for* The Last Billable Hour?
WOLFE: Not really. There were things I learned about the computer industry very generally that ended up in *The Last Billable Hour* but there were no specific cases that I worked on.

MURPHY: *Did you write any novels before law school?*
WOLFE: No. I had never written anything longer than a short story.

MURPHY: *That had been published?*

WOLFE: No. I only tried to publish one story right as I was realizing that writing wasn't exactly zooming along for me the way I had hoped. That was when I decided to make a switch to law.

MURPHY: *In* The Last Billable Hour *you have a number of events involving various lawyers. In particular Leo Slyde, who does various sleazy things towards his clients. Did you think that this would be a bad reflection of lawyers for lay people?*

WOLFE: I think I assumed that readers are sophisticated enough to know that you exaggerate in order to make a book work, to make it interesting. Also, from my experience many lawyers have a fairly poor reputation among lay people anyway and I'm not sure that anything I wrote harmed it.

MURPHY: *There is sort of an overriding theme in the book that money is more important than principle. Did you find that to be true in your practice?*

WOLFE: I felt that the acquisition of money was a very big motivating factor among many of the people that I worked with. I don't mean in my firm in particular, but in terms of my experience with the civil practice of law around here generally. That is not to say that I think I dealt with unprincipled people. I think that a lot of them were motivated to acquire wealth, but I don't think that they necessarily sacrificed principle along the way.

MURPHY: *Who did you think your readers would be while you were writing the book?*

WOLFE: I wasn't sure I'd ever have any readers. This book was something I did for myself. I knew it was fairly hard to get anyone to even look at a book and I wasn't sure that I'd be able to get anyone to look at mine. So, in terms of imagining a large readership, I didn't really think about it much. The people I did think about were certain specific lawyers whose intelligence and perspective I respect. I guess I was hoping that I would communicate with these specific individuals. Once I sold the book, I felt that the book might have a pretty big readership among lawyers, but I know that wasn't particularly what my publisher thought.

MURPHY: *How did you go about getting your book published?*

WOLFE: It was a very unusual experience. I've never heard of another one like it. I worked with a partner at Wilson who knew an editor named Jared Kieling at St. Martin's from their days at Princeton. When the partner heard that I was writing a book he told me I should send it to Jared. I had decided not to do it because it seemed embarrassing to try to take advantage of some personal connection. However, I was working on my book one day and Jared called me and asked if he could see the manuscript. Of course, the answer was "absolutely" and it turned out that he liked the book and bought it.

MURPHY: *Most of the book is told from the point of view of Howard Rickover the young associate who just joins the firm. Except there are a few passages in which the point of view is from the inspector Sarah Nelson. Why did you flip flop there?*

WOLFE: That was a hard problem for me. I originally wanted to do it all from one point of view because I felt that for a beginning writer it was a less complicated way to tell a story. But there were a couple of pieces of information that had to come into the book and Howard had no way of knowing them. So I ended up submitting the original manuscript with two scenes that were from Sarah's point of view, which of course my editor jumped on immediately and said that won't work. I either had to build Sarah in earlier or eliminate her entirely. I decided to bring Sarah in earlier. I did a fair amount of rewriting to include her earlier in the book.

MURPHY: *Did you rewrite in the romantic tension between Sarah and Howard?*
WOLFE: There was some of that from the very beginning but it was something that my editor wanted me to pursue. So yes, there was more of that in the final draft than there was initially.

MURPHY: *One interesting element of Howard's personality is his love of gourmet cooking. It is commented on frequently in the book. Was your inspiration for that character trait Robert Parker's Spenser?*
WOLFE: Actually, I've never read Robert Parker. No, my inspiration for that is a gourmet cook that I know.

MURPHY: *Did you start out with the idea of writing a satire?*
WOLFE: No.

MURPHY: *Do you consider your book a satire?*
WOLFE: I do. And it developed into one fairly quickly. But I didn't particularly start out to write a humorous book. I think it just developed that a lot of what I had been witnessing for several years was funny.

MURPHY: *You have one of the more interesting murder weapons in literature, the message spindle. How did you get that?*
WOLFE: I had decided on a character that I was going to kill, and I was standing by my secretary's station one day. I was picking up my message spindle and playing with it and I thought this would do it. And it did seem like it belonged in the law firm environment so that's what I used.

MURPHY: *The method of death is pericardiocentesis. Did you have to have a medical consult to get the particulars of that form of dying?*
WOLFE: Yes. And the medical consult was a friend of mine who was at dinner with me one night and I was telling her that I decided that maybe I was going to stab my victim with a message spindle. She said, "you know, there is a really clever way that you could do that" and she described it to me. Then she brought me a book that was put out by the American Heart Association that's used by paramedics in emergency situations that described it.

MURPHY: *One of the interesting things about the book that I found was that many of the clues that you lay along the road are ones that are more clues to the victim's character than to the actual murderer. Was this a planned technique?*

WOLFE: I know that once I got started with my book, the thing that interested me most was describing character. I think it's what I like to read about the most and it was certainly what I was most interested in working with. The plot became a vehicle to describe certain character traits that I thought I had been witnessing for a number of years. So in that sense perhaps the technique was deliberate.

MURPHY: *You mentioned the problem you had regarding getting information in through Sarah Nelson's point of view. Did you encounter any other problems in technique while writing the book that you hadn't anticipated?*
WOLFE: I anticipated that I was going to have a real struggle to make the story come together at all and I did. When my editor read my first draft, he felt that I needed to work on character's motivation to enable the plot to flow smoothly. I had to make it clear, for example, why Howard would agree to become so involved in something that wasn't his job when his job was overwhelming him. That was a big factor. And I spent a fair amount of time trying to make that motivation clear. My editor also felt that Howard should have been much more suspicious of Sarah all along than I had made him in the original draft. So that was another thing that I felt I had to work on.

MURPHY: *Suspicious in the sense that she was using him?*
WOLFE: Yes. He should have suspected that she wasn't just spilling everything about the case to him in a straightforward way.

MURPHY: *Were you influenced by any mystery writers in putting your book together?*
WOLFE: I don't think I could say that I was except for one aspect of Elmore Leonard, who is a writer I tremendously admire. I tried to be influenced by his dialogue. I think he is very good at realistic dialogue because he leaves out the parts of sentences that people don't say. I studied his dialogue and tried very hard to imitate it even though I have very different types of characters than he does.

MURPHY: *Were you trying to approximate the speech of lawyers in your dialogue?*
WOLFE: Oh yes.

MURPHY: *Did you encounter any special problems doing that?*
WOLFE: I don't think so. I felt that I reached the point where I could almost close my eyes and listen and hear how my characters would say things. So I felt that it worked fairly well.

MURPHY: *One of the interesting themes of the book was the ascension of Connie Valentine to partner in the firm and the problems and obstacles she had to go through. Did you find that same sort of obstacle course for a woman attorney in your practice?*
WOLFE: As far as partnership specifically, I never got close enough. I was there for four years and it's a seven year partnership track. Certainly my firm has women partners. And really the only thing I would know about obstacles are things that I have heard. I know, for example, a very big thing in many law firms is having client-getting capacity and I believe that is often a harder thing for women then it is for men. I think that may be a factor. But in terms of prejudice against women per se, I did not observe

that within my law firm. I observed it with judges a number of times but not within my law firm.

MURPHY: *Are there any interesting examples of prejudice with judges you want to relate?*
WOLFE: One example that comes to my mind is that there was a pregnant lawyer who was arguing in front of a federal judge when I was observing. Right in the middle of her argument he stopped her and he said, "How old are you?" And she told him how old she was and he said something like, "You don't look old enough to be a lawyer." The women said, "Well, one of us isn't", which caused laughter and eased the tension in the courtroom. But I can only suppose that with the client sitting there it did not make the woman look especially professional to her client.

MURPHY: *As you were going through* The Last Billable Hour, *did you have in mind any particular themes you wanted to express?*
WOLFE: The theme that developed is that the pursuit of power and money to the exclusion of other things is bad for human beings, and I guess that sort of permeates the book.

MURPHY: *You mentioned there were no mystery writers who really influenced the plot of this novel, but were there any writers at all who influenced your style?*
WOLFE: In a way I would feel arrogant saying that well known wonderful writers influenced me. But I can tell you who I wish influenced me. Flannery O'Conner who I think is quite wonderful. Henry James. Recently I read Patrick Suskin's *Perfume* which is not only a great thriller, but makes brilliant use of concrete metaphor to describe psychological states in a way I personally don't think I've seen since I read Kafka. I think he's very good. Larry McMurtry, a number of his books I've liked quite a lot. I also like Margaret Atwood. There is another mystery writer who I like very much and that's Tony Hillerman, who writes of course about contrasts between Navajo and mainstream American culture. I think his books are very interesting.

MURPHY: *Do you have plans to write another novel?*
WOLFE: Yes. I'm working on another one now.

MURPHY: *Is that on the legal profession?*
WOLFE: Yes.

MURPHY: *Can you give a hint on the plot of that one?*
WOLFE: I'm staying in Silicon Valley and this time there is going to be more involvement with clients than there was before and it's going to involve the biotech industry.

MURPHY: *Is it going to be a mystery as well?*
WOLFE: Yes.

MURPHY: *And do you plan on continuing to write in the mystery vein?*
WOLFE: I'm not sure. I have part of a plot for a mainstream novel. For now I have put it aside to work on my mystery and I'm not quite sure what I will do after that.

MURPHY: *What kind of routine do you have for writing your books?*
WOLFE: The one that I established when my daughter was five months old was that I would have twenty hours of child care a week. I would work on my book until I got a call for some kind of legal work that sounded interesting because I needed some income. So I would stop writing and use my twenty hours to work as a lawyer until I completed a project or projects and then I would go back to writing. I anticipate that I will continue doing the same, although last year I began having deadlines to meet to get the book out and for that reason I stopped doing legal contract work.

MURPHY: *Do you plan on continuing to practice law in the foreseeable future?*
WOLFE: I would like to and I think there will come a time when I will work full time as a lawyer again, but it probably won't be while my children are small.

INTERVIEWS

THE NON-LAWYERS

CLIFFORD IRVING

Clifford Irving's novel, *Trial*, is the story of Warren Blackburn, a young criminal defense attorney in Houston, who is caught in an ethical dilemma when he learns that the two murder cases he is defending are related. As Blackburn begins to prepare both cases for trial, he uncovers a single piece of evidence that can acquit one defendant and sacrifice the other.

A prolific author of both fiction and nonfiction, Irving is most famous for his *Autobiography of Howard Hughes*. In 1971 Irving claimed Hughes had authorized him to write a biography. Although Hughes had been a recluse for a decade, he denounced Irving in a telephone conference. Forced to return the $765,000 advance, Irving also was convicted for the hoax, and spent fourteen months in federal prison.

Irving is a graduate of Cornell University.

This interview took place in 1991.

FICTION: *On A Darkling Plain* (1956); *The Losers* (1957); *The Quick and the Loving* (1957); *The Valley* (1960); *The Thirty-Eighth Floor* (1965); *On a Darkling Plain* (1972); *The Death Freak* (1979); *The Sleeping Spy (1979); Tom Mix and Pancho Villa* (1981);*The Angel of Zin* (1983); *The Losers; The Valle; Trial* (1990); *Final Argument* (1993); *The Spring* (1996)

NONFICTION: *The Battle of Jerusalem: The Six-Day War of Jun, 1967* (1967); *Fake! The Story of Elmyr De Hory, the Greatest Art Forger of Our Time* (1969); *Spy: The Story of Modern Espionage* (1969); *Autobiography of Howard Hughes* (1971); *Clifford Irving: What Really Happened; His Untold Story of the Hughes Affair* (1972); *Project Octavio* (1977); *The Hoax* (1981); *Daddy's Girl: The Campbell Murder Case* (1988)

MURPHY: *With all the lawyers writing courtroom dramas these days, what made you take on a book like* Trial?

IRVING: I had written a book called *Daddy's Girl*, a true account of a brutal 1982 double murder in Houston and the ensuing trials. I spent about a year and a half in Houston researching and writing. When I finished I was still immersed in the fascinating and absurd world of criminal justice. I knew many lawyers and judges and I had their confidence. Momentum carried me into *Trial*. There was a tremendous amount of leftover research. I had recorded trial proceedings, sometimes with permission and sometimes without. I felt that many issues I had discussed in *Daddy's Girl* needed further elucidation and there were many issues I hadn't touched on that I wanted to deal with. I came out of the *Daddy's Girl* experience with at least half a dozen plots for books and *Trial* was the first one.

MURPHY: *Did you find any difficulty switching from true crime to fiction?*

IRVING: No, I was fed up with true crime by the time I finished with that book. I was fed up with getting into arguments with district attorneys and judges who didn't like what I had written about them and also didn't like the feeling that they couldn't control my actions.. When I began writing *Daddy's Girl* I made it clear to all the lawyers that anything they said which wasn't specifically off the record, I could use, but interviewees tend to forget the stipulations. The prosecutor was particularly annoyed with me when the defense called me as a trial witness - because my investigative research proved that other witnesses were lying. I didn't seek that kind of involvement, but I couldn't really avoid it. When it was over, I thought, I'm going back to my study in Mexico and shut the door and write a novel, and nobody is going to interfere with me while I do it.

MURPHY: *Other than the work you did in preparing to write* Daddy's Girl, *what preparation did you do for* Trial?

IRVING: I did a lot of interviewing of lawyer friends of mine. Not so much formal interviewing, but we would be talking at the dinner table sometimes and I would say, "Do you mind if I record this?" They almost always said, "No, go right ahead." And so I had a ton of good background material. I talked to people endlessly and read as many books as I could on the law. Most of my research came from one-to-one dealing with lawyers. There was a criminal defense attorney in Houston who took me around with him for three straight days on his round of appointments and settings in various courts and let me sit in with him in the office when he interviewed clients. Of course, he asked their permission first and they all agreed with the understanding that it wasn't to be used for any non-fictional purposes. That I would observe whatever confidentiality was operative. Some judges let me sit in chambers during conferences. People got used to me and they trusted me.

MURPHY: *Did you find yourself hindered very much by the fact that you aren't a lawyer?*

IRVING: Yes and no. Not being a lawyer, there was a great deal of technical stuff and jargon that I didn't understand. But also there was a great deal I was able to challenge things most lawyers take for granted, such as the concept of confidentiality. That led directly to my plot for *Trial*. Lawyers love to talk. When you are with a gang of lawyers at night, even if they are with their wives and husbands, ninety percent of their conversation is about law cases and courtroom gossip. Occasionally, they get on to other subjects, but only with reluctance. In effect, it was easy to do the research. I had a lot of fun.

MURPHY: *In* Trial, *the protagonist, Warren Blackburn, tries to maintain the confidentiality of communications with his client, even though he doesn't want to. And in the end, he really, in a way, breaches some client confidences. Is that what you mean when you look beyond what lawyers normally look at?*

IRVING: I tried to look deeper, not beyond. I had the liberty, since I was a novelist and wasn't dealing with the life and death interest of a real-life client, to stretch the law to its extreme, and also the privilege to make my protagonist, Warren Blackburn, deeply concerned with the moral issues - whereas very often I found lawyers didn't give a damn. Many had a fixed idea of what the moral issues would be and they could make their decisions in a few seconds. I could take liberties and I could go deeper than most lawyers often do. I'm sure there are many lawyers who struggle with such issues but I found for the most part, they don't.

MURPHY: *The dust jacket for* Trial *summarizes the two cases that Warren Blackburn is handling and, it seems to me, gives away a lot of suspense by telling us the two cases are related. Did you object to he publisher doing that?*
IRVING: No, I wrote a good part of the dust jacket copy. And that's probably a hangover from the fact that in an early draft of the novel you knew from the beginning that the two cases were related. And I didn't see any sense in writing the novel and pretending that they weren't. Otherwise, I felt that the reader was going to wonder, 'Why am I reading about two such disparate cases?' I felt the strengths of the book didn't come from the surprise, but from the reader's wondering how is the lawyer going to get out of the mess he's in and resolve the dilemma of the two cases being so stunningly related. So I wanted the reader to know the secret as early as possible.

MURPHY: *Blackburn eventually does, without giving away the ending, manage to effect justice as well as maintain his integrity as a lawyer. One aspect of that, which I thought your consultants may have objected to, was that he never tried to withdraw from either case.*
IRVING: You're right, that was the first solution that most lawyers gave me. They said, 'Well, I'd get out of the case. I'd withdraw.' And I said, "That's all well and good, but I don't have a novel if my hero does that." Besides, there's an element of cowardice to withdrawing. It's saying, "I can't face this. I can't fight it so I'll step out." And I tried to set up a situation in the book where it was extremely difficult for Warren to step out because he knew the lawyer who took his place would plea bargain and the innocent defendant would get 40 or 50 years. So I made Warren take the higher road, make the more difficult decision, hang in there and stay with the case. But, of course, I knew that he was going to be triumphant in the end. That's why fiction is so much more uplifting than life.

MURPHY: *The women in* Trial *are generally portrayed negatively. You have Judge Lou Parker, who shouts at Blackburn 'This is my courtroom' and she wants to run the proceedings and push them towards a plea bargain; Blackburn's adulterous wife, Charm, who has no charm; Johnny Faye Boudreau, one of Blackburn's clients, a racist, murdering owner of a topless nightclub. Why such a negative portrayal of women?*
IRVING: It wasn't meant to be that way, but I became aware in the writing that this was happening. And in effect, the inclusion of Maria Hahn, the court reporter, was meant to offset the negative attitude toward women that the book seemed to have. One of the problems that I faced was that I wanted a woman judge and Judge Lou Parker in the novel is based on a couple of judges I know in Houston.

MURPHY: *Are they woman judges?*
IRVING: Yes. And most of the lawyers I knew were well aware of the problem of these women judges. But it wasn't any malice on my part. I am certainly not anti-women. Johnnie Faye Boudreau is based on a woman now serving a life sentence in a Texas penitentiary. And I didn't have it in for Charm. I had respect for Charm and didn't try to write a negative character. Her adultery was a result of a vision that her

husband was falling apart in life and not the man she married. And maybe she was right in that. There was one rave review of the book by Caroline See in the Los Angeles Times who said that Charm was too perceptive for her own good. And in a way, that's what I meant. I'm sad about what happened to Warren and Charm. Indeed, in the first draft of the book they get back together again. But most readers didn't like that, so I succumbed to my constituency: my wife, my friends, my editor.

MURPHY: *The other case Blackburn is defending involves Hector Quintana, a homeless Mexican, who is charged with killing a Vietnamese father and husband. What kind of social statement were you trying to make here, having a Mexican and a Vietnamese as victims?*

IRVING: I noticed when I was in Houston - and everywhere else for that matter - that murders involving minorities, particularly blacks and Hispanics, are relatively unimportant in the eyes of the law. The trappings of justice are there but unless it's a high profile case, most cases are quickly plea bargained. Or, if they go to trial, they're moved with startling rapidity through the trial process. If a black kills a black, that is the least important thing that can happen in the criminal justice system. If a white person is killed, there's attention paid. I don't think I had that in mind as specifically as your question implied, but I knew it in my bones, having hung around the courts for a year and a half.

MURPHY: *There is another recent novel about the Texas criminal justice system,* Fade the Heat *by Jay Brandon that also negatively portrays the system. Did you find anything positive about the Texas criminal justice system?*

IRVING: Yes I did. I think the system is fine, but the people who run it aren't up to the mark. They're caught up in the problems of personal ambition. I didn't see anything wrong *per se* with Houston's unusual system of defending indigents, the appointing of lawyers by the judges as opposed to the existence of a public defender. It would work very well if people weren't venal and if the judges weren't in such a perverse hurry to clear their calendars. I suppose my greatest anger in Texas was at the judges - I saw judge after judge who would want to leave that courtroom before 3 or 4 pm because he or she was used to having a very short day. And therefore any lawyer who threatened to take a client to trial became a thorn in the side of the smooth process of what that judge considered justice. I found that reprehensible. I also found most of the prosecuting attorneys I met were mean-minded, small people. Not all, but most, and most is a hell of a lot too many. And a great many of the criminal defense attorneys were primarily interested in making money and moving their cases along rapidly. Not the ones who befriended me and helped me do the research on the book, but others whom I brushed up against. You know, all that is what I was angry about. Not so much the system but the human nature that inevitably fuels that system.

MURPHY: Trial *has received generally favorable treatment from the critics. Some, though, have called the book "lightweight reading." What is your reaction to that criticism?*

IRVING: The only review I read that said it was lightweight was Linda Wolfe, in The New York Times. Linda Wolfe probably thinks Hemingway and Scott Fitzgerald are lightweight because they're not deeply introspective and keep a rein on their adjectives. My prose may be smooth but there is a great deal of subtext, I feel, in the book. Things aren't said but are between the lines so the reader can grasp them. Sometimes a reviewer reads so quickly under time pressure that she doesn't get a chance to read the subtext, which a reader in the leisure of the living room can do. Anyway, William Safire, also in the New York Times, called Trial "novel of the year." So who do you believe, Linda Wolfe or William Safire?"

MURPHY: *Some of your earlier books mentioned in your biography, the notorious unpublished* Autobiography of Howard Hughes. *Why was this omitted from the bio in* Trial*?*
IRVING: My publisher cut it out.

MURPHY: *Any particular reason?*
IRVING: (Laughter) He's shyer than I am.

MURPHY: *I know you've written* The Hoax, *explaining the Hughes affair. For our readers who aren't familiar with that book, can you briefly explain what motivated you to write the* Autobiography of Howard Hughes*?*
IRVING: You're talking twenty years ago. It's awfully hard to remember motivation. I think my best memory is that I was bored. I thought it might be an exciting thing to do. I have to believe now it was a measure of my immaturity at the time.

MURPHY: *You wrote another book called* Fake: The Story of Elmyr de Hory, the Greatest Art Forger of Our Time. *I detect a lot of parallels between* Fake *and* The Hoax. *Did Elmyr de Hory inspire you?*
IRVING: "Inspire" would be hyperbole. He influenced me, I think, and having written that book in the late 60s I was involved for a time in the world of fakery. And I was fascinated by it. Undoubtedly some of that rubbed off on me and allowed me to make the moral lapse that led to the bogus *Autobiography of Howard Hughes*.

MURPHY: Do you have any plans to write more courtroom dramas?
IRVING: I'm in the middle of one right now. It's called *Unusual Punishment* and it's about a Florida lawyer, a prosecutor, who retires, becomes a criminal defense attorney. Ten years later he learns that in his last case, the man he prosecuted and sent to death row, was probably innocent. So he comes back to defend the man he once prosecuted. In that sense it's about the death penalty, because it does deal with the strange practices of primitive ritual murder - *lex talionis* - that we practice in this country.

MURPHY: *Does this have a Texas setting as well?*
IRVING: No, it's set in Florida, Jacksonville and Sarasota. I chose Florida because of certain bizarre aspects of their court system. In a Florida capital case, there's a bifurcated - if a guilty verdict is reached in the first stage, the jury goes on to deliberate and recommend a punishment. It can be either life in prison or death by electrocution. But the judge can overrule that recommendation. That's also true in tow other states: Indiana and Georgia. Indiana, in the last twelve years, has had one such reversal. Georgia's had four or five. In Florida, judges in more than eighty cases have overturned a jury's recommendation of life and told the defendant, "You'll fry." And many have. That's barbaric. That's frightening and anti-human. That's why I set *Unusual Punishment* in the Sunshine State.

MURPHY: *Is this a beginning of a new genre of writing for you?*
IRVING: I don't know. I take books one at a time. It's tempting to keep at it because one establishes a safe readership. But in a sense, every time I write a book I feel as if I were going on a journey. It's an adventure and I don't like making the same trip each time. So I doubt that I'll be able to write too many of these books. Maybe I'll have to write them alternately. I'll write something else after I finish *Unusual Punishment* and then write another book about criminal justice. I do have a bunch of ideas about novels dealing with lawyers and judges and courtrooms and, as you gather, I'm fascinated by the subject. But you need a break every now and then. Can't just tread in your own footsteps.

MURPHY: *Everyone insisted I ask you if you have any plans to write more autobiographies.*
IRVING: (Laughter) Just my own - in three volumes. I've had an interesting life.

JOHN LESCROART

John Lescroart's *Hard Evidence* features the unusual twist of a deputy district attorney who first prosecutes a murder case then, when that prosecution proves unsuccessful, turns around to defend the second suspect. While moonlighting at the Steinhart Aquarium, deputy DA Dismas Hardy finds a finger with a jade ring in the belly of a shark. After the finger is identified as belonging to Owen Nash, a wealthy Silicon Valley executive and martial arts expert, his mistress, glamorous call girl May Shinn, is arrested for the murder. Hardy wants the assignment but is forced to take second chair to Elizabeth Pullios, a sexy, ambitious prosecutor. When Hardy is ultimately fired, he decides to defend the second suspect, a former superior court judge.

Although not a lawyer, Lescroart did work for several years in the word processing department of a large Los Angeles law firm. He is a graduate of the University of California, Berkeley and lived for many years in San Francisco where he tended bar at The Little Shamrock, a Sunset district bar featured prominently in Lescroart's three Dismas Hardy novels.

This interview took place in 1993.

FICTION: *Sunburn* (1981), *Son of Holmes* (1986), *Rasputin's Revenge* (1987), *Dead Irish* (1989), *The Vig* (1990); *Hard Evidence* (1993); *The 13th Juror* (1994); *A Certain Justice* (1995); *Guilt* (1997); *The Mercy Rule* (1998); *Nothing But the Truth* (1999); *The Hearing* (2001); *The Oath* (2002); *The First Law* (2003); *The Second Chair* (2004); *The Motive* (2005); *The Hunt Club* (2006); *The Suspect* (2007)

MURPHY: *Your previous novels were primarily straight mysteries, and with* Hard Evidence *you've entered the legal thriller genre. What made you change direction?*
LESCROART: I don't see it as so much a change in direction as a kind of logical outgrowth of the character, Dismas Hardy. In *Dead Irish*, he was a burned-out case because of an earlier tragedy and he comes back to life during that book. Then in *The Vig*, he continued that process - he falls in love with his current wife - and finally in *Hard Evidence* he comes full circle. He gets back to his vocation, his family, and the life he was meant to live. I didn't in any way plan to jump on the legal thriller bandwagon.

MURPHY: *With all the lawyers writing legal thrillers these days, were you nervous at all about getting into this field?*
LESCROART: Yes. It's very strange because I have no prosecutorial or defense background at all. I have several friends in the District Attorney's Office in San Francisco and I was very interested in many of the cases I'd heard them talking about. But when I went ahead and tried to imagine doing a trial and all the courtroom stuff, it

was very challenging. I spent a lot of time actually in courtrooms, in the departments at Superior Court.

MURPHY: *The plot of* Hard Evidence *involves a wealthy Silicon Valley executive, Owen Nash, who was found murdered at sea. Were you inspired by any actual news events in coming up with this plot?*

LESCROART: No, but what's interesting is since I wrote it, several of the things that happened in this book have happened in real life. Not the least of which is that they actually found a shark almost within a week of the day that this book began. They found a shark almost precisely where I have him found: off the Farallones. He is brought to the Steinhart Aquarium, where he lives for two days. They have also recently found a hand washed up, believe it or not, on Stinson Beach. All of these pretty amazing coincidences have happened, even so far as where I predicted, or the book predicts, the exact day of the beginning of the end of the California drought. So it's been kind of weird seeing all this come to pass.

In terms of Owen Nash himself, he's just a character that I thought of quite a few years ago, and he became more and more larger than life as I worked with him more. I had a few drafts of this book quite a few years ago that I saved. First I had him being - not really a low rent guy - but almost like an owner of a television repair shop, and he just became more and more phenomenal. It's not a roman a clef in the sense that he's like a Donald Trump figure or anybody like that. He is a pretty unique billionaire, but he is definitely someone now that I feel like I know and I almost feel like he was a real person.

MURPHY: *Any chance of doing a prequel to cover the life of Owen Nash?*

LESCROART: That would be nice. You know, it's something I hadn't really thought of. I don't know. I think because everybody knows the fundamental truth of what a villain he is - and I think he is the true villain of the piece even though he's the ostensible victim in the book - I don't see it. I mean the back story on him is so perverse, that I don't see how I could create much sympathy for him. If I kept it in with the ending of *Hard Evidence*.

MURPHY: *Dismas Hardy finds the finger in the shark, assists in prosecuting the first suspect, May Shinn, then turns around and defends the second suspect. Did your lawyer friends express any disbelief over this kind of a conflict situation?*

LESCROART: Almost to a man and a woman, they said it would be a challenge to make it believable. One of the San Francisco DA's, a guy named Jim Costello, told me about a case where there was a District Attorney who was involved in prosecuting a Hell's Angel case. Then he left to become a defense attorney in the same case. Costello essentially gave me the way - and this is typical of so many of the DAs that have helped me out. He said in this case, of course, his representation was disallowed, but you could do the following. And he gave me a very plausible legal reason that Hardy could be allowed to do this, which was that he was second chair in that investigation never was affiliated with the defendant. Actually the only thing tying the two cases together was the victim, not the defendant or the second defendant. So this is an example of how these legal issues get resolved. I have it read by enough people and the ideas get bounced around, I'm pretty convinced that all the legal stuff holds up very well. Even though I know it's a little outrageous, but it's fiction, and it's fun.

MURPHY: *You actually have the parts of two trials in the book, which is unusual in legal thrillers. What did you do to try to avoid the boredom of repetition?*
LESCROART: The main thing was that I didn't have May Shinn get to trial. A lot of her case was police work and procedural stuff and then the background work of my other attorney in the book, David Freeman, who does the leg work himself and discovers the alibi. So you see a lot of the courtroom, but it's a little deceptive because there really isn't a trial going on. A lot of the stuff that's going on is behind the scenes procedural stuff. You really don't get into the "I object, Your Honor" type trial, until the second suspect's trial.

MURPHY: *You got a review in* The Chronicle *which I guess you'd call mixed. It praised the book but also commented on flimsy motives and things like Hardy getting involved in the case, becoming a prosecutor, then turning around and becoming the defense attorney, defending a former relative of his. How do you respond to those kinds of criticisms?*
LESCROART: I have to say, first: that's the only negative review I've gotten in the country.

MURPHY: *And it's at home ...*
LESCROART: At home, yeah. And, frankly, The Chronicle has always given me negative reviews. That review hurt, especially because it was in my home town, and I thought the review was not particularly on point. I thought it was a very schizophrenic review. To that extent, it didn't hurt me, but I want people to like my books and I certainly think there was nothing unreadable about *Hard Evidence* and nothing so implausible as to render it gimmicky or melodramatic even. It's a very real story, given that it's fiction, and I really went to great pains to make these stories real. And I am sorry that in my home town of San Francisco they don't seem to believe it. However, you know I was written up last week in the San Mateo Times and the reviewer said that this was much grander than a mystery novel, more than just entertainment and totally believable in every respect. So this is just part of being in the writing game.

MURPHY: *One of* The Chronicle's *comments was that readers would pick up on the murderer long before Dismas Hardy actually did.*
LESCROART: Some probably will, some won't. But this is not a mystery in the sense that, for example, Steve Martini's *Compelling Evidence*, was a mystery. This was very much more a character study. If you find out who did it maybe sixty pages before the end of a five hundred-page book, I don't really think that's horrible. And I didn't try to hold off until the very end because I also had to have a way to tie up the ending. You had to know where it was going a little bit sooner than with a straight mystery.

MURPHY: *This is your third novel involving Dismas Hardy. What makes him such an intriguing character to you?*
LESCROART: He has very real concerns. My publisher wants to have him in the mold of, say, Sam Spade, or a real private investigator type. From the beginning I have never viewed him in that light at all. I have viewed him as kind of a regular guy who

gets involved emotionally in most of the issues that people my age grew up with -- Viet Nam, the drug culture, all of that stuff. He's not a loner private eye type. And what makes him so great -- and I truly love this guy -- is that he's very real. He's married, he's got kids, he's going through a lot of what most of my friends are going through. And he's also involved in interesting cases. My writer friends are writing interesting books and my lawyer friends are trying interesting cases and they've all got real lives. And I think, in Hardy's case, I'm trying to make him be of out of the genre of that kind of hard-boiled, mystery guy. He's a regular human being with real feelings and a real life and real day-to-day problems and I think it makes him much more dimensional.

MURPHY: *The family aspect is prevalent in the books. Hardy's ex-wife comes in and out; he lost a son early in life, and he sees his former father-in-law frequently. Is the family aspect of these novels integral?*

LESCROART: Absolutely. It's who Hardy is. I think you can see it in the fact that he fell out of his career and his marriage through his first family breaking up. His son died, and it tore him apart so badly that it ruined his universe. And that's kind of the arc that I follow in these books, where his universe is being restored. The first step in the restoration of all of that cosmic stuff is putting his family back together. He's put to rest his first marriage and his relationships in that marriage and then he is free to start a new life. And there are a lot of actual references in the book to those exact issues.

MURPHY: *Hardy works initially with and then against the Assistant DA, Elizabeth Pullios, who is an attractive, single woman in the DA's office who has affairs with other members of the staff. Was this character designed as a contrast to Hardy, the "family man"?*

LESCROART: Absolutely. But this character also has her true life counterpart. I can't say real person, but she is certainly an amalgam of several women that I've run across, both in the law world and in the regular business world. I know this is perhaps a politically incorrect thing to say, but there are women who are nasty. Nasty and ambitious. And, as a matter of fact, there is a woman district attorney who I know who was engaged to a friend of mine. When he left the District Attorney's Office to go into private practice to do defense work, she in fact left him for that reason.

MURPHY: *She couldn't be with a defense lawyer?*

LESCROART: With somebody who was going to be a scum ball defense lawyer. This is true, and that's in fact the impetus for her character. I was out with this guy and he told me this story and I said "Well, there's my DA!" So, this is a real person. I think she's a blast to read about because she's a person you love to hate and that's nice.

MURPHY: *Hardy has a friend on the police force, Abe Lipski, a black Jewish detective. Why the interesting ethnic background?*

LESCROART: One of my best friends has the same background. He's a dentist in Santa Cruz and he's a wonderful guy and it's just such a strange background, I've given Abe Lipski a scar on his lips that my friend doesn't have. But other than that I just thought it was a great background and I love the jokes on when he has a white father and goes to places or refers to his father as white. There is so much posturing on the racial level that I just poke fun at from the inside on both sides, and I think Lipski serves that purpose really well.

MURPHY: *Your publisher and a lot of the reviewers have called* Hard Evidence *your breakthrough novel. What makes it your breakthrough novel?*
LESCROART: I hope it's a breakthrough novel. Most of Europe has bought it for pretty good money. It's got a movie option through Citadel Films, which is a division of Time-Warner. It's been picked up by Fawcett for paperback, and I think it's also just a bigger, more mainstream, read. This goes back to your earlier question about when you find out who did it. As I said then, I don't think it's a question of being a mystery. I think it's a mainstream read now and you can't put it in any kind of a noire, or hard-boiled genre way. You have to say, well, this is just a book. And I think that's why it's a breakthrough and I sure hope it continues.

MURPHY: Dead Irish, *your first Hardy novel, got a Shamus nomination. How has that helped your sales?*
LESCROART: I would say it had no effect in any way. I didn't even know about it, number one, until the Shamus nomination awards dinner. No one told me.

MURPHY: *Were you at the dinner?*
LESCROART: I was at the dinner only because it was in Pasadena, which is where I lived at the time. It was really funny because people like Sue Grafton and Larry Block came up to me, introducing themselves. They were nice and polite, I mean super nice, like we were going to be buddies, and I'm going "Wow. These are the stars! What are they talking to me for!" You know, there are nine hundred people there. Then they announce the nominees and they go Sue Grafton, Larry Block, John Lescroart.... And I go "Whoa. Good," But it has had no effect at all. It's been very weird. I don't know why. I think it was because it was a year even after the paperback came out or something. So, I'm hoping that other awards just kind of catch up. I think it's helped in the sense that people in the industry know that I got the nomination. So it's kind of given some credibility to the later two books, but that's about it.

MURPHY: *Are you working on any film or TV deals with* Hard Evidence?
LESCROART: I have the option for *Hard Evidence*, and I really would love it if that got picked up. Obviously, that would be a fantastic situation. But, my wife is going to be quitting work on May 1st and at that time I really intend to get into production work in writing. I'm going to try to write novels in the morning and really keep cranking because I think this is the time when the iron is hot and I intend to strike. I've got lots of connections now in Hollywood through this book and lots of people have read it and seem to like it quite a bit. My credibility is high, so I'm going to try to pursue what can be done with it.

MURPHY: *Are you working on another Hardy novel?*
LESCROART: Yes. A Hardy novel called *One For the Money.*

MURPHY: *What's that about?*

LESCROART: It's another trial drama set in San Francisco. Its theme is going to be the battered wife defense. I can't say that's really exactly what it's about, but it concerns a major insurance fraud and a battered wife defense.

MURPHY: *Is Hardy on the defense side again?*

LESCROART: Hardy is a straight defense attorney. In fact, he's working with David Freeman as his co-counsel on a murder case.

HAL LIPSET

For nearly half a century San Francisco private detective Hal Lipset worked on some of this country's most notorious cases, including Watergate and People's Temple. Many of these cases are recounted in Patricia Holt's *The Bug in the Martini Olive: And Other True Cases from the Files of Hal Lipset, Private Eye*. Holt, Book Review Editor for the San Francisco Chronicle, worked as an investigator for Lipset in the mid-seventies.

The title refers to Lipset's testimony before a Senate subcommittee on eavesdropping in 1965:

> The senators kept asking about the martini glass. I had the pointer on it, then I'd move it away, and a question from yet another senator would bring me back. This was an actual martini glass? they would ask. Oh, yes, with an olive as a microphone and the toothpick as the antenna, I would answer. And would it work with gin actually in the glass, they'd ask, or with an onion, say, in a Gibson martini, or a lemon peel....

The book was later released in paperback under a new title, The Good Detective. At the time of this interview, Lipset was still working out of his Victorian home on Pacific Heights, where this interview took place, and teaching a course on the fundamentals of investigation at the University of San Francisco School of Law, one of the first courses of its type in the country. Hal Lipset passed away in 1997.

This interview took place in 1992.

NONFICTION: *The Bug in the Martini Olive* (with Patricia Holt) (1981); (released in paperback as *The Good Detective*)

MURPHY: The Bug in the Martini Olive *talks a great deal about your work with electronic surveillance, and the innovations you've made in bugging and eavesdropping. One gets the impression that you spent a lot of time on electronic surveillance. Has it really been that great of percentage of your practice?*
LIPSET: It's next to nothing now. And it never was a great deal even in the 50's and the 60's when it was most prevalent - when it was a grey area - before the laws passed in '67 statewide and '68 federal. But in actuality, I really would not know how to solder two wires together. I'm not an electronics technician. What I did was see the benefit to society in its search for the truth - which we hope is what we're searching for - of the recording technique, the actual ability to take and preserve what somebody says on a recorded medium and use it in the legal milieu. I was an early person advocating the use of it. And I did, in fact, record literally hundreds of interviews that I had with people,

mostly where they were witnesses. And it was mostly one-party consent type of recordings. I knew it was being recorded and they didn't. And I did it wherever I could because I found that when I had to take the stand to impeach a witness who had given me a statement, that I was always attacked as a paid professional for the other side. While I felt that I was a non-biased objective investigator, just reporting the facts, the other side of any case would attack me as being paid by my client. They would claim that everything I had to say was suspect. I felt that the recording gave me a chance of proving the truth.

You've seen some examples in the book. There are literally hundreds of examples where tapes made that way were successful in getting the result that was more desirable for our clients. I think the California law is a knee-jerk reaction. Everybody thinks that a tape can be falsified and it's just not that easy to falsify a tape, as Mr. Nixon will tell you since it's exactly twenty years ago of the anniversary of Watergate, which proves the fact to me. If he could have falsified those tapes, he'd still be President. I just think that the tape is too good a means of getting at the truth and should be used more, not legislated out of existence.

It always reminds me of the way some tribes of Indians didn't want their picture taken by a camera, but we don't make pictures illegal. The best example is the fact that every year there has been a bill in the legislative hopper to make it illegal for anybody to take a video or motion picture of claimants who are suspected of malingering. The difference between the fact that you can't secretly tape record somebody now, which is the law, and the fact that there's still no law against taking photographs of somebody who may be a phony insurance claimant, is that the insurance companies have bigger lobbies than lawyers.

The lawyers, of course, were so asleep at the switch they didn't even fight the recording bill. That was passed because Jesse Unruh, who was the Speaker - the Willie Brown of his day - was actually recorded by a freshman legislator. And he said that will never happen again while I'm in the legislature. He put in that bill, twisted everybody's arm and it passed.

MURPHY: *What happened to all the old devices you used, the martini olive, the pens?*
LIPSET: I've still got a number of them. They were really never used. They were just devised to show the state of the art. The martini olive is a true story. They wanted something very catchy. They didn't know how catchy they were gonna get.

MURPHY: *Have you thought of opening a museum with all these pieces?*
LIPSET: Not really. The original martini olive transmitter stayed there at the Senate hearings. I don't know who's got it. Senator Long was the senator at that time. Bud Fensterwald was his administrative aid, who together with me helped dream it up. He's dead now. I don't know who's got the martini olive.

Novell, a computer software system, just ran advertisements in Time magazine and U.S. News and World Report. They ran double page spreads, advertising their Novell system. They used as a graphic the martini olive, the martini glass, the toothpick and a tape recorder in their advertisement. And it was funny; it came out just about the same time my book came out. And they never even knew, of course, that I was known as the inventor of that. Just the timeliness of it was very interesting.

MURPHY: *The book quotes you extensively. What technique was used to do this?*
LIPSET: The gestation of the book was when Pat and I sat down, she asked a few questions and I dictated twenty tapes. Then we were looking for a handle for the book. The only thing I knew was I didn't want a Louie Nizer book which said, thus and so and then I did a great thing. I didn't want that kind of a book. And we never could find the right handle for it. I dictated those original tapes in 1976.

MURPHY: *And it took that long to get it together?*
LIPSET: Yes, she finally got the direction and the way she wanted to weave my wife's diary into the book and the rest of it. She finally got it together about three years ago. Then we structured it. I read about eight chapters, and she sent it off, through an agent, and Little Brown bought it. That's how it happened.

MURPHY: *You mention the excerpts from your wife's diary. Were those verbatim excerpts?*
LIPSET: Yes. She was sort of keeping a fairly extensive diary, maybe with the idea of writing a book or something. But she died very young.

MURPHY: *Earlier you mentioned that this is the twentieth anniversary of Watergate. You did some work on the Watergate investigation. What was your role?*
LIPSET: My real role when I went there was to read everything. First, I was to immerse myself in what the facts were. Which meant that I had to read the Watergate trial transcript and everything that had been printed in the media. And remember, I was sworn in March the 8th, 1973. That was the day after Sam Dash was sworn in. The only staff people on the Watergate Committee at that time were Dash and a man named Fred Thompson, who was the Republican-side co-counsel, and a navy yeoman secretary, a woman, who had been brought in as the secretary for the Committee.

So my job was to read all that stuff and come up with a workable investigative plan. There was no plan. Dash was trying to understand the legal implications and find out how a committee investigator was supposed to function. And dealing with Senator Ervin and dealing with the other Senators and trying to get space and do the things you had to do to operate. Thompson was doing that same kind of thing. He was in the process of hiring an investigator to work for him. And we were being flooded with applications from lawyers and other people who wanted to become members of the staff. So when I had time I read applications and put them into piles of maybes, and this person looks good, and maybe we should do some more.

I wanted media information so I just called the Congressional Library and put a request in. And boxes of photocopies of news articles kept coming over. A lot of material. I read it all. I had a key to the office. I found an apartment across the street on the Hill, somebody's basement apartment. And I opened the office before 8:00 in the morning and I closed the office up at 11:00 at night, some fifteen to sixteen hours a day reading. It was a very tedious thing to do. But out of it I envisioned the investigative committee starting a three-pronged job with lawyers and investigators doing each part. One was the so called "dirty tricks," one was the "break-in at Watergate Headquarters" and one was the "tons of money," and what happened to the money. Those were the three areas the investigation had to go on.

MURPHY: *And you directed the investigation in those areas?*
LIPSET: That's what the plan was, that these three teams would be sent out to do their job and Dash and I would kind of oversee the whole thing and put out fires as they came up. Then eight days later - I mean we were still in the process of interviewing - Judge Sirica read McCord's letter. And that started a whole new thing. We had to go to work immediately on that. McCord was available to interview and we spent the entire weekend interviewing McCord.

And the next thing I remember was I was flying out to serve Herbert Kalmbach, Nixon's lawyer, and all the banks to freeze those accounts, because that's where some of the funds were coming from, as well as cash in the safe at CREEP.

Then I had to leave the Committee. The press was starting to get involved and was bringing up the fact that I had once been charged with a misdemeanor in New York City. I guarantee you Senator Ervin knew all about that. This is long after the Eagleton/McGovern thing and nobody went to Washington without his background being thoroughly known to everybody. I had known Sam Dash a long time. He knew all about my New York involvement. But everybody was happy. I didn't want to spend two years in Washington working for Watergate. Not at a reduced salary.

MURPHY: *Before Watergate you had an interesting case involving the Alias Witness Program. Tell me about that case.*
LIPSET: We had a man here in the Bay Area who took over Alvin Duskin's ladies garment firm, who borrowed $3,000,000 from a small business investment corporation back in New York. And was not who he claimed to be. He was a relocated witness who had testified against his bosses in the Mafia and was responsible for them going to prison. But we believed there was a multi-million dollar contract out to kill him. And he was guarded by Federal Marshals all this time and, of course, wasn't paying back the money he had borrowed. He had his wife and her family and everybody else on the payroll and was milking this company here in San Francisco. That turned out to be a lot of fun because we broke his identity.

MURPHY: *You made some changes in the Federal Witness Program as a result, I understand.*
LIPSET: I think we made a lot of changes. They started giving the witnesses a background that couldn't be penetrated. Instead of doing the silly things they were doing earlier. They didn't think anybody was ever going to look, I guess.

MURPHY: *After Watergate you got involved in another notorious case: People's Temple. You did some work for Jim Jones and for de-programmers as well. Has your work with the cults diminished since the 70's when it was more of a fad than it is nowadays?*
LIPSET: It diminished to practically nothing. The only time I'm involved now is when somebody thinks that they've got a missing teenager or a naive child the family thinks is

in the clutches of a cult. We've got to look for them. My past connections help me because I can usually find the answer without wasting a lot of time.

MURPHY: *Patricia Holt begins each chapter with a quote from a famous mystery writer - Dick Francis, Ross MacDonald for example. Are you an avid mystery reader?*
LIPSET: I like Dick Francis. I love John D. MacDonald. He's gone now. I read them all.

MURPHY: *Have you learned of any tricks for your business from reading mystery novels?*
LIPSET: No. They're just fun to read. I usually can figure out the answer when I'm about a third to half the way through.

MURPHY: *Holt also sort of compares you with the old mystery detectives and their code of ethics, honor and morals. She says time and again that you're in it only for the money. And that's the bottom line. Do you agree with her characterization of you in the book that way?*
LIPSET: I think Pat did a remarkable job in putting that book together and making it a very readable, fast paced, easy read. I like what she did. Everybody grows up and goes to work. It was the work ethic I was taught as a child. Isn't everybody in it for the money? You do something you'll hope you like to do to make your living. That's the life we're taught to lead, I think. Even with what happened in the 60's and the 70's and going on to the 80's, everybody I know leads a "normal life" - gets up in the morning and goes to work somewhere and brings home a salary, has family.

I think it's an oversimplification to say you're in it for the money. But I do say it with my tongue in cheek. Everybody gets out of work what they want to get out of it. But isn't everybody in it for the money? I mean starting with our friend President Nixon and going elsewhere. He only kept those tapes you know because he intended to make money out of him. And they were his downfall. His greed and his arrogance was his downfall. I don't think I'm greedy and I don't think I'm arrogant.

MURPHY: *Are there certain types of cases that you refuse to take?*
LIPSET: I would like to think so. But if you press me on what kind of a case I wouldn't take, the only way I could answer it is that if I take somebody's money, that I'm going to do something for them. That I'm going to accomplish something for them. And I occasionally have a client come in who tells me whatever their problem is and in evaluating the client, I get the feeling that I'm never going to be able to satisfy that person. And that's the kind of a case I don't take because there's no benefit to anybody in having that case. If a client is going to be the problem themselves, I don't want to be in it.

MURPHY: *The book describes many cases you've worked on and one gets the impression that all of your cases are glamorous. You travel to Switzerland to chase jewel thieves and work on Watergate, Jim Jones. I imagine there must be some drudgery and boredom in your job. Is that true?*
LIPSET: Yes, I think there are a lot of facets to the investigation business that are very boring. Surveillance is probably the most realistic type of job that you could consider just totally boring. To sit and watch a particular location, hoping to see someone coming or going, or sit there waiting for a particular person to come out and follow that

person to where ever they are going - is very boring. I remember sitting for five days in a location once, waiting to see something happen. And just about dusk on the fifth day the garage door opened, a car came around the corner, drove in the garage. The garage door closed and that car didn't come out for three days. Had I sneezed or chosen that moment to go to the bathroom, something happened that I'd been dozing, I might have just missed that. And that was the entire case - that car going into the garage.

That's drudgery and that's very very boring, but it's a very important part of an investigation. There are certain things you will only learn by surveillance and its something that you've got to put up with. It can be just as boring pouring through records, and yet records often flush out lots of information.

MURPHY: *What kind of tricks did you use during surveillance to keep yourself awake?*
LIPSET: You've got to fantasize forever and ever and ever. And you have to be able to sit and think, and just do something. Fortunately, I don't do much sitting out on surveillance anymore. I've paid my dues. There's somebody else around to do that. But it is a terribly, terribly boring way of spending a lot of time.

MURPHY: *You still do a lot of work for attorneys. How is your practice divided between civil cases and criminal cases?*
LIPSET: Insurance cases are all civil cases. So in civil cases it doesn't matter which side you're on. The work is still the same and its a matter of dividing your work into both a civil and a criminal practice. And I find that criminal is a lot more exciting, more fun. In a civil case, you know, the lawyer's either got to get himself a multi-million dollar verdict or he's a defense verdict where his client is not going to have to pay out a lot of money. It's a thrill always to win. That's the name of the game; that's what were in it for. By the same token, I don't think there's any greater satisfaction if you're working for a criminal defendant than that of hearing a jury come in with a "not guilty" verdict. That's a thrill. Normally that is just a lawyer and an investigator working against the arrayed majesty of the state or the federal government. And the odds are all on their side. But you are the only protection that someone who is wrongful accused of something has. So I find that still the most exciting moment for me.

The sad thing is quite often we never know the end result to a case. It's very much on my mind because I just recently learned a very sad thing about a childnapping case that I worked on in San Francisco, fourteen, fifteen years ago. The woman's parents were born in the Middle East. She married a man born in the Middle East. By the time their child was close to two, she was in the process in getting a divorce as well as custody of the child. Then the father illegally took the child back to the Middle East.

The mother came to me and wanted me to help get the child back. With my coaching the mother went to visit the father in this other country to get the lay of land. She was very bright, a courageous woman. She went over there basically to case the joint because this was in the battle zone area of Lebanon, where everybody walks around with an M-16 on their shoulder. It was in the hill towns. She phoned home every Sunday and reported. We had this code so I would ask her different questions. We recorded it so we could study what was said and not miss anything. She stayed for about two months. Finally she had all she could stand and came back. She was trying to convince him to come back with the child and he wouldn't have any part of it.

The family then decided they wanted me to try to get the child out. We did plan to do this. And you've got to mount those like a kidnapping to get them out. I have successfully done it in a number of countries. But in this case, because of where it is and everything else, I finally told the family, "I can try but this is a tough case and I'm not going to be able to guarantee you anybody's safety. We'll go in there and try to get them out. Your daughter's got to be there when this happens. And I can't guarantee her safety, I can't guarantee the child's safety and I can't even guarantee her ex-husband's safety. "Because if he starts using a weapon, everybody's going to be trying to protect themselves first." So we eventually decided not to go.

About a year later back comes the husband and claims that he and the child are in the United States. For $30,000 he will come and bring the child back and they will try to go back together again. He wants to open up a grocery story, some such baloney. It was an extortion because she went to meet him with the $30,000 and the child was not there. We got him arrested and tried for extortion and kidnapping the child originally. He got convicted and sentenced to four years in jail. We - meaning the family, myself, the court of hangers-on, the judge, everybody - thought put him in jail, return the child and we'll let him out of jail. In those days, nobody really wanted to put anybody in jail. Now they are starting to put parents in jail for this and I guess it's the only way they will ever get it straightened out. But he said "I can't give the child back. My mother won't let the child go. She says it's her child now." He went to jail and served close to two years of that sentence.

Now here's the sad part. That is all ancient history. That's over ten years ago. And I just recently heard the latest in this saga. The grandmother is now dead. The child has come back to this country. The father has remarried and has children of his own and he doesn't have any place for this kid. My client, the mother has never remarried, but so far as she's concerned this is not her child. The kid doesn't speak that much English. She hadn't seen him since he was two and he is now fifteen or sixteen. She's got no place to raise him. She's made a life without him. Now what the hell happens to that kid? So the kid was just used by everybody.

I hate to call the mother. That's sad. But I run into those kind of things every once in a while.

MURPHY: *Have you seen ebbs and flows of these kinds of cases with parents wanting to get back children?*
LIPSET: Yeah. I've seen a lot of it and I'm convinced this happened because they took fault out of divorce and stopped the fighting over money. In other words, supposedly they thought they were taking all fight out of the divorce by saying now its a dissolution and you each get half. They didn't realize that marriage and divorce has all to do with ego. And that people just have to fight when they're not going to be in love with each other any more. They have to have something to fight about. I think they fight over the children a lot strictly to use the children as a means of something to fight

over. If more women would say, "Hey, you take the kid" to the father, he wouldn't want the child so much then because men are not normally set up in their minds to take care of children as much as women are. It's just the way of life. And a man still sees himself working and likes to have a housekeeper, a nanny. He's got to supply a lot of people. I was, of course, left as a widower raising two kids so I know a little bit about it. But they were twelve and sixteen at the time. So I know a little bit about it. But I just see children being used as pawns in the hatred between the couple.

MURPHY: *Has the number of those kinds of cases been fairly steady since the start of no-fault divorce?*
LIPSET: I think so. Of course, now there's a new wrinkle. Now every time I hear of one of these cases, somebody is hollering molestation. That's the newest thing now. They say that either the father of the child is a molester of young children or the wife is a batterer or something. Most of the time, I think they make it up because there is a lot of it right now.

MURPHY: *You've been an investigator for nearly half a century. What does it cost to hire a person like you with all that experience?*
LIPSET: I don't get paid what I'm worth. I'm kind of unique, Stephen, because of when and how I got into the business. I got a unique education that I think should be a model for how an investigator should be trained. But I don't know how anybody else can ever get that education. I try to explain this to people who come in to work for me. But I can't pay them while they get an education like mine. And I don't see how anybody can get one today, except you're grinding out so many lawyers that more lawyers are going to become investigators. At least that will happen in my profession in the next twenty years.

I was very fortunate when I started in that I got to work on cases where I sat with the lawyer when the client came in, heard the initial conference, heard all the questions that were asked, got to get in with some of my own questions, went out and made the investigation, interviewed every witness - every witness that existed, hostile or friendly, operating on the theory that knowledge tells you what to do with the case. Took statements, made recordings, did whatever had to be done. Went to the scene, depending upon the kind of case. And eventually got to sit through the entire trial. I investigated the jury panel. I got to listen.

Today they have psychologists sitting in there advising you who to pick for the jury. I got to sit through all of that after having been out to every juror's house and seeing where they live. And having done some background on them. I got to listen to the voir dire and the selection of the jury and had some input. Then I saw the entire case go from opening statements through direct examination, cross, re-direct, re-cross - both sides of the case. Got to listen to the jury instructions. Got to listen to the final arguments. Was in the courtroom when the jury came in. If we won we bought the jury drinks and we got to talk to them for an hour or two after the case was over. If we lost I often got to go out and interview the jurors at their home or their place of business to find out why they voted the way they did, who they believed, who they didn't believe. Found out sometimes what we thought was important, the jury would pay no attention to - went off in some other direction. I sat through more cases than most lawyers try today in their lifetime.

MURPHY: *I wouldn't doubt it.*
LIPSET: Now, how can somebody else go and get that education today? I mean they'd have to go spend a couple of years hanging around a courthouse. They wouldn't have the chance to make the investigation. They can't do as much as I've done. The only thing I tell them is you go down there and at least listen to people being questioned on the witness stand. But they didn't have what I did - I was watching the witnesses that I interviewed and took statements from in many cases. I listened to them being questioned by counsel from whichever side.

But I don't know how anybody could do what I did. Back then I was getting paid $5.00 an hour. Now I get $100.00 an hour. And people that do what I do in New York and Washington and some other places are charging $200.00 an hour.

MURPHY: *The book contains over three hundred pages of your experiences. Is there one accomplishment in your career that you consider your proudest accomplishment?*
LIPSET: No, not any one. The glamour cases are always the ones where you sort of semi-worked as a law person. You know, chasing the jewel thieves. But I don't see myself as a policeman or a frustrated policeman, having done that in the army. I don't know that there's any one case that gave me more strokes than anything else. I just think of the satisfaction of having done a good job.

Some lawyer called me this afternoon before you got here and gave me a small assignment and said, "Oh by the way, I want to thank you for the job you did for me about two or three months ago." He came to me with some kind of a question about a bank that he didn't even have the right name for. And he knew that that bank supposedly was handling Soviet affairs in the United States. He wanted to find that bank and who they worked with in the United States. I was able to find it. I never knew if what I had gotten for him was a benefit or not. And here he was thanking me and telling me what it led to for him down that path. He was very pleased. That made me feel good. It gives me a reason for existing.

Another lawyer you would know called me because he needs a witness. The investigative staff in his office couldn't find this guy and I found him in like four hours of work. That's the kind of thing I like.

MURPHY: *You're apparently in good health, but like all of us you're going to pass away someday. What would you like to see as your epitaph?*
LIPSET: "He liked helping people." Or something like that. I'd just rather not look at it if you don't mind. I don't intend to go. I don't think I'm immortal, but I have an overwhelming desire to get back all the money I put into the social security system. I think I have to live another twenty years to get it all out.

ACKNOWLEDGMENTS

This is my first venture into the world of print-on-demand publishing and it has been a wild ride. When I first looked into publishing this book, many people in the publishing world said there was no market for a collection of legal fiction and nonfiction. In fact, I was told such a book would be difficult for booksellers to categorize and shelve. Should it be shelved as fiction? Nonfiction? Reference? Anthology?

Rather than fight the establishment, I decided the most prudent course would be to publish the book myself and market it online. Finding a full-service web site like lulu.com has freed me from the frustration and sense of helplessness dealing with conventional publishers. At least now I can exercise some control over the entire process of producing and marketing my own book.

As a result I have had to learn more than I ever imagined about formatting, design, printing, book covers, ISBNs, distribution, and marketing. I owe thanks to many people for their able assistance, especially Sheldon Siegel, the author of the Foreword, who has always been generous with his time and encouragement. Thanks also to Will Baker, an outstanding young designer and artist, for lending his talent to the design of the cover. You can view his work at http://desaturate.net.

As always, I am grateful for the support of my writing group - the talented authors Tom Beatty and Jeff Westmont - who pull no punches in assessing my writing, but always find something positive to say.

And a special thanks to Patty and our four children – Conor, Brandon, Tess, and Jake – who continue to supply me with ample material for future writing efforts.

ABOUT THE AUTHOR

Stephen M. Murphy is the author of the novel ALIBI and anthology of interviews of lawyer authors THEIR WORD IS LAW: Bestselling Lawyer-Novelists Talk About Their Craft. He lives with his wife Patty and four children in San Francisco where he represents employees in civil rights litigation. Visit his websites www.stephenMmurphy.com and www.LawyersWriting.com.

WHAT CRITICS ARE SAYING ABOUT STEPHEN M. MURPHY'S OTHER BOOKS:

THEIR WORD IS LAW: Bestselling Lawyer-Novelists Talk About Their Craft

"San Francisco personal injury lawyer Stephen M. Murphy has talked with dozens of JDs-turned-authors over the years, and in Their Word Is Law: Bestselling Lawyer-Novelists Talk About Their Craft, he gathers their pearls of wisdom into an anthology of interviews. Novelists, both famous and not, reflect on their craft in engaging terms, and Murphy is a fine cross-examiner."
Publishers Weekly

ALIBI

Murphy describes Manchester, New Hampshire, accurately. ALIBI is Murphy's debut thriller and an attention grabber from the first page. There are many twists, and a surprise ending. RECOMMENDED.
I LoveAMystery.com

ALIBI is one solid legal thriller & a grand read! ... What follows is courtroom drama at is best ... culminating in a stunning finish.... There is a touch of Turow & Richard North Patterson in the narration, & fans of those authors will definitely find ALIBI a really good read.
RebeccasReads.com

www.ingramcontent.com/pod-product-compliance
Lightning Source LLC
Chambersburg PA
CBHW020821260626
47169CB00003B/771